The Samurai's Daughter
MARY HIGGINS CLARK AWARD NOMINEE

"Massey deftly weaves fascinating historical and cultural detail into a suspenseful plot." —*Booklist*

"An absorbing cross-cultural puzzle." —*Publishers Weekly*

"Combining the legal mystery with Japanese history and antiques is a winning stroke for Ms. Massey. Intricately plotted and filled with Asian lore and customs, this charming love story is spiced with courage and danger." —*Dallas Morning News*

"The characters and details of Japanese culture and history are as appealing as ever, and fans will relish this while awaiting another one." —*Library Journal*

The Bride's Kimono
AGATHA AWARD NOMINEE

"Brimming equally with Japanese cultural lore and Rei's sharp comments on love, money, death, and silk."
—S. J. ROZAN, author of *Winter and Night*

"Astute character development and fascinating use of Japanese history." —*Booklist*

"*The Bride's Kimono* takes the reader on another humor-filled thrill ride with a heroine for the new age, Rei Shimura, the Japanese-American antiques dealer-cum-sleuth who must navigate between two worlds and two lovers—and around a corpse—as she solves the mystery of stolen antiquity."
—STEPHEN HORN, *New York Times*–bestselling author of *In Her Defense*

The Floating Girl

The Flower Master

"What Sujata Massey excels in, as evident from two previous Rei Shimura thrillers, is the arranging of plot details, interwoven with sprays of scene and freshly cut dialogue." —*Baltimore Sun*

Zen Attitude
ANTHONY AND EDGAR AWARD NOMINEE

"A gifted storyteller who delivers strong characters, a tight plot, and an inside view of Japan and its culture." —*USA Today*

"A very entertaining mystery." —*Publishers Weekly*

The Salaryman's Wife
AGATHA AWARD WINNER

"Sly, sexy, and deftly done, *Wife* is one to bring home." —*People* Page-Turner of the Week

"Massey gives us a clear-eyed look at Japanese daily life. An impressive first novel." —*Baltimore Sun*

Jim Burger

About the Author

SUJATA MASSEY was a reporter for the *Baltimore Evening Sun* and has spent several years in Japan teaching English and studying Japanese. She is the author of *The Salaryman's Wife, Zen Attitude, The Flower Master, The Floating Girl,* and *The Bride's Kimono.* Her books have garnered numerous awards, and critics have called her stories captivating, her writing clear-eyed and unique, and her characters complex, appealing, and wryly humorous. She lives in Baltimore, Maryland, with her family.

The Samurai's Daughter

Sujata Massey

Perennial

An Imprint of HarperCollins*Publishers*

A hardcover edition of this book was published in 2003 by HarperCollins Publishers.

HarperCollins books may be purchased for educational, business, or sales promotional use. For information please write: Special Markets Department, HarperCollins Publishers Inc., 10 East 53rd Street, New York, NY 10022.

First Perennial edition published 2004.

Designed by Nancy B. Field

The Library of Congress has catalogued the hardcover edition as follows:

Massey, Sujata.
   The samurai's daughter / Sujata Massey.—1st ed.
     p. cm.
   ISBN 0-06-621290-1
   1. Shimura, Rei (Fictitious character)—Fiction. 2. Women detectives—California—San Francisco—Fiction. 3. San Francisco (Calif.)—Fiction. 4. Americans—Japan—Fiction. 5. Japanese Americans—Fiction. 6. Antique dealers—Fiction. 7. Tokyo (Japan)—Fiction. I. Title.

PS3563.A79965 S26   2003
813'.54—dc21   2002068893

ISBN 0-06-059503-5 (pbk.)

04 05 06 07 08 ❖/RRD 10 9 8 7 6 5 4 3 2 1

Acknowledgments

I am grateful to the many kind and wise people who wrote to me, talked with me, and manipulated my pressure points as I wrote *The Samurai's Daughter.* In various parts of Asia, journalists Dan Bloom and Mark Schreiber, translator Akemi Narita, and author Christopher Belton were always able to find answers to difficult questions. I received a fascinating introduction to the world of Japanese acupuncture from licensed acupuncturist Zoe Brenner in Bethesda, Maryland. Shizumi Manule brought me to the hospitable and elegant Urasenke Tea Society branch in Washington, D.C., where I experienced a beautiful lesson in tea. Mike Tharp, West Coast bureau chief of *U.S. News & World Report,* was a wellspring of information on the issue of war reparations. For help with the grave Buddhist precepts, I thank Drew Leder, professor of philosophy at Loyola College in Baltimore, and for insight into blindness, Aryan Shayegani, an ophthalmologist at Wilmer Eye Institute at Johns Hopkins. My dear husband, Tony Massey, believed in the project, often relinquishing his leisure hours in order to give me the time to work. My sister, Rekha Banerjee, kindly opened her home to my two-year-old daughter, Pia, and me during a research trip. My mother, Karin Banerjee, kept Pia content so that I could get around San Francisco, and Donhatai Jirasingh kept her happy and entertained at our home. Consuelo Ramirez, cabbie extraordinaire, taught me the ups and downs of

San Francisco's streets. Helen Lee Dellheim shared legal expertise and friendship, as did many writer friends, including Marcia Talley, John Mann, Karen Diegmueller, Janice McLane, and Laura Lippman. My editor, Carolyn Marino, and my agent, Ellen Geiger, sent me on a mission to revise and shape the book into all that it could be—I am grateful for the advice.

While Shimura is a well-known name in Japan, Rei's ancestors and their actions exist only in my imagination—as does any relationship to the Imperial Family. For fascinating insights and inspiration regarding the historic elements of the novel, I credit Herbert P. Bix's *Hirohito and the Making of Modern Japan*, Sterling Seagrave and Peggy Seagrave's *The Yamato Dynasty*, and Rosy Clarke's *Japanese Antique Furniture*.

A beloved friend of mine from the mystery bookselling community, Paige Rose, passed away right as I was finishing my first draft of this book. I had always meant to dedicate a book to Paige, but sadly, didn't do it fast enough. So this book is for Paige, a year too late.

Cast of Characters

REI SHIMURA American-born but Tokyo-based collector and scholar of Japanese antiques.

TOSHIRO SHIMURA Rei's Japanese father, who practices psychiatry in San Francisco.

CATHERINE SHIMURA Rei's American mother, who decorates with a vengeance.

MANAMI OKADA Japanese boarder in the Shimura household.

HUGH GLENDINNING On-again, off-again beau who practices international law.

CHARLES SHARP Principal in the San Francisco law firm Sharp, Witter and Rowe.

ERIC GAN Asian-American translator and old flame of Rei's.

ROSA MUNOZ Now living in poverty in San Francisco, having suffered even worse horrors under Japanese hands during the war.

THE YOKOHAMA SHIMURAS Rei's family branch in Yokohama is headed by her father's younger brother, Hiroshi Shimura, a salaryman; his homemaker wife, Norie, is like a mother to Rei. Their son, Tsutomu "Tom" Shimura, is an emergency room doctor, and daughter Chika is an undergraduate at Kyoto University.

SHOU IDABASHI Private detective based in Tokyo.

RAMON ESPINOSA Rosa's friend from the bad old days in the Philippines.

MR. ISHIDA Tokyo antiques dealer who is a mentor to Rei.

MR. HAMAZAKI Managing director for Morita Incorporated.

DR. NIGAWA Internal medicine doctor at Kanda General Hospital.

MR. HARADA Tokyo lawyer and friend of Hugh Glendinning's.

Plus an assortment of students, teachers, assistants, policemen, and friends on both sides of the Pacific .

The Samurai's Daughter

1

"Way too salty. I bet the chef used instant dashi powder."

My judgment delivered, I laid down the chopsticks I'd used to spear a slippery cube of tofu from the unfortunate miso soup. The Asian-American waitress who'd served us passed by with a smile; apparently, she didn't understand Japanese. Well, this was San Francisco, packed full of people with faces that mirrored the world's races, but who often spoke only English. I guessed that I'd been saved.

"But this soup is so tasty!" Toshiro Shimura, my father, raked a hand through his salt-and-pepper hair. It was cut in a slightly shaggy style typical for a San Francisco psychiatrist—but was distinctly odd for a Japanese-born, fifty-something man. "Rei-chan, you don't realize how hard it is to find pure Japanese ingredients here. Anyway, I hear that in Japan a lot of the cooks now use bonito powder."

"Not *real* cooks. I grate bonito fish—you know, the kind that's so hard that it feels like a piece of wood." I closed my eyes for a minute, feeling nostalgic for the petrified hunk of fish resting in a wooden box in my tiny kitchenette in North Tokyo. "It's worth the extra effort because then the soup tastes like it comes from the sea, not the convenience store. Now, Dad, where were we? The ten grave precepts of Buddhism. The ones your grandfather felt were so important to live by. I thought it was interesting that he had them on display."

"Yes, they were recorded on a calligraphy scroll. I think it originally came from a monastery, but it hung in the office where he worked. Unfortunately, I don't know where it is now."

"Do you recall, approximately, what it said?"

"The precepts. You know them, don't you?"

I rolled my eyes. "I know some of them, but not all. You didn't raise me Buddhist, remember?"

"But you did take an Eastern religions class at Berkeley, yes?"

"It was so long ago, Dad. Just tell me. This is an oral history project, not a go-to-the-library project. I remember the first one: Don't kill. The next: Don't steal. And then the one about not lying—"

"Well, the precept against lying is actually the fourth, not the third, if I remember correctly. And in Japan, it's always been considered allowable to tell certain kinds of lies out of compassion, or because that lie serves a greater good."

"Well, I'd agree with that," I said. "What was the third one, then?"

"It's a precept against sex. Misusing sex, to be exact. That would cover situations such as rape and extramarital sex and—"

"Fine. Ah, what's number five?" I wasn't going to pursue the subtleties of the Buddhist rule governing sex—that was just a little too up-close and personal. It had been two years since I'd last come home to San Francisco, and I wanted to leave on as good terms as I'd arrived.

"That, if I remember correctly, is not to give or take drugs."

"But priests drink sake all the time!" I pointed out.

"Well, a person may take sake, but not in an amount to cause intoxication. My grandfather drank sake at supper, but only a single glass."

"Would you say in general that laypeople's interpretations of these rules were looser than that of priests? I mean, Zen priests don't eat meat, but most people in Japan do. But how is it that people are allowed to eat meat, when the first precept is against killing?"

"That's the rule I *thought* my vegetarian daughter would jump on." My father laughed. "The answer is that killing animals in self-defense, or to eat them, is permitted. It's just not right to kill them for sport."

"Aha. So the basis of the rule is that an animal's life is valued only when it might be threatened with involvement in a game, say hunting or cockfighting," I said. "I'm not sure I agree with that. A death is a death, to me. But the rule certainly provides an interesting look at the Japanese mind."

"The Buddhist mind," my father corrected me. "And as you know, Buddhism has its origins in India, and these laws are known to Buddhists in all nations. They are universal."

I put my notebook aside for a break, because as much as I'd complained about the noodles, I was hungry for them. Actually, my feelings about food, my hometown, and my father were about as mixed up as the Buddhist rules.

San Francisco was a typical tourist's dream, but in my mind it was a far second to Tokyo, my adopted home. Sure, the architecture in San Francisco was superb. But how could you enjoy it with all the rolling power blackouts? My parents' lifestyles had changed dramatically since California had faced its energy crisis—their huge Victorian home was no longer lit up welcomingly in the evenings, not even now, at Christmas, when my mother once had routinely lit electric candles in all sixty windows.

Tokyo didn't have such problems yet. And when there, it was easy for me to live simply, keeping my appreciation low to the ground, for things like the miniature Shinto shrines decorated with good luck fox statues, and the gracious rows of persimmon trees that line the ugly train tracks. And then, there were the Japanese people: the serene older generation moving through their own private dances of tai chi in the city's small parks, and the serious kindergarten students striding off to school wearing the kind of saucer-shaped hat and tidy uniform that hadn't changed since the 1920s. Not to mention my father's brother, Uncle Hiroshi, Aunt Norie, and my cousin Tom, who had become an important part of my life: so important that I planned to hightail it out of America before December 31 so I wouldn't miss New Year's Day with them. The sad truth was that I found staying in an eight-bedroom house with just my parents depressing. Even though there was one more person with us—Manami Okada.

Manami was a thirty-year-old pathology fellow from Kobe. She had been living with my parents for about a month, following a desperate call from a University of California at San Francisco administrator to my father, the unofficial godfather of the school's Japanese community. My father had explained to me that Manami was what the Japanese called a "girl in a box"—someone whose family had sheltered her too long. Not surprisingly, her housing situation in San Francisco was a bit too open for her tastes. One of her apartment-mates was a lesbian, the other a Hostess cupcake junkie; these were the reasons, anyway, that my mother offered me for why my father and she had taken pity on the unworldly young doctor and offered her one of the third-floor bedrooms for the token payment of $100 a month—which was one-eighth of what Manami had been paying for her previous apartment share.

Well, I knew that junk food could lead to murder—San Francisco was where the famous Hostess Twinkie legal defense had originated—but I didn't have any biases against gays. I'd viewed Manami with a great deal of skepticism when I'd met her about a week ago, but I had to admit she seemed pleasant. She was quiet, polite, studious—all those Japanese daughter qualities that I lacked.

She was serving her first year of residency, so she was usually gone all day, and often worked late at night. When she was home she joined us for meals, but chose to spend her quiet time behind the closed door to her room on the third floor. Her room was next to the big storage room where among the many boxes and trunks there was one holding items from my father's old life in Japan. I'd gone through the papers slowly one evening, hearing an odd splashing sound on the other sound of the wall; it took me a while to realize that Manami was trying to bathe in the traditional Japanese way, pouring buckets of water over herself rather than using the shower.

"What are you thinking about?" my father asked.

"Manami. I wonder if she's any happier with us than with her old roommates."

"Perhaps you should ask her."

I shook my head. "I don't want to be so direct. Maybe I'll just try to see if she perks up at the chance to help me with some ideas for my project. After all, since she's so old-fashioned, she might very well have lived a life in Kobe where they're still using traditional objects in the home."

My line of work is Japanese antiques. I buy them for people living in Japan who still care about old things, as well as for some American clients. I also do some writing and speaking on the topic; that's what had brought me to the U.S. on this trip. Since I'd made enough from my recent work in Washington, D.C., to pay a few months' rent on my tiny apartment in an unfashionable section of North Tokyo, I'd decided to take a sabbatical from antiquing to engage in a personal history project. I hoped to make a record of the style in which the Shimuras had lived before the massive modernization that came in the 1960s. I was interested in such things as the way the Buddhist precepts were followed in the normal daily routine, and also in the artifacts of that life: the cooking pots my grandmother used, the quilt designs, the landscape design of the camellia garden that had surrounded the old house in West Tokyo.

As I ruminated about the project, the restaurant seemed to vanish. Since we were sitting on *zabuton* cushions at a low table, we could just as soon be father and child in old Japan—an eager, boisterous child with a reserved father. Though of course in old Japan, the likelihood was next to none that a twenty-nine-year-old daughter would have the luxury of a gossipy restaurant lunch with her father. I would be taking care of my family—and perhaps sewing the quilts and cooking the dishes that my descendants would nostalgically admire.

"Sorry. I've just been paged." My father gave me a rueful look and unclipped the phone at his waist. In the years that I'd been gone, he'd become a total technophile; the only problem was he rarely remembered the importance of recharging his combined phone/pager. "It's your mother, as usual."

"I bet she has a shopping errand for you." I knew my mother was on the verge of running out of votive candles. She'd made especially elaborate holiday decorations this year because she and my father were hosting a party for ALL, the Asian Language League, on December 26.

As my father punched in our home number, I watched his fingers, stockier than mine, but the identical light golden color. Many children of Japanese and Caucasian unions turn out to have milky coloring, but I had the same complexion as my father and Uncle Hiroshi and my cousin Tom. My hair was more brown-black than black, though, and I couldn't say my nose was Japanese. In the United States, I was often assumed to be foreign-born; in Japan, I was assumed to be Japanese until people realized I couldn't read.

I stopped pondering my weaknesses, because my father had gotten through. He greeted my mother by name. Then, after a long pause, he spoke. "How soon? And she doesn't know yet?" My father listened a bit more, shook his head, and then handed the phone to me. "Here. The news is really meant for you."

I felt my stomach drop. Perhaps the emergency meant that she'd gotten a call that something terrible had happened back at my Tokyo apartment—a water pipe had burst, or the electricity had been turned off. I'd been away from home too long.

"Are you sitting down?" my mother asked with an odd mixture of breathlessness and pain, as if she'd run up Fillmore Street in her favorite Bally heels.

"Yes. Just tell me—"

"He's coming!"

"What?" For a minute, I was puzzled, until I figured out He might mean Jesus. To hear this kind of talk coming from my mother was a surprise—she had always been a typically low-key Episcopalian. Carefully, I asked, "Is this about Christmas Eve?"

"Yes! And he'll be here, and so we must prepare."

I saw my father watching me intently, waiting for my reaction. What was his issue? "Mom, you know I've never been that comfortable at the cathedral. Spirituality, for me, is more private—"

"*He* doesn't mind going—it turns out he grew up in the Church of Scotland! I'm so pleased he's coming that I've already put in a call to Williams-Sonoma to get a plum pudding. It's traditional in Scotland as well as England, apparently."

"Oh!" At last I understood the identity of the being in question: Hugh Glendinning, my on-again, off-again beau. We'd just said good-bye in Washington a few weeks earlier, when he flew off to China on business and I went back to my parents. "Are you talking about Hugh? Did he call from China?"

"Yes, and he said his cell phone was stolen so that's why he hadn't contacted you. He was calling from a hotel in Shanghai to say that he should reach San Francisco around noon tomorrow. He's got about a week's worth of work here, and his firm had booked him into the Mark Hopkins."

"The Mark Hopkins," I moaned, imagining what a great escape it would be for both of us—a beautiful room with a view of Nob Hill, room service, and a king-sized bed.

"Don't worry, sweetie. After I invited him to stay with us, he agreed to cancel the reservation. I also canceled the UPS man who was coming to pick up the box you were sending to his office in Washington—you can just give him the present while he's here, and I've already put flowers in the guest room on the third floor."

"That was very kind of you." Now that I understood he'd be sleeping directly over my parents, and within spitting distance of Manami, I stowed away all my fantasies about trysts.

"It's my pleasure, darling. I'm so pleased that he'd rather stay with us. Some of your old beaux were nervous about spending time with us, Rei. Not this one. He said he couldn't imagine a more wonderful invitation, and he understood *completely* about Daddy's being conservative enough that he'd have to sleep apart from you—"

So she was going to blame it on my father, I thought wryly. A good-cop, bad-cop practice. Whatever. After another minute of hysterical exuberance from my mother, I managed to make my good-bye. I'd noticed that my father was looking at his watch.

"Happy?" he asked after I'd handed back his phone.

"Of course I'm happy. But I don't want you to think that because he's here I'll stop talking to you, or working on this family history."

"Actually, I wouldn't mind if we took a break."

I shook my head. "With that kind of attitude, there would be no oral histories. We'd never know the experiences of slaves, of Holocaust survivors, of Civil War veterans—or the Shimuras! Come on, Daddy, you know I have a lot more work to do."

"As do I," my father said, raising his eyebrows as he looked just beyond me. He was signaling the waitress for the check, when we'd barely started our main courses. "I'm sorry to tell you this, but my office overscheduled me. I'm going to have to go to see five extra patients, starting at one. It's a quarter of one right now—I must leave."

"Of course," I said, watching my father slurp the remnants of his soup. He put a twenty on the table and left me to finish up the *zaru soba* and his seafood tempura.

I didn't believe my father's excuse for one minute. He was upset about something: either my history project, or my lover's arrival. Or both.

2

San Francisco International Airport always gives me a bad feeling. The INS inspectors give me trouble just about every time I return from Japan, even though I'm a U.S. citizen. Hugh would have to face them carrying a European Union passport, with his last stop having been China. This mix of origins might raise their suspicions. On the other hand, he had a great Scottish accent—and he was used to airport hassles. I told myself not to worry too much.

Because of the holiday, it took a long time for me to find a parking space. Once inside the airport, I went directly to the lobby outside the customs area exits; it was already twenty-five minutes after Hugh's plane had landed. I saw him right away. He was chatting animatedly on a pay phone with a small pile of leather suitcases beside him. More than a few people did double takes as they passed by. Hugh was like a human version of a golden retriever: tall and strapping, with a red-gold mane that flopped in his eyes— eyes as dark a green as the peaty bogs in his Scottish homeland. Looking at Hugh as I walked toward him, I was filled with the same old mix of desire and a certain exasperation with myself for being a sucker for the twenty-first century version of Braveheart.

Hugh spotted me, and gave me a smile like the sun. He hung up the phone, and in the next instant he was kissing me as if he'd been away for two years. For someone who'd been flying for hours, he tasted surprisingly fresh—like a mixture of toothpaste and oranges, two things I like very much.

"Sorry I'm late—I didn't think customs would be so fast for you," I said when we finally broke apart. I glanced around and sure enough, we had an audience.

"They were brilliant! Some angel in a blue uniform waved me into the American citizens line, and I was through in five minutes."

"But you're not an American! Considering the current security situation, that shouldn't have happened—"

"She must have known I'm in love with one. Maybe that counts." Hugh smiled down at me. "By the way, I arranged to have a box with some things from the Washington office sent by overnight delivery to your parents' house. Do you know if it arrived?"

"Yes. It came this morning. Just in the nick of time, I bet, with Christmas Eve tomorrow." I grabbed the plastic duty-free bags off the top of his luggage pile—bags that I bet held gifts for my parents. Hugh spent much of his life traveling, so airports were his chief shopping centers.

"Your mother said she'd cook on Christmas Day, but I hope I can take care of some of the other evenings: restaurants, theater, et cetera. I've got a decent dining budget from the firm—can you tell me beforehand any family favorites?"

"Well, my favorites and my family's are different," I said, ruefully thinking of my lunch in Japantown with my father. "I'm a little behind the times, having been away for so long. There's a raw-food restaurant that's super-hot, but I still love a vegetarian organic restaurant called Greens."

"Isn't that the restaurant cookbook you used to use in Japan—the book with the infamous quinoa timbale recipe?"

"I can't believe you remember that!"

"Of course I do. No quinoa available in all of Japan, so you had me smuggle a baggie of it from New Zealand!"

"Don't talk like that," I whispered, as I saw heads turning everywhere. "Even though this is California, not *everyone* knows what quinoa is. Someone might think it's contraband—"

"No, the truth is it's a biological weapon." Hugh exploded in great honking laughter.

"Time to go," I murmured, trying to seem casual and unruffled as we passed an airport police officer who was giving the two of us a head-to-toes stare.

"Right, darling. I'll keep the good news until we're riding on the cable car and you're showing me the sights."

I hadn't traveled by cable car, of course; the cable cars ran only on a few streets within the city, not all the way out to the exurb where the airport was. I'd used my mother's Japanese SUV, which should have had plenty of room for luggage, but was actually stuffed with enough evergreen roping and candles to burn down San Francisco again. These were all last-minute holiday decorations she had yet to put up.

"It's fake pine roping," I explained. "My mother bought a lot to decorate the hall for this party we're having December twenty-sixth. I should have warned you—it's going to be big."

"Boxing Day—that's the day we have our parties in Scotland." Hugh sneezed again. "Ah, that aroma. It definitely reminds me of certain rural parts of Japan."

"I miss the Japanese winter smell of sweet potatoes roasting," I said.

"*Yakiiimoo!*" Hugh called out the potato roaster's mournful cry in such a perfect baritone that I looked at him in amazement. In the next instant, I was almost sideswiped by a larger SUV barreling up behind us. I cut to the right just in time.

"I hate this city," I muttered, slipping an old U2 disc into the CD player. As Bono crooned about finding the real thing, I cast a sideways glance at Hugh—who was looking out the window. Well, there was a lot to see. California Highway 101 ran from the airport to the city, offering vast, shining expanses of blue sea and green hills. I had to admit this was the Bay Area at its most scenic.

"Why so many flags?" Hugh asked, and I followed his gaze to a car ahead of us decked out with tiny American flags that fluttered in the breeze.

"Patriotism," I said. "Apparently it started after the World Trade Center attacks, and never stopped. Several of our neighbors hang the flag outside their houses."

"I see them on billboards, too," Hugh said. "Funny thing, that

patriotism. Where's the line that keeps it from turning into nationalism?"

I glanced up at the billboards, trying to see what he saw. Maybe
because I was American, the flags didn't stand out sharply to me.
What I noticed was that the billboards in general had become
fewer. During my last visit two years ago, the billboards were all
hyping dot-com businesses. Now, many of those software pio-
neers had gone bust like the long-lost gold rush entrepreneurs of
1849.

"Watch your left!" Hugh bellowed, and I had to bring the SUV to
heel. I'd almost drifted into the next lane. After so many years away,
I had to keep concentrating to stay on the right side of the road, and
I had to think twice about directions. Highway 101 was my constant
reference point, an often slow but surefire route into the city that
became Van Ness, from where I could cut out at Japantown, then
take Laguna for the bumpy ride up to Pacific Heights, the beautiful
and expensive neighborhood where my parents had been lucky
enough to find a bargain twenty-five years ago. As we drove on,
Hugh kept up a barrage of questions. Where was Coit Tower?
Fisherman's Wharf? The Golden Gate Bridge? The hippies?

I addressed his last question first. "You have to go to the Haight
to see the few old hippies who are still alive. Now, *this area*, which
is called the Mission, is a mix of Latin American families and yup-
pies—kind of like Adams-Morgan in Washington. Interestingly
enough, one of the city's best Italian restaurants is here—"

"So where's the most romantic place in the city?" Hugh interrupted.

"Hmm." I had to think hard because I'd never had a serious
relationship while living in San Francisco. "I—I'll have to work on
that. Why is it so important?"

"Well, actually, Rei, it's Christmas." Hugh fixed me with an
intent gaze. "I've brought two presents for you. There's one I'll
give you in front of your family, and the other one is private. I'm
seeking a good place to give it to you."

"Ah," I said, making a quick, private prediction of absurdly
skimpy lingerie. "You're right that we'll need to be out of the
house to have any privacy."

"If that's the case, could we stop somewhere for a few minutes? Can you park the car somewhere?"

"Hugh, the grade on this hill is forty degrees. If I stop now, I'm liable to roll backward—I hate stopping on hills."

"Okay, can you go around the corner, find a parking lot or something? I must speak to you about something before we reach your parents. It's urgent."

I shot a nervous glance at him, turned the corner, and noodled along until I reached the parking lot of a Malaysian restaurant I'd never visited. Feeling guilty, I took the only spot available, between a gleaming green Volvo wagon and a rust-spotted VW bug painted in psychedelic colors. Old and new San Francisco—with the foreigners in between. I clicked off the music and then, after a moment's reflection, turned off the car. From Hugh's serious expression, I could guess we would linger for a while.

"All right, Rei. You'll be the first outside of the firm to know. I'm relocating."

I sighed in exasperation. "You're always relocating. You can't live anywhere more than six months, can you?"

"No, this time it's for longer than that. And I'm going to Japan."

I shut my eyes, and then opened them. I wasn't dreaming.

"You weren't expecting this." All of a sudden I could hear the hesitation in his voice.

"It's wonderful news," I said, meaning it. "Are you sure this isn't the Christmas present? If so, I love it more than anything else I'll get this year. Or next."

"Well, it certainly seemed like a gift when our senior partner asked if I wanted to do it."

"I don't understand. I thought the firm in Washington loved having you there to do all their U.K.-American business. Did something go wrong?"

"Nothing of the sort. Andrews and Cheyne have joined with another big firm, Sharp, Witter and Rowe, to file a class-action that will hopefully send me back to Japan." There are other forms involved, too, but we'll be the leaders—"

"Sharp, Witter and Rowe?" I sat up straight. "Ooh, bad karma. The principal partner, Charles Sharp, has a daughter I went to school with. Janine Sharp. I couldn't stand her! She was so snobbish and uptight and—"

"It's not Janine I'll be working with," Hugh said. "Just Charles Sharp! I'm meeting him and the translator who will be assisting me this afternoon."

"But today is Christmas Eve," I said.

"Yes, I know, and I'm sorry. I'll be off on the twenty-fifth and twenty-sixth, but in order to do that, some groundwork should be laid today. It's a massive, long project ahead of me, with plenty of billable hours. Once we get to your house this evening, we can properly cele—" a giant yawn broke up Hugh's speech—"brate."

"I'm afraid the celebration is going to be a celibate one." Meeting his quizzical expression, I explained, "My mother and father assigned you to a third-floor guest room, and there's a prim and proper Japanese pathology fellow staying in a room across the hall from you. Unless she's working at the hospital, and my parents are out too, there won't be the slightest chance for us."

"Her name is Manami, right? Your mother told me about her. I've been entrusted, in fact, with fixing her up."

I snorted and put the car in gear. As far as I was concerned, there wasn't much more to talk about. "I can't think of anyone you know who'd be appropriate. Those rugby players are too earthy—"

"I was thinking of a nice Japanese lawyer. I'll be meeting quite a few on this case."

"Good. I'd like to hear more about it." I pulled back on the familiar road toward my parents' house. In the old days, I'd walked this route home from school, and there hadn't been many diversions; but now Fillmore, as well as Union, was packed with tantalizing cafes and shops. As I'd viewed the scene in Pacific Heights today, it had seemed that a lot of people took cafe sitting as a kind of career. Well, maybe that was the only option if they were out of work.

"I wish we could stop in one of those cafes to really talk," Hugh said, following my gaze. "But I've got to get through that meeting first. If I just could drop off my things, have some tea, a shower, and a shave, I'll be off and back as quickly as I can."

"How will you get there?" I turned onto Green, my parents' street, which had a handsome assortment of late Victorian through Edwardian and 1920s houses. Almost every house wore an elaborate holiday decoration on the door—ranging from Colonial-style wreaths adorned with pomegranates and oranges to silvery wreaths of eucalyptus leaves. Now, with the influx of techno money, everything was in perfect taste; but it was sad that many of the families I remembered from childhood were gone. Some of them had been driven out by skyrocketing property taxes; others had sold because they couldn't ignore the windfall that came from selling to the new titans of industry.

"Taxi. I'm sure there are plenty trolling through the area, given that the British Consulate's here. Is this San Francisco's version of Embassy Row?"

"No. This is strictly a residential block—there's no consulate around. I don't know which building you're talking about." I didn't look where Hugh was gazing, because I was waiting out a tour bus blocking access into a neighbor's driveway, which I needed to pull into so I could neatly back across the street into my parents' driveway.

"Oh, is it the ambassador's private residence, then?" Hugh sounded worried as I completed my maneuvers and turned off the car. Now I followed his craned neck to look at the tall, extra-wide three-story white house defined by Grecian pillars and an elaborate portico—a portico from which hung ornate swags of evergreen roping, in the center of which was a full-sized Union Jack. I shook my head. My mother had somehow created this last flourish without my noticing.

"Actually, it's our house," I said in a small voice. "Didn't I tell you that my mother is gaga about flags? She flies them to welcome international guests. You can imagine how over-the-top the house looked when we had psychiatrists visiting from five foreign countries—"

"Oh, my God," Hugh said. "This is your *home*? It's a bloody palace! An American castle on the highest peak in Pacific Heights—"

"I suppose with the pillars you might think of a palace, but this really isn't the best or highest point in the neighborhood. This house was a real fixer-upper when my parents bought it from the city twenty-five years ago. It's not one hundred percent renovated." Suddenly I was flooded with doubts. It was an old house, with erratic water pressure, creaky floors, and radiators that sometimes clanged all night long. "You can still change your mind and go to a hotel . . ."

But Hugh had already picked up all his bags and was striding for the front door.

3

"Oh, you're just in time for lunch," my mother called out as I hurried to catch up with Hugh, whom she'd already admitted into the foyer. It was a large, square room with a vaulted ceiling that was hung with a massive Tiffany chandelier. The chandelier was the only thing lit, given my parents' strict energy rationing; at least it cast a warm glow on the walls, which had been decorated with antique painted screens showing birds alighting in trees during different times of the year. Hugh took all this in, as well as the parlor just beyond, with its tall Venetian mirrors, old Baltimore bell-flower veneer tables, and a pair of peach velvet sofas that my mother had recently bought to lighten up the place. In the foreground was a nine-foot spruce decorated with purple and silver balls; all the packages underneath were purple, silver, or green. My mother was so serious about her color scheme that she'd rewrapped all the presents I'd wrapped in her special papers.

"Mrs. Shimura, hello. I—I had no idea your home would be like this." Hugh's voice was as hushed as if he had entered a house of worship.

"Catherine," my mother said warmly. "And it's just a mix of family things."

"These screens you have mounted on the walls—are those from Rei's father's family? How unusual to have so many linear feet."

"You're right. Well, that's what you get when you marry into a samurai family." A look passed between my mother and Hugh, and I felt a flush of embarrassment. For an instant I was back in old Japan, or in any one of the many countries where a girl's worth was related to the dowry her family could provide. I loved my family's Japanese treasures enough to want to document them, but I didn't like the cavalier way my mother was talking—and the hint, not so subtle, of what our family could offer Hugh.

"Ah, good morning!" A tiny voice piped up from behind, and I realized Manami had joined us. She bobbed her head, and her shoulder-length black braids brushed the tops of her white lab coat. She wore it over a sensible blue wool turtleneck and blue-and-green plaid pants. I loved Manami's serious style, just as I loved her sweet demeanor. Maybe there were ten million girls like her in Japan; in San Francisco, there weren't enough.

"Good morning, sweetie. You must have had a good night's sleep—it's almost two," my mother said, beaming at Manami. "Hugh, let me introduce Manami Okada, whom I told you about on the phone."

"*Hajime mashite*," Hugh said, bowing slightly. It was the standard Japanese greeting for a first meeting.

"Ah! You speak such excellent Japanese!" Manami's eyes widened.

"I don't," Hugh said, chuckling. "I just lived in Tokyo for a while . . . and hope to be returning. So you're the doctor? Gosh, you hardly look old enough."

"Everyone says that, and I don't know why." Manami frowned. "I'm thirty, and I earned my MD several years ago. We have a slightly different training pattern than in this country. We study faster and become doctors at a younger age."

"But you came here for some advanced training, I heard. When you're done with residency, do you want to stay on?" Hugh asked.

"Not at all. I plan to return to Japan. I hope the pathology training here could perhaps add, how do you say, edges?"

"An edge!" I smiled at her. Just the previous night, I'd spent a few hours working on slang and colloquialisms with her. Once an English teacher, always an English teacher. "Yes, I'm sure overseas pathology training will be noticed, especially since you're doing so well."

"Oh, I'm not. I'm a very poor student—"

"Well, that's not what my father says. He would have loved to have a daughter like you." I spoke without jealousy, just the knowledge that came from being a decade past high school—where I had done just enough in school to make the top 10 percent, yet not so much as to infringe on a busy social schedule. I'd thought it was healthy, but the fact was, I never really lived up to what my father thought I was capable of. Manami, on the other hand, had forsworn the pleasures of San Francisco society for the serious pursuit of medicine.

Manami looked at her watch. "Excuse me. I must go. I slept so late today—I was on call yesterday, and felt tired."

"Of course, darling. Do you want to take some salad in your lunch box?" my mother offered. She was clearly as protective of Manami as I was.

"I couldn't trouble you," Manami said, but her eyes brightened.

"Come in the kitchen and we'll put it together." My mother rose, rolling up the sleeves of her cashmere sweater as if she was getting ready to do some serious cooking. "Hugh, Rei will show you the dumbwaiter so you don't have to lug your things upstairs."

I picked up the lighter suitcase and went into the kitchen, where the dumbwaiter was.

"So you don't need a butler to get things up and down, eh? I feel as if I've stepped into a BBC period drama." Hugh gaped at the mahogany door I swung open in the kitchen that revealed the dumbwaiter's compartment. "You've totally shocked me, Rei. This is like some kind of bizarre Anglo-Japanese paradise. I can't imagine a more beautiful setting for Christmas."

"Well, a snowy locale would help. Can we do the Japanese Alps next time?" I still didn't know whether to be pleased or mortified at his reaction to my home.

"Hugh, your family must be missing you dreadfully right now, just as I imagine Manami's is her." My mother stroked Manami's head briefly, and the young woman pulled away slightly. It didn't surprise me, because most Japanese don't like to be touched in a familiar fashion by people outside their families. I made a mental note to tell my mother to be less hands-on with Manami. Out loud, I reminded my mother that Hugh had to get going. As I'd expected, she protested. "Why not have a quick lunch? I made a nice Caesar salad—"

"My body clock's still too confused to let me be hungry. I'm trying to hang in so I'll have an appetite for supper."

My mother nodded. "Good. You'll eat supper here? I planned to serve at seven, but could make it later—"

"Seven's perfect. And thank you so much, Catherine. You can't imagine how tired I am of restaurant food."

Manami slipped out with her packed lunch box, and my mother escorted Hugh upstairs for the grand tour. Like a docent, she pointed out the original plaster moldings on the second floor, and the front staircase used for family, and the back staircase used for our nonexistent servants. On the third floor, she showed how the old servants' rooms had been turned into guest quarters. She identified the closed doors that led to Manami's bed and bath, various storage rooms, and an extra guest room that had a bath connecting it to Hugh's guest room, which had once been my own little study.

The dollhouse was gone, and so was the tiny desk where I'd painstakingly drawn the *kanji* characters that were taught to me at Japanese Sunday school. My mother had painted the room the color of ferns and decorated it with a few perfectly placed groupings of antique maps and prints of scenes in old San Francisco. She'd made up an old Empire campaign bed that I could already tell would be a few inches too short for Hugh with an antique quilt and a profusion of fancy pillows. But Hugh wasn't even looking at the bed—his attention was taken by the wide mahogany desk with chairs on either side that occupied the room's center.

"An old partners desk," Hugh said, touching its smooth surface. "This is what every junior lawyer would love to have someday. And such a gorgeous patina."

"I can find you a desk that's similar," my mother said with a gleam in her eye.

I had to practically drag my mother out of Hugh's room so that he could get going on his shower. While he washed, my mother and I had salad and sourdough toast—my favorite local treat—in the kitchen, and by the time I'd loaded the dishwasher, Hugh had come down to telephone for a taxi.

"I'll be back by late afternoon," he promised, kissing me at the door and giving my mother a wave.

After he left, my mother sighed. "This is going to be the best Christmas ever."

"I think so too." We squeezed hands for a moment, and I thought about how I'd thought the house was too empty before. Now, with Hugh around, things seemed just right.

My mother went back to decorating, and I slunk upstairs to my room to examine the slides I'd made from photos of some Shimura family heirlooms. The first was a close-up of a sword that was crafted for one of my ancestors during the late 1500s—the Muromachi Period, when there were still frequent wars between different feudal states. My father had said that it had been used by one of his direct ancestors, a Shimura nobleman, in defending the castle of his cousin—who happened to be the daimyo, or feudal lord, of a little-known wood-producing region. Our ancestor had lost his arm in the battle, but retained possession of the sword. I winced, as I always did when picturing this story, and began writing.

Shinto, the ancient religion of Japan, fostered a belief that swords contained the soul of a samurai, and thus were religious objects worthy of worship at a family's altar. In the Shimura household, a legend was told about the heroic samurai Jun Shimura, who lost an arm in the defense of a family stronghold. His sword was carefully kept in its original sheath and hung for display several times a year, times at which the family bowed down to pray before it.

I laid down my pen. I had an antipathy to weapons. In my opinion, a rice pot that had served the family through lean and lavish times was the kind of object worthy of family worship. I'd even revere a quilt patched together from old blue-and-white robes called *yukata*; my father had told me about such a quilt that his great-grandmother had made, and that he and his brother had slept under for many years, until it finally wore out. That was the problem, exactly: Crockery broke, and fabric frayed. The delicate things that I cared about perished, while the hard things like swords survived.

I wandered down to the second floor, hoping to take a closer look at the sword, to get more excited about it than I felt. I knocked on my parents' bedroom door and my father called for me to enter. He was sitting on a chaise with a checkbook in hand.

"I thought you had to work this afternoon," I said.

"There were a few cancellations. Now I'm sorry I rushed out of lunch. Is your friend safely arrived?"

"Yes, but he already had to go somewhere for a meeting. Dad, I actually came to your room to take another look at the sword." It was hanging over a tall dresser.

"Would you like me to take it down for you?"

I shook my head. "Let's do it later, when Hugh's here. He might find it interesting. Anyway, since you're here, maybe you can answer a few questions. How did you bring it into this country?"

"It was quite difficult," my father said, sighing. "My parents wanted me to have it, but the verification of its status with the government office seemed too daunting. So instead of going through the proper channels, I gave it to an American friend to carry, a military doctor who was being repatriated after the Vietnam War."

"So, it was important for you to have the sword here, even though you don't worship it—at least, not that I can recall."

My father pressed his lips together. "Sword worship, some may say, is part of the Shinto religion. To me, it means other things. I cannot worship a gun; how can I worship a sword?"

"I feel that way, too," I said. "But why, then, does it hang on your wall?"

My father sighed. "The temperature in the storage room is too uneven. And your mother likes the metalwork on the scabbard."

I suspected there was another reason, but I could tell that he wasn't going to be helpful. I shifted gears. "Hugh liked the crane screens downstairs—the ones that are mounted on the walls in the foyer. I've never known who the artist was. Do you have any idea?"

"None whatsoever. I'm not a good person to talk about it, as I don't really care for it."

"I see." My father was so peculiar. "How did the screen come into family hands? Was it from the old feudal days, or was it a more recent purchase, in Kyoto or somewhere like that—"

"My great-grandfather acquired it. I'm almost sure he didn't buy it, or if he did, he paid much less than it was worth."

"Sounds as if he shops the way Mom and I do."

My father stiffened. "Exploitative is hardly how I'd think of you two."

I bit my lip. "That's a harsh thing to say about good antiques shoppers. Whether it's us or someone dead."

"I don't know if this was taught in your master's degree courses in art history, but my country appropriated quite a lot of art and gold from other Asian countries."

"During the occupation of Korea, you mean?" I struggled, trying to figure out my father's trajectory. "Our screen is not Korean."

"It's Chinese. The Japanese military are said to have secretly entered Peking in 1900 and removed gold as well as treasured artworks from the imperial archives. The screen is so fine—much finer than a professor could afford. For that reason, I've always thought the screen probably was looted from China and given to my grandfather as a gift."

"But that's even better," I said. "It's such a dramatic story! A stolen treasure, maybe."

My father shook his head. "When a country loses its culture, it loses its soul. What kind of a place would China be today if it still had all its treasures? Would it be more humane?"

I snorted, thinking that once again, my father's idealism was out of control. "Do you think we should give back the screen to the Chinese government?"

"Not the government. The people!"

I pointed out that the government in China was actually called the People's Party, and that the Chinese family who'd owned the screen had to have been obnoxiously wealthy landowners, but my argument was a rhetorical one.

I finally understood what my father was saying—and it made me uncomfortable.

4

Just after three, my mother interrupted me in a half-doze at my desk.

"Hugh's on the line."

I picked up the cordless phone she'd brought, mentally preparing myself for bad news. He'd be delayed, probably; that was the life of a corporate lawyer.

Instead, he said that he was through with his meeting and was calling to see if I was game to run an errand with him, then head out for a drink with his colleagues at the Mark Hopkins.

"This is weird," I said. "You've never included me in so many things before."

"Well, after we broke up the last time, I went through the twelve-step program for bad boyfriends, and I learned a lot of clever strategies—"

"Don't joke about that." Somehow, I didn't like the word *strategy* connected to our relationship.

"Why not? I think it pays off to become reformed." His voice softened. "By the way, can you pick me up outside Sharp, Witter and Rowe? It'll make things easier than if I return to Pacific Heights again."

"I'll ask my mother if the car's free."

My mother agreed to lend me the Infiniti, as long as I was careful on the hills. She knew I was deathly afraid of slipping back-ward, because I'd practically burned up the transmission on the Camry they'd let me drive when I was in grad school. My mother also asked if I would pick up a special order of votive candles at Williams-Sonoma, and recommended that I change out of my jeans, since I would be going to one of the most glamorous spots in the city for cocktails.

"There are going to be tourists there," I protested. "Tourists can wear anything!"

"But we are longtime residents, not tourists, dear."

Honestly, American mothers were as bossy as the Japanese, I thought as I stared at my closet a few minutes later. Most of my career-girl clothes were at the cleaner's, so what I had to choose from were leftovers from college and high school days: things like off-the-shoulder *Flashdance* T-shirts, straight-leg Calvin Klein jeans, and various miniskirts.

The micro-mini and jeans didn't fit anymore, but I was able to squeeze into a Commander Salamander black velour dress that ended at mid-thigh. All my old shoes were gone, so I went into my mother's closet and came up with a pair of soft black suede boots that reached the knee. Now I was hardly exposed at all.

I thought I looked rather presentable when I pulled up outside the handsome old brick building where Hugh was waiting. But when he tumbled into the seat before me, he seemed too stressed to notice. The joking ease he'd had on the phone was gone.

"Thanks for coming," he said. "It turned into a rather difficult afternoon."

"How so?"

"After a brief meeting with everyone here, the translator and I went over to interview a potential plaintiff. I felt so bad about the whole thing that I wanted to stop in somewhere to get her a Christmas gift. Do you think we have time?"

I looked at my watch. "Sure. But you should have booked my mother to help you. She's the only one who loves shopping as much as you."

"Well, one of the stops is the opera house, for tickets I ordered for her and your father, so I'm glad she's not along. After that, we'll get the goods for my client. I need to get her one of those things that boils water for tea and soup—"

"An electric kettle," I said, heading toward Sutter. Williams-Sonoma would sell one, and I could get my mother's candles there, too.

"Right. I'll buy something for Manami there, too. And after that's all accomplished, I need to buy food."

"Food? Our fridge is packed to exploding."

"Not food for the Shimuras, food for . . . my client."

I rolled my eyes, knowing this trip was going to be a lot longer than I'd first thought. It took the better part of an hour and a half to hit the opera house, Williams-Sonoma, and the Real Food Company. This San Francisco independent gourmet-to-go shop was seemingly packed with last-minute shoppers wanting complete Christmas dinners for ten. As we waited for service, Hugh and I argued the merits of everything: green beans almondine, wheat-berry salad or pasta salad, and whether or not to get her a cranberry-stuffed Cornish game hen.

"Californians are fifty percent more likely to be vegetarian than other people," I said. "In my high school class, I'd say the majority of girls lived on yogurt."

"She's not that privileged," Hugh said.

"Oh, really? I think this lady is pretty darn privileged to have us running all over town like this." I wished I could bite the words back after I'd said them, because his expression tightened. "I'm sorry, Hugh. It's just that you rode into town a few hours ago hell bent on romance with me, and now we're going to be late for drinks with your friends at six, and shepherd's pie with my parents at seven, all because of an errand for your important woman client that can't wait till after December twenty-sixth."

"I'm sorry, Rei, but I've simply got to go there tonight. I wanted to bring you with me, but if you don't want to come, maybe you should go back."

I threw my hands up in the air. "Seeing that I'm your chauffeur, I have no choice. But hey, you can place your order now. Your number's come up."

In the car twenty minutes later, Hugh took my hand. "I could ask one of the others to run me by after the drinks, but then I'd probably be late for dinner with your family."

"I said I'd take you to all your appointments." I grumpily put the car in gear. "What's the address?"

"Sixth Street, the four-hundred block. It's an old hotel called the Blanchard."

"Sixth Street is close to the Tenderloin." I shot him a curious glance. "Who exactly is this woman?"

"You'll see."

I shook my head and kept my thoughts to myself. I knew the Tenderloin in passing—specifically, when I was trying to get from the city out of town on California 101. Now I was driving through it with the intention of stopping, something my parents wouldn't approve of in the dusk. At least there were plenty of small businesses around. In addition to the adult video and film houses, I saw fleabag hotels, Cambodian and Vietnamese restaurants. And of course there were the SRO hotels—the single-room-occupancy places built in the nineteenth century to house Chinese workers. Over the years these buildings had fallen into slum conditions, and whole families were now living in rooms really intended for one person. With San Francisco rents as high as they were, though, this was all that many immigrants and working poor could afford.

I reached Sixth and made a right turn, passing a liquor store, pawnshop, and adult video emporium.

"It's the white building just up on the left side," Hugh said.

"Sorry, but it's a no-parking zone. Let me go around the corner." I passed the building, which was really more a patchwork of gray and white, given all the flaking paint, and made a right into the narrow lane I'd noticed.

I found a small spot and squeezed the behemoth SUV into a small spot between a beat-up Oldsmobile and a taxi.

"Great area," I said, turning off the car. "Can I go in with you? I don't want to stay here alone."

"I'm glad you want to come in," Hugh said. "I didn't know what to expect, given your mood."

"I'll be on my best behavior," I said sarcastically, before he kissed me.

"Mmm. That's better," Hugh said, and it was. My anger had slowly evaporated since I'd seen the client's neighborhood. She was obviously needy, and I felt ashamed of being so grumpy.

Hugh lugged two shopping bags of take-out food, while I carried the gift-wrapped teakettle around the corner and into the vestibule of the building. I paused, looking for a place to buzz for entry upstairs, but Hugh said, "Don't bother. It's unlocked."

We trudged over the old linoleum, passing the various levels. I curiously looked down each of the corridors, the walls scrawled with graffiti and punctuated with doors decorated with scuff marks and many locks. I imagined the long-dead Chinese workers crammed behind each doorway and shuddered.

On the third floor, from behind the first apartment door we passed, came the sound of people arguing in a language that sounded Asian and tonal: Thai? Vietnamese? I had no idea. Coming from the next apartment were the stereo-enhanced moans of a pornographic movie. At least, I hoped it was a movie. Then there was Rosa's door. I could hear the faint strains of a Chinese opera song being played on the radio.

Hugh knocked loudly. No response. He knocked again, and again, and then, faintly, there was the sound of shuffling feet coming toward us. The door creaked open, though the chain remained in place. A section of a small face, as brown and wrinkled as a walnut, appeared. The eyes were bloodshot but sharp.

"What is it?" she asked.

"My name is Hugh Glendinning. Remember, I was here earlier today, Madam, the interview for the case—"

"I know who you are. I thought you got what you needed."

"We did, thank you very much. We . . . ah . . . brought you a gift—nothing big, but something to mark the holiday and my . . . ah . . . appreciation of the time you gave us." Hugh was talking rapidly, which made his accent more pronounced, more difficult to understand.

The woman snorted but her expression softened. "I don't need gifts. All I really need is food, since those meals people do not come on holiday—"

"Well, food is what we brought." I spoke up firmly, bringing myself into the conversation. "My name is Rei. I'm Hugh's friend."

The woman looked me up and down, nodded, then slid the chain off the door and opened it. I followed Hugh, taking a minute to murmur my thanks to this slight figure wearing a faded pink cotton housedress that stretched almost to her ankles. Her bare arms were little more than skin and bones; I imagined that a strong gust of wind coming through the drafty window by her television could topple her. She appeared to be somewhere between eighty and one hundred. I couldn't tell, because I was used to well-kept, healthy Asian women who usually looked a decade or two younger than their age.

"I am lucky you came. The meals people will not come to help me tomorrow," she said, looking at all the plastic containers Hugh was unloading onto her table. There wasn't much else on it, just a Pacific Gas and Electric bill that said Rosa Munoz, which I guessed was her name. Munoz . . . It sounded Spanish. I could have sworn she was Asian, from the shape of her eyelids, and the straight silver and black hair pulled back into a knot. I wondered how she was going to pay it. I couldn't recall if the government still allowed non-citizens to receive Medicare. So much had changed in the United States since I'd moved to Japan.

"It's our pleasure," Hugh said. "I remembered you said your stove was broken. Now you can at least have something good to eat for Christmas, and maybe even make yourself a cup of tea."

"Ah, yes. I can have a tea party."

From the way she raised her eyebrows, I could tell she was being sarcastic, but it seemed lost on Hugh.

"Do you have relatives in the area, Mrs. Munoz?" Hugh asked.

"Oh, no. Never married, never had children. Like I say to you this afternoon, I'm the only one of my family who got out of the P.I. I could never marry, after what happened to my body."

The Philippines. Ah, I was beginning to put things together. A large number of Filipinos had helped the United States during World War II, and had been given the chance to emigrate afterward. Her name, Munoz, must trace back to the history of Spanish colonialism in the Philippines. What didn't make sense to me was the connection between Hugh and Japanese companies.

"May I show you how to use this electric teakettle? You can fill it from the tap, but remember not to let water hit the electric plug." Hugh took the kettle out of its box and handed it to Rosa. She held it awkwardly with her gnarled fingers, and now I was glad we'd gotten her the smaller model.

I glanced out the window, through which I couldn't miss a movie house marquee whose letters were in purple and red neon—all except for the T in ADULT, which had burned out. I kept fixedly looking outside because I didn't want Rosa to see the tears welling in my eyes. This was Christmas Eve. A broken-down old lady shouldn't be alone in a miserable rented room. Now I knew why Hugh had brought me here, and I felt embarrassed by how irritated I'd been to run around for gifts. We should have brought her much more. At the very least we should have given her blankets to stave off the chill, and a new wastebasket to replace the overflowing plastic shopping bag.

I turned back at last to look at the two of them. She and Hugh were sitting on an old, sunken love seat together, talking in low voices. I drew closer and leaned against the wall, since there was no other seating.

"It was kind of you," Rosa said, the stiffness and reserve that had initially been in her voice fading. "I begin to think you might really be able to help."

"I'll find that old friend of yours in Japan, I promise," Hugh said softly. "That is, if he's still alive."

"Buried alive," Rosa said. "Buried alive. They said it was because she was sick, and we could all catch it. But I knew it was because she saw."

"She?" Hugh whipped a small device out of his pocket, and turned it on. A mini tape recorder. He was always at work. "I must have misunderstood, because I thought your friend was a man. The name was Espinosa, right?"

"No, no. Ramon Espinosa is different. This was Hiroko. The girls all had to use Japanese names. I don't know her real name.

Does she understand Tagalog?" Rosa suddenly turned to me.

"No," I said hastily. "I'm not Filipina. Actually, my heritage is half Japanese."

Rosa nodded. "Yes, that's the way, isn't it? You couldn't help it. They just came and took what they wanted. Hurt everybody."

I flushed, realizing that she believed my mother had been raped. Oh, God. She'd lost her grasp on time if she thought I'd been conceived during the war. I nervously looked at Hugh. I was starting to put things together. She'd been hurt. I wanted to know more.

"My father was just a baby during the war. He didn't hurt any-one, but still, I'm very sorry for what his country did in the Philippines during the war. I know the military was rather . . . harsh."

"Miss Munoz, you were saying that Hiroko died because she saw something," Hugh said. "What was it she saw, some atrocity? An act of violence?"

"It was always violent. Didn't I tell you that already?" Rosa clicked her tongue and looked at me. "No, I tried to explain before. I'm not sure of the English word, what was it in? Got . . ."

"What was in what?" Hugh asked.

"I'm not sure of the English—"

She broke off at the sound of glass shattering. I went to the win-dow and looked out, but saw nothing. I said, "Probably someone dropped a beer bottle."

"Or worse," Hugh muttered, and snapped off the tape recorder. "I'm sorry, Miss Munoz, but we'd better go. I didn't intend for this to be a formal interview, anyway. I'll come back to continue with the translator on the twenty-seventh. And I'll do my best to find a repairman to fix your stove."

"I can't afford that—"

"I'll pay."

She nodded, looking satisfied. "What's his name? I don't open the door to nobody I don't know."

Hugh looked understandably blank, so I jumped in. "It will be someone my mother uses. I can telephone you with the name."

"Okay. That would be good, because my landlord doesn't do

anything about the stove. He says appliances are provided in as-is condition."

"It's my sincere wish that after we've won the class action, you won't ever need to worry about that landlord again," Hugh said. "You'll be able to move somewhere quite comfortable."

Rosa waved her hand tiredly. "I won't hold my breath for that."

"Don't, then," Hugh said. "But because of your willingness to speak out, it's going to happen. Thank you. And merry Christmas."

"Do you have a card, Hugh?" I asked. "Let me put down my name and my parents' address and phone for her, just in case."

After I'd scribbled my name on the card, I handed it to her.

She studied it carefully. "Shimura. I know this name."

"Do you?" I paused. "There are a lot of Shimuras around. The ones here aren't like the ones you might have known in the old days."

She shook her head and repeated, "I know that name."

Who was he? A soldier who hurt you?

But I was afraid to ask her those things, and it was time to go. My question would have to wait.

5

When we'd escaped the sad, beaten-down building, I turned to Hugh. "I'm sorry for being so grumpy earlier. I understand why you wanted me to meet her."

Hugh squeezed my hand. "As you can guess, she had some hard times during the war. I heard it all for the first time a few hours ago, with a translator at my side. It was so bad, Rei, she still bears a grudge against the Japanese. But not you, Rei, I'm sure of it—"

"Tell me what happened to Rosa," I said. We'd reached the car, and I quickly unclicked the remote-controlled lock so that we could get in. I wanted to get out of the neighborhood as fast as I could.

"Forget her name, Rei. I didn't mean to let it out."

"It's not your fault. I read it on a bill on the table."

"I see. Well, just keep it between the two of us, all right?" Hugh shot me a wary look. "In 1942, when the Japanese invaded the Philippines, Rosa was thirteen. She was the daughter of a rice farmer living in a village in the southeastern section of the country. As the Japanese moved through her village, her entire family was killed. She was spared because she agreed to join a group of girls who worked at a brothel that served the Japanese forces."

"Comfort women," I said. The word was a Japanese invention— an innocuous title for the most horrible kind of work around. Comfort women were kidnapped from Korea, China, and the

Philippines and forced to serve anyone in the Japanese military who paid for them. The brothel owners applied the fees the comfort women earned against their living expenses, and of course, the women never earned enough to win their freedom.

Hugh sighed heavily. "Rosa, being so young, had a particularly terrible experience. She submitted to fifteen men a day, everyone from regular privates to the medical officer supposedly in charge of her welfare. The women were customarily allowed a few days' rest a month because of menstruation, but because Rosa hadn't begun, she never had a break."

"She told you that? Oh, my God." We were stopped at a red light, so I took my hands off the wheel and put my face in my hands. I understood why Hugh wanted to file a class action on the behalf of all these brutally abused people—but I knew that the class action could easily fail. In the last few years, a group of comfort women had pressed the Japanese government to pay reparations, but the government refused to do it. Some concerned Japanese citizens had set about raising funds to give to the comfort women survivors, but the gesture hadn't been appreciated by most of the women. They wanted an admission of government guilt. I reflected that if the Japanese government—the sponsors of the military—didn't feel enough guilt to compensate the women, who else would? And would the comfort women accept money from anyone other than the government?

Hugh touched my shoulder. "The light changed."

I put my foot hard on the gas, since this was one of the steep sections of California Street and I was desperately afraid of falling backward. When we were securely moving ahead, I told Hugh to continue.

"Finally, she escaped through the help of one of her officer-customers who felt sorry for her, paid off her supposed debt to the brothel, and found a spot for her at a Japanese company operating in another part of the Philippines. She wouldn't have to provide sexual services, just hard labor. She said that even though she had less physical strength than the men, because of what she'd been through in the brothel she had learned to turn off mentally when bad things were happening. The male slaves had a harder time with it. A number of them went insane or committed suicide, or simply succumbed to death. She only knows one male survivor from her group who's still living, the man we mentioned whom I hope to find in Tokyo. Apparently he was blinded. I assume he's living in as desperate a situation as she is."

"Okay, I understand there are a number of these people who were hurt during the war. But I know the Japanese government is standing behind a peace treaty it signed after the war that indemnifies it from actions. Who's going to give Rosa all this money you're hoping for?"

"Some of Japan's largest companies. There's a modern electronics company that sixty years ago used Rosa and her friends to work in the mines, and another company—it's an overnight delivery service now—that used the shipping line it owned in those days to transport the slaves. The list goes on. And we're optimistic the Japanese companies will be easy to hit, given that there is a precedent of successful class actions filed against German companies that used Holocaust victims as labor."

"But Germany's different from Japan," I pointed out. "Their government was also willing to pay reparations to the family of concentration camp victims. It's a country that admits war guilt freely. Japan doesn't."

"Do you think the Germans would have admitted guilt if they hadn't been pushed?" Hugh's voice rose. "The point is that America never pushed Japan for justice; for political reasons, the U.S. government refuses to do it. But lawyers don't have those boundaries. They can take up the fight for social justice—"

"And cash," I said. "You aren't doing this pro bono, are you? You hope to make pots of money for your firm in Washington, just as Charles Sharp does for his firm right here."

"Are you saying this, Rei, because you don't want me to do it?"

I was quiet, remembering Rosa's face. "No. But you've got to admit there's more than goodwill motivating you."

"Certainly. Just as your father doesn't only practice to help the underprivileged, but to own and furnish a house that rivals a minor estate. And you, my dear, charge your clients more than enough to keep a roof over your head and MAC lipstick—"

"Enough, enough, we're here," I said. I stopped the car in the driveway in front of the hotel, and a parking valet moved quickly to attention.

"Are you sure you want to come up and meet them?" Hugh said in a low voice as we got out.

I took his hand in mine. "Yes. I won't put them on the spot, because that wouldn't be fair to you. But count on my listening carefully and giving you my private opinion later on."

As we passed a hotel doorman in a sharp navy uniform, I was flooded with nostalgia. How much the same, and how different, the hotel seemed now that I was no longer eighteen. I'd been frightened by the doorman's once-over then, worrying I wouldn't be allowed in to go up to the famous bar on the fourteenth floor. I'd made it there, but had been carded and left in disgrace.

In the softly lit bar at the top of the hotel, we checked our coats. I stood next to Hugh, looking out at the sprinkling of people at the intimate tables that ringed the room. There weren't many people having drinks at a hotel on Christmas Eve. As I'd expected, most of them were casually dressed tourists. My little black dress would make me look like a lounge singer, or worse. We had to go halfway around the restaurant before Hugh spotted his party—a Caucasian man in his fifties wearing a proper business suit and a younger Asian-American wearing a sweater and khakis.

"So glad you could join us," the older man said, making a gesture of half-rising for us, but not coming up all the way. Hugh shook his hand and that of the younger man.

"Charles, Eric, this is Rei Shimura. Darling, I'd like you to meet—"

"*The* Rei Shimura?" the Asian-American interrupted Hugh in mid-sentence.

I turned from Charles Sharp, whom I'd been blasting with a megawatt smile. Who was this other person who knew my last name? He looked too young to be one of my father's acquaintances, but he didn't look like anyone I remembered from Berkeley.

"Rei, may I introduce Eric Gan," Hugh said in his iciest, most BBC voice—as if he'd seen Eric's inspection of me, and been annoyed. "He's providing language interpretations for the interviews I'll be conducting while in town."

I looked more closely at the young man, who had black hair snipped in a close, trendy hairstyle around his angular-featured face. He was just a few inches taller than I, and looked the way I imagined my brother might—if I'd had a brother.

"I guess you don't recognize me," Eric said.

I smiled politely as I raced through all the associations that made sense. Eric Gan. The name was familiar, definitely part of the memory bank. He was too young to be one of my parents' contemporaries. He could only be someone I'd studied with, or known socially, or—then I got it. Eric Gan. I'd practically forgotten his name, because it had been so long ago.

"Eric! From ALL Japanese class!"

"Yeah." Eric turned to the others. "We were both in Mrs. Yamada's Japanese class for years. We had an independent study project together when we were fourteen."

"That's right, so we did. Oh, Eric, I'm sorry I didn't recognize you right away. It's been so long, and you're, well, a *man* now. And a multilingual lawyer at that." I beamed at him.

"Oh, I'm not an attorney. As your *boyfriend* said"—Eric gave Hugh a playful glance, emphasizing the word—"I'm just an interpreter. When you and I were at ALL together, I was just doing Tagalog, Japanese, and Mandarin, but I went on to pick up Cantonese, Vietnamese, and Bahasa Malaysia—"

"Bahasa Malaysian. That certainly is impressive," Hugh said, pulling out a chair for me.

"Bahasa *Malaysia*, not Malaysian." Eric wrinkled his nose at Hugh. "It's a subtle thing, but that's the way foreign languages work."

"Ah, the waiter's here. Let's order our drinks," I said hastily. Eric always had had a snide side to him—that's why I'd never been close to him, though we'd experimented a bit in our early teens. I ordered a wine spritzer, since I was driving home, and Hugh ordered his usual whisky with water on the side. When the waiter departed, Charles Sharp asked me what ALL was.

"The Asian Languages League," I said, settling back and feeling grateful for his diplomacy. "It's a nonprofit that was formed in the early seventies by Asian-American families who wanted their kids to have exposure to the languages of their heritage. It was also a bridge to all the Asian immigrants coming in."

"Let me make a note of it," Charles said, taking a small notebook from his breast pocket. "ALL. That could be a good source to notify about our services for potential plaintiffs—"

"My father's the group president right now. Hugh can talk to him about it." Feeling cheered by how well things were going, I sipped my spritzer. I'd have liked to have another, but I knew I was going to have to be more careful about drinking than I was in Japan. There, I never drove; here, I was in command of my mother's SUV.

"Dr. Shimura's quite a guy. Have you met him yet?" Eric turned to Hugh.

"Yes, in Washington a month ago."

"They called him the daimyo back when we were kids. Still do, probably."

"'Daimyo'?" Charles Sharp asked, giving Eric a slight frown.

"A daimyo is a Japanese lord, the kind of guy who had the samurai at his beck and call, who in turn extorted money from the peasants." Eric took a hefty swig of his beer. "You should have seen Rei's father during the league's annual fund-raiser. My mother kept the phone off the hook for most of December, she was so afraid of being forced to give up more than she could afford."

"That doesn't sound like my father. He was completely mild-mannered," I protested.

"Think back to a certain Sunday afternoon in the spring of 1986," Eric said, winking at me. "I'm sure Rei remembers, but she might not want to talk about it."

"What a good memory you have, Eric," Hugh said. "With your attention to detail, I'm going to expect the translation work to be world-class."

"Eric's top-drawer," Charles Sharp said with an edge of irritation. "He's done about a dozen survivor interviews for us already, and there have been no complaints."

"Will Eric be following Hugh to Japan to assist with the interviews there?" I asked, knowing what I wanted the answer to be: No.

"Probably. After all, he's a trusted member of our team."

"Thank you, sir," Eric said, then turned to me with a smile he must have thought was seductive. "Guess you can show me around Tokyo in the off hours, Rei."

"We'll do our best," I said faintly. "I'm sure that once home, I'll be as busy as Hugh is. I'm working on a history project and I have an antiques business on the side . . ."

"Oh, really? I collect Asian antiques," Charles said. "Where is your shop?"

We chatted on about the business I'd set up hunting for pieces that people dreamed about, but couldn't find. I tried to say enough to steer the conversation away from the dangerous territory where it had been, but not so much as to seem like an egomaniac. At last, I said, "Enough about me. I'm interested in hearing the long-range goals of your project. Hugh hasn't told me much, but I sense it's going to take some terrific teamwork between his firm in Washington and yours."

"Yes, we're relying on Hugh and his understanding of the Japanese psyche to help us along in Japan, just as Eric is so useful with Tagalog speakers. I understand the interview with the potential plaintiff went very well. I'm looking forward to seeing the transcript," Charles said.

"I'll have it for you by the time we meet again," Eric said.

I waited for Hugh to mention that he had some new details from the tape he'd made during our recent visit, but he didn't say anything. Then I remembered that my voice was on the tape. Maybe he didn't want to reveal that I'd been along on the visit. I wished Charles would say more about the case, but I had to be sure I didn't reveal that I knew more than was proper.

"So, what are your plans for Christmas?" Charles Sharp turned his gimlet gaze on me.

"Well, I'm visiting my parents here for the week. The goal is to give them and Hugh a chance to get to know each other."

"Yes, and as the new boyfriend in town you can imagine how nervous I am." Hugh glanced at his watch. "Actually, sir, Rei's mother is expecting us for shepherd's pie in ten minutes. We're going to have to beg your pardon."

"Have you become a meat-eater, Rei?" Eric asked as I stood up to gather my things.

"No. I've gotten my family to use Quorn in place of ground beef. It's the most amazing, all-natural protein source—"

"It's a fungus that grows underground in England," Hugh said, grinning. "The weird thing is it actually tastes good."

"Uh-huh," Eric said, looking about as unconvinced as Charles Sharp. "Anyway, you don't have to worry about serving that at the party. I'm bringing a tray of my famous vegetarian *lumpia*."

"Which party?" Hugh asked, knitting his brow.

"The Shimuras invited me to their party," Eric said, sounding triumphant. "ALL has a holiday gathering every year, and this year it's at their place."

Feeling conscious of the one person in the cluster who had been left out, I said, "Mr. Sharp, our house is open to you as well. Please come—my parents would love to meet a neighbor."

"Do you live in Pacific Heights?" He sounded surprised.

"Yes, on Green Street. You'll know the house from the flag waving out front."

"The rising sun?"

"At the moment it's the Union Jack, because Hugh's with us."

"Well, Miss Shimura, I'll try. I live over on Washington Street myself. We're not much for flag-waving there."

"I'll take the elevator down with you," Eric volunteered. When we got to the lobby, he didn't go his own way but waited around while the valet pulled up with my mother's SUV.

"Nice wheels, Rei."

"Oh, they're my mother's."

"You never have your own car. I remember your mother's old Camry well—the backseat especially."

As Hugh turned to gape at me in horror, I snapped, "It was the backseat because we were fourteen years old and had to be driven places!"

I stormed over to the driver's side and slammed the door. I would have burned rubber getting out of there, if the valet hadn't been standing in the way because I'd forgotten to tip him.

6

"I'd laugh if it didn't hurt so much," Hugh said. "Three weeks ago I was trying to make peace with your last ex-lover, and now I learn there's another one to get used to."

"Eric wasn't technically my lover. We were just kids, believe me."

"If that's true, what did your father walk in on that day in 1986 that was so damn marvelous Eric Gan's never forgotten it?"

"It's all goes back to those language classes," I said, deciding that I would have to be forthcoming—but that I'd put things in the most gentle terms possible. "Eric and I were so far ahead of the others—Eric in terms of his *kanji* knowledge, and me because I spoke good colloquial Japanese—that we'd been given independent study assignments. We'd finished our projects early, but instead of telling the teacher we were done and needed more work, we played hooky. We would hang around my house, since my parents usually were out doing things together on Sunday afternoons. My parents were smart enough not to trust me with a house key, but they didn't realize that I was small enough to fit in through the milk door. On more than one Sunday, we slipped in that way. The last time we did this we were fooling around in the kitchen. We provided a real eyeful for my father, who it turned out had been home."

Hugh was starting to smile. "Jesus. What happened then?"

"Unfortunately, Eric tried to escape through the milk door, but he moved too fast and got the rivets of his Levi's caught on a nail. He actually had to slip out of his jeans to get free, and in the process he got scratched on his bottom and started howling with pain. Ultimately my father got involved in examining the injury—"

"Oh, my God. There should be a law against that kind of thing." Hugh was laughing so hard that I could see tears forming in the corners of his eyes. "In this politically correct city, maybe there is a law."

"Thanks for understanding." I kissed Hugh on his cheek. "I'm sure that Eric's coming to that party just to rib me, but you don't have to worry that he's any sort of threat. He's such a phony. The truth is that his famous vegetarian *lumpia* comes from a Filipino grocery, though he always tries to pass it off as his own. If you want to get back at him, you should ask him his recipe."

"I'll try to take the higher road. But you can't blame me if I ask him if he's traveled through any milk doors lately."

"Just don't say anything to my parents about this. I think they've forgotten."

"I wouldn't dream of it." But from the glint in Hugh's eyes, I knew he really wanted to.

"Here you are!" my mother trilled as she opened the front door to us. I had to knock because, even at my age, I still didn't have my own house key.

"The shepherd's pie smells divine. Far better than the frozen ones that have been sustaining me for the last few years away from home," Hugh said, ambling toward the kitchen.

"We'll be eating in the dining room," my mother called after him.

"I'll be there in a sec. Rei wanted to show me an architectural detail in the kitchen first."

I hurried after him, muttering under my breath, "Don't you believe me? The door is in the wall right behind the kitchen table—"

"It's not that I don't believe you—I want to see the size of the door. I'm curious about exactly how small your bottom was at that time. Not to mention Eric's."

"Yes, you can rib him about it if he gets obnoxious with you again," I agreed.

The view under the kitchen table, though, was obstructed by a long red-and-green Christmas tablecloth—and by my father, who was seated at the table reading *The Annals of Psychiatry.*

"Oh, hello, sir!" Hugh stopped short, and I bumped into his back. "I mean, Dr. Shimura. I apologize for the interruption—"

"Not at all," my father said, rising and stretching his hand out to grasp Hugh's. "I've been hoping for your return, because Catherine's shepherd's pie came out of the oven five minutes ago. And please call me Toshiro. Otherwise, I'll feel as if we're having an office visit."

"I hope that won't be the case. I mean, I've got my imperfections, but one of the things I pride myself on is good mental health, though Rei's the one I can credit for keeping me so happy." Hugh gave me a fond look, which made me blush.

"Hugh, would you care to try a California cabernet?" my mother asked. "I've been waiting for the last two years to open a certain '97 from the Sonoma Valley."

"It sounds scrumptious, but I'm likely to nod off if I have more alcohol. I had a small whisky at the hotel which hit me like a ton of bricks."

"Don't worry, then, we'll save it for tomorrow's Christmas lunch," my mother said.

"Mom! What about me?" I demanded.

"Wine? Oh, that's right, you're old enough to drink. I almost forgot. Manami never touches wine," my mother said, giving a fond glance to the young woman, who had been quietly walking around the table pouring water into everyone's glass.

"Here, let me open the bottle," Hugh said, taking the bottle from my mother, who was struggling with the fancy corkscrew I'd given her a few holidays back. "I'll take a taste, because who knows when I'll ever have the chance for a Sonoma '97 again?"

"Many more times, if you stay in this neighborhood. And pour a big glass for me—I've had quite a day."

As we settled around the twenty-foot-long mahogany table—
my mother had already put in the extra leaves, given that the ALL
party was a few days away—she told us about her day. The problems had started when the plum pudding had arrived smelling
off. The deliveryman was gone by this point, so she'd called
Williams-Sonoma to arrange for a replacement, but they didn't
know when he could come back. Then, while looking for Asian-
themed cocktail napkins at Gumps, she'd also noticed a lavish display of Japanese kimono sashes. "Three hundred dollars per obi,
Rei. While you're here, darling, you should go in and get an
appointment with them, see if you could become their obi
importer. Why, out of the collection you've amassed for yourself,
surely there are a few dozen you could part with."

The story of my mother's day irritated me; it seemed so trivial,
given what we'd seen of Rosa's life. I frowned and said, "Right
now, the thought of selling my own collection doesn't really
appeal to me. I mean, we've lost so much of what Dad had." I
turned directly to my father. "Didn't you sell some old family possessions back in the seventies?"

"Why would I do that?" He frowned at me.

"Of course you did!" My mother rapped him playfully on the
knuckles, then spoke to all of us. "We sold a few things that were
worth money but didn't have deep emotional significance back in
the mid-seventies to put together enough cash for a good down
payment on this house. I sold an old Baltimore quilt that had
belonged to a great-great-aunt, and Toshiro sold a document that
belonged to his grandfather. Of course, it would be nice if we still
had those things, but we had to do what we could to get a decent
roof over our heads."

"'Decent' isn't the word for it," Hugh cut in. "It's a beautiful
house. And if you bought in the seventies, the appreciation in its
appraised value must be tremendous."

"Well, thank you for the compliment. And the truth is, the
house *has* risen in value—much more than the quilt and the letter
could have brought if we went to Hopewell's today. It would be
unheard of today for people like us to be able to buy a house in

this neighborhood. It turned over mostly to computer people a few years ago, though now some of them have had to sell, so it's back to CEOs and lawyers again."

"Speaking of lawyers, Charles Sharp lives around here," I said. When my parents looked blank, I added, "Charles is one of the principals in Sharp, Witter and Rowe, the law firm Hugh's consulting with right now. Oops. Is it all right that I said that, Hugh?"

"Sure," Hugh said. "I'd like to get their thoughts on the case as well. Although I must warn you, it's not a particularly pleasant dining topic."

"Really? Do tell, we're all grown-ups here, it's all right!" my mother said, giggling. Clearly, the wine had gone to her head.

Hugh shook his head. "All right. In a nutshell, what's happened is that Andrews and Cheyne, the firm I work for in Washington, have joined up with the local firm Rei mentioned to mount a class action seeking reparations for the Asian and American victims who were slave laborers of Japanese *zaibatsu* during World War II."

"But isn't a *zaibatsu* an animal? Pig or . . ." My mother drew her perfectly waxed brows together as she struggled to remember her basic Japanese.

Manami, who had been silent, was now hysterically laughing, her hand in front of her mouth as if that would hide it. She gasped, "Not *buta!* No, no!"

"What did I say?" my mother demanded.

"*Buta* is pig," he began. "A *zaibatsu* is a superpowerful Japanese company such as Honda or Sony or my own former employer, Sendai," Hugh explained. "But these companies aren't named in the suit—"

"Who is?" Manami asked.

Hugh shook his head and smiled. "That is something I can't tell you. At least, not until we've spoken with them and decided for certain to file the class action. I can tell you about our plaintiffs, though—these are very old women and men who suffered unthinkable abuse at the hands of the Japanese during the war."

"We've always been interested in social justice," my mother said, regaining her composure. "Rei was still a pea in the pod when we were marching against U.S. involvement in Vietnam, but she was right there, bouncing along in a Snugli as we drew attention to injustices against Mexican farm laborers, Native Americans, and Angela Davis!"

Manami looked puzzled; clearly, these names and issues meant nothing to her. I resolved to give her a minicourse in seventies liberalism later on.

"I'm relieved to hear you're sympathetic to this project," Hugh said. "I've been trying to stress that it's not an attack on Japan, but rather on the *zaibatsu* companies profiting from abuse of powerless people."

"So what did these *zaibatsu* do?" my mother asked.

Hugh told them some of the details about Rosa—without mentioning her name—and about others who'd told their stories before, to other people, but who had passed away and were thus unable to reap any benefits from the class action.

My mother's eyes were large, and I saw her glance nervously at my father, who, despite the alcoholic flush on his cheeks, looked quite grave.

Manami had a similarly serious face. I sensed she wanted to say something, and when Hugh stopped talking, she did. "Actually, it is incorrect that the Japanese government forced the girls to do it. The facts remain that the brothel owners invited them. These people were not even Japanese. Some of them were Korean and Chinese—"

Hugh waved a dismissive hand. "Yes, the Japanese hired people who came from the comfort women's home countries and thus were more likely to be able to convince them to leave their own lands and go work in the brothels."

"Well, then, why aren't *those* governments in trouble?" Manami, with her braids, looked like a child—but a feisty one. It was the first time I'd heard her disagree with anything, and I realized she was finally getting used to our family's open style.

"Manami has a point," I said. "Hugh and the lawyers should go after the brothel owners as well—it would be another way for the comfort women to get reparations."

"Even if a former brothel owner is alive—which I doubt—it's not likely that he'd have the kind of money to pay victims that the *zaibatsu* groups would. I'd like to follow every path possible for the victims, but this particular detour would simply waste time. The *zaibatsu* are sitting ducks. Or pigs, as your mother so aptly pointed out."

"What do you think, Dad?" I turned to my father, who'd been quiet.

"Over the years, I've overseen the psychiatric treatment of some comfort women in my practice," my father said. "But this business about the companies is new to me."

"Nobody thinks about it," Hugh said. "Not until the Holocaust victims rose up against the German companies that used them did this issue come to light and seem like a possibility for Japan."

"But I thought you liked Japan." Manami regarded Hugh with clear confusion.

"I do, Manami. I love the people, the way of life, the land. But there are people within the country that did horrible things to other people because they thought those people were subhuman. They thought they got away with it. Sixty years later, we're going to tell them that they can't."

Hugh had been speaking so passionately and quickly that his Edinburgh burr had made his English hard to understand; I could tell from Manami's blank expression. So I translated in Japanese as best I could, and she nodded.

"You have a strong feeling, Hugh-san. Very strong."

My father cleared his throat. "This is no doubt a shock for Manami, please remember this. The topic is not common conversation in Japan, now or when I was growing up. When I grew up in the postwar era, finding enough food, and heat, and hoping for a chance to rejoin the world economy were the things that my parents worried about."

"Yes, as we say in Japan, water washes things away," Manami said "We must concentrate on Japan being the strong caretaker of modern Asia, to build for the future."

Hugh nodded politely, then turned right back to my father. "So you actually counseled female patients living in San Francisco who were comfort women? Do you know if any of them are still alive?"

My father shrugged. "I'm sure that some are. We tried to start a group therapy program in the seventies, but it ultimately floundered because so many of the women were too ashamed to voice their experiences. There is a cultural insistence on the purity of Asian women—as you must know," my father added a bit archly.

Right on, Dad, I said to myself. *Let Hugh think you believe I observe all the ancient Buddhist rules.*

"About your patients," Hugh said to my father, interrupting my thoughts. "They could receive significant financial benefits from joining the class action. May I share our recruitment letter with you and any colleagues you think have handled similar populations?"

My father shook his head. "Sorry, but that would be inappropriate."

"Why?" I asked, because Hugh's skin had flushed and I could see he had been embarrassed and shocked by my father's response.

My father's eyes glinted in a way that I knew meant bad news, and he began speaking rapidly—so quickly that his Japanese accent became more prominent, a sure sign of his stress. "First, I worry this suit is like opening Pandora's box for patients who have, over the years, come to terms with their grief and learned to become high-functioning." He paused. "I cannot encourage patients to become involved in an enterprise with no likelihood of a successful outcome. Finally, the whole enterprise is a conflict of interest, since it could potentially enrich my own family via my daughter." My father cleared his throat. "That is, if you plan to marry her."

"Dad!" I shot a reproving look at him and then said to Hugh, "You don't have to listen to this. You don't have to stay in this house, either."

Hugh's face was now beet red, but he held up a cautionary hand. "Sorry, but it's my fault entirely. I asked a question, and your father was good enough to answer me candidly. I disagree entirely with his first and second points, but I do agree with him on the point of marriage." He turned to me. "Of course I want to marry you. For ages I've wanted this." He glanced at my parents and said, "I've asked her repeatedly. She's just, um, delayed her decision."

"Please excuse me," Manami blurted. "Then you may have your family moment."

"Manami, I apologize. It was a lovely dinner, Mom. I'm sorry, but I have to take a break." I stood up, ignoring the napkin that had fallen from my lap to the floor. I had to leave. I felt utterly humiliated that my father had called Hugh on the carpet about our relationship within an hour of their renewed contact. Now I was beginning to get a sense of why Eric Gan had been so terrified of the man he called the daimyo.

"Where are you going, honey? It's raining!" my mother called as I headed for the front door. Everyone else was frozen at the table.

"Anywhere but here!"

Hugh followed me to the door and caught me by the arm. "I'm not going out, and I wish you wouldn't either."

"But what are you going to do alone with them?" I was aghast.

"I'm not alone—Manami's here, and I'll ask her to help me wash up. And then I'll make tea for everyone. After I've got enough caffeine and sugar in me, I'll try to find something to say to your father that might convince him I'm not a gold-digging, ambulance-chasing bastard."

"Oh, Hugh. You don't need to try." Even though we were clearly visible to my parents, sitting thirty feet away in the dining room, I gave him a quick kiss and whispered that I'd sneak up to his room later to find out how things had gone. Then, loudly, so they could hear, I said, "I'm just going to walk a few blocks to clear my head. I'll be back in fifteen minutes."

"Is it safe to walk around here in the dark?" Hugh asked.

"Safe as houses. There's a carolers' group going around, anyway—I'll trail them."

I walked around behind a bunch of people, half dressed in North Face jackets, the others in fur, singing "Good King Wenceslas"—it was an upscale caroling group, with an emphasis on English and Latin songs. Despite the mist, I didn't cool off. I knew I was going back to a house where my normally mild-mannered father was planning to engage in a long, drawn-out process of tormenting both my lover and me. *God rest ye, merry gentlemen, indeed.*

When I rapped on the door a half hour later and my mother opened it, everything was still. The dining room had been cleaned up, and I couldn't see my father or Hugh in the front parlor.

"Your father's reading in the library," my mother said in a low voice. "Hugh went to bed. And so did Manami."

"Not together, I hope."

"What kind of a comment is that?" my mother demanded. "Manami's a nice girl."

"So am I," I retorted. "Why didn't you let Hugh stay in my room?"

My mother wrapped an arm around me. "Don't fret. It will just take time. Your father's seen himself as the primary man in your life for almost thirty years. And Hugh has his own issues to work through."

"Such as?" Of course, Hugh wasn't perfect, but I was the only one allowed to say that.

"When Hugh knew you in Japan, he thought you were a poor girl, didn't he?"

"Mom, nobody says 'poor' anymore, they say 'low income.' And I have no idea what he thought—"

"Well, in Tokyo you live rather modestly, but now he's entered your family home and been hit over the head with the understanding that you grew up with plenty of comforts." My mother stroked a stray hair away from my forehead. "Put yourself in the poor man's place. He might feel he needs to prove that he's got the resources to care for you properly. The last thing he'd want to do is give us the feeling he's a sleaze."

"Enough already!" I couldn't risk hearing more, so I hurried up the stairs, unsure of why I felt so agitated. We weren't rich. My parents had made a canny real estate investment in the seventies, but that was all. My mother drove an Infiniti, not a Lexus. My father clipped coupons. And my parents had made a bizarre gesture of taking in a foreign lodger for $100 a month.

We were a seriously odd family. Perhaps seeing my background, Hugh would decide I was more trouble than it was worth.

But when Hugh crept into my room later that night, whispering endearments and engineering me into a position that wouldn't rock the antique bed, I realized that I didn't need to worry.

He loved me, as I did him.

It would just take the rest of them some time to catch up to us.

7

Christmas morning. It was six, the hour I always awoke as a child. In the old days, I couldn't wait to get to the needlepoint stocking my Baltimore grandmother had made for me. But today, I knew that Hugh would be sleeping in, given his jet lag, and I didn't want to open my stocking alone, so I headed for the kitchen to make coffee.

My father had beaten me to the task. He looked up from his usual seat at the kitchen table. "Merry Christmas."

"To you as well." I didn't meet his eyes, just poured myself a cup of coffee.

"Why didn't you come to talk with me yesterday evening when you got home? I had no idea how long you were out in the streets."

I dropped four sugar cubes in my coffee. "Couldn't you have asked Mom?"

"I did eventually. But I wanted to apologize to you myself for saying what I did about the marriage. It's not that I'm pushing for it, I hardly know the man at all—"

"You mean—you don't like him?"

"I do, chiefly because he seems to care a great deal about you. In fact, I'm sure that you could convince him to turn down this assignment."

"You don't understand! He leapt at it as a way to go back to Japan—to be with me."

"Why couldn't he return to the company he used to work for? He apparently had a good time working for Sendai, a top *zaibatsu* company—now he's seeking to bankrupt a company just like it. Manami's father works for a *zaibatsu*, as do most people's fathers, husbands, and sons. Can you imagine how an attack on a *zaibatsu* will play in the Japanese papers?"

"I certainly can." My private thoughts from the previous day came back to me. My father had made some very logical points. And in fact, I'd had my doubts about the law firms' motives being completely altruistic. I'd argued that to Hugh, and now I was defending him to my father. Whose side should I be on? I couldn't decide. "Let's lay the matter to rest for the holiday, okay? I don't want to go through this with Mom and Hugh again."

I heard footsteps coming down the stairs—my mother's light tread, followed by a heavier one and the sound of laughter. I went to the stereo and turned on the old recording of *Amahl and the Night Visitors*. Christmas was on.

Santa had filled everyone's stockings with fruits and home-made truffles. My parents were stunned by the opera tickets Hugh had given them; my gifts were smaller—a first edition of *Snow Country* for my father and a 1920s purple silk kimono for my mother—but they kissed me and said the gifts were perfect. I explained to Manami that the black cotton turtleneck I'd given her should enable her to pass for a real San Francisco hipster; she nodded and said it would keep her warm, anyway. Hugh had given her a map of San Francisco with all the bus routes outlined on it, since I'd told him she couldn't drive. My parents gave Manami a generous gift certificate to the Gap, and Hugh a new cell phone with our home number stored in memory. I had worried about Hugh's presents for a long time, and I gave him the new Bryan Ferry CD and an antique traveling gentleman's desk that I'd gotten at auction with my mother a few days before.

The things I received were all nice. My parents presented me with a huge set of engraved stationery—perhaps a hint that I should write more—and Manami shyly presented some bath salts from Hakone. From Hugh, I received *The Rough Guide to Scotland* with a tartan G-string tucked inside that my mother blithely assumed was a bookmark. It was just as well.

"The private present comes later," he whispered in my ear before we sat down to breakfast. But when would there be time? It was off to Grace Cathedral after breakfast for the morning service. Hugh went eagerly—he'd grown up in the Church of Scotland, which was practically the same thing as Episcopalian, which my mother was. My father professed to follow no religion, like most Japanese, but over the years, attending occasionally with my mother, he'd made quite a few good friends at Grace. Manami went out of tourist curiosity. I had to confess I was the only one there who went out of duty.

While the choir sang in a single, ethereal voice about the arrival of Christ, I stood silently in the midst of them, thinking that I felt more at home at the Yanaka Shrine in Tokyo. The shrine was Shinto, part of Japan's ancient worship of ancestors and nature. Not God. A couple of Sundays a month I'd take myself through its faded crimson-orange *torii* gate and perform the ritual of washing my hands, clapping them twice, and then disappearing into myself for a few moments. Yes, I thought of my parents, and my grandparents before them, even though this was not our ancestral seat. I thought of everyone I loved. Overwhelmingly, though, the miracle of the shrine was its proximity, the fact that it was part of my ordinary life. It reminded me that I'd reached the goal I'd aspired to since childhood—living in Japan. That was what I wanted more than money or love.

After the service ended and people had dispersed, we walked the cathedral's famous labyrinth—a giant carpet woven with a medieval design of curving paths that people moved along in prayer, sometimes stopping to kneel. It was a copy of a real out-door labyrinth in Chartres, France; Hugh had actually been there, and was describing it to my mother. My father stood at a spot where he could gaze out beyond Grace's heavy doors into the gray San Francisco day. I moved slowly along the carpet's path to the center, lost in thought.

If I loved Japan, how could I support Hugh's suit? Yesterday, I'd been so moved by Rosa's story, and so excited by idea of the class action. I wanted justice for the comfort women and slaves—that was without question. But Hugh's work would create tension in my social circle. I would still have my good Japanese name, but I wouldn't be a samurai daughter anymore. Instead, I'd be an enemy of Japan Inc.

Manami wanted to buy postcards at the cathedral's gift shop, so we went downstairs and then finally back out to the car.

"Does it feel like Christmas?" my mother asked as my father steered us all back to Pacific Heights.

No, I thought. *The day is gray and depressing and feels like a portent of more bad days to come.*

"Rather!" Hugh said cheerfully. "It rains in Scotland. The only thing I'm missing is the bogs, but perhaps if I get a good close look at the Bay later on, that'll do it."

"Have you called your parents yet?" my mother asked.

"Actually, no. I'll do it right away when we get back—they're nine hours ahead."

On the short but hilly ride home, my anxiousness slowly turned to nausea. The backseat of the Infiniti, sandwiched between Hugh and Manami, was the wrong place for me. And my mother was talking about salmon, which made it all the worse.

I was the first out of the car when we got back to Green Street, gasping for cool, rainy air. I walked up the steps to the house, hoping against hope my mother hadn't chosen the salmon just for me, because I didn't know if I could eat it.

I waited by the door, deep-breathing, as Hugh came up behind me.

"Hey, what's the rush? Your father lent me his key ring—which one is for the door?"

"The old Yale one," I said. But the moment I fit it into its keyhole, the door popped loose from the frame. "It's unlocked. Whose fault was that?"

"What?" my mother said, coming up behind me. "I'm sure I locked it earlier."

"What a perfect time for a break-in," I said. "Christmas morning, while the presents are lying around downstairs and the family's away at church. We must have been watched by someone."

"You're jumping to conclusions," my mother said, going straight into the house. "Let me count the silver in the dining room. You all can see if the presents are still here." Yes, the silver was there. The ceramics were still in the cabinets and on the sideboard, the unwrapped presents were in the parlor, and in the kitchen a $20 bill was lying neatly on the Welsh dresser where my mother had left it. The checkbook was in the drawer.

Nothing was wrong.

My mother laughed with relief, although my father began chastising her for being careless enough to forget to pull the door all the way closed. She was the last one out the front door—she had to have been the culprit.

Feeling glad I wasn't the one to blame, I sank down in a soft sofa in the library.

"Well, now that it seems everything's all right, would anyone mind if I made a phone call? It's getting late in the evening in Scotland, and I usually talk to my parents on Christmas."

"Oh, you must!" my mother exclaimed.

Hugh took his new cell phone out of his jacket pocket. "This really was awfully handy. Thanks again."

"Unfortunately, it's not on an international calling plan yet," my father apologized. "I thought you might want to choose the carrier you were using before?"

"I did that already," Hugh said, smiling. "Before we went to the cathedral, I took a few moments."

"But you must use our home phone. We signed up for an excellent international calling plan when Rei went overseas—"

"Even to the U.K.?" Hugh looked dubious.

"Ten cents a minute. We'll be offended if you don't use it."

"Thanks," Hugh said, and began dialing the old black-and-white phone that had been in the library for as long as I could remember.

"I'm going to be sick," I said. "Sick from nerves."

Hugh grinned at me. "They'll love you just as much as I do. But speak slowly, hey? The Yank accent will throw them."

Hugh talked for the first ten minutes, and then handed the phone to me. I shouldn't have worried because I could barely get a word in edgewise. Which was fine with me—Hugh's mother had a gorgeous lilt that was similar to Hugh's, but more charmingly colloquial. "Happy Christmas, but why aren't you here with us?" she began. "When are you coming to visit? We need to finally clap eyes on the gal that's stolen our eldest son's heart—"

"Stolen," I heard echoing somewhere else, with a Japanese accent.

Stolen?

I turned my head to see that Manami and my parents had entered the room. My mother was pantomiming for me to end the phone call.

"Pardon me, Mrs. Glendinning, my mother has something to say to me." I rolled my eyes at my mother, completely irritated.

"My name's Lydia, dear. Please use it if you like and—"

Hugh took the phone from me. "Mum, there's a small problem here, so we're going to have to ring off. No, don't worry, I'll get back to you in a few—oh, right, it's the middle of the night. I'll call you tomorrow. Right. Lots of love to everyone."

"Someone has been in my room," Manami said in a small but angry voice when the phone had been hung up at last. "The papers on my desk are disorganized. And someone looked inside my backpack!"

"It's very strange," my mother said.

"Manami, I hope you don't suspect me," Hugh said. "Catherine showed me your door, so I knew not to go inside it—"

"I did not mean to lay blame that way," Manami said, but she kept her eyes to the ground.

"Remember, everyone, the front door was unlocked," I said. "We thought a thief would be interested in the valuables on the first floor, but maybe not. Maybe it was someone who has a thing for Manami—you know, a person from the hospital—"

I looked at Manami with her schoolgirl braids, and, on this day, in honor of the holiday, her neat gray skirt. She was not overtly sexy, but she might appeal to someone who liked the fifties school-girl look.

"Before we jump to conclusions, let's look in all our rooms," my mother said. "And the bathrooms, too—most house-breakers are junkies."

"Good point," I said, already halfway up the stairs. "Someone might very well know there are two doctors in the house and expect them to have hoards of Xanax."

That theory didn't pan out. My room was untouched, as was my parent's. But when Hugh came down from the third floor, his face was serious. "Just as Manami said, someone was up there and went through my suitcase and the drawers of the desk. I can't figure out what's gone; I'll have to spend a few hours searching."

"Your briefcase? Was that touched?" I asked.

He shook his head. "Fortunately not, because that's where all my legal notes are. I'd brought it downstairs earlier because I had to find the information on my telephone account. After I was through linking the cell phone to the provider, it was time to go to church. I didn't have time to go up to the third floor, so I left it under the Christmas tree. See? It's still there."

"It looks like a Christmas present," I said, regarding the oxblood leather briefcase half-hidden by some torn wrapping paper.

Hugh picked it up and opened it. "I'll go through it carefully, but it seems as if everything's here."

"Do we still keep a key under the hibachi on the front steps?" my father asked my mother.

She nodded. "Yes, I put it back out when Manami came to live with us, just in case she came home when we weren't here one day and was missing a key."

"I have not used it at all," Manami said.

"I'll see if it's in its proper place." My father went out of the house, and then came back in. "It's gone."

I glanced at Manami, whose face had gone pale. All of a sudden I felt what she had to be feeling—that this place that she'd thought was safe really wasn't.

"You should call the police," I said.

"Oh, I feel like such a fool to have left the key there. The police are going to scold me, aren't they?" my mother fretted.

"They're not going to be happy to come out on Christmas, especially if nothing was stolen but a house key," my father said. "They were so annoyed with us last month when we called about that loud group of teenagers. I hope we don't get the same officer."

"Maybe it was those teenagers," Hugh said to my parents. "They could have removed the key as a prank. That's the kind of thing the local lads did back in my day."

"But if it was teenagers, why didn't they take anything?" I mused aloud. "I can understand them skipping the antiques, but what about CDs or cash or electronic equipment? Why did they just snoop on the third floor?"

"We need to have our locks changed," my father said. "I'll get on the phone to see if there's a locksmith working today. I expect we'll have to pay a premium."

"And I'll call the police," I offered. "You never know whether any other houses on the street might have been hit. If there's a pattern, it could be easier to catch whoever was here."

I made my call, but was startled that the police weren't willing to come to our house. The matter of a missing house key and rustled possessions was deemed small enough for me to just relate the details over the phone. They took down the details for an incident report they said we could give to our insurance company, should we want to make a claim for the cost of having the locks changed. Finally, I was warned not to keep keys in safe places outside of houses, because no place was truly safe. Yes, I agreed. I'd tell everyone in the house.

8

Two new locks and four keys to match cost a breathtaking $800, something my father grumbled about all through lunch. At least the locksmith had come. Our castle was impenetrable again. Still, my parents were so depressed that I thought they needed a change of scenery. I reminded them of their invitation to a neighbor's open house around the corner, and they departed with the plan to organize everyone there into a neighborhood watch group.

Manami went upstairs to search her room again, just in case she'd missed something that had been taken. I sat down in the kitchen with a bowl of warm water, the silver polish, and some soft cloths; I'd promised my mother I'd polish her antique Stieff silver tea service for the forthcoming ALL party. Hugh sat down across from me, working on e-mail from his laptop computer.

"Domestic bliss," I said as I finished rubbing the sugar bowl to a sparkle.

"It would be, if I weren't so on edge," Hugh said. "I've received an e-mail from Charles Sharp ordering utmost confidentiality. I hate to think what might have happened if my briefcase had been stolen. We came close to utter disaster."

"No thief would know what to make of your notes," I tried to reassure him.

He pressed his lips together. "Well, it didn't happen, that's the important thing. But I'm on edge. Let's go out, do something more cheerful."

I agreed wholeheartedly. I placed all the finished silver on the sideboard, and then ran up the two flights of stairs to check if Manami wanted to come along.

"No, thank you. I'd rather stay here and read," Manami said somberly.

"What about dinner—would you like to go out with us?"

"Oh, no. Today's food was enough. It was delicious, but so heavy. If I become hungry, I will boil some Japanese noodles."

Feeling secretly relieved that I'd now have some time alone with Hugh, I went downstairs to tell him we were at liberty.

"Great. Do you think your mother would mind if we borrowed her car? I'd like to see something more of the city, especially since I have to work tomorrow."

"I'm sure it's no problem," I said, going into the kitchen to find my mother's car keys in the dresser. "What do you want to see?"

"Well, I'm a bit embarrassed, because it's so touristy . . ."

I winked at him. "Let me guess. The Golden Gate Bridge?"

I was right, of course. It wasn't a particularly good day to see the bridge, because of all the fog and the fact that it was getting late; however, there would be no rush hour traffic, given that it was Christmas. I brought a travel mug of tea for each of us and a map, just in case we became lost. I didn't feel as sure on the streets as I used to. My plan was to take Van Ness to Lombard and drive through the Presidio. We would wind up in Sausalito after we'd crossed the bridge. I would find a place open for dinner there, and spend a few more hours away from home.

A household intrusion shouldn't shake me up this much, I thought. I'd suffered worse in my lifetime. But the truth was, the house on Green Street had always seemed like a sanctuary to me. Now it had been violated. We had new locks and a set of special keys the locksmith swore couldn't be duplicated by anyone but my parents, whose names would be on register at the shop. But that didn't seem like enough.

"You're so quiet," Hugh said, taking my hand.

"I'm sorry Christmas turned out this way," I said. "You would have been better off in Scotland."

"Not really," Hugh said. "Can you stop?"

"Stop what?"

"The car."

"We're still a few miles from the bridge." In fact we were just driving through Presidio, an old military installation that was one of the city's prettiest parks.

"Please, Rei."

There was something in his voice that alerted me that this was really serious. Ready for bad news, I turned off into a parking area. I pulled over in a spot marked reserved, and turned off the car.

"If we walk down this trail, you'll really see the water," I said. I led him around a massive stand of eucalyptus that had been planted long ago to camouflage the layout of the base, and there we had it: the Pacific Ocean, gray-blue and endless.

"Two more days and I'll be flying over it," I said.

"Soon enough, we'll be there together."

"Just like old times," I said.

"But I don't want it to be like the old times," Hugh said.

Aha. So he was going to break something to me. What? I had a feeling of panic. Was he so pressed with work that he wanted to postpone our relationship?

Hugh didn't meet my eyes. He was busy digging in his pocket, taking something out. When I saw the small red parcel, a wave of relief rushed over me.

"I thought the G-string in the book was the private present," I said.

"No, that was a joke," Hugh said.

This isn't. That was the unspoken message. My fingers tore clumsily at the paper. I had once opened a box like this expecting a ring, and it hadn't been. I had no idea what could be within this box—earrings? A pendant? I wasn't going to expect anything, I swore to myself.

"You look grim," Hugh said.

I didn't answer, but let the wind carry away the last shreds of paper and looked down on a faded blue velvet box. It had to be family jewelry, I thought, and my heart began pounding.

"My grandfather gave this to my grandmother in the early thirties," Hugh said. "If it's too art decoish for you, we can change it—"

"No," I said, after I opened the box and saw the ring lying nestled on creamy silk. A rectangular emerald was surrounded by tiny pavé diamonds set in narrower rectangles. The band was a luminous metal that I knew had to be platinum.

"No?" Hugh breathed. "You mean that you don't want it?"

"No, that's not it. I said no because I wouldn't dream of changing it! Oh, Hugh, it's exquisite."

"This is the fourth time I'm asking you to marry me," Hugh said.

"Fifth," I said, laughing. "Four's an unlucky number, remember?"

"Will you?" He took the box from me, and took the ring out of its cushioning.

"Of course." I found that I was choking up. "I didn't expect this, but I do—I do want it. I want you always."

As we kissed each other, I had the strangest feeling of being in a play—maybe it was because of the perfectly styled setting in front of the Bay, or because it was Christmas. But I knew the way I felt about Hugh was sincere. He had grown and changed so much for the better in the few years that I'd known him. I hoped I had, too.

I felt the ring slide on my finger, and it rolled about a little loosely.

"It's too big," Hugh said mournfully. "Well, I should have expected that. My grandmother was a big woman, six feet tall."

"They can resize it at Hopewell's," I said, sniffling a bit. "I'll go there tomorrow. Do you want to come with me?"

"I have to work," Hugh said gently. "That's why I was so hellbent on getting this time with you today. Tomorrow I work, and the day after you go back to Japan. I wanted to settle things."

"Your timing is auspicious," I said, smiling at him. "I wouldn't be surprised if we could start sleeping under the same roof in my parents' house tonight."

"Do you really think so?" Hugh's eyes gleamed. "Well, let's go back and tell them. I'm too excited to continue sightseeing."

"Can you imagine," I said as we ambled back to the car, "how my mother's going to spring into action? The question is whether she's going to push for a wedding right away, so we don't get cold feet, or make us wait a year so she can organize things perfectly."

"I wonder—oh, shite." He broke off, and I followed his line of vision to my mother's car. The passenger window had been thoroughly smashed. Thousands of tiny bubbles of glass on the street made me think, absurdly, of Christmas stars. "Rei, I'm sorry. I shouldn't have insisted you stop—"

"It happens. Life in America, you know." I walked up to the car and looked in. "The question is what was stolen. I hope my mom didn't have anything valuable in the car."

"Oh," Hugh said. "Wow. Look, my new cell phone and even that little shortbread tin I brought with us is gone. We're completely cleaned out."

Fortunately, he'd left his briefcase at home, just as I'd left my backpack. The break-in was more of an annoyance than anything else.

But it was the second break-in in the same day.

I found it hard to believe it was a coincidence.

The police didn't come out to solve this crime, either. Once again, a phone report was the order of the day. Though, as Hugh pointed out, if they'd come and seen where I'd parked, I'd probably have gotten a ticket for parking in a reserved space.

"Two bad things have happened to us in one day," I protested over the phone to the sergeant on telephone duty. "It seems as if it could be a pattern!"

"Well, lady, do you have anyone in your life who doesn't like you? Ex-husband, ex-best friend, someone with a vendetta?"

The truth was, I had recently seen Eric Gan, and it seemed clear that he was annoyed that Hugh and I were together. But his livelihood depended on working on the class action with Hugh; it would be stupid of him to stalk us. After a long pause, I said, "No."

"Well, I'll write up an incident report to use for—"

"My mother's car insurance. Yeah, yeah. I know."

I was afraid of what my mother would say about her smashed window, but she was surprisingly unfazed. The emerald on my finger had done enough, apparently, to mitigate all the trouble. And she didn't see a link between the two break-ins, because of the different locations of the events.

"What do you think, Dad?" I asked him when we were alone—my mother had gone to start the dumbwaiter to transfer Hugh's luggage to my bedroom.

"I think . . . you should take your time, not rush into anything," he said.

"You mean about thinking there's a link?"

"No, I'm referring to your very sudden engagement."

So he was talking about our personal news, not the break-ins. I took a few deep breaths and said, "Dad, last night you put Hugh on the spot about not having . . . serious intentions. Now we've told you what we thought you wanted, and you don't want it—"

"Just a minute!" He held up a cautionary finger. "Please don't put words into my mouth. I'm only saying you're both going through significant milestones regarding work and moving. To add another element of stress like a wedding might cause problems for both of you."

"I can't imagine what kind of problems. Unless it would mean something like you and Mom not coming to the wedding."

"Is that a threat?"

"No," I said to my father. "It's just that if you're unhappy, you might decide not to come."

"How many months until you plan to actually go through with things?"

I shrugged. "There is no plan yet. We'll talk about it in Japan."

"I like him, Rei. Please believe that. It's just that you've only recently rekindled the relationship. Why not give it a year?"

"I'm almost thirty," I said to my father. "Hugh's already there. How long until we're grown-up enough to make our own decisions?"

All night, I tossed and turned in bed next to Hugh; I'd decided not to tell him what my father had said because I didn't want to make him even more paranoid.

I lay in bed, listening to the twanging noises of the old radiators and the occasional creak elsewhere in the house. My worries about whether Hugh and I would ever be accepted by my father turned to a nagging sense of worry about things. I hadn't been able to find a glass repair shop willing to fix the window until tomorrow, so the car was essentially sitting open to anyone in the driveway. I also wasn't sure if my parents had remembered to lock the door with the new keys after they'd come home.

I got up quietly, went out into the hallway, and turned on the lights, which offered reassuring illumination as I tiptoed down the stairs. I walked to the front door and checked it. Locked. Ditto for the back door. Looking out the kitchen window, I saw that the car was indeed in the drive. There was nothing more I could do to feel safe.

As I made my way upstairs again, I used the kitchen staircase— a simple wooden one that once had been used by servants. As I paused on the back end of the second floor, I heard a new sound.

It sounded like sobbing, stifled in a pillow, and then more quiet sobs.

Manami. Was she crying because she was missing her family? Or was it because we'd forgotten to check in on her when we'd come home?

I started up the stairs to her floor, and the cries quickly stopped. She must have heard me coming.

I spoke softly outside her door in Japanese. "Manami-san? It's Rei. May I come in?"

"No," came the answer, broken and Japanese. "I'm sorry that I woke you."

"You didn't. I was already awake. But I'm worried about you. Is there anything I can do to help?"

A gusty intake of breath, and then her voice, faint but in better control. "No, Rei-san. I was just . . . feeling strange. That's how it is for me in America sometimes."

I couldn't force my way in, so I went downstairs and crawled back into the warm place next to Hugh. Well, I had a project now. I would figure out what Manami needed to feel like part of our family. Maybe the act of doing so would take away the heavy disappointment that my father had caused me on a day that should have been my happiest.

9

Project Manami got off to a weak start the next morning. I put on a robe, left Hugh to take his shower, and went downstairs. I had it in mind to bring a cup of green tea and some *senbei* crackers to Manami's bedside. Then I'd invite her to come along with me to Hopewell's, where I would kill two birds with one stone: get the engagement ring resized, and find out what I could about the old Japanese letter that my parents had sold in the seventies.

In the kitchen, all I found was my mother, already in action. She was rolling out scones. I could smell some baking in the oven, and there were three trays waiting on the counter.

"Your father already left for the hospital," she said when she saw me setting up a pot of green tea.

"It's for Manami, actually."

"She's out, too. Your dad was going to give her a ride to campus, but she must have left even earlier. Do you want a scone?"

So Manami was gone; I wouldn't be able to take her to Hopewell's. "Thanks, but I'll wait for Hugh."

"That's nice. You may have two each; the rest are for the party."

"Oh, that's right. The Boxing Day party is this afternoon. What do you need help with?"

"Well, I noticed you did the silver yesterday, sweetie; thanks for that. I think . . . well, the baking's under control . . . maybe if you could pick up the sushi for me? Oh, darn, the car window. I almost forgot. You can't possibly drive."

"I'll take the bus then. And Mom, there's someone coming to fix the glass this morning. Hugh and I already gave him a credit card number; don't you try to pay for it, okay? We feel so terrible about it—"

"Don't, sweetie. It's a small price to pay for the sake of your engagement."

"Speaking of workers, do you know someone who could repair or replace a stove? Before we leave, we want to see if something can be done for—for a client of Hugh's. She's living in the worst place imaginable, and can't get the landlord to do anything about her stove."

"That's very sweet of you, Rei. I must say that you're doing a lot to try to help everyone. It'll be a great loss when you're gone."

"Not to everyone," I said roughly, thinking of my father.

"I think you're wrong. But anyway, Emil Sonnenfeld is the person I'd recommend, because he's usually been able to help me within twenty-four hours. Shall I call him for you?"

"That would be great. I'll give you the address." I handed my mother the card on which I'd written it down on Christmas Eve.

"What's the tenant's name?"

"Mom, I'm not supposed to divulge that. Just tell him that if it's an old Filipina lady, he's got the right place and should send the bill to you. I mean, to me, in care of your house."

But my mother wasn't interested in issues of payment. "She's from the Philippines? For heaven's sake, why don't you invite her to the Asian Language League party."

"I'm almost positive she's not a member. The dues would be too high, anyway—"

"She'll be my guest, then. What's her number? Shall I call her?"

"Let me do that," I said. "Or better yet, Hugh. He's the one she really knows and trusts."

"Good morning, good morning." It was Hugh, dressed for business in a gray flannel suit. "Who is the soul who's crazy enough to trust me?"

"Our—I mean your—client," I said, struggling for balance as he swept me into his arms for a kiss. He reeked of the Caswell-Massey toiletries my mother had stocked in his bathroom. "My mother came up with an electrician who might be able to fix the stove."

"Thank goodness you remembered. I'd practically forgotten." Hugh sounded rueful.

"That's what wives are for!" my mother said archly. She was smirking as if she'd enjoyed the display of public affection.

"That's sexist, Mom," I said, but I couldn't deny my relief that at least one person in the family was excited about the engagement. "Anyway, I'll get the sushi on the way back from Hopewell's. I'm going there to check into Dad's letter."

"Which letter?" my mother asked.

"The one he mentioned selling back in the seventies. I just want to find out what it was, in case there's something I should follow up on."

"Oh, that. Well, when you're there, be sure to ask for my friend Mary Jamison. She's been working there for as long as we've been their clients; I'm sure she'd help you. Oh, and the person who does jewelry evaluations might be able to help you resize your ring."

"Do you think they'll charge much?" Hugh asked. "Darling, let me give you something to cover the cost—it's not right that you're paying anything toward that ring."

"Hugh, I'm sure they won't charge, because she's one of us," my mother said.

"One of whom?" Hugh raised a quizzical eyebrow.

"Our family. We've done so much business with them over the years, they will just be happy to see Rei. Especially if she dangles a promise of bringing them some wonderful consignments from Japan."

An hour later, I was showered, dressed in a violet wool suit, and heading downtown on the no. 1 bus. For a change, my twenty-year-old outfit fit right in. The society matrons riding the bus alongside me were all wearing clothes from bygone days. Sitting around us were a sprinkling of tourists in teal and purple athletic wear, as well as members of the nose-ring mafia who probably had jobs on Filbert Street. It was a perfect San Francisco moment, and reminded me of why I was occasionally bored by life in perfect-taste Japan.

I jumped off the bus at Sacramento and Larkin and walked

south a few blocks to the intersection with Sutter Street, where Hopewell's Auction House had stood since the late nineteenth century. I'd been in just the previous week to get the gentleman's traveling desk for Hugh.

I went straight to the back desk and asked for Mary Jamison, the veteran appraiser my mother had mentioned. She had always reminded me of my mother—she was about the same age and wore the same kind of pageboy hairstyle, only red; and she'd dressed entirely in black, year round, for as long as I could remember.

"Darling, look at you!" she said, gesturing toward me. "Love the suit. And the ring—are you engaged?"

I slid off the loose ring that I'd slipped on my finger just before entering. "I'm almost afraid to wear it. It's a bit large. It was my fiancé's grandmother's ring."

"I can take care of that for you." She held out her hand. "Oh, you're going to have to tell me all about him. Is he local?"

"No. He's from Scotland."

"Oh, the one you bought the traveling desk for. I adore Scottish men; that actor, Ewan McGregor—"

"Hugh's bigger." I caught myself. "Heightwise, I mean."

"Well, that's nice, too." Mary laughed knowingly. Only in San Francisco would ladies my mother's age feel so at home with the ribald. "I'm sure he's simply gorgeous. I'm very upset you didn't bring him with you today. I assume he's here for the holidays?"

"Yes, but today he's working. He's doing something with Sharp, Witter and Rowe." I made a face.

"A lawyer." Mary sighed. "Well, there are worse things than having a man who's still got work to do. Around here, so many people have lost employment that you wouldn't believe it."

"I've noticed," I said, thinking about all the people in the coffee shops. "Actually, I want to ask you about an auction that was held a long time ago. My parents sold a letter here in 1976. It was from a government official, which is why I'm interested."

"We could check the sale catalogs," Mary said. "Tell you what. Why don't you go over to the jewelry counter and let Gary fix the ring for you. I'll see what I can dig up."

Gary used something remarkably low-tech—a cigarette lighter—

to warm the platinum and then reshaped it to the exact size of my finger. We were both admiring the way it looked when Mary came back.

"Here, I've got it," Mary said, waving a catalog that had been discolored yellow with age. "There was a sale in July of that year, and your father's letter was probably item number 453, which we described as a rare scroll containing the signature of Emperor Hirohito, dated 1928."

"Emperor Hirohito?" I stood in the center of Hopewell's, the bustle around me fading into silence. I felt my heart drumming under the tight violet wool suit. This was the first I'd ever heard that my family had any connection with Japan's most notorious leader—the emperor who led Japan into war and, following Japan's defeat, hung on to his imperial seat for over forty more years.

"Yes, Hirohito," Mary answered. "As you know, there's always been a terrific market in letters signed by heads of state—not to mention royalty."

"What else can you tell me about it?"

Mary scrutinized the catalog. "There's not much of a description of the letter's contents, but it was authenticated by an appraiser. Though I can't speak for certain about how he did the authentication, it probably was done based on a careful analysis of the stationery, the seal, and, of course, the signature."

"Who appraised it?" I asked.

"Oh, in those days we used John Nishida. But he passed away two years ago." Mary sighed. "All I can really tell you is how much it sold for."

"Of course. And the buyer, if you've got that," I added, trying to sound casual.

"It brought nine thousand dollars. Regarding the buyer, I'll have to check elsewhere in the office for that record." Mary looked at me. "If I tell you who bought it, what will you do with the information?"

"Nothing much. I want to see the letter and transcribe its contents for a family history project I'm doing. So far, the family holdings I've analyzed have just been decorative arts objects. This letter would add a personal and political element that would be very interesting."

Mary raised her eyebrows, turned, and disappeared again. While I was alone, I collected my thoughts on Emperor Hirohito. The late 1920s was just before Hirohito launched Japan's march to conquer Asia. The letter, I bet, had originally been the property of my grandfather, who was a professor of history at Tokyo University. He was born in 1902, so he would have been twenty-six at the time it was written—either finishing up graduate school or just starting his career as a teacher.

When Mary came back, she said, "You're in luck. I know the buyers are still alive and well in Marin County, because they came in for a sale a few months ago. We've got their number in our Rolodex." I must have brightened too much, because Mary added, "I'd better be the one to call them. Otherwise, they might feel their privacy is being violated."

"How would I make them feel that way? I'm not angling to buy the letter."

"Imagine a clever thief who could go around to auction houses and gather information on who owned what, and where they lived. I know you're not a crook—but they don't." She paused. "I'll call them for you."

"Thanks," I said, sighing.

I left Hopewell's feeling frustrated about wanting something, but not knowing exactly what it was.

10

I was so preoccupied by the Hirohito development that I almost forgot to pick up the sushi. I had to yank the bus's stop cord quickly and hurry back a block to my father's favorite Japantown restaurant—the one where we'd recently eaten.

Only in America, I ruminated while waiting for the waitress to bring the sushi out from back. Only in America would a Japanese restaurant aspire to serve so many food groups—sushi and tempura and teriyaki, not to mention the noodles I'd complained about. I doubted a chef who was good at frying tempura would be equally facile at rolling rice and fish in nori. The fact that the restaurant tried to do it all, instead of trying to master one cuisine, gave me a rush of homesickness for Tokyo.

My aunt Norie Shimura—the wife of my father's younger brother, Hiroshi—was an excellent cook. The scent of her slow-simmering stews wafted out of her house and onto the street, a pleasant invitation to me on my frequent visits. Inside, the round table in the dining room covered by a blue-and-white hand-blocked indigo print would be filled with an assortment of odd-shaped bowls and plates, all filled with things like her own pickled daikon radish and cucumbers, sweet, rich pumpkin cubes tossed in a ginger-soy sauce, and always, a saucer of tiny whole fish that would be sprinkled on top of the food for extra crunch.

In doing oral research, I'd learned that a lot of Norie's recipes were direct descendants of recipes from Hiroshi's mother—my grandmother, Toshiko Shimura. Norie had to learn to cook this way because she'd married into her husband's family household. And Toshiko's recipes had in turn been her mother-in-law's.

I was yanked back to the present when the waitress bringing my order turned out to be a blue-eyed blonde with a nose ring. "Here's your order!" As she spoke, she ticked off an order slip. "Twenty pieces each of cucumber rolls, California rolls, egg, tuna, shrimp, and filly."

"Filly? Do you mean *horse*?" My annoyance was swiftly replaced by shock. In certain regions of Japan, horse sashimi was a specialty, something I didn't eat but knew was really indigenous, traditional food. I hadn't dreamed that raw horse meat would catch on in California. Was it legal? Did the animal rights people know?

"No, no! *Philly* rolls. As in Philadelphia. You know, cream cheese and smoked salmon? Your mother specifically requested it."

"Oh. Never mind." I winced. I liked smoked salmon, but cream cheese?

One thing I had to say about American sushi was that it was cheap. For $59.99, the blonde loaded me up with 140 pieces, all arranged in concentric circles on two huge foil trays. I'd gotten so much sushi, in fact, that it was too much for me to handle on a bus. I sprang for a taxi instead.

My mother held the front door open as I came slowly up the walk. "Sweetie, the car window's fixed. Why didn't you call me to pick you up instead of taking a taxi?"

"It doesn't matter," I said. "Where do you want me to put this?"

"Basement fridge. And how was Hopewell's?"

"Well worth the visit. They resized the ring for free, like you thought they would, and they were able to tell me Daddy's letter was actually a scroll written and signed by Emperor Hirohito."

"Emperor Hirohito? My goodness!" My mother blinked, just as I'd done upon hearing the name. "Whatever did the letter say?"

"I don't know. It was sold to some collectors, whom Mary is going to contact for me. Can you believe Dad went and sold something like that?"

"Like what?"

I spun around and found that my father had entered the room. Immediately, I demanded why he hadn't told me that Hirohito was the author of the letter he'd sold.

My father sighed. "I didn't want you to become overly excited, since we don't own it anymore. Besides, I never thought of it as a prize possession."

"A scroll from the Emperor of Japan to our family isn't a prize possession?" I said dryly. "Apparently it sold for nine thousand, which seems like a lot, but if you'd only waited to sell until after he died in '89, you'd surely have received more."

"Thanks for the good advice," my father said, and walked out of the room. Obviously, I'd touched a nerve.

The telephone rang then, and my mother picked it up. "It's for you, Rei. Mary at Hopewell's."

I dove for the phone and said, "I can't thank you enough for getting back to me so quickly."

"Well, the news I have isn't what you wanted. The couple who bought it actually wound up selling it on their own in 1990."

"The year after Hirohito died. Well, that makes sense."

"The interesting thing, Rei, is they said the buyers were a Japanese university archive. So if it's in an archive, it's probably available for public inspection."

"Do they recall the school's name?"

"They said Showa or something like that. She wasn't terribly clear on it."

"I bet it was Showa College. And I know the place quite well." The college was a small, expensive institution that had a history of international exchange. It had been founded to honor Hirohito, whose reign in Japan was called the Showa Period. Showa College had a strong program for foreign students and a foreign film series in the summer that I always followed. It made sense that the school would be interested in the letter. And I could easily visit Showa College once I'd returned to Japan. I thanked her and got off the phone to face my mother.

"I'm still on the trail, but I'll have to wait to find out what the letter says until I get back to Japan."

"Well, I'm glad you can put it aside for a little while. I'm a bit frantic doing the last-minute prep for the party. Can you help me?" my mother asked.

I did, and before I knew it the time was five o'clock. Japanese are notoriously punctual—they were among the first arrivals. I laid out Mrs. Kono's tray of *inarizushi* and Mrs. Tanaka's sweet bean cakes. A group of Chinese ladies bearing buns stuffed with savory minced pork were next. A large group of Koreans came after them with succulent grilled beef on skewers—beef I wouldn't taste with my mouth, but did, covertly, with my nose.

My father came back and greeted his guests, all the while avoiding me. It was an old move of his that I remembered from my angry adolescent days. I ignored him back and kept my eye on the door, looking for Hugh. Finally, at ten past six, the front door opened with a gust of cold air, and both Hugh and Eric Gan entered, carrying bags with the name of an Asian grocery on them. A girl was with them—clearly Asian-American, with waist-length hair, granny glasses, and a big smile. As she wiggled her fingers at me, I recognized her as Julia Gan, Eric's older sister.

While Hugh and Eric got their shopping bags organized on the potluck table, Julia and I caught up. She had always been an idealist during our childhood, and her current employment showed that she had stayed true to her character. She was working as a director of a shelter and hot-line program for Asian women who were victims of abuse.

"They were tiny when I joined them, only working with South Asians," Julia said. "But in the last four years, we've lined up hot-line volunteers who speak Korean, Mandarin, Cantonese, Vietnamese, and Tagalog." She ticked off the languages on her fingers. "Too bad you're not here, Rei. You could help us with Japanese; we're still looking for someone to do that."

"Why not Eric?"

Julia snorted. "My brother's male, if you haven't noticed. *Men* are the ones who have abused our clients. When a woman makes a frantic cry for help, she wants to talk to another woman, preferably someone from within her home culture who will not make sexist or ethnocentric observations."

I hid my smile at Julia's Bay Area–speak. My parents, with their Mid-Atlantic and Japanese backgrounds, had never quite learned to talk this way. "Okay, I get it. And actually, I might have someone who can help you, but it would have to be on a very limited basis. We have a Japanese boarder, Manami, who I think hasn't really integrated into the culture here—"

"Give her this card. We'd love to meet her," Julia said, handing me a small piece of red cardboard with the name Lotus Listens on it.

"Why is your hot line called this?" I asked.

"The lotus is a plant associated with tranquillity," Julia explained. "And listening, of course, is what we do best."

"Has Eric told you much about the class action?" I asked. "He's been talking with older Asian women who were victims of abuse. It's not like they're in an imminent situation of danger, but . . ."

"But they need ongoing support against PTSD," Julia finished. "Exactly right. I think your dad's hospital had a program like that for women some time ago, but it was closed down. I wonder why."

"Hallo, darling." Hugh had finally threaded his way through the crowd to me. "Sorry to be late."

"We were so busy it didn't matter. Did you talk much with Julia about the class action? It sounds as if her hot-line workers might be able to follow up with support for the women you're meeting."

"Super idea," Hugh said enthusiastically. "Why didn't you think of it, Eric?"

Snip, snip. I looked at the two men, and from their postures, I understood that the words Eric had uttered on Christmas Eve had started a war between them.

"The class action's confidential," Eric said, scowling at Hugh. "And if Charles knew what you and Rei were broadcasting all over town, he'd be pissed as hell."

"'Pissed'? You mean, he drinks?" Hugh wrinkled his brow innocently.

"'Pissed' means 'angry' in American slang," I said to Hugh, who probably hadn't misunderstood Eric's comment at all. "Um, it's good that you're here. We need to talk, but as you can see, it's a madhouse. I don't know how—"

"Why don't you help me put my work paraphernalia upstairs," Hugh suggested.

As we started off, Eric Gan made a loud cackle. "Don't stay up there too long. I can warn you about Dr. Shimura creeping around and spying."

"Thanks, but I know my dad-in-law's habits quite well already," Hugh said with an easy smile. Score: Glendinning one, Gan zero.

"Father-in-law?" Eric screeched after us. "You mean, you got *married*? When did you have time?"

"Not quite yet. But we are engaged," I said, turning around to face him.

"The wedding will be in the new year, I'm sure." My father's voice had come from behind us, startling me.

"What's this?" Mrs. Chow, the current treasurer of ALL, had sidled up next to my father. "Do you mean to say that Rei is finally getting married? Why didn't you tell us? We would have brought an engagement present!"

My father looked at Hugh and me with an almost apologetic expression. "I was planning to introduce Hugh, in some sort of manner, to the group. I suppose now that the beans have fallen, I should formally announce it."

Beans have *been spilled*, I thought—but didn't dare correct my father's English. And the truth was, I was wearing a splashy ring. But it was San Francisco, where nose rings and *bindi*s got more compliments than a simple emerald on a finger.

"Ah, that's nice, but may I put away my things first?" Hugh pleaded.

"Why don't you leave your coat and briefcase in the library," my father instructed. "Come with me, please—we shall stand together in the hallway. Where is my wife?"

"Um, excuse me—Toshiro—"Hugh said, obviously having trouble using my father's first name—"given what happened the other day, I'd rather put it somewhere less public."

"Go where you like, then," my father snapped, and Hugh, completely red-faced, went up the stairs without another word. I had never seen him look so embarrassed. *Why?* I thought with a pang.

He'd seemed proud to be my boyfriend in the old days. Was my family, so humiliatingly intense, changing that?

"Dad, he has a good point," I said when Hugh had gone. "The case could be jeopardized if anyone snoops in the briefcase."

"You mean—you don't trust our friends?" My father shook his head at me. "You've changed."

But the Asian Language League had, too. There had to be close to a hundred people in the house, and most of them looked unfamiliar to me. About fifteen years had passed since I'd been fourteen and taking Japanese language classes. But some things never changed: the preschoolers, for example, who were making a game out of playing hide-and-seek under the buffet table, and the elementary-age children picking all the expensive bits of fish off the sushi, and the teenagers hanging out in the back staircase by the kitchen, wanting nothing to do with the adults.

Which was how I felt, too. I was still trying to explain to my father how he'd better chill out when Hugh made his way downstairs. Instantly, my mother tapped a crystal goblet with a silvery *ting*. Her call drew people to the foot of the grand oak staircase, where they looked up expectantly at my father, who was standing on the bottom step, dwarfed by Hugh on his left. I stood on the right, trying to stop from fidgeting.

My father started off simply, introducing himself as the group's chairman emeritus and my mother as the continuing hospitality coordinator. He welcomed back the longtime members—"I do not like to say old," my father joked, to gentle peals of laughter—and the newest.

"Whether or not you have Asian blood, you have a place in the Asian Language League's family," my father said, his voice rising slightly. "We welcome all, as our name suggests. If you are interested in taking or teaching a class not offered, please speak up."

He went on to talk more seriously about the group's ongoing support of Julia's Lotus Listens project and the Asia in the Schools initiative that sent ALL members to visit classes in Bay Area public schools.

I wanted to catch Hugh's eye, but it was impossible with my father between us. Anyway, he seemed to be listening intently. I guessed he hadn't had a clue about how passionate my father's civic involvement was. *All the more reason to run away*, I thought bleakly.

"And now, I have very auspicious news for the New Year. I would like to reintroduce my daughter Rei, who is with us for the holidays. Rei is one of ALL's very first students, and I think it is a credit to her fine teachers that she learned enough Japanese to live and work there for the last five years."

There was a polite scattering of applause and warm smiles. I thought about how ordinary my father's description of me had been. He hadn't said what I did for a living, or even that I'd been a good student of Japanese. He'd reserved his praise for my teachers. Was it just Japanese manners at work, the manners that made it important not to praise one's children for their abilities—or was it a lingering reaction to the recent arguments we'd had?

Not daring to look at my father, I kept my attention on the crowd. I began to recognize a few faces. My first Japanese teacher was there, smiling warmly at me. How old she looked, as old as Rosa Munoz.

"The man next to me is my future son-in-law, Hugh Glendinning." My father pronounced the last name slowly, as it was so vastly foreign. "Hugh is a native of Scotland, but he has worked in Japan, and plans to work there again, on a most important case that will surely be of interest to many here."

"Please, let's not bore them," Hugh said in his soft brogue, but my father soldiered on.

"Hugh is trying to file a class action suit on behalf of Asian people who had their civil rights violated by the Japanese during World War II. This issue may be of interest to some of our families, so please take the time to speak with Hugh if you like. People may have different reactions to the prospect of this lawsuit—as we have had in our own household." My father coughed slightly. "Still, I am proud of my future son-in-law's concerns about justice for Asian people."

When my father finished, I wanted to hide under the buffet table with all the toddlers. He could have broadcast the news from a megaphone on Coit Tower and had the same effect—or, for that matter, sent a press release to the local Asian cable TV channel, since Mandy Oh, a Chinese-American woman who worked there, was at this event. I spotted her now. She had a gleam in her eye and was heading right for Hugh.

"How could you?" I said to my father.

"All I did, was announce your engagement." There was a hurt look on my father's face. "I'm trying to show you my support—"

"Why did you say there was a mixed reaction in this house? You're making it obvious that you don't approve."

"You're too sensitive, Rei," Hugh said. "It's not a big problem. I'll make the best of the, um, free publicity."

"Well, it might be more than you bargained for," I said. "That woman in blue coming your way is a TV reporter."

Hugh followed my gaze to Mandy, who was trying to advance but was temporarily blocked by two tiny Vietnamese ladies bearing massive platters of summer rolls.

"Oh, no. I don't think I'm ready for that. Everything's got to be cleared with Charles—" Hugh's face had paled.

The door knocker sounded.

"Don't they know it's not locked?" I said.

My question was answered when the door swung open, revealing a blue-uniformed policeman.

"Oh, someone must have parked illegally," my father said. "Let me go and settle things."

"Don't avoid me," I called after my father. "I'm still mad at you."

He conferred with the policeman for a minute, and then came back with an odd look on his face.

"Uh, Hugh. The police."

Hugh was busy talking to Mandy Oh, and looked distracted by my father's greeting, but kept on going. "Yes, madam, it's an issue that is of interest to the community, but at this point the company cannot be named—"

"Hugh, they want to talk to you."

I shook Hugh's arm. "Did you and Eric park somewhere you shouldn't have?"

"No, we actually taxied it," he said.

"We got a call from an electrician who was sent on a job to the residence of a Ms. Rosa Munoz." The police officer had reached us. He flipped out his identification card quickly, but his name was short enough that I caught it. Ali. Officer Ali, with skin the color of café au lait, closely cropped hair, and a ruby earring in one lobe.

"I'm the one who made the call, actually. Did she not want to let him in?" I asked.

"She *couldn't* let him in," the officer said.

"Oh. Did he upset her in some way?" Hugh asked.

"No, that's not it." Ali frowned at us. "If you people would stop interrupting me, I can tell you what I have to say. It's not good news."

"Bad news," I said, unable to stop myself. "You aren't saying that she's dead?"

His expression told me that was exactly the case.

11

"What makes you think that?" Officer Ali demanded.

"It was an educated guess. When you said it was bad news," I added.

"Nobody's certain of the lady's identity. That's why I came for Mr. Glendinning here." Officer Ali offered the business card that had Hugh's name and my parents' address handwritten underneath, as party guests crowded around.

"Let's find a private place to talk," Hugh said in a low voice. "I'm afraid it's rather, uh, chaotic right here."

"Who died?" someone in the crowd said loudly. Then they all took it up, pressing in closely to eavesdrop.

It seemed as if Officer Ali didn't like this any more than Hugh, because he suggested going out to the cruiser to finish the conversation.

"Actually, there are plenty of quiet rooms upstairs," I suggested.

"Glendinning is her attorney, correct?" the officer asked pointedly. I nodded.

"Then he's the only one I need."

"How about me? I was in on all the interviews." Eric Gan had come up behind us. "Are you also her attorney?" the cop asked Eric.

"No, I'm a translator—"

"Okay. The answer is no, then."

"I'll see you both in a bit, Rei," Hugh said quietly, and went to get his coat.

Now I had a bad feeling in my stomach. The last time the police had taken Hugh away to discuss something, he had wound up in prison.

I was left behind with Eric, and a feeling of doom. Eric offered a *lumpia* to me, but I shook my head. "I couldn't possibly."

"So how did you get so involved?" Eric asked me, as the party moved back to its regular pace.

"We stopped by on Christmas Eve to bring her some food and a small gift. One of us had the idea of having her stove fixed—I can't remember who now." I felt utterly distracted.

"Did she know you were Japanese?"

I smiled wryly. "She did. Actually, she said she knew my name. This made me think that one of the men who had hurt her must have been a Shimura."

"Or," said Julia, who had come up and put her arm around me, "she had gone to the post-trauma women's group at your dad's center and remembered his name from there."

"He never said he treated her," I said.

"Well, he can't! He's a psychiatrist—he has to maintain physician-patient confidentiality," Julia said. "I'm sorry, Rei. I wish I had known more about this woman than what I just overheard. She's one we might have been able to help."

I couldn't answer. I didn't know what to say. Rosa, dead. If she could have hung on a year, she would have had money. But she might have died right after that point. There was no certainty about anything.

Mandy Oh, the reporter, appeared with her notebook flipped open. She had already scribbled several notes. I hoped, rather futilely, that the notes were just a story about ALL.

"I need to talk to your fiancé about the class action for tomorrow's news broadcast," she said. "When can I bring my crew? And do you want to do it here or at the law firm?"

I swallowed hard and said, "Mandy, I really can't make plans for him."

"Sure you can—you're the wife!"

"Not yet," I said. "But just between us, I think you'll get a better story when he's, uh, ready."

"Did you know," Mandy said, giving me a furious look, "that as a representative of a minority community media organization, I am frequently not even invited to press conferences? I'm not considered real media, you see. And here your friend is throwing out tempting bits of information about a story that *directly* impacts our community, and he won't give me the story?"

"It's gotten so complicated, Mandy . . ." I broke off. I had to think of something to distract her, to put a better face on things. "Actually, I do have a scoop for you. I'm working on a personal family history of the Shimuras. I have slides of family artifacts and quite a few reminiscences about how my grandparents and their grandparents lived in Japan. You know, the kinds of quilts they slept under, the dishes they ate from, the letters they received from notable people of the period. I'd be happy to give you an exclusive on this if you like."

"That's just soft news; I couldn't sell it to my bosses," Mandy said. "Anyway, I'd better circulate to get some more color. Bring Hugh to me when he gets back with that cop—or else."

I stared at her as she retreated.

"Whew," said Julia, "she wants a story. Can't say I blame her."

"Well, why doesn't she want to write about your hot line or something? I'm sure you can use the publicity," I grumbled.

"She has. Every year she does that story. Mandy Oh is our hero. I mean to say, *shero*. We've switched to that term lately."

The rest of the party passed in a blur. I was surrounded by well-wishers from the old days. Half of them asked about the wedding plans, but the others were all abuzz about the lawsuit. I tried to say as little as possible, and threw myself into picking up all the leftover plates and glasses. People began to leave around eight. By nine the two dishwashers were going, with all the tables and surfaces cleared and five bags of trash headed for outdoors.

"This is unbelievable, Rei," my mother said. "I can't believe how much easier life is with you around. I know this sounds crazy coming from me, but wouldn't it . . . wouldn't it be nice if you and Hugh could live here with us, just like a real Japanese extended family . . ."

"Thanks," I said, too upset to protest.

"We could do over the third floor entirely as an apartment for the two of you. You could even have one of our parking spaces in the driveway—"

"We're going to live in Japan," I said, trying not to cry.

The doorbell rang.

"Who now?" my mother wondered aloud.

"Maybe Hugh's back," I said, and went to the door. Remarkably, he was. I gave him an inquiring look, but he just shook his head at me.

Hugh had been away only about three hours, but he was transformed. His whole being seemed to sag; his suit was wrinkled, his skin looked paler, and his expression had a hollow kind of sadness.

"You were gone for a while," I said. "What did they do to you?"

"Nothing. They thought I should be the one to make a positive ID on the body, since I was her lawyer and there was no one else who was closer. After that, I stopped in Washington Street to see Charles Sharp and talk things over with him."

"Had she—been hurt?"

He shook his head. "It didn't look like it, thank God. They think it was natural causes, a heart attack or something, but they'll do an autopsy just to make certain."

"But I can't believe it's natural. People live through their seventies in good health all the time now—"

"She's not another Mr. Ishida," said Hugh, referring to my septuagenarian friend in Tokyo who was vigorous enough to practice tai chi.

"Okay, she's not. But think about the coincidence of the break-in at our house and the smashed window of my mother's car. Maybe someone was searching for something . . . information about Rosa. And once they got it, they killed her."

"We'll wait for the autopsy," Hugh said, but I could tell from the way he looked at me that he thought I might be right. We'd known each other too long, and had had too many hard experiences with unnatural deaths, not to expect the worst.

"What is it?" My mother was suddenly standing just a few feet away.

Hugh cleared his throat. "I've had some bad news. My client passed away. I was taken to the morgue to make the identification."

"Oh, my darlings, I'm sorry," my mother said. "You obviously cared about her a great deal, since you were going to the effort of fixing the stove—"

"What about that stove?" I was still unable to quite believe my foul-play theory. "What if—the electrician screwed things up and it was the gas that killed her?"

"No, the electrician found her already dead when he entered the apartment. She was still warm, but wasn't breathing. She was in her chair, slumped over. It seems as if she'd died in the midst of eating—the police said there were takeout food containers and soy sauce on the table." Hugh looked at my mother. "Catherine, I'm sorry. I'm not really up for talking anymore."

"Not to me, but how about Toshiro?" my mother exclaimed. "He's quite good with issues of grieving and loss—"

"Not now, Mom." I took Hugh by the arm as gently as if he were an old lady Rosa's age. "We're going upstairs."

In my room, Hugh lay motionless on the bed. I sat in the chair across the room, staring out the window. Across the street I could see mostly darkened houses, with only one or two rooms glowing with light. In them, people sat in front of computers or televisions, tuned into other worlds. Our house was uncharacteristically blazing with light, but my spirit was dark.

At last Hugh spoke. "Somebody once advised me never to enter into personal relationships with clients. I understood that to mean the obvious—don't have affairs. But now I see it means more. Don't walk into people's homes unbidden, don't give them things, and don't try to remake their lives . . ."

"You didn't do anything wrong."

"Who knows? She was doing fine until we showed up with the promise of making her final days better. Maybe it was what your father said about stirring up old memories for her. That could have caused enough stress for a heart attack."

"Maybe the class action stirred up old memories for someone else," I said.

"What do you mean?" Hugh turned his face and I could finally see his red eyes.

"Both the American and Japanese governments have argued against giving the comfort women a chance at getting reparations, right? Neither side wants to upset the cozy relationship between the two countries. And those are just the governments themselves. There must be thousands of like-minded people in the U.S., and millions in Japan. If Rosa's death had happened after my parents' party—after all those Japanese-American guests heard about the plan—I would wonder if one of them had done it."

Hugh reached out and stroked my arm. "Get some sleep, darling. You're so tired you're turning racist."

But he was a fine one to tell me to sleep. Hugh tossed and turned plenty, and since my single bed was too small for both of us, it made drifting off impossible. Finally I told Hugh that I needed to sleep somewhere else, with more space for my body, in order to function the next day. Hugh kissed me and said a mournful good-bye as I carried my pillow up to the third-floor guest room where he had been sleeping. I didn't like to leave him, but I knew it was for the best.

There was a sliver of light under Manami's door, which was slightly cracked open; as I moved down the hall the door was closed quickly, and I heard her put the hook on it, locking it tightly. I smiled to myself, realizing that she must have thought it was Hugh, and she was protecting her modesty.

"Manami-san, it's just me. Rei," I called to her quietly in Japanese.

The lock came undone, and she peeped out at me. I had a flashback to Rosa doing the same thing at her apartment door.

"I'm sleeping in Hugh's room," I whispered. "I think I'll sleep better."

"But your parents!"

I realized then that Manami didn't know anything about the engagement. "It's okay. He's sleeping alone in my room, and I'll be up here near you. I hope you don't mind?"

"Of course not. I'll be—more comfortable. I've been afraid," she said.

"Oh, sure, the break-in would make anyone nervous." I'd almost forgotten about it, because of what had happened to Rosa. "Well, good night."

"Just a minute, Rei-san. I'm going to the hospital early tomorrow morning, so I won't be able to say good-bye to you when you and Hugh-san leave for Japan."

"Yes, we can say our good-byes now, but you should know that Hugh will still be around.

"Oh? Why isn't he going with you?"

"Well, there's been a—complication. Remember the class action suit Hugh described at dinner the other night?"

Manami nodded. "Oh, yes. The one against the Japanese companies."

"Well, the lead plaintiff for the case suddenly died. Hugh's not entirely sure the lawsuit will come together." I decided to withhold what I'd been thinking about the death's being unnatural, because, as Hugh said, there was no evidence yet. And Manami was such a timid soul; the last thing I wanted to do was frighten her.

"Oh, so you cannot both be living in Japan. How sad!" she exclaimed.

"I hope it can still work out. I don't know if you heard it from anyone, but we decided to get married. It happened when we were out yesterday afternoon. He gave me an old family ring."

"Your mother told me tonight." She smiled slightly. "Congratulations. Your ring is very pretty. And please don't believe things are ruined. Hugh-san worked in Japan before for a *zaibatsu*. Your father already suggested that he could do that again."

"Hugh did like working for Sendai, though it was very long hours and a lot of travel. But this new job was so much more . . . meaningful! He felt he would be doing something to right a wrong that had been made."

"Right wrong? What does that mean?"

"It's colloquial . . ." I struggled for a minute to find the words. "To right a wrong means to correct something bad that happened before. Hugh felt that if he could get Japanese companies to pay money to these people they'd hurt during the time of war, it would make everyone feel better. Not everyone agrees with that, of course. Well, good night, Manami. I have to get my rest tonight, because I've got to get up early for the airport."

"Good night, Rei-san. *Ii tabi, wo.*" She spoke the phrase that meant, "Have a good trip" with the proper cheerful emphasis.

But I doubted that I would.

12

My father made me a Japanese breakfast the next morning: Miso soup from a packet, sliced yellow pickled radish, sticky rice in sweet tofu skins.

"This was kind of you," I said in Japanese as I sat down across from him and put the bowl of soup to my lips.

"Will Hugh be able to eat it?" my father asked.

"Sure. But he'll make a cup of regular tea, too, to help him wake up." Indeed, I'd shaken awake the exhausted man a few minutes before, and he was now in the shower.

"I made coffee for you. But it's probably better to take it after the breakfast."

"Right. So the tastes don't clash."

"Speaking of clashes," my father began.

I held my hand up. "Never mind. It doesn't matter. I was upset yesterday, but there are worse things to worry about today."

My father held my gaze for a long moment, then said, "Your mother told me about Hugh's client. Why did she die?"

"I don't know. Maybe Hugh will hear today." I paused. "There's something that's been bothering me. One of the last things this woman said to me was she knew our family name—Shimura. I didn't think much of it until Julia Gan pointed out that she might have been seen at your clinic in that old support group program."

"Julia? I can't comment on any patients who might be alive—"

"No, I don't mean Julia. I mean the old Filipina woman. Because she's no longer alive to have her privacy violated, I don't think Hugh would mind me telling you her name. It's Rosa Munoz."

My father sighed. "It was a long time ago. Names can be tricky. I'll have to check."

"So the name doesn't ring an immediate bell?"

"No, it doesn't. But I tried—I tried to keep a low personal profile with the project, given my name. I thought it might be too stressful for the women to think a Japanese doctor was involved, given that they had all known Japanese doctors while they were in sexual slavery—"

"I see. You mean to say that you knew the military doctors were complicit in the scheme."

"That's right. Their chief interest was the health and stress relief of the soldiers." My father sounded bitter. "Their relationship with the women was pretty far from the Hippocratic oath."

I sat for a minute, thinking. "I'm surprised, after all you've said about your own work, and your feelings, that you didn't want Hugh to pursue the class action."

My father sighed. "Look what I tried to do. It failed. I know that for him, the stakes are even higher. Already a woman's died, maybe from stress—"

"It could be something else," I said. "Someone might have killed her to stop the lawsuit. When the autopsy's done, we'll know."

"Do the police suspect Hugh?" my father asked.

"No, I don't think so. Why would they?"

"Well, he was the last person to see her."

"I was with him! He wasn't alone," I said.

"Yes, but they didn't take you for questioning—"

"It wasn't questioning, it was making the identification." I set down my soup bowl with a bang. "Hugh was her lawyer, Dad. He's above reproach. I can't imagine you would think him possible of—anything!"

Hugh chose that moment to lumber through the doorway, carrying both my suitcases. "I couldn't figure out how to get the dumbwaiter to work," he said.

"If a man can't operate a dumbwaiter, how could he kill a woman?" I blazed at my father.

"Sorry? Kill whom?" Hugh looked from one to the other of us in confusion.

I sprang up. "Hugh, let's go. If I don't leave now, I'll miss the plane. We can get coffee on the way."

"But I like the tea here," Hugh protested.

I stared at him. Obviously, if he was willing to sit in the kitchen and drink tea in my father's presence, he hadn't heard the gist of what my father had said about him. "Fine," I said. "But like I said, I'm going soon. I've had enough."

I strode out and up the stairs to my bathroom. I would brush my teeth, take away the horrible taste of my father's soup, and suspicion.

"What is it, Rei?" Hugh bounded up after me, and caught me in the hallway.

"Yes, darling, what's your plan for the morning?" My mother popped out of her room, blow-dryer in hand.

"I'm a bit—stressed," I said. "As you know, this happens whenever I have to travel somewhere. What I think would be best for everyone would be that I just cab it to the airport. I've already said good-bye to Dad."

"Just wait!" my mother said. "Wait a half hour, and Daddy and I will drive you. There's room for Hugh, too."

"I'm expected at the office," Hugh said. "I'm not going to be able to take her. But you're not going, Rei, till I've gotten to the bottom of what's wrong."

"Something's wrong?" my mother asked. And the sight of her angular features, softened by concern, were enough to make me want to weep.

"Dad thinks the police suspect Hugh," I said.

"Yes, your father's very worried. But of course, he thinks it is unjustified suspicion. He knows Hugh would never hurt anyone, especially since—"

"It's in my interest that she be alive. Because I'm a greedy, ambulance-chasing bastard," Hugh said bitterly.

"Chill out, kids," my mother said. "Toshiro has never said anything about ambulance chasing or greed, nor has he said that Hugh's a killer. He's just, I repeat, worried about the police. Remember how they behaved in the sixties? Well, you don't remember, you weren't alive then. But we do. We're all on edge. As I said to Toshiro last night, we just have to wait for the autopsy. The autopsy will show that she died of natural causes, nobody's fault but Mother Nature's."

"Would that be the case, Catherine," Hugh said. "Would that only be the case."

I took the ride to the airport from my parents after all. I was still not really clear on whether my father suspected Hugh or not, but I didn't care. I just wanted to get back to my old life, where there was nobody I cared about enough that I could get shaken to the core.

The flight was a good one, as far as I was concerned. No terrorists on board; for that matter, nobody in the two seats next to me. I was able to stretch out and sleep, a fitful slumber in which an old woman with dark eyes floated in and out. Her lips were moving; she was trying to say something that I couldn't understand. *I don't know the language,* I thought, and began a frantic search for Eric Gan. But he was nowhere.

I touched down in Tokyo late in the afternoon; technically, it was the next day, although I'd left San Francisco in the morning and reached Tokyo early in the evening. I gave my heavy suitcases to the airport delivery service to handle getting them to my apartment, and then rode the train an hour to make my way home.

I had just enough energy to slide the key into the lock and my body onto the futon. Then I was asleep.

As exhausted as I'd been, I still woke up early the next day. Very early: 5 A.M. The Family Mart convenience store wouldn't be open at that hour, so I would either have to eat the dried bonito fish still in its box on the kitchen counter—the aged specimen I'd boasted about to my father—or break into the foil-wrapped packet of cookies I'd taken off the plane, and forgotten to declare at customs, the previous night.

I cranked up the Tokyo City Gas space heater and settled down a few inches away from it with the cookies and a cup of green tea. Lack of central heating notwithstanding, the apartment was as comfortable as a thick Japanese acrylic sock—the kind men wore in winter with thonged sandals, a habit I'd taken up myself, since my shoe size in Japan was more masculine than feminine.

I'd painted my living-dining-kitchen area in a warm persimmon, which dramatically set off the old lacquered chests and tables I'd refinished. Everything was unusually neat, as I'd taken pains to tidy up before leaving for America two months earlier, but there was a thick layer of dust on all the old wood. Dutifully, I dusted every surface, coughing at the clouds I whipped up. I was going to have to do a lot more cleaning with the New Year a few days away. At the end of each year, students cleaned their schools, salarymen washed their cars, and housewives turned over their houses top to bottom. It was all to welcome the *toshigami*—the god of the New Year—into their homes, for the promise of prosperity and happiness in the coming year. The changing of the calendar was a time to pay off debts and lay to rest all the old problems for a clean start.

The thought of starting over reminded me of Hugh's class action. It seemed a bit absurd to be calling on a Japanese Shinto god for help with a lawsuit against Japanese big business, but I couldn't escape my heritage—and the idea that with a bit of careful preparation, the class action might succeed after all.

I thought about the name Rosa had mentioned to us: Ramon Espinosa. He was her Filipino comrade who was supposed to be living in Japan.

I called information, spelling out the name Espinosa to the operator. No luck. I should have expected that. Mr. Espinosa was probably a retired laborer without many comforts. I pondered whether it would be preferable to be a broke foreigner in San Francisco or Tokyo. Both were terrifically expensive cities. But San Francisco embraced a myriad of cultures—Tokyo didn't. Ramon Espinosa had chosen a hard lot in life, to stay in Japan instead of returning to the Philippines—that is, if he was still in the country.

If he were alive, there would be a police record of his presence. And if he'd died here, that record would exist as well. Japan was mad for keeping records. Searching the nation's local ward offices for such records, though, would take months. To get it done quickly, I'd need to ask a professional for help.

I flipped open the telephone book for my district—in Tokyo, there are so many people, you can only get a phone book covering one's own ward—and looked in the business section for detectives. Private detectives were plentiful, because families frequently used them to research their children's prospective marital partners. I doubted PIs worked on Sundays—it was the only day of the week Japanese people rested—but at least they'd hear my message first thing Monday morning.

I spent the rest of the morning making telephone calls to business associates, leaving messages that I was back in town. There was another call I should have made, to my parents, to let them know I'd safely arrived. But I told myself it was too late—they'd be in bed already, asleep. Better to call them another day.

Around eleven, I decided to venture out to the Family Mart convenience store a few blocks away. I stepped out into typical January weather—mid-forties, sunny, and dry. Everything on my tiny street looked the same as always. Two bicycles leaned against the wall of the apartment house, unchained because nobody would ever steal them; the fan shop's exterior was decorated with a line of potted plants struggling to stay alive in the forty-degree weather; and the ever-present wet spot on the sidewalk outside the tofu shop had not dried. As I walked, I passed my neighbors; the Tanakas carrying their young baby toward the subway, old Mrs. Yuto cleaning the outside of her windows, Mr. Haneda polishing the chrome on his car. Yes, the New Year's cleaning was on, full force. I resolved to buy extra cleaning supplies at Family Mart.

I'd wanted to see my dear old friend Mr. Waka, who was usually behind the counter at this Family Mart franchise, which he owned. Mr. Waka always had a ready hand to give me candy or advice on my life. But his son was there, saying that he was filling in while Mr. Waka was home with the flu.

"It's been a difficult winter for illnesses, *neh*?" Kenji said, while wiping his nose with a tissue.

"I didn't know that your father had a flu! Please give him my best regards and tell him that I finally returned from America. I've been away over two months—too long entirely." I felt strangely desperate to have someone recognize that I'd been gone.

"Oh. Well, please take care," Kenji said, using the hand that had wiped his nose to load my little plastic shopping bag with the food and the cleaning supplies.

"Right. And please say hello to your father for me," I said, thinking the younger generation just wasn't as fastidious about hygiene as their elders.

As I entered my apartment I heard a voice talking into my answering machine. It was Hugh, telling me he was having trouble getting a flight booked. Without bothering to take off my shoes—a big no-no, if anyone Japanese had been watching me—I dashed into the living room to lift the receiver.

"Hello," I said breathlessly, just as Hugh hung up.

Damn it. I played the whole message, during which Hugh said that Rosa's autopsy results had come back, revealing a cardiac event—in other words, a heart attack; a typical elderly person's death. Hugh went on to say that since nobody had claimed a relationship with Rosa, the law firm was being asked to clean up her effects. If it went quickly, he could fly to Japan within the next day or two.

So Rosa had died of natural causes. I should have felt reassured. Now I didn't have to worry about the New Year bringing a police investigation. The matter was cleaned up, dealt with. But it was too bad I couldn't have caught Hugh on the phone and pressed him for details; I felt quite unsatisfied.

I was distracted for a while by the delivery of my suitcases from the airport. I got right to unpacking, and as I was finishing up, the phone rang again.

On the other end was my aunt Norie.

"Oh, welcome home, Rei-chan. When you come tonight, don't

forget to stop by the *senbeiya-san* in your neighborhood. Can you bring your uncle's favorite crackers?"

"What? I don't remember making plans." I had no idea what Hiroshi's favorite style of *senbei* cracker was, either.

"It is Sunday evening. You always come on Sunday evening for supper."

"But—how did you know I was back?"

"Your father telephoned to remind us. Actually, we would have been happy to meet you at the airport, but he told us he thought you could manage."

"Did he sound angry with me?" I asked.

"Angry? Of course he's not angry. Why, did you do some—misbehavior?"

"No, just the usual." I pressed my lips together. "I'll see you tonight."

At my aunt and uncle's place, a welcoming light shone over the door, and there was a large urn holding pine, bamboo, and plum—nature's trinity to celebrate the New Year. I was transported back to all the other New Year's times when I would go to see my aunt and uncle and cousin, when the kind of problems I had were with my job, not with my status as a free woman.

Of course, the door was unlocked. I slid it to the side and sang out, *"Tadaima,"* the traditional greeting that means "I'm home." Technically, I shouldn't have said it, because I wasn't an actual household member, but I called it out because I was feeling hopeful. A quick patter of light footsteps, and my cousin Tsutomu, whom I thought of as Tom, was there. He liked me to call him Tom because it made him feel exotic. Japanese people all called him Tsutomu, or, more typically, Shimura-sensei—the honorific at the end marking his status as a doctor at St. Luke's International Hospital.

"Rei-chan." He drew me into a swift, tight hug, then stepped back to look at me. "What happened?"

"Nothing," I said. "I'm just tired. I would have liked to rest from four o'clock on today, but I couldn't resist coming to Sunday night supper. Where's Chika-chan? Isn't she home for the holidays?"

"She's out with her friends," Aunt Norie said, coming out of the kitchen to give me a hug. "She's been with us a week. Since she's so grown up now, she says this neighborhood is too boring—she wants to play in Tokyo every evening, and it's with a fast crowd from the Kansai area. Sending her to Kyoto was stupid—now she's trying to turn into a Kansai girl, obsessed with clothes and so loud, *ara*, you wouldn't believe the way she talks!"

Norie was referring to the classic divide between Eastern and Western Japan—the Kanto and Kansai regions. Kanto, the section that encompassed Tokyo and Yokohama, was regarded as stable and tasteful. Kansai, which was the seat of Japan's original capital, Kyoto, and its true business mecca, Osaka, was different. People in Kansai talked more loudly, and had their own slang; they spent more money on clothing, and women felt free to wear sexy shoes and more vibrant colors than their sisters in Tokyo. The Japanese said it was the combined forces of Kyoto's past royal image and the big money merchant culture of Osaka. I didn't know if this was true, but I couldn't fault a Yokohama girl for wanting to pick up some Kansai style. I hadn't seen Chika since she'd gone off to college three years earlier, so the change, I knew, might very well be dramatic.

"Chika will be here New Year's Eve, Rei, but don't worry about her right now," Tom said. "You look so tense. Did something happen in America?"

"Let her come in out of the cold and relax before you interrogate her," Aunt Norie chided, securing the bag of sesame crackers she had requested I bring. "Rei-chan, thank you so much for remembering."

"A lot happened in California," I said, stepping up onto the living room floor and giving my aunt a long, hard embrace. I'd missed her so much.

"Well, please inform us, Rei-chan. Your father only said that you were coming home at last." My uncle Hiroshi came forward to greet me with a slight bow, rather than an embrace. It was awkward for him to embrace me—even if I was his brother's daughter. Hiroshi had thick salt-and-pepper hair just like my father's, but it didn't hang too low. It was cut neatly, the way most salarymen wore their hair. Hiroshi had worked for the same bank since college, then been made redundant after thirty-five years. Since then he'd found new work in the business office of an electronics company, but he was not a section head, as he'd once been. This wasn't the way they'd expected Japan to treat them. Still, the prospect of Norie working to make up for the economic shortfall was unthinkable. My aunt had once tried to find a part-time job, but the only businesses interested in her skills were supermarkets. She preferred to teach *ikebana* classes, taking a token cash payment from each student. Besides, she was so busy cooking for her family, I thought, as I sat down with everyone at the cozy round dining table dominated by Norie's propane-powered tabletop cooker. After the cooker's flame glowed blue, she topped it with a large clay pot called a *nabe*. She had made *donabe*—a light, seafood-based broth into which we all dipped shrimp, clams, mushrooms, and scallions.

Eating the nourishing *donabe* gave me the rush of confidence I needed to begin to tell them I was engaged to be married. I was nervous because it had taken them well over a year to get used to Hugh the first time around, and then when we'd split, they'd blamed it all on him. But they were quietly positive, and Norie even volunteered to help me shop for the right hotel in which to hold the wedding.

"We're interested in a smaller gathering at a shrine," I said. "I thought of the one in my neighborhood, if they'll have me, or another one that's important in Shimura family history."

"Your aunt and I married at the Yasukuni Shrine," Uncle Hiroshi said.

"Isn't that the right-wing shrine where people go to honor those who died in World War II?" I made my comment a question, for politeness's sake. I knew for a fact that the current prime minister had made a visit there, which had set off a firestorm of criticism from liberals, and praise from conservatives.

"It's the place where *all* who gave their lives to Japan over the course of our wars lie," Hiroshi explained. "And since our old family household was nearby, it became the shrine where our family made donations and prayed."

Norie put down her chopsticks. "It was fine for a wedding thirty years ago, when the political issues were quiet. But who knows what the conditions are like now? When the prime minister visited, the whole world watched. It could be quite difficult for Hugh-san and Rei-chan, because I'm sure they will have hundreds of guests, some of whom wouldn't be comfortable."

"I wouldn't marry there," Tom said. "I would have a simple ceremony in Guam or Hawaii, followed directly by the honeymoon!"

"You're one to talk," Hiroshi said. "No girl in sight, and you refuse to talk to the matchmaker your mother found for you."

"Ah, I'll check with Hugh first," I said, trying to deflect attention from my poor cousin, who at age thirty-two was getting old for marriage. "There's a slight chance he'll be flying in tomorrow."

"Oh, then he must come for New Year's Eve," Norie said, and then a general discussion of menu ensued. She would serve the traditional *toshi-koshi soba,* long buckwheat noodles meant to guarantee long life and happiness—my favorite—as well as the tiny sardinelike fish that you were supposed to eat whole—not my favorite. There would be fresh *mochi* cakes made from rice she'd pounded herself. Afterward, everyone would walk to pray at the neighborhood temple.

"You know, it sounds great, but he might be very, very tired upon arrival," I said. I hadn't liked the way he'd pushed himself so hard when he arrived in San Francisco. "Can we let you know that day if we're coming? And before I forget, Uncle, I must ask you some family history questions. I recently learned there was a scroll signed by the late emperor that belonged to our family. Do you know anything about it?"

"Oh, yes. That letter actually came to my father. He was so proud when he received it that he would take it and hang it in the most important alcove of the house on the anniversary of his father's death."

"That's interesting," I said. "I wonder why that day."

"Well, the scroll was actually a condolence letter about the death of his father—your great-grandfather, Shimura Kazuo."

"How amazing!" I said. "What was the connection between Great-Grandfather and the emperor? They couldn't have been friends . . ."

"No, of course not." Uncle Hiroshi smiled at me as he used his chopsticks to deftly dip a shrimp into the *donabe*. "Your great-grandfather was a renowned man of letters. He had met with Emperor Hirohito when he was young and had not yet ascended the throne. But the emperor remembered your great-grandfather many years later when he passed away. He wrote a beautiful letter of condolence that my father considered his most important possession. After his death, that scroll was passed on to your father, who was the eldest son."

"I see." I paused, knowing that what I'd say next might shock Hiroshi. "Actually, my father held on to the scroll until the mid-seventies, but at that point he decided to sell it to raise money to buy our house."

"Oh! He never said anything to us about it." Hiroshi stared at me.

"Well, the end result is it was bought by Showa College, and they have it safely stored in their archives. It's good, don't you think, that it's available to the public?" I was desperately trying for something to mitigate the act committed by my father.

"But it is our family heritage," Hiroshi murmured. "Does he still have the family sword? Or did he sell that, too?"

"Oh, no," I said. "He treasures that very much. It hangs in a place of honor on his bedroom wall."

"Bedroom wall?" Hiroshi said, with a little laugh that didn't conceal his pain. "When my father owned the sword, it was specially displayed at our household altar at special times only. Every year my mother placed *mochi* cakes and an orange on a special plate in front of it."

"I'll record that in the family history. Thank you, Uncle." As I spoke, I noticed that Hiroshi had completely forgotten about the shrimp he'd dipped into the broth. Its floating body had curled up into a ball—which is what I wanted to do, too.

13

Monday morning, I was at the post office right as it opened, desperate for two months' worth of mail. Once I had it, my life could properly restart. The clerk was gone for a while, finally staggering back with two large crates. I dragged both boxes outside and flagged down a taxi to take me the quarter-mile home. The ride was short, but expensive. With a base price of close to $6 for merely entering a taxi, I was $10 poorer when I got out at home. The only mercy was that Japanese cabbies didn't expect tips.

Opening the door to my place, I heard the phone ringing. Why was it that when I was home, nobody called, and when I was out, everyone did? I raced up onto the tatami mats, forgetting about my shoes once again.

"Hello?" I said breathlessly.

"Anno, Idabashi desu ga . . ."

A Japanese man, sounding startled by my English, had begun to introduce himself. It took me a few moments to realize that this man, Mr. Shou Idabashi, was one of the detectives I'd called. He must have been like me, I figured, trying to take care of all his business before the New Year's holiday shutdown. I told him that I was looking for an aged relative of a friend. When I told him it was a foreigner, he sighed happily; foreigners weren't that hard to find, since they were all registered with the police.

"If Espinosa Ramon-san is still living, I can probably have his data for you within a few days. How far must I follow the trail? I will interview the man if you want to stay out of the situation and maintain your privacy," Mr. Idabashi said in polite Japanese.

I told the detective thanks, but I'd prefer to talk to him myself. He told me where to wire the advance payment, and I went straight out to my bank to do it. Then I returned home and made a call to Showa College, where the library department clerk said that yes, the letter existed, in the form of a scroll, and I could make an appointment to see it the next day. I hung up, triumphant. In twenty-four hours, I would know exactly what kind of business Emperor Hirohito had with my grandfather.

In the meantime, I'd work on the stacks of unpaid bills and invoices I'd brought home from the post office. I'd been able to pre-pay Tokyo City Gas and Nippon Telephone and Telegraph before my trip, but many other debts had accumulated. Fortunately, my bank statement showed evidence of two payments that clients had wired me while I was gone. I wasn't broke, because I'd been very careful with my expenses in America. The most expensive thing I'd purchased was a Gianni Versace men's belt, for my best friend Richard Randall, and if he were a gentleman, he'd reimburse me.

It was two o'clock, and I longed to put my head down on my pillow, but I knew that to beat the jet lag, I would have to stay awake. I dialed Richard at home.

"Can't wait to get together, sweetie, but I have to teach two classes first," Richard said. "Why don't you meet me around nine-thirty at Club Isn't It. It's ladies' night, so you'll get in for free."

"I'll fall asleep before that! Can you meet me for lunch tomor-row?" I pleaded.

"No, because it's New Year's Eve. I'll be running around buying booze for the party at Simone's. You're coming, right?"

"I'm sorry, I didn't know about it. I've already got plans."

"What, eating *soba* noodles with your aunt and uncle?"

"I was going to do that, but instead I'm waiting to see if Hugh makes it into town. I was thinking a bottle of champagne and fresh sheets on the bed would be enough for me."

Richard sighed. "Rei, you're acting like an old woman—when do you turn thirty?"

"In the new year," I said sourly. Richard was always rubbing it in that he was five years younger. I reminded him about his fancy belt, and that if he didn't come to get it, I'd spank him with it.

"Ooh, please. But I do want the belt for the party. Tell you what: I'll meet you at your place late tomorrow afternoon. I'll style you for Simone's party, and then we'll go."

On New Year's Eve day, my appointment at the college library was set for ten-thirty. I was up at six, so I had plenty of time to exercise, wash, and even blow-dry my hair. At a quarter of ten, I was slipping on my shoes when the telephone rang. I had a suspicion it was my parents, so now I was stuck with a dilemma. Answer, and miss the train and be late for the appointment at the library. Not answer, and let the rift between us widen.

I picked up the phone, and it was Hugh.

"How did you get here so fast?" I asked.

"No time to explain. I don't want to miss the next train into the city, to get to you. Which train should I use, JR?"

"No, no, I live in the old section of town, so better take the Keisei Flyer to Keisei-Ueno Station. From there, just take a taxi to my apartment. Oops, you'd better not. I have to go out for a big appointment right now and I won't be back for a couple of hours."

"How can we meet, then?"

I looked at my watch. "If you catch a train within the half hour, you'll be at the station by eleven-thirty. I think I could meet you at twelve. Could you amuse yourself playing pachinko or something?"

"My eyes wouldn't stay open. I think the best thing for me would be to get a coffee."

"You can get one at the Royal Host in the station. I love you."

I rushed off to Showa College with a lighter step and a happy heart. I beamed when I met Miss Tokuma, the librarian. She had a pleasant, round face that reminded me of a Japanese folk character called Binfuku. I had a little collection of Binfuku masks hanging in the entry to my apartment, but of course I couldn't tell her that. Instead, I praised her efficiency in locating the Hirohito scroll so quickly.

"I've followed its trail all the way from California," I said. "I faced so many obstacles there, I thought I'd find them here as well. But you've agreed to see me on the last day of the year. That was very kind."

"I have the scroll right here for you." She held up a long acid-free cardboard tube. "We will view it together."

She led me over to a window, where we sat at a table completely free of books or people. There was a little RESERVED sign on it, which made me think of restaurants. The sign must have had plenty of power, because all the other tables were overcrowded with young people reading, writing, and punching away at laptops. Some of the students were lying across their books, obviously asleep. Since it was school vacation time, I imagined that these were the few who had overdue papers. In Japan, there was a desire to clear debts before the New Year came. For these students' parents, the debts were financial. For the students themselves, the debts would be to their teachers.

Miss Tokuma indicated that I should sit down, so I did. She took a chair across the table from me and drew from the large cardboard tube a silk-covered cylinder that I guessed housed the scroll. Then she unrolled it, carefully placing four glass weights on each corner of the two-foot-long paper.

The paper was bordered in black, and its top was the pattern of a sixteen-petal embossed chrysanthemum. I'd seen this chrysanthemum carved into gates of the old Royal Palace in Kyoto, but nowhere else, until now. It was against the law for anyone but the royal family to wear, or display, the sixteen-petal chrysanthemum. A thrill ran through me. I kept darting glances back at the emblem as I slowly read what I could of the text.

The scroll was handwritten in a flowing calligraphy going from top to bottom and right to left. I made out a few words, but that was it. My reading level was still nowhere near an adult's. I recognized only the characters that formed my grandfather's name and a few other words.

Miss Tokuma had risen up behind me to read over my shoulder. She was silent for a while, then said, "The language is very special, of course, since the words are from the Showa Tenno himself."

Miss Tokuma had used an expression that referred to the name of Hirohito's reigning period, instead of saying the name Hirohito.

"Tokuma-san, I'm really sorry, but as I mentioned to you before, I came from California."

"Yes, yes, I understood."

"I mean to say that I grew up abroad and regretfully never learned to read Japanese. I would be very grateful if you could make a photocopy for me and I could bring it to a translator."

Her round face lost its jovial expression. "I'm sorry, but that's not possible. The paper is too fragile to spread out on the photocopy machine. It could be contaminated by trace elements left on the glass."

Miss Tokuma began rolling up the letter. I wanted to grab it and hold on, but that would only have made her more nervous.

"Oh, I apologize for not understanding the situation. Could you translate it for me, please? I mean, if the calligraphy isn't too difficult to make out."

She stiffened at that, and said, "Shimura-san, this is Showa Tenno's fine hand. Of course it is legible. It is a national treasure."

I bowed my head. "Please, Tokuma-san, I have such poor Japanese. I long to understand the letter's content."

"I would help you ordinarily, but please consider the situation. This is the last day of the year, and the library is quite busy. My duty is to return to the desk to help the many students needing assistance. It would be best if you come back in five days, after the New Year's holiday is over."

She was lifting the weights off the exposed scroll, readying it to go back into its hiding place, when a shy voice spoke up.

"Excuse me. May I help?"

The voice belonged to a boy with close-cropped hair and tired-looking eyes. He looked all of twenty years old. I couldn't imagine how he could help until I realized he could, of course, read.

"If it's not too long, I can read it to you. I like to practice my English—I have oral examinations coming up."

"Oh, how lucky for me," I said. "And if you read it to me in Japanese, I would be happy to spend some time coaching you for your oral examination."

"Silence is the rule in the library," Miss Tokuma said. "However, if you keep your voices low, I will allow this student to do the translation for you."

I thanked Miss Tokuma profusely and got down to business with the boy, who introduced himself to me as Yoshi Endo.

"Let's see," whispered young Mr. Endo, taking the seat next to me. "It looks like this is a condolence letter—from the last emperor to someone called Shimura Junichi."

"My late grandfather," I said.

Mr. Endo raised his eyebrows. "Really? The letter is dated August fifteen, 1938, Hayama, Japan. That's where the imperial summer villa is," he continued.

I nodded, encouraging him to go on.

Yoshi Endo read: "To Shimura Junichi-san, I offer my sincere regrets on the passing of your father, Professor Shimura Kazuo. As you know, your father instructed me in Japanese history and political theory for three years when I was a young prince. Your father had a depth of knowledge and a gift for clear explanation. Shimura-sensei also had a generous heart and a devotion to his country that is a model for all Japanese today. I will never forget the teachings of your father, and I pray that you will find peace at this difficult time."

The student looked up from the scroll. "That's the end. Was Shimura Kazuo the father of Shimura Junichi?"

"That's right." I said.

"Did you know him?" Mr. Endo asked, and then slapped his head. "Of course you didn't. This letter says he died in 1938!"

"Right," I said absently. It was a few years before my father was born. His own father, Junichi, was a young professor at the time. With all that was going on politically, it impressed me that Emperor Hirohito had taken a moment to think of a teacher from the days of his boyhood. And the fact that my great-grandfather had taught him was fascinating to me. I hadn't known the emperor had taken classes at the University of Tokyo. It didn't seem natural for him to be taking classes with commoners, especially since there was a Peers' College for the noble and royal families of Japan to attend. Why had my great-grandfather taught him? What were the circumstances?

"I thank you so much, Endo-san. You can't imagine what this means to me," I said.

"Shimura-san, you're very welcome. Actually, I'm the one who is honored. Why don't you bring your notes about the letter to the New Imperialists Club meeting! The others would be excited to learn something new about Showa Tenno."

"Who are the New Imperialists?" I raised my eyebrows.

"It's the junior committee for the political group. People who love the emperor and dream of restored powers. If you're second-year or older, you can be nominated to join."

He was talking about the right wing—the ones who wanted to give the current emperor more power and to make Japan's self-defense forces a regular military outfit capable of waging war in other countries. I tried to hide my shudder, because I understood that he had made his invitation out of nothing but goodwill—and the mistaken impression, which did flatter me, that I was a nineteen- or twenty-year-old sophomore. "Actually, I'm not a student here, so I don't think I could go."

"All right. Well, nice to meet you, and happy New Year," the student said, bobbing his head and standing as if to go back to his work.

But I hadn't forgotten my promise. "Happy New Year to you, but now, isn't it time to let me help you prepare for that oral examination?"

14

I spent about half an hour listening to Mr. Endo discuss the narrative structure of *Paradise Lost*. When I finally stumbled out, I was filled with visions of hell and running slightly late for the meeting with Hugh. At the station, I passed down the wrong hallway before finding the Royal Host coffee shop. It was fifteen minutes after twelve, and he wasn't there. I sat down in an orange vinyl booth to wait.

Royal Host was a perfect example of an American fast food restaurant adapted to Japanese tastes. You could get a hamburger or an *okonomiyaki* squid pancake. I wasn't in the mood for much so I ordered a "hotcake" and coffee.

The syrup was artificial maple—unpalatable to a girl who had grown up spoiled by the real stuff from Vermont. I pushed aside the hotcake to sip coffee and watch the flood of travelers in the station corridor, looking for an easily recognizable tall figure with red-blond hair. At twelve-thirty, I began to worry. He'd called me before ten. Two and a half hours was plenty of time to get into the city. Maybe he'd gone to Royal Host early and left before I arrived.

I asked the waitress—who was looking disgustedly at me for staying so long with an empty cup—whether she'd seen anyone fitting Hugh's description. No, she answered, then made a check with the other staff in the restaurant. No white foreigners yet that day; the only foreigner had been a *Filipin-jin* very early in the morning.

Too bad I hadn't seen the Filipino, I thought, because I could have chatted him up to get more information on Filipino neighborhoods in Tokyo. I ordered a sandwich and lingered for another thirty minutes until the lunch hour rush came and it was no longer fair to keep a table to myself. I left a note for Hugh in case he showed up later. It was rather detailed, with my address written out in Japanese, and with instructions to show it to the cabdriver.

I rode the short hop on the subway to Sendagi Station and walked home. My neighbors along the street had cleaned their windows and washed their cars. A few doorways were decorated with twisted straw roping tied with many small white paper strips. The strips signified troubles that people hoped would be over in the New Year. I could have used about ten of these: one over my door, and the rest on every window.

So much for the happy New Year. I would stay home that evening. I was in the mood neither for noodles with the Shimuras, nor tequila with Simone and Richard. I felt too unsettled to go out.

I opened the apartment door and headed straight for the telephone. Sure enough, the answering machine's red light was blinking. Three callers had left messages. The first was my father, wishing me a happy New Year in a voice that sounded tentative: neither warm nor cold.

The second call was from Hugh, who apologized profusely for not showing up at Royal Host. He said that en route to Tokyo, he'd received a call on his new cell phone—a message from the law firm about a plaintiff's address. He said he felt duty-bound to stop in, since it was right on the way. He left the cell phone number for me, asking that I call him after three.

I clicked my tongue in annoyance. I was glad that Hugh wasn't lost, but it seemed clear that he was back to his workaholic ways. Still, I could understand his eagerness to make contact with the plaintiff, who I guessed was probably Ramon Espinosa. But what he would accomplish without a translator, I couldn't imagine.

The next phone message was from the detective I'd hired, Shou

Idabashi. He said he had some information for me about Espinosa, and left Espinosa's address and telephone number in Kanda.

Perfect timing, I thought, and got ready to go out again. It was just after one—the odds were that if I made it to Ramon Espinosa's, I'd be there in time to help Hugh if he was still on site.

Kanda wasn't that far, and it was also one of my favorite districts in Tokyo, with a main street filled with lots of shops that sold used books. Of course, for someone who couldn't read Japanese the opportunities were limited, but I had bought many antique books with beautiful covers and endpapers and others illustrated with amusing woodblock print pictures. I also frequented a few bookstores with English language sections, like the Tuttle Company, where I would sometimes hide out for hours in the stacks, looking for the latest English women's novels, or mysteries written by Americans. The Tokyo booksellers charged double for foreign books, which was the reason I tried to read covertly without paying to take books home.

I turned off the main street leading from the station into a smaller one with a fire station, and then turned again to find the street Mr. Idabashi had described.

Mr. Espinosa's apartment building looked as if it had been built about twenty years before—old by Tokyo standards, where things were often torn down within ten years. The building wasn't what was typically called a "mansion"—those apartment blocks were more like the Western ideal, supertall and wide—but it looked very nice. It was in better condition than the old stucco building I lived in, and it had the pleasant addition of balconies attached to each unit. The futons airing on the balconies were bright and new-looking, and there was a row of shiny bicycles parked in a rack near the door. The bikes had all the old traces of mud washed off for the New Year. As with most apartment buildings, each apartment had its own external entrance. Outdoor staircases ran up both the east and west sides of the apartment block.

I entered the vestibule and saw the mailbox with Espinosa written in katakana, the Japanese phonetic alphabet used for foreign names. I trudged up the building's concrete staircase to the third floor, where I presumed apartment 31 was located. I thought I'd caught a hint of Hugh's Grey Flannel aftershave, but it turned out to be fragrant incense wafting from unit 32, which was labeled with the family name Moriuchi.

Briskly, I rang the buzzer on Mr. Espinosa's door.

"*Hai?*" a strong-sounding male voice called out. The Japanese inflection, in this small word, was perfect; it didn't sound like a foreigner speaking.

"My name is Shimura Rei," I answered in the proper Japanese backward fashion. "I'm looking for Espinosa-san, please."

The door swung open, and I faced a figure smaller than I—a man with deeply creased skin the color of strong tea and a head that was bent lower than mine. He was wearing a white coat with a high collar and styling that reminded me of the way dentists used to dress. He bowed immediately, and I bowed back. As I straightened to look at him again, I noticed that his eyes were hidden behind black glasses.

He was blind, I realized suddenly. And not being able to see me meant he had no idea who I was. "Espinosa-san, I would like to explain who I am. I am a Japanese-American who has come from California to speak to you about something very important. I carry news about an old acquaintance of yours—"

"Oh?" Mr. Espinosa sounded pleased. 'Please come in, then."

I slipped off my shoes and followed him into a room with a long metal doctor's table covered by a white towel. There were also bookcases and tables stacked with small boxes made from brass, steel, and carved woods. There was a calendar on a wall with dates punched out in dots that I realized had to be Braille.

"You're a doctor," I blurted. "I should have addressed you as 'sensei'—I'm sorry."

"Oh, I'm just an acupuncturist," Mr. Espinosa said, laughing. "And only since after the war. I am hardly an expert."

"'Only since after the war'? That's fifty-seven years. I would say that's plenty of experience."

"Do you see the tea table to the right, with cushions around it? Please make yourself comfortable, Miss Shimura. Tell me, have you had acupuncture treatments before?"

I had to crane my head to see around a tower of boxes, but sure enough, there was a tea table with a couple of new-looking black-and-red cushions around it.

"No, I haven't had a treatment before," I said. "As I mentioned, I come here with news."

"You are a young lady, but you are not pain-free, I would think," Mr. Espinosa said. He sat down next to me, and without saying anything picked up my wrist and held it—picked up my wrist, when he couldn't even see me. He must have used his sense of hearing to judge the location of my body, I realized with amazement.

"Are you tired?"

"Yes, but it's just because I came back from the U.S., and have jet lag."

"Any pains anywhere?"

"Around the knee sometimes, but that's from running—"

"Pain on either side of the knee might also be a symptom of a liver problem. It's quite serious. It can also impact relationships . . . Do you have frustration in your relationships, Miss Shimura? A temper?"

I looked at the blind man sitting with such a peaceful expression at my side, and understood that he must have already had a deep talk with my fiancé I sighed and said, "You're correct about that, I'm afraid. You must have spoken to Hugh."

"Who? I did speak to a *gaijin* on the telephone, Miss Shimura, but he did not mention you."

I caught my breath. "Then how do you know all those things?"

"I feel the flow of energy at your pulse. If I did an abdominal examination, I would know more about how I can help you. Right now, I can already make a guess that the wood nature in your system is off-balance. But since you are not here for treatment, can I give you tea?"

"No, no, I don't want to trouble you," I said, out of rote politeness. Actually, a cup of green tea would have soothed me and given me something to hold while I thought about how I'd bring up the topic of Rosa.

"It's no trouble at all," Mr. Espinosa said, and he moved with a measured pace toward the tiled counter and range at the back wall—what passed for a kitchenette in Japan. With his left hand he lifted a blue-and-white ceramic teapot that had been drying upside down on a plate rack, and at the same time, he pulled a tea canister from a cupboard with his right. He shook the equivalent of two tablespoons of green tea into the teapot, then brought the pot to the table before me. He moved next into the center of the room, where he lifted a steaming cast-iron kettle from its perch atop the space heater. Kneeling at the tea table, he filled the teapot with the boiling water and then replaced the kettle on the space heater. All had been accomplished without a false step. I realized that even with the benefit of twenty-twenty vision, I couldn't possibly have served tea to a guest so quickly.

"*Itadakimasu.*" I murmured the word that was the standard Japanese grace, and I sipped. The tea was very good—as good as the tea my elderly antiques dealer friend Mr. Ishida served. In more than a few ways, Mr. Espinosa was reminding me of Mr. Ishida.

"Mr. Espinosa, since you haven't met yet with my friend Hugh, I'm not sure how much I should tell you. I think he has a good deal to explain."

"As do you," Mr. Espinosa said calmly.

I nodded before remembering he couldn't see the gesture. "Yes. But first, I have to ask: Did you ever know a woman called Rosa Munoz?"

For the first time since I'd arrived, his face moved. The sagging skin around his mouth trembled. "Rosa. Oh, yes! Do you know her?"

"She survived the war and emigrated to California—San Francisco, which is my hometown. I met her on Christmas Eve."

"How wonderful! And is she well?"

There was no easy way to do this. And he couldn't see my face, pick up the cues that anyone else could have. I said simply, "I'm sorry, but she died just a few days ago."

He was silent for a long time. "She must have been seventy-five. Well, I suppose it is a blessing that she lived that long at all."

He knew her age. What an incredible detail to be able to calculate rapidly, after all the years. They must have been good friends, or more.

"She had a heart attack," I said. "It was incredibly tragic, because she was close to coming into some money, and a better life. At least, that was what we were hoping for."

"What do you mean?" He stiffened visibly.

"She was poor," I said cautiously, wondering where I'd gone wrong. "She had worked as a cleaner, and the apartment she lived in was very shabby, in a rough neighborhood. She had nobody to take care of her, but we were trying to change that."

"'We'?" Ramon Espinosa repeated, as if confused.

"I shouldn't say 'we.' I—I knew Rosa, but I'm not a representative of the law firm that's been in contact with you."

"You mean—that firm in San Francisco," he said.

"Yes. I presume you offered to give testimony?"

"No, I didn't." His voice was quavering. "They found out about me somehow, and passed a message on through the Acupuncturists' Association. But I never agreed to talk."

This was something I hadn't expected. But I sensed it wasn't right for me to try to talk him into anything. My father had said that bringing up traumatic memories could send people over the edge.

"Oh, I'm sorry. I've misunderstood everything," I said. "Should I leave?"

He shook his head. "Please tell me about Rosa first. What did she say to the law firm?"

"All I can speak for is what she said when I was there with her," I said. "Rosa told my fiancé—a man named Hugh Glendinning, who was hoping to meet you—that she would testify about everything she'd been forced to do during the war. Hugh's goal was that the Japanese company that enslaved her—and you—would pay reparations that would make your lives easier, and that this would set an example for the human rights struggle worldwide."

"Rosa's situation was far worse than mine," Mr. Espinosa said. "She was, ah . . ." His voice trailed off. I imagined he was too genteel to say "a comfort woman."

"I do know the terrible exploitation of her," I said, choosing to speak euphemistically to keep him at ease. "There hasn't seemed much chance for reparations from the Japanese government that fostered the brothels. The law firm thinks it's going to be much more rewarding to sue the company that used Asians and American POWs to dig its mines."

"That's when I met her," Mr. Espinosa said. "We were both digging a tunnel. It was unusual for a young lady to do such hard work, but she had said she'd do anything not to have to return to the, ah, hotel where she'd worked with the other ladies. She was able to get the transfer, she told me, because she knew a high-ranking officer who arranged things."

"Do you remember his name?"

"Oh, no. Just a typical Japanese name. They didn't see each other after the war."

"Rosa had such a hard time after the war," I said. "Yes, she managed to reach California, but she didn't find a stable and respected position. She cleaned a bar for years. The apartment building where she lived was like—" I stopped, because I couldn't find words to describe it. In Japan, nobody had housing as bad as the tenement I'd visited.

"Still, Miss Shimura, she and I were so fortunate to survive."

"But you were treated so badly, and not paid a salary." I paused. "You are obviously a very forgiving person, but if you chose to tell your story truthfully to this lawyer, it could mean money and justice for everyone else, not to mention yourself."

"You want me to stand up against this nation where I have earned a good living since the war?" He paused. "The pain for me is gone. What happened to my eyes was terrible, but one of the managers took pity on me and brought me to Japan after the war, and enrolled me in an acupuncture school for blind people. I made many good friends in that school, and I have wonderful patients and neighbors. All Japanese, Shimura-san. Things would have been more difficult if I'd been sent back to the Philippines after the war. I'd not live long as a blind beggar there."

Suddenly, I saw the story behind the dark glasses that he wore. Perhaps it was an accident in the mines that had blinded him. The company had not thrown him out, but had provided for him. As it had prospered, so had he.

"You feel so grateful to the company for helping you after the war that you would never testify against them," I said.

"Yes, that's the truth of it. Thank you for understanding."

"I—actually, I feel pretty slow about the whole thing. I apologize for bothering you."

"No, don't feel that way. I'm sorry to disappoint you. As I said, Miss Shimura, I know that you have trouble with your knees. If you like, you can come here sometime for a complimentary introductory treatment."

"I'll keep it in mind, thanks," I said, taking the business card he offered. "I'll leave you my card too, in case you change your mind." I handed it to him.

"I will have my assistant read it to me," he said. "Thank you for your visit. I had not thought of Rosa for a long time, and while I am sad to hear the news, perhaps it is a blessing she is away from the bad place you mentioned."

It wasn't until I left, and was almost all the way home on the train, that it dawned on me that I shouldn't be feeling so warm and fuzzy about my short visit with the gentle Ramon Espinosa.

Ramon Espinosa had been cared for by Morita Incorporated after the war. He was grateful to them. Now he had a dangerous piece of information—information that a foreign lawyer was planning to sue Morita. I'd given out Hugh's full name, and because he was listed in Martindale-Hubble—the "who's who" of lawyers—it would be a snap to trace who he was, and for whom he was working.

The question was, did Ramon Espinosa still have a close contact at Morita Incorporated—someone whom he'd feel close enough to tell?

15

"Happy New Year!" Richard Randall screamed in my ear. The party at Simone's tiny flat in Shibuya had quickly outgrown its confines, and we had spilled into the street.

"It's not time yet," I said, checking my watch. I'd made the decision to take Richard's party over the *soba* noodles at Aunt Norie's just because I could get back to my apartment easily the same night. Norie had said she understood why I'd changed my plan, and hoped I'd come for the ceremonial New Year's Day meal the next day.

In the meantime, while nursing a glass of bad white wine, I'd been calling my answering machine at the apartment to check if there were more messages from Hugh about his whereabouts. I'd called the number he'd given me at three o'clock, but he hadn't answered. And my answering machine hadn't recorded any messages. I was starting to think that perhaps I should have sat at home so that when the call came, I'd be there.

Richard thought it was no big deal, of course; he'd pressured me to go out with him because he wanted his new belt and because he wanted company. After Richard's comment about how staid and thirtyish I was becoming, I felt reluctant to stay at home. I was also reluctant to be a homebody because I was annoyed with Hugh for missing our meeting at Royal Host twelve hours earlier.

Surely he could have kissed me hello first, then gone on about his business.

I eyed Richard, a small blond sprite wearing a black leather jacket open over a T-shirt sporting the *anime* character Princess Nausica. On the bottom, he wore vintage Levi's highlighted by his new black belt trimmed in gleaming nickel. He looked exactly the same as when I'd met him five years ago, when we'd been roommates and fellow English teachers at a kitchenware company.

I was wearing something Richard had never seen before, and loved: an old crushed velvet dress from college that had turned up in my suitcase. I had a feeling Hugh had packed it when I wasn't looking. The dress was purple and only went to mid-thigh, and had the habit of creeping up when I danced. Now that we were outside, I'd covered the dress with a black Persian lamb swing coat that had belonged to my Baltimore grandmother in the 1950s. It had seemed like the perfect wrap when I'd left early in the evening. It wasn't lined with much, though, so I was starting to freeze.

"Richard, why don't we go into a bar or something. This hanging out on the street is no good. Somebody's going to call the police, I'm sure."

The way most of my old friends looked translated to hoodlumism in Japan. Pierced noses and ears, strategically ripped denim, black hair that was dyed yellow, and vice versa—these were the looks of typical Japanese teenagers, but not of twentysomethings. By the time most Japanese reached their late twenties, they were working at respectable jobs, and had looks to match. But Richard and Simone and their ilk had freewheeling jobs teaching English part-time and serving drinks in bars. About the most respectable person in the bunch was a guy from Yokota Air Base, and that was because of his sheared military haircut, not his behavior—he'd pulled up to the party in a van with a telltale military license plate, decorated with offensive bumper stickers that I hoped few Japanese could translate. Since his arrival, he'd proceeded to drink an entire six-pack of Budweiser—he'd brought plenty of cheap booze from the PX—and was working on another.

"Richard, I think I'm going to call it a night," I said. "I'm still tired from the jet lag."

"What's the point of going out for the New Year if you leave before midnight?" Richard protested.

"Not much, I guess. I think I'm just too worried about Hugh not showing up. Seriously, what if he's gone to Ueno Station again?"

"The trains stop running in fifteen minutes," Richard said. "If he's there, he's going to have to leave. Unless he wants to sleep in the tunnels, ha-ha."

Richard's mention of the tunnels made me think of Ramon Espinosa working in the mine. Ramon, who was loyal to the company that had allowed him to be blinded in an accident, and might be telling them, on January 3 or whenever they reopened for business, about Hugh's plan.

"Seriously, Richard, I'm going to head out. You don't need me here—you're having a great time with all the others."

Richard and everyone else gave me last, boozy hugs and early New Year's kisses, and I moved off, rapidly, because I wanted to catch that last train out of Shibuya Station back to northeast Tokyo.

Roppongi used to be the ultimate party spot in Tokyo, but in the last few years, Shibuya had taken over the prime position. Endless high-rises were packed with tiny nightclubs, which spilled over with young Japanese. On the streets, they were grooving to music that blared from shops and restaurants on the ground level.

I hurried past a glowing billboard for Puffy's latest album, and then one for Morita Incorporated. The ad was of a young woman in shorts and a skimpy tank top, lying on her back on a pine floor, her legs tossed up in the air. Morita's new model of cordless telephone was in her hand, and a perfect orchid leaned in a terra-cot pot in the corner of the room. There was nothing else.

Nothing else. The dream in so many Japanese ads was of space, simplicity, comfort; but I couldn't help thinking now of a lost generation of women on their backs—comfort women, women who when they were worn out from those labors were shepherded into the mine-building project for the benefit of the Morita Power Company. These women, of course, were mostly Filipina and Chinese and Korean—not Japanese, like the young model on the billboard. No, I thought, stopping to stare a minute longer. The model had Occidental eyelids.

Half-and-half models had been popular in Japan ever since the teenaged Rie Miyazawa showed her semi-American face in the late 1980s. *The ideal for advertising, but not the ideal for real life*, I thought, giving her one last annoyed look before moving on. I was half and half, and what had it gotten me? I'd never had any lucrative English teaching jobs, because I looked too Asian. Not to mention I didn't have the height and youth and beauty to break into modeling or acting anytime soon.

I soldiered on toward the station. Several light-haired foreigners were inconsiderately blocking my path; I would have to dash into the street and risk being run down by a motorcycle or car. Everyone was out tonight, cruising.

Just as I reached them and was deliberating whether to bull my way through, as most Japanese would have, or just say "Excuse me," they cut into a fashionable restaurant called Grapes.

It had a clear glass front, but I could see a rosewood bar with gleaming brass taps behind it, though most of the people at the bar had wineglasses. It was an older, wealthier-looking foreign crowd than I ran with; they looked to me like stockbrokers and investment bankers.

I'd met that crowd years before through Hugh, and not really fit in. But I'd envied them—for their cost-of-living allowances that allowed them central heat, the chance to shop at all the best department stores, and opportunities to meet friends for drinks in places such as Grapes, which Richard had said charged about ten thousand yen, or about $100 U.S., for two glasses of wine and an hors d'oeuvre.

As I gave one last amused look at the convivial scene in Grapes, I caught a flash of red-gold hair. I was missing Hugh too much, I thought, as I paused again to study the back of the man in the bar with the thick, slightly wavy hair. He was wearing a black waxed-cotton coat with a corduroy collar, just like Hugh's Barbour.

I felt a prickle of unease, and instead of proceeding toward Shibuya Station, I walked through the glass door of Grapes, just to double-check.

Hugh Glendinning was seated at the bar, one khakied leg crossed over the other, bent attentively toward someone smaller sitting next to him. I didn't have to crane my neck to know it was a woman. A *girl*, to be honest—she didn't look older than twenty-one. She must have had super connections to land herself a seat at a sophisticated spot such as Grapes on New Year's Eve. She was wearing a yellow sweater-dress that showed off a slim figure, and had crossed her legs to reveal that she was wearing sharp stilettos that made my own high heels appear modest. She was what people called a parasite single, a young Japanese person who lived to dress fabulously, and who spent all her income on pleasure.

Several ideas flashed through me. The first was that it was typical of Hugh to find out Tokyo's hottest new hangout within twenty-four hours of arrival, and to be there with an office lady from his old company. That was the most charitable interpretation of the girl that I could make. The excitement I'd felt upon finding him was definitely tinged with paranoia.

I twisted the emerald ring—this was becoming my new nervous habit—and walked forward, silently rehearsing my greeting. But before I had to break the ice, Hugh had swiveled around on his stool and was beaming at me.

"Darling! You got the message after all."

"I didn't," I said, backing away from the embrace he seemed to be threatening me with. "I just happened to be walking by—" I decided not to say "to go home," because it sounded too pathetic to be turning in as early as this on New Year's Eve.

"Ohisashi buri, neh?" the girl with him bleated, then lunged forward unexpectedly and snuggled her arms around me. "Long time no see" was a weird thing for someone I didn't recognize to be saying to me. And I could only guess she was hugging me because she was drunk, since the Japanese didn't touch people casually.

I patted her back quickly and set her on her feet, looking into her face. Who in the world was this person? I wished Hugh would introduce her, but he'd bounced up and gone looking for another bar stool. Apparently, I was being invited to join their tête-à-tête.

"Rei-chan, let me see the rock." The girl grabbed my left hand and ogled. "Oh, very nice. That's the kind I want. Oh, and one just like him. He's a sweetie!"

Well, the competition was awfully friendly. Calling me little Rei, even though I should have been Shimura-san to her. Hugh must have been talking about me. I hadn't needed to be jealous after all. I smiled warmly and asked, "Is this the first time you've met Hugh?"

"Yes, of course! Mama sent me to find him, after giving me a perfect description."

Mama. Now my back went up. Was she some kind of bar girl or hooker with a Mama-san employer?

Hugh came back. "I can't find an extra stool, love. Why don't you take my stool so you can sit next to your cousin." He stood up, stretched, and sighed. "You won't believe the wild-goose chase I went on today. I got a voice mail left on my phone that the guy we were looking for—you know, the potential plaintiff—was at a certain address in Kawasaki. When I got there, I found out it didn't exist. Imagine me with my pitiful Japanese trying to find out from the neighbors if this person ever lived there. Of course, he didn't. What I'd like to say to the paralegal who sent me out on the road all day for nothing—well, I can't say it, not in front of your cousin."

Cousin. He said it again. Was Hugh's mystery woman my cousin Chika—Norie and Hiroshi's daughter, and Tom's little sister? She'd been seventeen the last time I'd seen her. If this was her, say she'd grown up would have been an understatement.

"Rei-chan, what's wrong?" the girl asked. "Are you ill?"

"Chika? I—I didn't recognize you." I leaned over and hugged her again, this time with feeling.

"None for me?" Hugh made an expression of mock anxiety.

"Later," I said, giving him my first real smile of the evening.

"Well, Chika is a good sport. She's delayed going to her friends' New Year's party to escort me to your apartment. Apparently, your aunt had a key and directions."

"You're awfully far from my apartment," I commented.

"This was to be our meeting place. The Toyoko Line comes to Shibuya, as you know," Chika said. "I told Hugh-san to meet me in this place so I wouldn't get cold waiting outside."

Or targeted by a rapist, I thought, taking a sip from the glass of champagne the smiling Australian tending bar set before me, unbidden. It was good—the first decent booze I'd had all night.

"Good, isn't it? We had a glass of that already. Don't worry, I checked to make sure she really was twenty-one." Hugh winked at the bartender.

"I would have guessed twenty-five," I said, and Chika smiled. She was still young enough to want to look older. I turned to Hugh again. "Anyway, I'm so glad you made it! But before I get totally looped, I've got to bring you up to speed."

"Actually, Rei, why don't you leave that till later, after we've seen Chika off."

"I can get to the party myself," Chika protested. "It's just a few blocks away."

Hugh and I exchanged amused glances, and I realized all of a sudden what it might feel like to be parents.

After I finished the glass of champagne, we did walk Chika to the party. It turned out to be more like a mile away, but at least we saw that the guests were really her age, and not the older lecherous types I'd feared they'd be. After we said good-bye to Chika, we placed a quick call to Norie on Hugh's cell phone to let her know where Chika was. Then midnight struck, and the temple bells began clanging. Hugh and I kissed—our first real kiss of the night, and of the New Year.

The subway was definitely closed by now, so we went straight to a busy corner to wait for a taxi. In a low voice, I told Hugh about how I'd met Ramon Espinosa—and how doubtful I was that he'd want to be part of the class action.

"Let's go back together and I'll take a try," Hugh said. "Tomorrow. We can bring him a New Year's present."

"I don't like that idea," I said quietly. It reminded me too much of what we'd done with Rosa.

"Why not?" Hugh squeezed my hand. "It doesn't have to be anything big, since you say he's comfortably off. But there's got to be some kind of good luck gift for the New Year that would be appreciated."

"It would seem like a bribe. Or, at the very least, he'd have to return the favor."

"I see," Hugh said. "Oi, there's a cab stopping. Can you believe our luck?"

It had only been twenty minutes, so we were lucky indeed. As we got in and settled ourselves, I thought more about how we could approach Ramon Espinosa again. He had said he'd take me as an acupuncture client. I explained my idea to Hugh.

"He seemed most excited to work on my knee. He said my problems there are a manifestation of my wood liver."

"You're right, it's a good excuse to go back. But you'd better tell me what a wood liver is—I don't want you missing out on hospital treatment if you're seriously ill—"

"I don't think it's that extreme. All he said is a wood liver can cause me trouble in my relationships—"

"Our relationship is perfect."

But not the one I have with my father, I thought. "I'm glad you're happy with me. And I'm willing to take you back there with me. But let me make all the introductions. I think I'd be better in a dominant role—"

"I so agree," Hugh said, and from the look in his eyes, I knew he wasn't thinking about the plaintiff anymore.

16

When I woke up New Year's morning, I was naked, yet so much warmer than usual that I thought I was back in America. Then I recognized the lumpy futon under me, and Hugh's shoulders and head a few inches away. There is no better thing in the world than waking up with someone you love—someone who's already done the thankless job of creeping out into the cold to turn on the space heater and brew tea.

Hugh was on his side, facing away from me, reading something; I ran my fingers down his bare back to let him know I was awake—and appreciated his presence.

"Good morning, darling." Hugh rolled around to kiss me. "Finally. I've been up since five."

"A few days ago, I was waking at four. But it does go away. Spending the day in sunlight helps."

"I know," Hugh said. "And even though it's gray out, I'm racing to go. Even though you said Ramon Espinosa doesn't want to take part in the lawsuit, I want to talk to him. How early do you think we can appear at his flat?"

"Um, we're expected at my aunt's today for New Year's lunch. Since we missed last night's noodles, this is really crucial. Could I take you to Ramon Espinosa's afterward, when we're coming back into town? Mid-afternoon's a proper time for a New Year's visit, I think."

"You probably think I'm a piranha," Hugh said, sighing.

"I used to think that, sometimes," I said. "But now that I'm in love with you, I tolerate it. However, I really think you're not going to get what you need from Ramon. You'll see when you meet him. He's quite content with his life. He doesn't want to dredge up old memories."

Hugh was silent for a minute. "So, I won't ask him about that. Maybe, though, he'll have names for me of others who might want to do it."

I nodded, but I didn't really agree. I didn't want to think about it. The first thing on the agenda was getting Hugh in the right frame of mind to talk to my relatives, who hadn't seen him in almost two years. I insisted that he wear a suit, and I did as well.

"It's not a bloody wedding," Hugh grumbled as he rummaged about in his suitcase for a fresh shirt.

"No, it's not. But it is the most important holiday of the year. You'll see."

It was a glorious New Year's lunch. Aunt Norie had outdone herself, preparing in advance twenty-five perfect dishes, arranged with precision in the three antique lacquered boxes that had been used for New Year's foods by the Shimuras since the turn of the century, when my great-grandfather's mother had bought the set from a famed lacquer artist in Kamakura. I took some notes on their history and used Tom's fancy new digital camera to snap some pictures of the boxes, so beautifully filled up with food.

While Hugh and Tom caught up on old times, Aunt Norie fussed over Chika, who appeared unusually sleepy, with her head flopping down and her eyes closing. Chika was a far cry from the glamour-puss of New Year's Eve; this morning she merely looked like a kid who'd stayed out too late, had had too much to drink, and was living with the consequences. I wondered how she'd gotten home from her party; had she caught a ride or waited until New Year's morning, when the trains ran again?

I longed for a moment alone with my younger cousin, but Norie wanted to immediately open the fine bottle of Fukushima sake that I'd brought to toast the holiday. As my aunt offered the carefully warmed spirits in tiny, dark blue lacquered glasses, everyone said *Kampai* except for Chika, who had a big glass of water next to her untouched cup of green tea. She'd taken no food. I could understand why a hungover person might not want to chew a grilled giant prawn with its head and whiskers still attached—or the tiny squid that had been cooked to the point that they curled into the shape of pinecones. Hugh was eyeing these things a bit nervously himself. Below the din of voices, I encouraged him to try the safe bets: sweet, sake-simmered root vegetables, the fancy hard boiled eggs, the grilled salmon, and the daikon root and carrot that had been knotted together to look like a New Year's rope. Everything Norie had prepared was symbolic of different elements of nature, which in turn were symbolic of the New Year and good wishes for the future. This was the kind of Japanese cooking that I admired most and had already spent many pages chronicling for my family history.

"Have you decided on the shrine?" Norie asked me in English so Hugh would understand. "Or do you want a wedding hall? Some wedding halls can do Shinto, Buddhist, or Christian ceremonies—all three if you like! And of course, they can rent you all three gowns."

"What's this about three wedding gowns for Rei? Isn't that rather . . . fancy?" Hugh asked Norie.

Chika coughed in her napkin as if she were dying. Norie shot her a reproving glare, then explained, "Oh, no, three is normal, Hugh-san. At a Japanese wedding, the bride wears a kimono for the Shinto ceremony, a white wedding dress for the reception, and a short, colorful formal gown when she and the groom lead off the dancing."

"Um, that is more than I would need," I interjected. "I was thinking of finding a vintage wedding kimono somewhere."

Uncle Hiroshi chuckled. "If your grandparents were alive, they would be upset at your wearing old clothes for a wedding."

And even more upset at my choice of a foreign groom, I thought. The whole topic was making me uncomfortable, so I decided to steer the conversation away from nuptials.

"I finally went to the library and read the letter that Hirohito sent us," I said. I waited a beat for everyone to quiet. "You won't believe how well he knew Great-Grandfather!"

"You mean, Showa Tenno," my aunt corrected with a smile, so I knew she wasn't trying to embarrass me.

"Sorry," I said. "I forgot, we do it differently in the West. But did you know that Great-Grandfather was his teacher? Actually, he taught the emperor Japanese history back in the thirties."

"*Ah so desu ka,*" Norie said, shaking her head gently. "I knew Shimura-sensei was a famous professor, but not that he'd taught the emperor himself!"

"He wasn't a teacher, but a private tutor," Uncle Hiroshi said.

"So, that's it! I couldn't understand how the past emperor could have studied with Great-Grandfather. But if it was a tutoring situation, that's more befitting royalty," I said.

"The emperor had a number of tutors—all leading scholars carefully chosen," Hiroshi said. "Our ancestor discussed the importance of Japanese history with him."

"Why didn't you tell me this before?" I asked.

"I thought you knew it already. You know more about our family than anyone, *neh*?" Hiroshi said.

I paused, wondering if that was a slight jab. But I pressed Uncle Hiroshi to tell me more. He told us that Kazuo Shimura—during the time he was a star professor at Tokyo University—was invited by the Imperial Household Agency to teach the fifteen-year-old crown prince history. He had been a natural choice because he had written a popular textbook on the history of the Meiji Period.

I hadn't known about the textbook, but from my own brief studies in the political history of Japan, I knew that the military government officials who controlled Hirohito's education hoped that the crown prince would want to become an emperor who would finally fulfill expansionist dreams.

"Did you ever read Great-Grandfather's textbook?" I asked Hiroshi as Norie went into the kitchen to warm up the chestnut and bean soup she'd prepared for dessert.

"Yes, years ago. We have a copy. I think it's with some old papers and photographs, but I'm not sure."

"After we've finished eating, may I look around for it?" I asked. "Just tell me where the family history materials are, and I'll be very careful."

"But you can't read Japanese. How will you find it?" Uncle Hiroshi asked.

"I'll help her with that," Tom volunteered.

"Good plan," Hugh said. "While you do that, I'll have a chance to sit down with Aunt Norie and look at the Japanese bridal magazines she's bought to help us with our wedding preparations. But can we still try to get back to Tokyo around three?"

"What do you have to do in Tokyo? Do you need me to help with directions again?" Chika asked.

It was the first thing she'd said during lunch. I sensed she was angling for a way to go back to the city. What was wrong with Chika? Was she going through a normal rebellion, or was there some deep unhappiness between her and her family?

"Rei knows how to get there. It's a place I need to see for my work. Too boring to explain," Hugh said. Obviously, he didn't want to bring up the class action with them. But it would have to surface, sooner or later.

While I helped my aunt clean up, Chika lay down on the couch with a compress on her forehead, too tired to participate. Then I joined Tom in the search of Uncle Hiroshi's file cabinet. We found the family documents amidst other things—old gas and electric bills, the deed to the house, and countless bank statements.

"Ah, here's something." Tom pulled out a thick brown envelope and began rummaging through it. "It looks as if these are all newspaper clippings, university programs, and so on about Great-Grandfather. Have you seen his picture?"

"No, and please be careful! That material is so delicate," I said as Tom held out a fragile old piece of newspaper for me to see. It was an article printed in tiny kanji, and next to it was a photo of an unsmiling middle-aged man. He wore a coat and a skinny tie, and his hair was parted sharply to the side.

"The article below announces that Professor Kazuo Shimura has become the tutor of Crown Prince Hirohito. So—I guess it's really true what my father said."

"Did you doubt him?" I asked.

"Not exactly. But I found the story so surprising that I thought it might have been exaggerated—perhaps by his father to him. You know how stories change as they pass from person to person."

I nodded. "Will you read the article to me?"

Tom read aloud in Japanese as I scribbled at a breakneck pace. Kazuo Shimura, professor of history at Tokyo University, had been appointed to tutor His Royal Highness in Japanese history on the recommendation of the Imperial Household Agency. He was one of the crown prince's five tutors, all of whom were respected names in Japanese academics. The author of the article opined that Dr. Shimura's great scholarly knowledge of the Meiji Period would be of value given Japan's new role as leader of all nations.

"Why do they say that?" Tom asked. "Emperor Meiji ended the Shogun system. I think the Shogun culture is what made Japan special. Why didn't they talk about studying Tokugawa and all the others?"

"Ah, your samurai roots are showing," I said. "Samurai and shoguns weren't the model by the early twentieth century—Kaiser Wilhelm was. And I would think that the government officials grooming Hirohito thought Emperor Meiji was a perfect example since he beat the Russians in a war at sea and had hoped to conquer Korea, though he had to defer that dream because of a number of complications relating to lack of capital."

"I'm impressed that you knew all this, Rei. I haven't read Japanese history since I was doing entrance exams for university. And then I was just learning dates and names, so it's all a haze to me."

I tried to hide my pleasure that my Japanese cousin thought I had a good sense of his nation's history. "Well, I had to take history as part of my master's degree, and that was fairly recent."

"It's clear that Father knows a lot, but he apparently didn't think the stories were worth telling until you began asking questions. I'm glad for what you're doing, Rei. I wouldn't be surprised if you uncover enough past glory that we could call someone up at the Palace to give us a private tour." ❦

"Why would you even want to visit the Palace? From what I see on TV, the royals don't have that much to offer in the way of fun. In the past, though, it was different—Prince and Princess Chichibu were known to roller-skate through the hallways."

"If Princess Masako left the crown prince for me, I guess I could take her Rollerblading," Tom said, his eyes twinkling.

"Do you really think she's cute?"

"Oh, I'm not serious. But I think it's a shame that such a formerly lively and smart person has changed her life so dramatically after marriage. Fortunately for her, she gave birth to the baby princess."

"Yes, if the imperial line had ended, it would have been a national tragedy," I agreed. The loss of a continuously ruling dynasty said to have begun with the Sun God would have made even a cynic like me weep.

Tom was saying something. It took me a second to click back and hear him. "Do you really want to do it?"

"The translation? Sure. If it's not too much trouble for you to do it, I would love to have it, verbatim, for the family history."

"That's not what I was asking," Tom said softly. "I wanted to know if—if you really felt ready to be married. I like him, but . . . well, I'm so used to being your being *you*. Free-spoken and active."

I smiled at Tom. "Hey, I'm not becoming some sort of princess. Nobody's going to tell me to stop working or start procreating. It's just—formalizing a commitment we made a long time ago to each other."

Talking about commitment reminded me that I'd promised Hugh the chance of an afternoon visit to Ramon Espinosa. It was already three. "Thanks so much for showing me the article, Tom. We have to go now."

"All right. But now that I've gotten into this file, I'll look through a bit longer. Who knows, maybe the actual textbook is buried at the bottom of this mess. That would be interesting to read, wouldn't it?"

"It would." I hugged Tom; the movement felt awkward, because I hadn't done it much. Because I grew up in a different country from him, and perhaps because of the slight age gap, I'd always found my cousin a little bit alluring. It wasn't that I'd wanted to date Tom—but there'd always been something between us that was close and special.

I put away thoughts about how my relationship might be changing with Tom as Hugh and I rode the Toyoko Line back to Tokyo. Hugh was intent on figuring out a way to get to talk to Ramon Espinosa without making the old man feel threatened. In the end, we bought him a box of beautiful tangerines from a vendor outside the Kanda train station, having decided to present it as a small token for the New Year. We also decided that I should be the one to make the initial contact.

I rang the buzzer, but unlike the day before, he didn't immediately respond.

"Espinosa-san?" I called out.

Now I heard something: a huge bang, as if something had fallen down—and then silence. Hugh and I looked at each other nervously.

"Are you all right? It's Rei Shimura and a friend," I called out.

"We'll wait and give him time to answer," Hugh whispered to me.

But as long as we waited, nobody came. Five minutes passed, and I grew antsy.

"I wonder if he's all right," I said.

"Maybe the door's unlocked. Most Japanese don't worry about those things, do they?" Hugh asked. He wiggled the doorknob, which was locked. Still, it was a flimsy Japanese lock, not a dead bolt. I remembered something my college roommate Lily had done when one of our friends had passed out drunk in a dormitory bathroom with the door locked. She'd used a flexible plastic card—in that case, it had been a cafeteria meal card—and fished it into the doorjamb, then wiggled it a few times until the lock popped.

"What are you thinking?" Hugh looked at me as if he had read my mind.

"Don't worry, you're not responsible. I'm doing it on my own," I muttered. Then, quite loudly, for the benefit of the neighbors as well as the man inside, I called, "Espinosa-san? I'm going to come in to help you. If you don't want me to do that, please say so!"

Silence.

"I'll do my best to get in then, okay?" I searched through my wallet, rejecting my credit cards as too hard, then finally coming up with an old plastic library card that bent nicely. I slid it neatly into the narrow space between door and frame, and gave a gentle shove. The lock popped with a satisfying click, and I turned the knob and stepped into Mr. Espinosa's apartment.

"You're unbelievable," Hugh said. "But I really shouldn't be here, seeing this rather, um, illegal procedure—"

"Don't worry, if I'm arrested you won't have to defend me." I cracked a smile at him, feeling triumphant over my accomplishment, and eager to go in.

17

Before, the overwhelming aura of Ramon Espinosa's apartment had been of tidiness; despite the many boxes and utensils, everything was in its place. Now, I saw the heavy metal boxes strewn across the room and short, thin steel needles showered across the green carpet like dandelion seeds in early summer. The long acupuncture table was on its side, and the kettle lay next to it, a small river of water flowing from its opening and onto the floor.

Could he have suffered an epileptic seizure and wreaked all this damage? My heart was hammering as I continued my walk. "Espinosa-san?" I headed toward the back room, which I hadn't seen during my visit. He had to be in this room, or in the bathroom.

The bedroom was set off from the main room by sliding paper *fusuma* doors, cracked slightly open. I peered through, with Hugh right behind me.

I had expected to see Mr. Espinosa sleeping, or dressing, or doing anything that might cause us both to be embarrassed. What I wasn't expecting was the sight of him on the floor, lying on his side with his eyes closed.

He had to be hurt. Hugh and I exchanged glances for a split second. I threw the door all the way open so that we could get to the fallen man.

I picked up his wrist and felt that his skin was cooler than mine. I searched for a pulse, and felt something very, very slight.

"He's alive!" And thank God we'd broken in.

"Damn it, I must have left my mobile at your aunt's," Hugh said. "Telephone, where is it—"

"Here." I'd already darted off to the phone lying by the bedside table. I picked it up, but there was just static.

A new fear gripped me. There had been no storm, no earthquake, no good reason power should be out. The moment after I thought about this, my eyes went to the open window. That's why the room was so cold. Someone had broken in through it to attack Ramon Espinosa. Probably the banging sound I'd heard was the intruder going out the window once I'd surprised him by calling Ramon from the front door.

I looked out the window, and saw that Ramon's balcony was next to the balcony of another apartment and that just a few feet beyond that was the external staircase. If the intruder was even slightly physically fit, he could have made it to the staircase within a few seconds—an easy getaway.

Hugh's voice, sharp and frantic, brought me back. "Rei, what the hell are you doing looking out the window?"

"Looking to see if—" I cut myself off, the enormity of the situation sinking in. "What are we going to do?"

"I'm going to try CPR." Hugh knelt over Ramon. "Call an ambulance."

Without saying anything more, I ran out and banged on the next apartment's door, the one that said "Moriuchi." A gentle-looking woman of about fifty opened the door to me. In the small space behind her, ten people were sitting around a low table upon which rested plates of tangerines and sinbei crackers. Everyone stared at us. "I'm very sorry to bother you, but your neighbor, Espinosa-san, is unconscious. May I use your phone to call an ambulance?"

"Oh, no!" Mrs. Moriuchi looked horrified. "Dear Mr. Espinosa. Let me bring the phone to you." She hurried into the kitchen and came back with a cordless phone. I dialed 119 and made my explanations, asking for both police and medical help.

After I'd clicked off, I caught my breath and explained that I thought someone might have been in the apartment and hurt him, then used the balconies and the outside staircase as an escape route. I asked if they'd seen anyone pass by on the outside of the building. Nobody had, but their New Year's table faced a family altar—not the window.

I hurried back to the apartment to see how Ramon was faring, with Mrs. Moriuchi and her husband following. I hadn't performed CPR since I had taken a baby-sitting course back in the early '80s, so watching Hugh, I wondered if he was doing things right. With his mouth on the old man's, he was exhaling twice and then, after catching his breath, pushing down on Ramon's chest a number of times.

"Two breaths, ten compressions," I said. "Are you doing fifteen?"

When he came up to do the compressions, he gasped, "Ten for children, fifteen for adults. And you can help me with the compressions."

I kneeled over Ramon Espinosa, trying to press the life back into him; my knees felt as if they were going to shatter, they ached so much. But I kept pushing. My pain was nothing compared with what he'd gone through, what Rosa had gone through. They'd lived through so much, only to die like this, after I'd seen them.

After I'd seen them. A shudder ran through me as I kept working. Rosa had died after Hugh and I visited her; again I'd made a visit to a war survivor, and now he was at death's door.

I pushed and cried silently to myself. So unlucky. Had this come to pass because I hadn't prayed at the shrine? The people from next door had come in and were standing at the door behind me, clucking with worry. I couldn't hear what they were saying over the pounding in my ears. If Mr. Espinosa turned out to have heart failure, he'd have died of the same thing as Rosa: a coincidence that some might think made sense, given their ages—but one that I couldn't believe.

Ten minutes later—I knew because I'd checked my watch when I'd called 119—the paramedics arrived. They strapped an oxygen mask on Mr. Espinosa's face and slid a stretcher underneath him, then strapped him tightly onto it. As they carried him down the staircase at a rapid clip, the police came storming up. They gaped at Hugh and me, and then, apparently deciding we couldn't have been the ones in charge, turned to the Moriuchis.

"Did you find him?" one of the policemen gravely asked the couple.

"No," Mrs. Moriuchi said, "it was due to the concern of the young visiting couple that we learned."

"My name is Rei Shimura," I said. "I'm the one who called. And my friend tried to give him CPR, but we're worried it might not have been enough."

"What's happened to him is not so clear. They will make all necessary examinations at the hospital. By the way, are you the gentleman's daughter? If so, you can ride along to the hospital."

I was confused by the police assumption, but after a minute understood. It was New Year's Day, a day of family celebration in Japan. And I probably looked somewhat foreign to the cop, too. Though I wanted to ride in the ambulance, I knew that if I were found out to have lied about my identity, it would haunt me later on.

"I'm a new friend of Espinosa-san's. I had come to pay him a New Year's visit." I went on to explain about the locked door and how I'd used a library card to gain entrance. The cop's eyebrows went up at that, so I hastened to add that the sounds I'd heard inside made me think that the old man had fallen down.

"Then, when I saw the mess on the floor, and the overturned table, I knew he was in trouble." I walked back to the bedroom, illustrating my theory. "You can see from the open window how the person probably got inside and back out again."

"We will run print tests on those places, and also of you and your friend."

"I understand," I said. I shot a glance at Hugh, who was looking nervous—as if he'd gotten the gist of the conversation. The problem was that he had his fingerprints on record with the Japanese police. Although he'd never been technically charged with a crime, the fact this fingerprint record existed would raise red flags.

While the police swept the apartment for evidence, Hugh and I walked over to the police station in Kanda. We were fingerprinted, then let go without incident. Maybe the old fingerprint record wasn't an issue. We walked the half-mile to the hospital to wait for news of Ramon.

"If only we'd gone to see him in the morning, as you wanted," I said to Hugh as we sat in small vinyl-covered seats in the waiting room. "I was so wrong to put it off."

"I don't think so," Hugh said. "Because we came when we did, we interrupted someone who very well might have killed him. The timing was right . . ."

But this January 1 had been stamped with violence, and perhaps death—the worst way to begin a New Year.

When Dr. Nigawa, the cardiologist in charge of Ramon's care, came to see us in the waiting room five hours later, I was the one who did all the communication. Hugh had warned me that he wanted to keep a low profile. The less his legal interest in Ramon was exposed, the better for everyone.

Dr. Nigawa informed us that Ramon had suffered a stroke and then lapsed into a coma. He had suffered damage to his heart, and the CPR that Hugh had given him had probably saved his life. The brain scan they'd run had shown no evidence of brain damage, which was a positive. Still, his chances of emerging from coma were only 10 to 20 percent.

I explained it all to Hugh in English, and then asked if we could see the patient. But Dr. Nigawa said only family members were allowed.

"He has no family," I said.

"Oh. Well, then, we'll have to see. But in a few days—not tonight."

I didn't see how we would disturb a man already in a coma, but I knew there was no point arguing. And Hugh pointed out, as we left the hospital in the dark, that the policy would at least ensure that nobody else could get to see Espinosa—that the person who'd attempted to kill him wouldn't get to finish the job.

We made it back to the apartment at 1 A.M., which meant it was 8 A.M. in San Francisco. I'd told Hugh I wanted to talk to my parents about what was going on, and he agreed.

"Rei, this is a surprise." Over the long distance line, my father's voice sounded clear—and cautious.

"Are you in a rush to get off to work?" I asked.

"Goodness no, it's New Year's morning here. A bit early, but I'm awake and available to talk. Your mother's still asleep, though."

Something about the strain in his voice made me think the call was not welcome. Maybe he was still annoyed with me over the drama of my departure. "Um, Dad, I tried to call you earlier to wish you and Mom well, but I only reached the answering machine."

"I heard your messages. I'm sorry I didn't call you back. Things have been a bit difficult here."

"Oh? What's going on?" I flashed a look at Hugh, who was stirring a pan of warm milk on the stove.

"It's Manami. I think she was more depressed than we knew, because she's done something very strange—she's left the pathology program."

"What? She just quit?" My own story would have to wait, I could tell.

"She left the program, and our house, two days ago. We don't know where she is, and we're quite concerned."

"What did her supervisors at work say about her?"

"She was fine. Everyone liked her very much. It just doesn't make sense at all. And what's awful is she doesn't know the area. We have no idea where she would go. With the type of visa she's on, she could be thrown out of the country if the university reports her missing."

"But if she's missing, how can they throw her out?" I was irritated by the limits of his thinking. "Dad, are you—really sure she left voluntarily? Do you think she might have been abducted?"

"Well, she left us a note written in Japanese saying she was sorry but needed a short vacation to regain her spirits for the New Year. She left while she was in the middle of a rotation, which is unheard of. It makes it quite difficult for her colleagues, since they'll have to cover for her."

"Is there any evidence she left willingly?" I watched Hugh take the warm milk and pour it over a slice of bread in one of my exquisite old blue-and-white bowls. He was making British comfort food again. He raised his eyebrows toward me, as if to offer to make me a bowl as well, but I shook my head and made the gesture of sipping from a wineglass.

"Well, one of her suitcases is gone from the storage room. We haven't gone into her closet or chest of drawers, because those things are private, but the coat and shoes and backpack that she usually kept downstairs are gone, too."

"Did you call the police anyway?" I asked, as Hugh brought me a glass of a mediocre Hungarian red—my house wine, now that I was back in Tokyo and paying exorbitant prices.

"Do you think I should? Knowing what I told you about the visa, I'm not sure." My father sighed. "I keep rereading the note, the words 'a little time.' In my mind that implies she'll return to me. Does it to you as well?"

"Yes, it does, but, Dad, the way things have been going, I'm starting to think that anyone I meet is marked for death." I felt as bitter as the wine swirling in my mouth.

"Tell me," my father said, so I did, in as logical a fashion as I could, given the circumstances. I described how Hugh and I had found Ramon Espinosa on the verge of death, and how I worried that he might have been attacked—which made me paranoid all over again about Rosa's death.

"That's interesting." My father was silent for a moment. "You know, I didn't tell you about something I did . . . because I thought you wouldn't approve."

"Really? That sounds exactly like *my* behavior."

"Well, the fact is . . . I had an old friend in the pathology department at the medical school who went over to work in the office of the medical examiner a few years ago. I, uh, made a call to him, to ask for a copy of Rosa Munoz's autopsy. He gave it to me without question. I thought you'd be angry because of all that sensitivity regarding the class action—so I didn't tell you."

"Why did you want to have the autopsy?" I asked, feeling Hugh's eyes on me.

"I feared for both of you," my father said. "I thought things could somehow get twisted around and either of you could be held responsible for the death—if not by the police, then by the community. I felt it would be good for us to know what the medical evidence was. Just in case."

Ironically, of course, the fact that my father was in possession of a confidential document could have landed us all in trouble. "That's okay, Dad. I'm not angry, I promise you. But I thought the results of the autopsy were common knowledge."

"Well, I wondered about the elevated level of potassium chloride. The examiner thought the level was a reaction to the stress of the assault on the heart, but when Manami and I sat down together to look at the numbers—I consulted her because of her pathology specialization; I hope you don't mind—she agreed with me that it was a significant finding."

"Really. How so?" As I talked, I searched for a paper and pen. This was information I was going to share with the Japanese doctor as soon as I could.

"Well, there is a chance that the chemical potassium chloride might have been intentionally introduced into Rosa's system and triggered the heart attack, though of course it would have been hard to slip her much of it at one time because it's so salty. She could have taken it intentionally, as a suicide."

"Dad, can you fax me the autopsy, and could you hold on for a second? I need to check on something with Hugh."

"Yes, madam?" Hugh raised an eyebrow.

"Didn't you tell me that when you went to see Rosa's apartment after her body had been removed, there was a container of soy sauce on the table?"

"Sure, and lots of Asian take-out food that had begun to spoil." He wrinkled his nose.

"Did you throw it away?" I asked.

"Yes. I put it in a trash bag I found under her sink, and then I chucked the whole lot into a bin behind the building. Why? Did I do something wrong?"

I sucked in my breath. "Of course not. It's just that there's a chance that food might have provided a clue."

"Well, I didn't throw away everything on the table. I was a bit rushed, so I left the soy sauce in its bottle, and maybe another sauce I'd found."

"Do you think it's still there?"

"If the cleaning crew hasn't made it in. I left instructions for the firm to have someone go in as soon as possible."

"Rei?" My father's voice brought me back to our long-distance conversation.

"Dad, sorry. I was just asking Hugh about what he saw in the apartment when he was sent to take care of closing it up. He saw lots of Asian take-out food and a bottle of soy sauce on the table. Wouldn't those foods be a good way to camouflage a salty poison?"

"Not just good—perfect. But I have to warn you that poisoning through food usually takes a while to work," my father said. "That is, if the poisoner wants the death to look natural."

"Still, is there a way you can get the police to go in and look at any and all food left in her apartment?"

"I don't know. I could say something to my friend in the Medical Examiner's Office. Then the onus wouldn't be on me."

"Dad, I'm sorry about loading this on you at such a difficult time. With Manami gone and all."

"Yes, it's very worrying. I telephoned her parents and they said they hadn't heard anything about her going on any vacation. She usually telephones or E-mails every day, so they were quite panicked."

"I think you should tell the police she's missing. I mean, isn't that what the family wants?"

"They were torn, knowing the situation of her visa. If the police know she's in the country yet not working, they will contact the INS. So if Manami comes back feeling ready to give the hospital another try, it could be too late—she could be expelled from the country for staying here without working."

"So it sounds as if you tend to believe she really ran away from the program. That she's not dead or anything."

"I don't know. I have such a difficult choice to make, not knowing if she's just on holiday or really missing."

"Let's try to find her on both fronts," I said. "Give me her parents' number, and I'll call and see if I can get any leads on where she might go within the U.S., if she wanted to take time off. And you can take one of those photos of Manami we shot at Christmas, reproduce it on flyers, and post them around town with our phone number. You know, the same way that parents do for runaway children," I said.

"How depressing to put our houseguest in that context. And by the way, Rei-chan, I'm grateful that *you* never ran away."

I laughed. "When I was a teenager I saw enough miserable-looking runaways living on the streets in Haight-Ashbury to know better." I paused. "Dad, I don't think I really made it clear when I called before . . . that I'm sorry for my blowup when I was leaving California. I didn't treat you with respect."

"I don't expect you to be a Confucian daughter," my father said, sighing. "I wouldn't want you to be like Manami, withholding so much that she feels she needs to run."

After we said good-bye, I told Hugh everything my father had said and let him know that I was beginning to wonder if Manami's disappearance was another piece in the puzzle. What did Manami, Rosa, and Ramon have in common? All had been acquainted with me. All had vanished, been attacked, or died shortly after I'd met them.

"It's really something," Hugh said. "But be careful how many people you tell this to. You don't want to wind up a suspect in an international criminal case."

"If I come forward right away, I'm not going to look bad," I said. "Just helpful."

Hugh was quiet for a while. Then he said, "I agree the message should be . . . passed on to the authorities. But it's got to be through a means other than either of us going to the police. And it's got to be a method that keeps our names, as well as that of the law firm, confidential."

"I don't know how that could be done," I said.

"Neither do I. At this point, there's nothing we can do but sleep on it."

18

The next morning, I still had no answer to the problem. Hugh invited me to go out and take a run with him, but I was too frustrated. I placed the call I'd promised my father that I'd make to Manami's parents in Kobe. A man answered immediately, as if he'd been waiting by the telephone.

"This is Rei Shimura, a friend of Manami's. Is this Mr. Okada?"

"Yes, it is." His voice sounded polite, and calm. "My daughter is not living in Japan now, she's in the United States studying."

"Yes, I understand that. Have you had word on her safety?"

"What do you mean?" came the response.

I paused, taking in the strangeness of the response. Even though I'd introduced myself up front, Mr. Okada might not have understood that I was one of the San Francisco Shimuras who already knew that Manami was missing. I also thought his initial response—"*she's in the United States studying*"—was awfully mild for someone with a missing child.

"Hello? Excuse me, are you there?" Mr. Okada's voice continued.

"Yes, I'm sorry. There was a distraction here. I'm calling from Tokyo," I said.

"Oh! You are one of her university friends, then?"

"You could say that."

I didn't lie often, and as I spoke I was glad he couldn't see the expression on my face. I was breaking a rule—not just a Buddhist rule my father had told me about, but one of my personal ones about being forthright and honest.

"Ah, I really need to get in touch with her about something— quite an important matter. A potential job," I improvised. "Can you tell me where she can be reached?"

Now he paused a moment too long. "I'll contact her and ask her to call you back."

"Why can't I just call her wherever she's staying? With—a host family, I presume?"

"She is no longer there. That family treated her so badly she decided to leave."

"Really. What did they do?" I swallowed hard. I hadn't expected this.

"Ah, she said their personal habits were immoral. They were Japanese-American, but much more American than Japanese. My daughter felt unsafe and is looking for a new place now. I can take your number and have her return your call."

"Please do that," I said coolly. This time, I gave my last name as Shimada, to secure my disguise, but gave my real Tokyo phone number. I wanted Manami to call me. I had to hear from her mouth what had been so unkind about my family, and why she'd run away, leaving everyone to worry about her. And at the end of it all, if I still felt the way I did now, I would give Manami Okada a piece of my mind.

It was too late to wake up my parents with this news about Manami, so I tried to remember the other things I had to take care of in Tokyo, things in the here and now. I called my cousin Tom's house, and he picked up. I explained to him about Hugh's missing phone and asked if he could look for it.

"He did forget it," Tom said. "But unfortunately, I think Chika-chan borrowed it. Just for the night, she said, because she was staying over with a friend and wanted to be able to reach us if they went out and had any trouble. She said she'd reimburse Hugh the cost of any calls she made."

"I'm sure that won't be necessary—unless she called Timbuktu.

But please, when your sister calls in, tell her that cell phone is Hugh's business lifeline, especially while he's here. I can only imagine all the people who've tried to reach him. I guess the best thing we could do is call the number and try to get Chika to drop it by to us—is she hanging out in Tokyo?"

"My parents think so." Tom lowered his voice. "But I doubt it. I think she's taken the bullet train back to Kyoto to see some boy and she might not even be home tonight. That's what kids do these days, they use cell phones so the parents can be in touch and they can say they're somewhere that they're not."

"Great. No chance of getting the phone for a while then."

"I'm sorry, Rei. But I do have good news about something—I kept looking yesterday, and I did eventually find Great-Grandfather's history textbook. I've already translated four chapters for you."

"Oh, Tom, that's wonderful," I said, though the last thing on my mind was researching my grandfather's life.

"I go back to work in two days. If you tell me your fax number, I can give you what I have."

I stared at the phone, wishing there were a way to contact Hugh in the middle of his run and get him to return, posthaste. The telephone rang, with its Caller ID feature showing a 415 area code—San Francisco. I picked it up quickly. Would this be my father calling me on his cell?

"Happy New Year, babe."

My heart skipped a beat at the sound of the man's casual English—and his American accent. It wasn't my friend Richard, that was for sure.

"Who's calling?" I asked stiffly.

"This is Eric Gan. I thought you'd remember my voice."

"Of course. If you want to speak to Hugh, he's actually out jogging right now. I could take a message, though."

"I'm not calling to speak to Hugh," Eric said. "I wanted you."

Oh, no. I thought he had gotten over his adolescent crush. This was going to be awkward.

"Really," I said. "What for?"

"I'm coming to Japan on business, you know. The same reason Hugh's there. I want you to promise me we'll have a chance to get to know each other again."

"I don't think that'll work, Eric. And I'm sorry, but I've actually got to get off the line right now. I was heading out somewhere."

"Really? Where?"

"I'm going to the hospital," I said.

"Oh, no! Are you sick?"

"It's—an injury, actually," I fibbed. "My knees have been killing me for a while, and I've just learned about a new treatment. But I've got to run—I mean, I must walk out the door. The taxi is waiting."

"Wait a minute, which hospital? I'll call you when you get there."

"You can't possibly call a Japanese hospital—"

"Why not? I speak the language, Rei. And if I can dial you in Tokyo, I can certainly dial whatever hospital you're going to. Just give me the clinic number. I'm sure you'll be waiting around for at least half an hour or so when you get there."

"Actually, I won't. The Japanese medical system is remarkably punctual and efficient. I'll catch up with you later, Eric."

I left a message for Hugh about where I'd gone and about what I was trying to get Tom to do for me, telling Hugh to share with him whatever information he felt he could. Then I dressed quickly, walked the few blocks to the subway station, and boarded a train to Kanda. I walked into the hospital's intensive care unit and asked to speak to Dr. Nigawa.

"Sorry, but Nigawa-sensei is making rounds," said a smiling young woman wearing a white uniform, an old-fashioned perky cap, and a badge identifying her as chief nurse Tanaka.

"Oh. In that case, can I sit with Mr. Espinosa while I wait for the doctor to get to him?" It was worth a try, I figured.

"Yes, actually, the policy has changed to allow special friends," Nurse Tanaka said. "We had two acupuncturists visit already today. Such sweet men—they were blind, too, like Mr. Espinosa."

"It must have been a poignant visit," I said.

"Yes, yes. But they were cheered when I told them about his nephew having called, the one from the Philippines who will be flying in shortly to visit."

"Oh, I didn't know he had a nephew! How lucky that someone got in touch with him." I was filled with a sense of relief. "I'd like to speak with Mr. Espinosa's nephew as well."

"I'll take your name and number and pass it on. Now the room you want is 53. You can stay five minutes—the doctor has asked us to keep visits short."

I went down the hall, thinking that limiting the visit to five minutes was awfully unfair to the two blind men, who'd probably gone through considerable obstacles to reach the hospital.

The door to room 53 was closed. I knocked on it tentatively, and heard nothing.

Well, of course. Mr. Espinosa couldn't call out if he was in a coma. I opened the door and walked in.

The room was dominated by machinery. From them, tubes sprouted to a tiny yellow doll of a man lying on a cot. Ramon looked dead, but I could tell from the machine tracking his heartbeat in a clear turquoise line that he was still alive.

I didn't last three minutes before tears were pouring down my cheeks. Every time I tried to stop and pull myself together, the sight of him lying there, unchanged, made me cry again.

Now I understood why the visiting time was limited. I turned away, deeply distressed, and took the elevator down.

It was just a short walk to Ramon's apartment building. As I'd expected, his neighbors, the Moriuchis, were at home. When I knocked, a ten-year-old boy carrying a remote control opened the door.

"Yuki, be careful! Do not open the door to strangers without asking. It could be the Kanda Ward Attacker!" Mrs. Moriuchi called from behind him. A second later, she appeared with a worried expression on her face. It softened when she saw me.

"Oh, I'm sorry. I didn't mean to offend you. I have been trying to make sure my careless son learns about safety."

"Oh, yes. I understand your wanting to be cautious about opening the door. What happened New Year's Day was so frightening," I said.

"Yes, it was a terrible thing. I'm so worried about our neighbor. Yuki-kun"—she waved her hand at her son, who had slunk off to sit in front of the television, and was channel-surfing with his remote control—"he is the saddest of all."

Mrs. Moriuchi told me that during the five years they'd lived next door to Mr. Espinosa she had often helped him with his accounting, and that once Yuki learned to read he had read letters and books aloud to the older man.

"I had to help with the difficult *kanji*, of course, but soon Yuki-kun began to learn more and more," Mrs. Moriuchi said.

I glanced over at the boy, who hardly looked like a model of intellectual zeal. He just looked like a normal boy who'd rather watch TV than do anything else. Casually, I asked, "Did Yuki ever open any letters written in Tagalog—the language of the Philippines?"

"I'm not sure." She raised her voice in her son's direction. "Yuki-kun, tell Shimura-san about the letters you saw. Were any from the Philippines?"

Yuki-kun didn't respond, so she walked over and stood in front of the TV set, repeating her question.

Yuki-kun looked around her and whined, "No. And you're blocking my view!"

"It's really important," I said, going over to the boy. I crouched down and looked at him. "Were there any letters from outside Japan?"

"I—I don't think so," he said, flustered by my in-the-face approach. "There were some strange letters, though, once you opened them up. Just pages of paper with holes typed in them."

"Braille," I said.

"Yes, every now and then he would read one to me. Those were from the other acupuncturists."

"What was the context? Did the letters talk about, say, hard times during the war?"

He shook his head.

"Okay, anything about a company called Morita?"

"No letters that I can think of. But Morita Incorporated is great! See, this is their latest model TV. It just hit the shops in Akihabara before Christmas—but we've had it since August," Yuki said proudly.

"Yes, yes. It's very nice." I shot a quick glance at the large liquid-crystal-display, flat-screen television monitor, which was showing a Japanese game show. I watched TV only for the news, and even that I didn't trust.

"It was a gift from Espinosa-san. He said he couldn't watch it and it just took up space," Mrs. Moriuchi said. "What a generous man. I brought him some meals, which he said he enjoyed, but it couldn't possibly match the kindness he showed us."

What was a blind man doing with a flat-screen television in the first place? I pondered the various possibilities before asking, "Where did he buy such a special television for you?"

"I don't really know. It came in a box from Morita Incorporated, but I can't tell you more than that. I assumed, because there was no other gift wrap, that it was a gift given to him, not something he bought."

A free television, after all these years of life in Japan. Mr. Espinosa's ties to Morita Electric had remained very tight indeed.

19

I made it home by late afternoon. Walking along the street, I bowed and called out a greeting to my neighbor, the elderly Mrs. Yuto, who was using a broom to sweep a few leaves that had fallen off one of the small, scraggly potted trees that lined the space in front of her house. I had no idea of the species of the plant, or its age; I imagined it had been there for years, just as she had.

Mrs. Yuto's tiny white brows drew together sharply at the sight of me, and she didn't return the bow.

I could have passed on, but I hesitated. Maybe I'd done something to offend her without knowing it. "Greetings, Yuto-san! I wish you congratulations on a happy new year."

She nodded, but said nothing.

"Uh, Yuto-san, is there some problem? I apologize if I've caused any trouble . . ."

"The police were here," she said in a low voice.

"To—my house?"

She nodded. "They spoke to that foreign man who was staying there."

"I see." The worst had come to pass. The fingerprints had been checked yesterday, and the police were interested in Hugh in connection with the attack on Ramon.

I went into the house. It was empty; not a sign of Hugh anywhere. I rushed back out. Mrs. Yuto was still sweeping, but this time there was a self-satisfied smile on her face.

"Did they take him with them?" I asked in a low voice.

"I don't know. I was inside doing other things, *neh*?"

"I see," I said, thinking how much she seemed to savor being the bearer of bad news. "Well, I guess that I'll check with the police myself."

"A good idea. These days, police are cracking down on illegal foreigners overstaying their visas."

I stared at her small, tight face and sputtered, "The person in my apartment is my fiancé, and while he is Scottish, he's here legally on business with an American law firm."

"He might like it better in those places, *neh*? There are more foreigners there."

A kid parking his bicycle was taking an overly long time—as if he was dawdling in order to eavesdrop. And I noticed that a woman a few doors away was also watching our exchange. As much as I wanted to say something nasty back to Mrs. Yuto, I knew that whatever I said would be repeated throughout the neighborhood.

I turned my back so the watchers couldn't see my expression, and gave Mrs. Yuto a disgusted glare. Then I set off for the neighborhood's police box, which was a stucco building about the size of a closet, close to the primary school on the hill.

Hugh wasn't there. In fact, the constable didn't know what I was talking about. Once I realized that, I quietly made my apologies for disturbing him and trekked back down the hill. If the Yanaka police hadn't taken him into custody, maybe it had been the police from Kanda, the neighborhood where Ramon Espinosa lived.

I walked toward the train station, with every step feeling an even greater sense of panic. I began running. As I ran, the soreness around my knees radiated. I was in the wrong shoes to be doing this. I was in the wrong neighborhood, the wrong life. I could barely see through my tears, but I knew people were watching. That made me run all the harder, until I smacked into something solid: a briefcase with the Mark Cross insignia on it, just like Hugh's. I looked up, and there he was, dressed in business clothing and looking just the way he always did—except for the fact that he wasn't smiling, but was craning his head to look past me.

"What is it?" he asked.

"I—I was headed for the train station. I was in a panic, that's the reason I was running so fast that I didn't notice you in my way—"

"Well, this is perfect timing," Hugh said, brushing off his brief-case and taking me by the arm. "I'm glad I caught you before you went out. Where are you going, anyway?"

"The police! I heard from my neighbor they came by to take you into custody—"

"Hold on," Hugh said, laughing. "They only came to remind me to register as a foreigner living in the district. Apparently I should have gone to the ward office to give my name and infor-mation."

"Oh! That's all?"

"Yes, yes, that's all. They were as cordial as could be."

I sighed. "So why were you gone from the apartment?"

"Doing my job! I was at the Imperial Hotel, where I've gotten a suite set up for Charles and Eric and me to work. They're coming in tomorrow, so I wanted to get a jump on things, make some important calls—"

"Chika has your mobile phone," I said. "I told Tom to have her give it back."

"Great. I could use it, though now I have some lines through the Imperial Hotel as well. Say, want to go out for dinner and catch up on all the news?"

I shook my head. "I'd rather go home. Want to do take-out?"

"Sure. Any decent sushi around here?"

"Do you really want sushi? I'm in the mood for something warm and comforting, like a big bowl of ramen."

"Can't we do both?"

In San Francisco a week ago, I would have said no. But now I felt easier about things. The neighborhood *izakaya* prepared noo-dle dishes beautifully. I knew that it also had an agreement with a sushi shop around the corner. It was possible that I could make one call to the *izakaya* to get both kinds of food, plus the supersized bottle of Kirin beer that was my favorite.

Hugh agreed enthusiastically to the plan, and when we got home he went into the bathroom to fill the tub while I phoned the restaurant to order noodles for myself and assorted sushi that included Hugh's favorites of sea bream, grilled eel, snapper, and salmon roe. As I recited my credit card number, I noticed a flood of papers on the floor next to the phone. A fax had come from my cousin Tom; he had translated the first few chapters of Kazuo Shimura's history textbook.

I wandered into the bathroom, where Hugh was up to his neck in aromatic water.

"Tom found the history textbook, and he's started a translation."

"Great. That's what you wanted, isn't it?"

"It'll be interesting to see how my great-grandfather writes about the samurai era," I said. "Knowing how much he cared about the family sword and all."

"Could I read it, too? I can use all the help I can get learning about Japan."

"Sure." I looked away from him, distracted by a sound. "I think the delivery boy's at the door. Let me get the food."

"Brilliant. But I'm not ready to come out of this tub yet," Hugh said.

"Don't worry. We can eat later."

I opened the front door, and sure enough, there was the delivery in a set of lacquered red boxes. They weren't real lacquer, of course, but hardy plastic—because the custom was, after ordering a delivered meal like this, to leave the empty boxes outside your door to be picked up by the restaurant's bicycle-riding delivery person the next day. It was much more effort for the restaurant than using disposable food containers, but I thought it was much more elegant this way.

I checked my watch. Five-twenty. I was almost depressed. Why did I bother spending an hour to make something like a bowl of ramen when a restaurant could do it so much faster? And it wasn't as if I saved any money by cooking things myself. Grocery store ingredients were just as expensive as the finished dish served in a restaurant.

I carried the two boxes inside. Hugh's sushi was obvious—it was in a lower, flat rectangular tray. Then there was my box, a taller one;

inside, I knew, was my bowl of hot udon, plus a side order of cold *zaru soba* I'd ordered in case the sushi wasn't enough for Hugh.

I carried Hugh's meal to the tea table, then returned for my food box. When I it picked up, I heard a pleasant hissing sound inside. The *udon* was really hot.

I opened up the boxes and placed the various covered dishes atop my own real lacquered pine trays. Then I added a few old Imari plates, ivory chopsticks, and napkins I'd stitched myself from hand-dyed indigo fabric. I took the cap off the liter bottle of Kirin and filled a glass for each of us. I read a bit of my great-grandfather's history, but I was really in the mood to eat. I went to the bathroom door to urge Hugh to end his bath.

"Yes, yes, I know it's here. I can hear it sizzling." He came out, tying the belt on his bathrobe, and drew me into an embrace. He smelled amazing—a combination of my own Kanebo soap, his Grey Flannel, and that sexy Hugh Glendinning smell that made me think of having him for dessert—after the *udon*, of course.

Reluctantly, I dragged myself back to the meal at hand. It was true—the bowl was hissing so much that its top was rattling.

"I wonder how they do it . . . some fabulous technology?" Hugh said, going to the table.

"Yes, hot noodle dishes are served too hot to be eaten . . . that way you can linger for hours. It certainly makes delivery work easier, too."

I knew it would be a while before I could put soup to mouth, but I couldn't wait to inhale the familiar aroma. This shop was one of the few places I knew that served a truly vegetarian noodle soup; the soup stock was not flavored with pork or chicken, but with rich red *miso* and dried shitake mushrooms. There was also a hint of chili that I loved. They called it Chinese Priest's Udon: "Priest" because there was no meat, and "Chinese" because of the spice.

I lifted the lid. A line of steam blew out at me with an odor that was noxious and choking—not the soy-ginger-garlic I'd been anticipating, but something that made my eyes water and burn. And in the split second before I shut my eyes, I saw there was no soup in the bowl at all—just a small black device that was spewing thick white smoke.

20

"Argh!" Hugh said, just before he started choking.

"Shut your eyes! It's . . . ga-ga-gas," I said between coughs. I couldn't smell it, but it cut into my airway and eyes like a knife. I shut my eyes instantly and began walking toward where I thought my door was.

"I'm trying—" I heard sounds of fumbling, as if Hugh were attempting to put the lid back on the bowl.

"No time. This is a gas attack," I sputtered. "Outside."

"Not dressed," he coughed back at me. "Two degrees—"

I reached out blindly, grabbed his arm, and pulled. Even though my eyes were tightly shut, they were running like faucets. I opened them a fraction to see where the doorway was. Once I had my bearings, I stumbled toward it, dragging Hugh.

When I tugged on the doorknob, I realized I'd locked the place up for the night. Damn. I struggled crazily with my three locks and finally got the door open and the two of us out on the step. Hugh was hyperventilating, and I was coughing. I couldn't see him, but at least I knew he was with me. And the noise he was making meant that he was alive.

"What the hell kind of special did you order?" Hugh coughed between each word.

"That restaurant is very reliable." I dissolved into another coughing bout.

"I guessed that," Hugh said. "You only order from reliable places, right?"

I buried my face in his terry robe, letting it absorb the tears. "Tear gas. Do you think that's what it was?"

"Don't know. I've never been gassed before, but my eyes are running."

"We need to call the police," I said.

"Shall we go to your neighbor? There's an old lady who was looking at me when the police came—"

"Mrs. Yuto!" I said. "Oh, no. We can't do that. I didn't tell you this before, but she's completely against our living arrangement. And she said all the neighbors were talking. We can't go to them, Hugh—we're all alone."

He caught me by the shoulders, and I slowly peeled open my eyes to look at him. "Rei, are you telling me none of these people will help us?"

I took a deep breath. I was beginning to be able to get in air again. "I'm not sure. This is a conservative neighborhood. It's not like Roppongi or Aoyama or even the part of Yokohama where my relatives live."

"Then let's walk to the police station," Hugh said, standing up. "Whoever did this should not get away with it."

Sergeant Nishimura, the constable on duty at the neighborhood police box, was sympathetic, but not overly worried. He assured us that if it had been Sarin, we'd already be dead. I suppose that should have cheered me up, but it didn't.

Nishimura, who was an organized fellow, sent a colleague to the crime scene and another to the restaurant. Apparently the delivery boy had dropped off a perfectly normal food order about five minutes before I'd opened the door. He said I hadn't responded to his knocking and he'd left because I'd prepaid for the food with a credit card, and thus he didn't need payment.

"Perhaps some mischief-maker may have acted right after the

food delivery. Shimura-san, do you think anyone in the neighborhood wishes you and your friend to have misfortune?"

"Sure I do. From Mrs. Yuto onward, apparently none of them like me anymore."

"Why do you think that?"

"Because I'm living with a foreigner. Why else?"

Sergeant Nishimura coughed delicately. "But you, Shimura-san, are a foreigner yourself. You've not reported any problems before. It must be something else."

I translated for Hugh, who had been looking impatient. When he heard Sergeant Nishimura's comment, he nodded. "Yes, your neighbors have always been fine. I mean, when I went out today, several people said hello in English and smiled at me."

I hugged my arms around myself. Hugh was such a hopeless optimist. He'd probably run into Japanese tourists visiting the neighborhood, not its real denizens.

The sergeant called a supervisor, who ordered an antiterrorism crew to analyze and air out my apartment. The tear gas capsule had already been removed, and was brought to us for inspection. The sergeant explained it was a common product marketed to women, security guards, and others interested in self-defense.

"Made in Japan?" Hugh asked, and I translated.

The sergeant shook his head. "This one is a U.S. manufacture. It could be purchased here or there, or many other points in between."

I thought more about this detail two hours later, when the police assured us that my apartment was again safe for inhabitation.

"Someone was watching for the food to be dropped off. Then, seeing I didn't respond to the initial knock on the door, he or she dumped out the soup, put in the tear gas, rang the doorbell, and ran off." I paused. Who knew that we were going to order in food, and that I wouldn't take it right away? Who walks around with a tear gas canister at the ready? Do you think . . . Morita Incorporated could be behind this?"

"Could be," Hugh said. "I wasn't aware that they knew anything about the class action plan. Maybe they got wind after my conversation with the police in San Francisco."

I shivered. "Are you saying someone in the SFPD with a pro-Japanese leaning might have contacted the company?"

Hugh squeezed my hand. "It seems far-fetched, but it's possible. I mean, we're talking about one of the world's most successful electronics companies. There could be substantial rewards for anyone who helped that company keep its status. And it might not have been a mole within the police—it could have been someone at your parents' party, or the person who broke into the house and rifled through my things . . ."

"What can you do?" I had no idea myself. I felt utterly hollow.

"I'll meet with them to lay the cards on the table," Hugh said.

"But how can you handle a meeting by yourself with all those Japanese executives?" I asked gently. "I know you used to do that kind of thing with Sendai, but you were all on the same side. Not to mention you had a translator."

"I'll do it with Charles Sharp, of course, and Eric will be there to do the translations."

"That's right. You mentioned that they'll be flying in tomorrow," I said.

"Eric's already here. Charles comes tomorrow."

So the forces were landing—for better or worse.

21

When life gets chaotic, sometimes the best escape is work.

I wasn't surprised to wake up at six the next morning and see Hugh, already dressed for corporate battle, sitting at my tea table with a pot of tea and lots of fax pages in front of him.

"Did something come in for you from San Francisco?" I asked, yawning as I stumbled into the room to join him.

"No. It's the translation of your grandfather's book—Tom sent the first few chapters."

"Oh, right. I glanced at it yesterday evening, but didn't have time to read it, considering all that happened." I went into the kitchenette to get myself a cup, then came back and sat next to Hugh. "Is it interesting?"

Hugh put down the papers and looked at me. "I'll say so. Actually, it's more provocative than anything."

"Don't tell me my great-grandfather wrote the sexual history of Japan," I teased, laying my head on his shoulder.

"No."

Hugh's brief, strained-sounding response made me stiffen. "What is it then?"

"Rei, your grandfather was a bit . . . Listen, I'm sorry. I won't say anything against your ancestors. Here, you read it for yourself. I'll bring your coffee."

"If you're trying to say Kazuo Shimura was a conservative, I already know that," I said. "He was a great scholar, but unapologetically nationalistic. That's why he was chosen to tutor Hirohito."

Hugh didn't answer me, just busied himself with the coffee. I started turning over the lined notebook pages. Tom had translated four chapters of the twenty-chapter book. I read through the introduction, which was dated 1931. It was fairly straightforward, though pedantic; my great-grandfather wrote, in a rather officious tone, that the lessons learned from the past would help Japan in the future, and that the great deeds of the ancestors should never be forgotten. The introduction ended saying that students should listen to their teachers, and parents and study history's lessons diligently.

Chapter 1 was titled "Reverence to the Sun" and outlined the proof that Japan's imperial family was literally descended from the Sun God. I didn't believe it was true; the fact that my great-grandfather had reported it as such must have been a direct reflection of the atmosphere around him. Emperor Hirohito's advisors knew how useful it would be to have a public fervently believing such things about their leader—it would allow them all complete power to do what they wanted in their wars.

The next chapter was a history of the different reigns in Japan. Scant attention was given to the importance of China in Japan's past—China, which had given Japan Buddhism, its system of character writing, and more. Perhaps my great-grandfather had overlooked all this because Japan was at war with China when the book was written; politics could cloud things. He wasn't too enthusiastic about the West, either.

"People call Europe and America the most advanced national powers; however, just as it is true the chrysanthemum is the world's most gorgeous flower, so Japan cannot be dominated, in either its national power or culture," I read with a sinking feeling. I'd heard that my great-grandfather had been a brilliant professor. But in my mind, "brilliant" meant original. I could only hope the book would improve in later chapters.

"What do you think?" Hugh asked, putting his own pages aside.

"So far the history seems accurate, if a bit prejudiced in its presentation. I wish he would have said more about the importance of China in building Japanese culture, but maybe he couldn't because of the political climate when this book was published."

"Oh, he says plenty about China later on. Just wait," Hugh said grimly. "Anyway, I'm going to have to put it aside to get over to meet Eric at the Imperial Hotel. Then in the afternoon, I've got to fetch Charles from the airport. If he's not too tired, I'd like to make a dinner reservation for all of us somewhere. Any ideas?"

"Why don't you leave it up to Charles to decide?" I said. After all, his company was footing the bill.

"He doesn't know the restaurant scene the way you do."

"If he likes fashionable Japanese food, you should try Kiku. But it's hard to get a reservation."

"I'll use my accent." Hugh winked and was gone.

I left a message on my parents' answering machine that I had reason to believe Manami was alive and well, and to call me for details. Then I showered and blow-dried my hair and went out to Sendagi Station to buy the *Japan Times*. I had bought it to check the real estate listings in the middle, but my eyes were drawn to a front-page article that reported that a crowd of Japanese nationalists—some party members and others students—had gotten into a fight in the park surrounding the Yasakuni Shrine yesterday afternoon. After they'd refused to obey police requests to keep to a certain area, a small melee had developed. The police had released tear gas, and ten people were treated at area emergency rooms for discomfort.

The fact that the police had struck against Imperialists was quite ironic, I thought. In the early 1930s, Japan's top military leaders were at first wary about the expansionist attitudes Hirohito's staff members were espousing, but what could they do?—he was the descendant of the Sun God.

I tucked the newspaper under my arm and got ready to pay the fare to Shinjuku. I knew this was the station closest to the office of Mr. Idabashi, the detective. I had been thinking that he was probably the only person in Japan who could have figured out the connection between Ramon Espinosa and me. For reasons of his own, he might have decided to get something from Ramon. The bowl of tear gas noodles might have been a warning from him to me to stay out of things.

I'd thought I could trust the detective, but the fact was, he hadn't been recommended to me. Private detectives were free agents; their motivations to do their work could be all kinds of things.

On the platform, I dug into my backpack for the receipt that came with the refund he'd given me, since he'd done the job in less time than I'd paid for. His business card was stapled to the paper; it included a minimap of Shinjuku on the back, with a big star marking the Fine Future Building that housed his office.

So he had a real office. Or did he?

I rode one stop to Nishi-Nippori and then changed to the Yamanote Line to Shinjuku. It was late enough in the morning that I had a seat to myself, so I hung my head and took the tiny catnap I sorely needed after my night of disjointed, troubled sleep. I opened my eyes a few stops before Shinjuku and half-focused at the row of commuters facing me. It was too late in the day for people to be heading to work; I imagined that the smartly dressed women in their thirties through sixties were heading for shopping and that the few businessmen interspersed between them were en route to see clients. My eyes slid back to one young guy buried behind the same edition of the *Japan Times* I'd been looking at earlier in the day. Not many Japanese read an English-language paper. Nor did they wear Bass Weejuns. I became curious enough to stand up and move toward the exit, even though Shinjuku Station was still thirty seconds away and I would not have to battle any crowds to make it out the door. As I edged along, the man turned the newspaper page, and as the veil was momentarily removed, I saw him.

"Eric? I can't believe it," I said. Even though Hugh had told me Eric had arrived the previous evening, I was so discombobulated by seeing him that I fell into the usual polite pleasantries. He looked proper—instead of his usual slouchy clothes, he was in a dark blue suit, white shirt, and yellow tie. It was an entirely appropriate business look for Japan.

"Wow, this is great, Rei." Eric grinned at me openly, the way he once had when we were friends in our youth. "I can't believe you're out by yourself like this—I thought you and Hugh were joined at the groin."

"A politer expression is 'joined at the hip.' And no, we aren't," I said frostily. He hadn't transformed into his younger self after all—he was still the same creep who had tried to embarrass me in San Francisco. I scrapped the offer I'd almost made to guide him to the Imperial Hotel, or wherever his destination was. *But wait a minute,* I thought. He was staying at the Imperial Hotel. Why was he on a train bound somewhere else?

"Shinjuku, it's Shinjuku. Don't forget your things—" the recorded announcer's voice said over the loudspeaker.

"Well, I've got to run. Better not get lost," I said, moving toward the door.

"Rei, don't leave the train on my account." Eric, to my horror, was following me off.

"I'm not leaving because of *you*—I'm going to my appointment. Why don't you do the same?" I shouted over my shoulder, trying to move along as fast as my high heels would permit.

"But—I'm going to Shinjuku too!" Eric declared. "We can go around together. I'm not very good at finding my way here, this being my first trip—"

"Well, let me tell you that Shinjuku is quite a hike from the Imperial Hotel. From this point on, it's about a half hour on the train—"

"I don't care if I'm late," Eric said, catching up to me and grabbing my arm so hard that I had to stop. More than a few people stared at us, and I wondered whether it was because two obviously Asian people were speaking English to each other or because we were squabbling—an unacceptable public behavior.

I stopped moving—since I bruise easily—and Eric let go of my arm and put his hands in his pockets rather sheepishly.

"I'm sorry, Rei. It's—well, this is the first time I've caught you alone. In San Francisco I couldn't manage it, and here I thought it would be impossible. Just hear me out, okay? Could we have a cup of coffee or something? We could meet later if you're too busy right now."

Eric hung his head a little, and I reminded myself to be gentle—for some unfathomable reason, he still had a crush.

"I doubt there will be time," I said. "Right now I'm dealing with quite a lot of problems."

"Well, I guess you can tell me about it at dinner."

That was right, Hugh was making reservations for all of us. I nodded, but didn't say any more.

I made quite sure Eric boarded the next Yamanote Line train headed southwest before I left the platform for the east side of Shinjuku Station. If he followed me to Mr. Idabashi's office, I could just imagine how bad it could be.

It was my first time back to Shinjuku in a while, so I looked at it with new eyes. Through the mid-nineties, many gigantic, high-style shopping malls had been built; now, the glass palaces were going up more slowly, and there were many signs offering sale prices in the department stores. Yes, it was the customary time of year for sales, but I knew the economy had weakened. As I walked toward Kabuki-cho, the pleasure quarter, I thought about the impact any trouble at Morita Incorporated would have on the economy. The first people laid off at big Japanese companies were usually women and part-timers. If office ladies lost jobs and couldn't shop, department stores would falter.

It was like making a pyramid of tangerines, a game I used to play when I was a child staying the summer in Japan. I built and built as high as you could go, and then my competitor, usually my cousin Tom, would remove one of the tangerines and the pile of fruit would collapse and roll across the floor. We were all dependent on each other; that was the game's lesson.

Already, I could see the impact that a depressed economy had had on Kabuki-cho. Many hostess bars had closed, now that there were fewer companies with generous entertainment allowances. The admission fee to sleazier places—soaplands and no-pants coffee shops—had been reduced, according to signs in the windows.

Mr. Idabashi certainly had chosen an unsavory location for his detective agency, I thought as I turned left into the little street that had been marked on his business card. Well, my goal was to see if there was the slightest inkling of impropriety about him. So far, things weren't looking good for him. At least there wasn't a red-light business in the Fine Future Building, I thought as I looked at the companies listed on a sign posted on the modest two-story, aluminum-clad building. It contained a travel agency, a wedding planner, and the Idabashi PI Service.

The three came together logically, I thought. Young people about to be married were likely to need PI services. Once a bride's parents had read an investigative report and approved the fiancé, they could walk a few steps to the wedding planner to get the ceremony set up, then a few more to the travel agency to arrrange details for the honeymoon.

I had hoped that the detective agency had a glass window in its door, so I could spy on Mr. Idabashi without raising his antenna; but there was no such luck. It was a steel door with the agency name on it in black letters. Across the hall was the wedding planner's office. This door did have a glass window. I glanced into a small, cluttered room painted pink and decorated with a little frieze of bells and flowers. Maybe I could get some information from the planner.

I opened the door, catching the eye of a woman in a pink suit sitting behind a large desk crowded with papers. She was wearing a telephone headset, into which she was talking to someone.

"Yes, yes. Blue roses, irises, and lilies of the valley." A pause. "For all of them." A sucking in of breath. "Let me check with the client. Thank you!"

When she put down the phone, I said, "Excuse me for disturbing you."

"Welcome to Sugo Bridal Service! I'm Sugo Nanae." She beamed at me as if I were her new best friend, and I realized that I must look like a potential client.

Well, I'd been thinking this was the way to go. "Ah, Sugo-san, I hope you can help me. I want to get married . . ."

A quick glance to my left hand, and Ms. Sugo said, "Well, it looks as if you've got a good start on the project. What a beautiful ring."

"My fiancé surprised me." I couldn't restrain myself from blushing a little. There was something about being in this super-feminine office that made me feel awkward and ill at ease. "Unfortunately, I can't remain engaged or even plan the wedding until my parents decide they like him. They don't know him at all, and they're quite nervous."

"I understand. How difficult for you. By the way, are you considering elopement?" She held out a folder to me. "We offer something called the wedding escape plan. There's an all-included package with hotel, wedding ceremony, and private luau. Hawaii is very convenient, and of course it's much cheaper than Japan."

"I—I couldn't elope. I guess I want to plan a real wedding, but I have this obstacle that my parents won't come through with money until they're satisfied I'm marrying the right man."

"You probably will need to order an investigation, then." I could hear the sympathy in her voice. "Why don't you talk to a detective who specializes in such matters? There's one right across the hall. Idabashi-san—he's very reliable."

"Is he—a kind person? I'm quite nervous. Frankly, I'd prefer to talk to a woman about this kind of thing—"

"Don't be nervous," Mrs. Sugo said. "He's easy to get along with, and he is discreet. He won't do anything to hurt the situation of whoever is paying his bill."

"I'm not sure I understand."

Ms. Sugo raised her eyebrows. "What I mean to say is, if your parents pay, it's his obligation to give them what they're asking for. But if you pay, he will do his utmost to come up with a report that works in your interest."

"Does he specialize in engagement surveillance?" I asked.

"I think he does a little of everything. He does corporate work, too."

"He's been hired by big companies?" If so, I would definitely have to worry that Morita Incorporated might have been a past client.

"Large and small, I'd think—just like my wedding service. I can deal with anything—traditional Shinto ceremonies, chapel weddings in Hawaii, you name it!"

"What kind of work does Mr. Idabashi do for the companies?"

For the first time, a flash of irritation—or was it suspicion—seemed to cross Ms. Sugo's face. "I have no idea. Weddings are my concern, not company business. But look, he's free now."

"How do you know?" I asked. I wasn't ready for a direct confrontation yet.

"Look out the door. He's come into the hall with a client."

I whipped around to see that two men were walking out of the office. The first was a small, gray-haired salaryman in a modest blue suit, and the second was a man about ten years younger dressed in an electric blue sharkskin suit. His hair was permed into tight curls, and his nose looked as if it had been broken more than once. His cheeks were pitted by the remnants of something awful—chicken pox? Acne? I wasn't sure, but I looked after him in awe as the two men headed down the short staircase to the street.

"Ah, I see Mr. Idabashi has gone out. Well, I guess it is lunchtime." She looked at her watch. "He usually takes a half hour."

"Oh, of course," I said, realizing that I was wearing out my welcome. "Didn't you think that client of his looked a little . . . unusual?"

"What do you mean? The client looked like a typical father of a bride to me."

"Do you mean to say that the older man in the blue suit was the client?"

"Was it blue? I didn't notice. Actually, I have no idea who his clients are, other than some of my brides' families."

"Was Mr. Idabashi the man with the curly hair?"

"Yes, indeed." She looked at me curiously. "What's wrong?"

I couldn't say that curly hair and pockmarked skin and brightly colored clothing are the marks of a gangster. Nobody even said the word *gangster* aloud. So instead I said, "I just realized I'm running late to my job. I must go now. Thank you for all the help."

"Please take some brochures with you. And I've got some more materials on upcoming wedding specials coming back from the printer that I can mail to you next week. Let me take your name and address." She opened a folder and picked up a pen. "Also, who referred you to my agency?"

I paused. "Um, my cousin referred me. But she wound up not going with your agency, so I don't think you would have a record of her name."

"I see. Well, I would like a record of yours, if that's not too much trouble."

"Ah, the problem is that I live with my parents, you see, and if they received any wedding-related mail before the inspection is over they might become angry."

"Ah, I understand." She pressed her lips together sympathetically. But please tell me your name for my guest log, so that when you call back I'll know you?"

"Shimada," I lied. I was doing this so often now, I was certain not to get to heaven—Buddhist or otherwise. "My name is Reiko Shimada."

"Very well, Miss Shimada, good luck to you and your intended groom. And please come back and see me when your parents have agreed to the union."

Why would a yakuza *become a detective?* I pondered as I walked through the streets of Shinjuku on my way back to the train station. To help other mobsters, say, collect on bad debts? If that were the case, wouldn't he have enough work to keep him from having to do general detective work, such as bridal surveillance and missing persons? He hadn't charged me very much money; in fact, he'd returned some of the deposit I'd made.

I was at my wits' end by the time I got home. I went straight to the phone to call Hugh. I explained my suspicions about Mr. Idabashi possibly working for unsavory people.

Hugh was less sympathetic than I'd expected. "Rei, that curly-hair thing is a stereotype. There's no reason to believe that Asian men with curly hair are gangsters—their hair just shows their parents might have intermarried. Anyway, how could Mr. Idabashi have been involved in what happened with Rosa in San Francisco? You hadn't contacted him until days after she died."

"I haven't figured it out, all right?" I was irritated with Hugh for his cool reaction.

"I see. Let's agree to disagree on your gangster theory, all right? And I want to tell you what Charles said on the limo ride in from Narita Airport. We have plans to meet with people at Morita Inc. tomorrow."

"That's what you wanted to do," I said. "But it's too fast, isn't it?"

"Not given all that's happened to our two plaintiffs."

"Hold on. You don't really think it was someone from the company who'd do something so . . . open?"

"I don't know. It makes a hell of a lot more sense than your suspicion about Mr. Idabashi. And regardless of whether they did anything to our plaintiffs, we've got to act as if we're not afraid of them. It's like a game—"

"Bullies standing up to each other on the playground," I said softly. It was a far cry from a tower of tangerines.

"What? Darling, aren't you with me on this?"

I sighed and said, "At this point, I don't think about the future of the lawsuit; I think about the people who've already been hurt, and the fact we might be hurt, too."

We made our good-byes and then I called over to Kanda General to check on Ramon Espinosa. He was still in the coma. I asked to speak with Dr. Nigawa, but he wasn't available.

Feeling too stressed to sit still, I pulled on sweats and went out for a run. This time my knee was better. I breathed easily as I loped along the sidewalk.

As I moved into the semi-dreamlike state of freedom that a good run can bring, I thought of the different ways in which I was lucky. I had my health, Hugh, and relatives who cared about me. Money . . . sure, it would be nice to have a decent bank account. I'd heard somewhere to do what you love, and that the money would follow. It seemed that only rich people said that. I'd never get rich by researching my family history and writing it up for nobody but the Shimura clan and myself. I'd probably have to shelve this project for a while and get back to the business of fixing up and selling old *tansu*.

The family history had seemed so important a week ago, with the discovery that a letter from Hirohito existed. But I was finding my great-grandfather a far less admirable character than I'd hoped. He was a pedantic, conservative scholar: nothing to brag about. *Why did the hard things have to survive?* I wondered again.

I didn't want to know about my great-grandfather's ridiculous beliefs. If only Uncle Hiroshi's files had been filled with old menu plans and garden designs. I'd built my life around the cultural traditions that made Japan humane: the elegant, fragile, admirable things. Things like that had survived in museums, but apparently not in my family's home.

22

Kiku is the rare kind of restaurant that gets terrific reviews in both the Japanese and English-language press—which makes it hard getting through the door. Even though it was half-empty, when I arrived every white-clothed table in the restaurant had a RESERVED sign on it. Apparently spaces along the vintage-looking zinc bar were reserved, too, because when I headed for a bar stool, I was immediately questioned by an black-clad gentleman about my intentions.

"My name is Rei Shimura. I'm meeting colleagues later on—"

"What are their names?" the maître d' said as he looked over my outfit. I was wearing a trim red wool suit I'd bought a few months ago in Washington, but it suddenly felt too loud and cheap for this subdued locale.

I hesitated, now paranoid about giving too much information. "I'm not sure which one called. Perhaps the reservation is in a foreign name?"

"We have many foreigners eating here tonight. In fact, it's so busy that perhaps you'd be more comfortable next door . . ."

"Glendinning, party of four." Who else was so good at making reservations?

The tightness on the man's face evaporated. "We have that

reservation, yes, so you may stay. We're still arranging the table, so please, why don't you wait for your group at the bar."

I nodded and sat down, delighted to be able to pull myself out of the fray of exquisitely dressed couples coming and going. Sake was the specialty beverage of the restaurant, with over a hundred varieties available from different regions in Japan. After some deliberation, I ordered a crisp sake from my favorite province, Fukushima, which came to me in a small glass filled with ice. It was the perfect partner to the *otoshi*, the small, predinner nibble they served alongside it—a spicy, tangy mix of mackerel and trout chunks. I couldn't have eaten fish this strong-tasting when I was in high school, but the longer I'd lived in Japan, the more I had become able to appreciate savory and strong flavors, especially if they were spiked with things like chilies and horseradish. I ate the fish as slowly as I could, hoping Hugh and the others wouldn't be too late. I had a feeling that it would be very easy to wear out my welcome at this place.

My worries faded in a couple of minutes, when I saw a small, silver-haired Japanese man come through the door. I'd have known that stoop-shouldered gait anywhere—it was the man I'd taken into my heart to be my grandfather, Mr. Ishida. Ishida-san was a real Tokyo old-timer, and a serious gourmet—which was why the maître d' was buzzing around him and treating him far more solicitously than he had me.

I waved to my mentor, who gave me a gracious half-bow. A place was found for Mr. Ishida next to me, and the bartender brought him a glass of sake and his own plate of *otoshi*.

Mr. Ishida asked me if I'd been away in the countryside. I guessed he was angling to see if I had bought anything good that he might be interested in taking off my hands; the thought that my mentor finally had enough trust in me to express his curiosity made me very happy.

"I wish," I said wryly. "I've been out of the country—actually, back in San Francisco, researching the Shimura family history."

"But your family's from here. You shouldn't have to go so far."

"Well, it was on the way back from that museum lecture trip I'd done in Washington." I explained. "I'd thought my father would have a lot to contribute, but I didn't get much. About the most interesting thing I discovered was that we actually once had something quite valuable—a signed letter by Emperor Hirohito. But he'd sold it."

"That must have been disappointing." Mr. Ishida was too cool to ask what price the letter had fetched.

"It was. Fortunately, the letter made its way to the archives at Showa College, so I did read it. But it was just a condolence letter, nothing of political or social importance. I'm afraid my history project has been a waste of time, not to mention that I'm not making a dime—or I should say 'yen'—from it."

Mr. Ishida regarded me through narrowed eyes. "But history is worth much more than money. It's our nation's heritage. The problem here is that nobody will speak up about his or her life. We say water washes everything away—that it's unimportant. So the stories, like pieces of old furniture, are lost."

Water washes everything away. Mr. Ishida had used a proverb that Manami Okada had uttered in San Francisco. Nobody wanted to talk about atrocities committed against others because that time was past; the water had washed it away. We were supposed to move forward and build strong new relationships based on a new Pan-Asian desire for peace.

I looked closely at Mr. Ishida. "I didn't know you felt that way."

He cocked his head to the side. "You know, there actually might be a market for what you're doing. If you could put your history together in some kind of multimedia presentation, a museum might be interested."

"Wouldn't that be nice," I said absently, watching Eric Gan come in through the door. He gave me his familiar, oily smile again. Just great. Now I was going to have to introduce the man I admired most to the one most likely to cause me embarrassment.

"Ishida-sensei, please let me introduce you to Hugh's colleague, Eric Gan." I did it all in Japanese, because I knew Eric was fluent. "Eric is visiting from the United States, and he is a Japanese-English interpreter."

"Very pleased to meet you." Mr. Ishida bowed. "I have a small antiques shop in the area. Rei and I have been colleagues ever since her arrival some years ago."

"Actually, I'm Rei's first boyfriend, not just a translator," Eric said, in a brash way that made me cringe.

"We're just friends these days," I amended. "Ishida-sensei, I believe you may remember my fiancé, Hugh Glendinning. He's the tall man with reddish-blond hair who has just come in the door."

Mr. Ishida turned and surveyed Hugh and Charles Sharp as they were pulling off their overcoats. He said, "Ah, there's a gentleman with money and taste. He was just in the shop earlier today to buy some porcelain. He also is considering a *tansu*."

"Hugh?" I asked in surprise. I didn't think he had much money to throw around at the moment.

"Actually, I'm talking about the other gentleman. His name means something that cuts . . . it's escaping me at the moment."

Feeling somewhat relieved Hugh hadn't shopped behind my back, I said, "That's Charles Sharp, but he lives in San Francisco. He's just here short-term."

"Sharp—how could I forget?" Mr. Ishida shook his head ruefully. "I shipped some goods to an address in San Francisco for him a few years ago. This time, he bought just a little Imari porcelain, but he's considering quite an important chest—I hope he takes that, too."

"Let's talk about it later," I said as Charles and Hugh began to thread their way through the crowd to us.

Mr. Ishida looked at me curiously, and I quickly explained, "He's my fiancé's boss. I want to make a good impression on him—why, hello there. Mr. Sharp, you must still be exhausted. How nice of you to let me come along to this restaurant—it's one of my favorites."

"Please call me Charles," Sharp said, looking at me. "We'll all be family, now that you will be Hugh's bride. And hello to you, Mr. Ishida. The plates have arrived already. Is Rei one of your customers, too?"

"Yes," I said quickly, because I didn't want to go into the depth of my complicated relationship with my mentor. My head was buzzing with what Charles had said about my being a bride. It should have made me feel warm and fuzzy, but it just made me feel stupid.

"I am relieved the deliveryman brought the plates already," Mr. Ishida said in his slow, precise English. "Did you open the package to certify they are in good condition?"

"Not yet, but I'm not worried. Your deliveries have always been perfect, whether to the Imperial Hotel or Pacific Heights."

Hugh put out his hand to Mr. Ishida. "Good evening. I'm Hugh Glendinning. I don't know if you remember me from a few years ago."

"Yes, I certainly do. I'm very happy you have returned to Japan. I apologize, but I must leave for my home now. Shimura-san, if you have a moment to visit my shop tomorrow, we shall finish that discussion about the auction."

By the time Mr. Ishida had paid his bill—he'd insisted on picking up my sake tab, despite my protestations—Hugh, Charles, and Eric were well settled at a table in the back of the restaurant.

The seating hadn't worked out the way I'd hoped. While I'd been gone, Charles had chosen the chair next to Hugh. I took the seat next to Eric without even looking at him. I scanned the menu for the tuna carpaccio that had been my favorite; it was no longer there, so I decided to have eggplant grilled with a miso topping followed by *ganmo*, a tofu ball simmered in a soy broth with potatoes. My goal was to eat so much I wouldn't have to speak to Eric.

Menu study took a while for everyone else. Hugh chose a grilled chunk of tuna cheek, and Charles a grilled red snapper–type fish called *kinmedai*. Eric went for the only thing that made me squeamish—"hot squid," a species of miniature squid that were electrically charged. In their afterlife, the squid were boiled and chilled with slices of mountain celery, greens, and mustard-miso sauce. I was sure Eric had chosen the electric squid to be macho, and resolved I would not taste it, no matter how aggressively he insisted.

"Did you already know Mr. Ishida?" Charles looked at me with something new in his expression after the orders had been taken.

"Sure. Everyone in Tokyo knows Mr. Ishida," I said cagily, not wanting to go into the extent of our close relationship. "He's the best man in town for *tansu.*"

"I've shopped there before. Years ago," said Charles, nodding at the waiter, who brought us a platter of crunchy *daikon* atop lettuce, garnished with a cod roe mayonnaise and flakes of dried bonito fish. Mayonnaise was a Japanese passion, but not one of my favorites; I passed on the dish, which the men quickly polished off.

"Charles's house is packed with Japanese treasures—you'd love it, darling," Hugh said between bites.

"Yes, you must come sometime for an education," Charles said, and I bristled. Clearly he thought that what he owned was out of my league.

"Is it just Japanese antiques you own?" Eric asked Charles. "Or have you gone for fusion, like this too-trendy restaurant?"

I shot a withering glance at Eric. Kiku was going to cost the equivalent of at least eighty dollars a person; he should have been grateful he wasn't paying for his electric eels, I thought.

Charles seemed to take it in stride. "Well, Japan is my foremost specialty, but I do have some Southeast Asian items I collected from Thailand and Vietnam over the years."

"What about the Philippines?" Eric said.

Charles smiled and said, "Not much to collect there except for rattan furniture. Or, I suppose, the shoes of a famous first lady."

Eric's face flushed. As much as my ex–childhood flame annoyed me, all of a sudden I felt for him, at a table in a fancy restaurant with white men who made far more money in a year than he would in ten years, one of whom was dismissing his family's culture.

"Oh, there's quite a lot of value in the Philippines," I offered. "The only dilemma is there's no way to get it out."

"And what are you talking about, specifically?" Charles looked at me with new interest.

"Gold." I said the word softly, so they all had to lean in to listen to me.

"The Philippines is better known for pearls," Eric corrected me. I wanted to slug him; didn't he know I was trying to save his dignity?

"That's the small stuff," I said. "What about all the gold Buddhas and gold ingots the Japanese looted from Asia during

World War II? A lot of it is supposed to be hidden in caves and tunnels in the Philippines."

"How did you hear this?" Charles Sharp asked. I could tell his interest was piqued, because his nostrils flared out a little bit, as if he'd smelled something good.

I wished I could have said it had been through my own scholarship, but it wouldn't have been true. "My father told me."

"Rei's father is a very interesting person," Hugh said. "Of all the Japanese I've met, he's the only one who wants to talk about the war."

"Well, maybe not the only one." Eric snorted lightly. "Morita Inc. is about to make a big-time attitude adjustment."

"What do you mean?" I took a sip of sake. "Oh, sorry. Don't tell me anything for which you'd have to kill me later on."

Charles Sharp gave me a half-smile. "Actually, Rei, the last thing I'd want to do is make an associate's wife unhappy. I wanted you to be here tonight because I'm asking Hugh to consider a shift from his current employer in Washington in order to join us as an associate. It would be partner track, with a generous starting salary and a high enough cost-of-living allowance to move into a top-notch building. There's one I'm thinking of that's close to the Imperial Hotel—"

I shot a glance at Hugh. His face showed that he was as stunned as I.

"Is this like one of those public proposals?" I said in the next split second, to fill the gap. "You know, the kind of scene where you ask someone to marry you in front of their family so they have to say yes?"

"Rei," Hugh said, turning almost as red as the pickled ginger on his plate. Then he turned to Charles. "It's, uh, quite an offer. Perhaps we can discuss specifics in private tomorrow."

"Eric, what are you working on next?" I said, realizing I'd made an error.

"I'm following Charles to assist with the preliminary interviews with a new group of survivors that we've heard about in the Philippines. That's a top priority, now that things are lining up so nicely with Morita."

"I'll join him when I can," Hugh said. "But for now, I'm here."

"That's reassuring." I pushed aside the *daikon*, which had tasted so good a minute ago but now was like soggy wood in my mouth. "So, Mr. Sharp, I understand you and Hugh have a big meeting with Morita Inc. tomorrow. Do you think they'll be surprised?"

"Surprised by what?" His eyebrows drew together in an expression of polite concern.

"Well, I'm curious whether *you* think they're already aware of the class action."

"You mean—because someone planted tear gas on your doorstep?" he said. He smiled. "I don't really know. The tear gas could have come from anywhere. There was a nationalist demonstration at the Yasakuni Shrine where tear gas was involved—yesterday, wasn't it?"

"You're up on the news," Hugh said. "I hadn't even heard about that."

"I didn't have a chance to tell you," I said, turning back to Charles. "Yes, I'm aware of the demonstration. Look at the potential link, though. You're going after a big Japanese company—the backbone of the nation. You're going to expose war secrets. Imperialists have to hate it! And they could have done so much more than the tear gas to warn us—they could have been the ones who killed Rosa and tried to kill Ramon. Even if they didn't do it with their own hands, they could have hired a hit man to do the job. You know, this country has a long tradition of that kind of violence-for-hire work, going all the way back to the samurai."

"It doesn't really matter what I think." Charles smiled blandly. "You're the insider, Rei. The one with an instinct for understanding."

I shook my head, sensing that I'd been too forceful and again lost my edge. "There's a saying about people who have lived in Japan for a long time," I continued in a quieter voice. "At first, you know nothing—the land and people are as inscrutable as all the stereotypes. Then, after a few months, you relax and you feel you understand. You engage happily in life, and tell your old friends in America or Europe or wherever you're from that you finally enjoy and understand the Japanese people. And then, just as things are going swimmingly, something changes. You lose your confidence and realize that you never understood this country and its people after all."

I caught my breath after I'd finished. I hadn't meant to be so self-revealing. But I'd been thinking about my neighbor Mrs. Yuto's no longer liking me, and the gas on the doorstep. I couldn't figure out what was going on in the country that I'd always loved—but didn't seem to reciprocate anymore.

23

The shadows seemed longer in my room later that night as I lay back on my bed in a woozy haze. I had gotten so depressed that I'd drank too much sake—not only at dinner, but afterward, when I beseeched Hugh to stop in with me for a nightcap at the seedy little *izakaya* around the corner from my apartment. I'd broken practically every Buddhist rule in the book, except for the ones regarding killing. At the rate at which I was going, though, who knew what was next?

"I'm a liability," I moaned after we'd come home and Hugh was helping me get into my Japanese long johns. "You're either going to have to divorce me or quit that firm."

"Divorce is out of the question, as we haven't even found the wedding site yet." Hugh stroked my cheek. "And as for the other possibility, I don't work for Sharp, Witter and Rowe yet—and I don't think I'm ever going to."

"Charles wants you completely under his thumb," I said. "And he's using COLA and that fancy apartment as the lure."

"Andrews and Cheyne *should* offer me their own COLA package," Hugh said. "I don't know why they haven't brought it up yet. Anyway, I'm lucky enough to have a fiancé with a charming flat."

"Yeah, the only problem is it's subject to attack from the neighbors. Or whoever." I curled under my covers, waiting for Hugh to get in. But instead, he sat down in the corner of the room and began pulling everything out of his briefcase. Then he put things back and closed the latch.

"What are you looking for?" I asked.

"My cassette player. Have you seen it?"

"No, but my Walkman's on the bookcase in my living-dining room, if you want to borrow it."

"I'm talking about my microcassette player," Hugh said. "I had it in my briefcase today, I'm sure. It's the one you saw me using when we spoke to Rosa on Christmas Eve."

"Oh, that tape. I'm surprised you didn't give it to the San Francisco police," I said, raising myself up on one elbow so I could get a better look at him.

"At the time they were talking to me, I didn't think what we'd recorded had anything to do with her death. But tonight, something you said jogged a memory. I want to listen to it again."

"Do you think someone removed it from your briefcase?" I asked.

"It could have happened. But the only time the briefcase was out of my sight was when I went to the loo. And at those times it was in the office suite we've rented, under the protection of Charles and Eric."

"What kind of protection is that?" I said.

"I agree," he said, coming over to sit on the edge of the futon. "It was damn stupid of me. When you said what you did about the gold tonight, I realized that both of them were acting too surprised to be believable. Charles should have known because of his interest in antiquities. And Eric should have known because of his heritage."

"You could go into work tomorrow and ask each of them if they've seen the tape recorder. Their reactions could be interesting."

"They'll both deny it, I'm sure."

"You never know—maybe you really did misplace it. Have you checked your coat pockets?"

Hugh shrugged and got up to go to the front of the apartment, where I had a tiny excuse for a coat closet that was mostly taken up by luggage. After a second, I heard laughter. "Thanks. You're right!"

"You found it there?"

"Yes, I must have shifted it to my pocket sometime—maybe because I was mistaking it for my lost phone."

An hour later, we'd played the short tape more than forty times. We'd also each written our own transcriptions of what we'd heard and compared. One passage seemed the most interesting—and of course, the hardest to figure out.

Rosa: Buried alive. Buried alive. They said it was because she was sick, and we could all catch it. But I knew it was because she saw.
Hugh: "She"? I thought your friend was a man. You said he was called Ramon Espinosa.
Rosa: No, Mr. Ramon is different. This was Hiroko.
Rei: You were saying Hiroko died because she saw something. Was it violence or some kind of atrocity?
Rosa: It was always violent. Didn't I tell you that already? No, I tried to explain before. I'm not sure of the English word . . . what was it in? Got.

After that, there was nothing of note except the sound of breaking glass outside. "What was the word?" Hugh slipped his arms around me. "Now I'm wondering if she said it before in the Tagalog interview she did with Eric. But it only came to me as a suspicion, following what you said tonight at dinner about the gold. I can't thank you enough for being there."

"Good," I said, nestling against his chest. "Now, can we get to sleep?"

"Let's work out the last sentence," Hugh said. "Or last two sentences, maybe."

"Hugh, your English is sounding suspiciously American. Wash your mouth with Aquarius Water and go to sleep."

"What was it in? Got!" Hugh said, stabbing at the paper with his finger. "She said it loudly and clearly. I suspect it's just the foreign intonation that made it sound like two sentence fragments to us."

"You think you understand something." I sighed heavily. "I'm afraid I don't. I guess it's because I'm so tired. . . . Can you tell me tomorrow?"

"Before you go to sleep, just look. Here."

I blinked my bleary eyes and followed his finger on the page he'd written in his elegant, loopy handwriting. And then I saw.

What was it in? Got.
In got
Ingot!

By the time I'd finally gotten it about the ingot, it was late enough at night in Tokyo that it was mid-morning in California. Hugh telephoned a paralegal at Sharp, Witter and Rowe to request copies of the tape he and Eric had made during their formal interview of Rosa—plus Eric's Tagalog and English transcriptions of the interview. Because the documents were confidential, the paralegal said, she couldn't fax them but they would go out with the overnight mail. Hugh would get them in two days if he were lucky.

"I don't know if I can wait that long," Hugh fumed after he'd hung up the phone. "And if they're so highly confidential, that might mean she'll automatically contact Charles about why I want them. And then he'll wonder if I can be trusted."

"If the paralegal is sending the papers, she trusts you," I said. "Who wouldn't? Now the challenge will be to find a trustworthy Tagalog speaker to independently verify Eric's translation of what was on the tape. And if it turns out he lied, it might mean . . ."

"Eric was involved in Rosa's death, because he knew she knew the location of the gold. The more I think about it, he's the one who came in late on Boxing Day to work—I didn't tell you earlier, because so many other things had happened, but Charles was quite annoyed that he wasn't there on the dot at nine that morning."

"I'm not wild about Eric," I said. "But I still find it hard to believe he's ruthless enough to have killed an elder from within his community."

"You're sounding awfully nationalistic," Hugh said.

"But in San Francisco's Asian communities, people feel so proud and protective of those who emigrated before them. And that's coupled with the traditional Asian reverence for elders." I paused, thinking it over. "Eric wouldn't have killed an old Filipina lady. What if he presented the transcript with all the information about ingots and Charles Sharp got interested? Maybe the reason Charles offered you all the goodies tonight is because he thinks he'll stay undetected if you're under his control."

"But Charles was in the States when Ramon Espinosa was attacked," Hugh said.

"So was Eric," I countered. "He telephoned me and the Caller ID showed the call originated in San Francisco. But either of them could have hired a hit man."

"Tell me more about that phone call," Hugh said.

I described what I remembered about Eric's phone call—the one in which I decided he still had a crush on me.

"He probably called you using his mobile phone," Hugh said. "I know he carries one. He could have been in Tokyo, calling you with his mobile, and it would still have said San Francisco because that's where the number is registered."

"Oh, really?" I didn't have a cell phone, and as a result I hadn't thought much about what one could do with them, other than irritate people around me.

"Let me look at your phone for a minute." Hugh pressed a few buttons. "Ah, here it is. Let me try it." He punched a few more buttons. In a minute, he spoke again. "Hello. Is it Eric? Great, Hugh here." He shot an I-told-you-so look at me. "Ah, yes, I know it's the middle of the night. Sorry. I just assumed you were awake with jet lag."

Hugh asked him about how they were gettting to Morita Incorporated the next day, listened to the answer, and then said good-bye. He looked at me in triumph and said, "Now we know that Eric could have been at home in San Francisco, or here, or some other country altogether when he rang you."

I didn't want t believe Eric had done it. I said, "I wish I could talk to my father. He might know something more about Eric's situation that could shed light on him doing anything criminal—"

"Don't do that yet," Hugh said. "We still don't know whether the transcripts Eric made are honest ones or not. I don't want to risk accusing Eric of a crime if he's done nothing. Morita Incorporated could be behind it all. And they'd love it, wouldn't they, if a poor young translator were made the scapegoat."

Hugh had a reasonable point. But at the same time, I knew that I couldn't sit and wait as patiently as he. It wasn't my style. And while Hugh had a bona fide business day to attend to, I didn't. In the long night during which we both tossed and turned, I thought about what I could do to find out the truth about Eric and Charles. The things that I came up with weren't all entirely proper—but they would lead to answers.

That morning, instead of seeing Hugh off at my door, I took him out for breakfast at Dunkin' Donuts and then walked with him to the train station. We enjoyed a brief but warming embrace before his southbound Chiyoda Line train pulled in. It was a cold morning, I noticed, after he left. My breath flew up in small smoky gusts as I stood on the platform, shifting from foot to foot, waiting for my own northbound subway train to come on the opposite platform.

When I got out of the train a half hour later in Kanda, the sun had risen high enough that the temperatures were in the fifties. I warmed up as I power-walked to Kanda General.

Nurse Tanaka was on duty again. She was surprised to see me so early, but she didn't seem angry. She told me that Dr. Nigawa was making rounds, checking on how each intensive care patient had fared over the night.

"How is Espinosa-san?" I asked, and she lit up like Christmas.

"He improved yesterday. For only twenty minutes, but it happened. I know it, because I was there."

"He woke up for you?" I suppose it did make sense; they were the ones in constant contact with him.

"Yes, he did." Again, Nurse Tanaka beamed. "I was there with a junior nurse, and I'd instructed her to bathe him with a pleasantly scented soap. Soon he began twitching one side of his face. At first we thought it was random, but then we realized he was trying to say something to us!"

"Oh my. What did he say?"

"We asked, 'Do you want the soap?' and he made two twitches. Then we asked, 'Do you want us to use cold water?' and he made one twitch. We asked if he was communicating yes or no, and he twitched twice again. To say yes."

"Did you bring in the police then?"

"The police?" Nurse Tanaka looked stunned at my question.

"Yes, because, well, he was attacked. He might have been able to give some yes-no answers about his attacker."

"I didn't think of it, to tell the truth. We were more focused on his recovery. By the time Dr. Nigawa came to see him, he'd fallen asleep. But the doctor said there is every chance he will come back to us."

I was disappointed they hadn't pushed to find out who had hurt him; but I could also understand their first priority was Ramon's health. I asked if I could go in to see him.

"Yes, but you haven't heard the end of the story! We told him the names of the people who had come to visit him. He reacted *most* strongly to your name."

That made me nervous. I asked, "But what about his nephew?"

"Nothing. I mean, he twitched no, but I imagine that just meant he didn't know him very well. But I think he really did want to see you. Maybe he will wake up for you this morning."

"I hope so," I said, and then went off to see him. He'd reacted to my name. Did that mean he thought I'd brought the trouble to him—or that he wanted to finally tell me the things he wouldn't say before?

When I got to the bedside, Ramon looked much the same as he had before—his face as crumpled as ever, his eyes closed. After speaking to him and getting no response, I reached out and touched his hand. His skin felt as dry and shriveled as it had before.

"I know you're getting better," I said, just in case he could hear, but his muscles weren't working. "Just take your time. I'll be here for you. Don't worry about anything."

"Ah, good morning." I heard a male voice at the door, and I turned to see Dr. Nigawa. He picked up the clipboard at the foot of Ramon's bed.

"Good morning, Nigawa-sensei. I'm so glad you're here. I have a few questions about Mr. Espinosa's health."

"Of course. But if it's about whether he'll ever completely emerge from the coma, I can't tell you. I'm afraid the nursing staff became overly excited yesterday and interpreted random movements as communication."

"Were you there to see it?" I asked.

"Ah, no. I arrived after it was over."

So there was no reason to believe the nurses had overreacted, I thought. But I didn't say that to Dr. Nigawa.

"Excuse me for a moment. I must take his vital signs," the doctor said.

"Sure." I stood up and walked to the side of the room by the windows, to give the patient and doctor privacy during the examination. "I wanted to ask you about his blindness. Since his medical history is here, I wondered if you could tell me the background information you have about it."

"Well, I can tell you he did not lose his sight while living in Japan," Dr. Nigawa said, putting his stethoscope against the patient's chest. After a minute, he wrote something on a chart and continued. "He came here as a blind immigrant from the Philippines after the war. He was training as an acupuncturist, apparently. So he always had a roof over his head, and food—despite having no family members to support him."

"Does the record include the reason he went blind?"

Dr. Nigawa thumped Ramon's knee with a little hammer. It didn't move. Then he said to me, "As I recall it, the medical record said injury had caused the blindness."

"Do you think it could have been violence?"

"Well, obviously it was a different doctor in the forties who recorded his initial history, so I don't really know. However, Espinosa-san had never said anything like that to the doctors who treated him earlier in his life."

"Can you guess anything by the condition of his corneas?"

"No. His eyelids, didn't you notice, are sewn permanently closed."

I bent over to look closely at Ramon's eyelids. There was a line of reddish-yellow scar tissue where his eyelashes would have met the thin skin over the top of his cheekbones. That must have been the site of the stitches. "Who do you think would be capable of doing such a horrendous thing?"

"A doctor, I'm sure. Particularly in the old days, when glasses were scarcer and the sight of a person walking around with opaque corneas might have made others uncomfortable."

So that's how he saw it—an act of social responsibility. I saw it otherwise. For the doctor in charge of slave workers at Morita Incorporated, sewing up the burned eyes of a war slave might simply have been the best way to cover things up. Literally.

Dr. Nigawa was talking. I dragged myself out of my horrible visions of the past to hear what he was saying. "Shimura-san, please understand that the blindness might be the smallest of his problems. Even if he comes out of this coma, he is unlikely to walk or move much. His future is quite bleak. There are very few hospices in Tokyo, and he has no relatives in Japan. I don't know that he is strong enough for a transfer back to the Philippines—"

"I agree!" I'd heard a story that sometime in the past, Japan had shipped off hundreds of its own handicapped people to live in the Philippines, just so they were not Japan's problem anymore. I didn't know if it was true or not—but the thought of Ramon going there made me queasy. "Ah, I can open his apartment back up for him, and get nurses to give him round-the-clock care. I'm sure his neighbor, Mrs. Moriuchi, could help with that, too."

"Miss Shimura, the situation you are suggesting will be astronomically expensive. I don't think you understand what you're offering."

"'It wouldn't be me paying. He is due some money that may be coming within the next year. I'll look into it." Class action money. If one of the plaintiffs could push the case through, Ramon would come into money without having to speak a word. "Once I find the money, I'll make sure Espinosa-san is able to live where he's comfortable. Whether it's his own apartment with live-in nursing care or a hospice, we'll find something!"

Dr. Nigawa coughed and asked, "Do you have any legal status with the patient?"

I shook my head. "Not yet. And I bet I know what you're probably thinking—that I could just be after control of the money. It's not like that. In fact, when he becomes lucid again, maybe he could be asked about this question of power of attorney. He might be comfortable giving it to his neighbor, Mrs. Moriuchi. Do you think you could ask the nurses to follow up on this?"

The doctor was silent, then nodded. "It is true that I would like to have someone with whom to discuss his treatment. But perhaps a relative would be more committed than a neighbor."

"The blood relative lives in another country, and probably doesn't speak Japanese—"

"Oh, but he does. I spoke to him myself. Still, what you say about the distance between our hospital and the Philippines is important." Dr. Nigawa sighed. "Very well. I shall alert all our nursing staff to ask our patient about this matter of power of attorney, should he regain consciousness. And perhaps you in turn can ask Moriuchi-san if she is willing to provide such service."

"Fine. I'll ask her today." I was cheered by the doctor's openness and spirit of cooperation. "There's just one thing. I don't like Mr. Espinosa being unguarded like this. What if the person who tried to harm him in the apartment comes back to finish the job?"

"But nobody has asked to see him except for two other acupuncturists, the Moriuchi family, and yourself. Although, as I already mentioned, his nephew, telephoned from the Philippines."

I kept my gaze on Ramon, whose chest gently rose and fell in slumber. How peaceful he looked. "I'm curious about this nephew. Has he been in touch with the police?"

"I don't know. All we talked about was his uncle's condition—whether he'd be able to speak again."

"Since the nephew lives in the Philippines, how did he find out his uncle was in the hospital?"

"He didn't tell us. Perhaps a mutual friend advised him of the situation."

But the Moriuchis had told me that Ramon had never received letters from the Philippines. Who was this nephew who'd suddenly emerged from the woodwork? The fact that he claimed to be Filipino but spoke Japanese made me think again of a perpetrator within the ranks at Morita Incorporated—someone inside Japan with easy access to information about Espinosa-san's whereabouts and condition. Here again, Eric Gan fit the bill.

"Are the media still calling about Espinosa-san?" I asked.

"Yes, we've had a few calls fielded to our public affairs office."

"Are you releasing the news he was conscious for a few minutes?"

"Well, to tell the truth, the interest has died down. But we would certainly provide that information if asked."

"I don't like that at all," I said. "If it's publicly known that Espinosa-san has the capability to communicate, the attacker might hear about it, and worry that he could give away his identity."

"But I told you, Shimura-san, the nurses did not even ask him about the attacker. It's not their business." Dr. Nigawa's voice rose slightly. I realized that I might be wearing out my welcome, but I persisted.

"That fact might not have been mentioned on the news. Well, if Espinosa-san wakes up again, I really hope somebody will try to find out who hurt him." I pondered the ways of doing it. "What about audiotapes? Since he was able to hear, why couldn't we bring in some tape recordings of different suspects' voices?"

"It sounds as if it's a matter for the police, Shimura-san. But it's certainly a good idea. I think you've thought this out very carefully."

"Not really," I said. In fact, I felt my brain had been asleep for the last week. I was just beginning to think.

24

The Imperial Hotel is considered by most people to be Tokyo's finest. To be honest, I can think of half a dozen other hotels that are prettier and more Japanese-looking, but the Imperial has the advantage of actually being close enough to the Palace to offer views of its grounds. It had once looked like an old Edo Period villa—that was in its first incarnation, when Frank Lloyd Wright had come to Japan to design it. Unfortunately, that old structure had been scrapped to make a boring high-rise. Still, when you walked in you saw, right away, a sexy cocktail lounge with low-slung red chairs and wonderful art deco pendant lamps that were Wright relics from the original building. I would have loved to stop in for a sherry and people-watch, but I had my mission very much in mind.

I'd reached Hugh an hour earlier at the rented conference room that he, Charles, and Eric were sharing. He'd been in a hurry—Charles and Eric were already in the lobby trying to locate a cab, and he had picked up my call as he was about to go out the door. After ensuring that he was alone, I asked him for the name of a Japanese attorney who could write a power of attorney agreement and then casually slipped in a question about Eric's and Charles's hotel room numbers. He knew them, as he'd called on both rooms earlier.

"Don't say a word to them about my call," I said.

"Of course not." Hugh sounded irritated. "But don't tell me you're planning to make calls on them when we come back this afternoon. You'll just get me in trouble."

"Okay, I won't do that." I made a kissing sound and hung up the phone before he could ask anything more.

I thought my plan was clever. Chika didn't agree.

"You mean—I've got to pretend I'm married?"

"The most beautiful young bride in the world." I'd reached my cousin by calling Hugh's cell phone. She had just returned to Yokohama, but still had the phone turned on.

"But I don't have the clothes!" she protested.

"Go into your mother's closet and pick out anything. Then sneak out the back of the house so that she doesn't see you leave."

"Rei, I can't pull it off. I'm no good at lying—"

"You lied about where you went last night, right? All the way to Kyoto on the bullet train, and your parents think you were in Tokyo. You'll be great."

I don't know if it was my implied threat, or her curiosity, but Chika arrived at our meeting spot outside Shibuya Station an hour later. We met at the statue of Hachiko, a famous dog who for many years came to the station to meet her master in the evening, even after he died. I'd had some exciting meetings under Hachiko's bronze nose in the past—but this meeting only made me nervous. Could I pull off what I wanted to do, and with such a reluctant accomplice?

Chika had done what I'd ordered her to do. She arrived dressed in Aunt Norie's clothes. She wore a pair of perfectly tailored mauve slacks with a matching jacket, a silk blouse, and low-heeled pumps.

"I'm so embarrassed," she groaned as I came up to greet her.

"Where's your scarf?" I asked; everyone knew that a knotted silk scarf was the emblem of a married woman. Fortunately, I was prepared. From the pocket of my own conservative wool blazer—Talbots, vintage 1990, unearthed from the bottom of my closet—I pulled out a sheer beige voile scarf. I fussed around Chika's neck with it and she sprang back, causing the scarf to tighten. She made a strangled sound, and suddenly everyone was looking at me.

I loosened the scarf and loudly asked my cousin to tell me again what kind of bow she wanted.

"As discreet as possible," she wheezed. "Do you know how dowdy these scarves are? We look like we're over forty!"

"Not quite," I said, smiling back at my cousin. I picked up her right hand. "Oh, good, you have rings. You can lend me that gold one, and put these two on your left index finger, but put the others in your purse."

As we rode the Hibiya Line toward the Imperial hotel, I explained the situation. Both of us were wives—Chika was married to Eric Gan, and I to Charles Sharp. We would tell the front desk clerk that we had forgotten our room keys and our husbands weren't in.

"But won't they remember that the two men came in without wives?" Chika wondered aloud to me.

"Well, it's a big enough hotel that there will be plenty of front desk staff. Charles Sharp would be the more memorable guest, I think, and Hugh was with him when he checked in. They were tended to by a gentleman called Noguchi-san. We'll just make sure not to ask him for help."

The scam went smoothly. We got the keys from a young woman who smiled knowingly at the big Mitsutan shopping bags I'd thought to bring along.

Once we were in the elevator, I told Chika that she could feel free to go shopping in the hotel's arcade or to have a coffee at my expense in the lounge.

"Are you joking? I went to all this trouble to help you, and I can't go into my husband's room?" she demanded.

I hadn't told Chika why I needed entry to these places. She didn't even know who Charles and Eric were. Still, the thought of her watching me snoop through Charles's and Eric's possessions made me uneasy.

"I have only a short amount of time to get things done," I said. "I don't even have enough time to explain it to you—" I was whispering, because we were headed down the hallway to the rooms. We had only an hour, maybe, before there was a risk of the men's return from the meeting at Morita Incorporated.

"Let me come along," Chika nagged. I didn't answer, because as we approached the end of the hall, a problem became clear. The hotel maids were cleaning rooms all along the hall. They'd know we didn't belong in Charles's and Eric's rooms.

"Oh, I forgot something," I said loudly to Chika. I turned around and went back to the elevator, swinging my shopping bag.

"What?" She followed me inside. "What did you forget?"

"We can't do anything now. The cleaners would see us. But at least I have the keys; I can come back later."

"But if you keep the keys, how will the people staying in the rooms be able to get back in?"

"These are spare keycards, Chika. I'm sure the men already had their own keycards that they took with them."

"So you're still planning a break-in," Chika said when we'd left the hotel and I'd thanked her again for her services.

"It's not a break-in, just a look-around—and I'll thank you very much not to tell anyone about our adventure," I said.

"I won't," Chika said. "But if it's not a break-in, why are you visiting strange men's rooms? Are you going to cheat on Hugh?"

I choked back a laugh. "Why would you think I'd do a thing like that?"

"Sneaking into hotel rooms . . . knowing strange men's names . . . it makes me worry."

I smiled at Chika. "I promise you I have no romantic interest in these men. If anything, I'm looking into their backgrounds to protect Hugh. I'm not sure if they're—all right."

"Oh!" Chika said, and a smile spread across her face like sunshine. "That's not so bad then. I really like him, Rei-chan; we all do. In fact, I would like a boyfriend like that for myself if you weren't interested."

"I believe it," I said, looking at my beautiful cousin, who was untying the scarf I'd put on her. "Yes, I completely believe it."

After I'd bought Chika lunch and we'd said our good-byes, I attacked the next item on my agenda: Mr. Ishida. The rickety wooden building that he called both shop and home wasn't too far from the northeast Tokyo neighborhood where I'd once lived. I usually went to Ishida Antiques with a light step and an excited feeling, not knowing what I'd find behind the door. It was definitely a place for in-the-know shoppers, which made it interesting that Charles Sharp was his patron.

After we'd said our hellos and settled down to cups of his famous tea—a delicate blend from Kyoto—my mentor asked me what I needed from him.

I sighed. "I wish it were as simple as an auction recommendation. But I'm afraid that what I'm going to ask will be harder for you to give."

Mr. Ishida smiled. "Actually, I keep auction recommendations quiet. Too much competition from the younger generation of antiques dealers, *neh*?"

I laughed. "Actually, my request is not related to business. I want to know a little bit more about your impressions of Charles Sharp, that man who came into the restaurant last night."

"*Ah so desu ka*," was Mr. Ishida's response. He put his cup down and sat a minute. "He's a very good customer. He's bought from me before."

"Much more than I've bought, I know," I said.

"Yes, but he is a famous older lawyer and has a heavier purse. He chose some beautiful Imari porcelain yesterday."

"I thought you also said that he bought a *tansu*?"

Mr. Ishida shook his head. "He asked me to put it on hold. He'll know in the next day or two if he wants to buy it."

"Oh, he's shopping around, then."

"I think so. But it's a very rare *kaidan-dansu*; I don't think he'll find another. Come, let me show you."

I followed him into the back room, where the staircase chest Charles was interested in rose seven feet tall—all the way to the room's ceiling. Its seven steps were all fitted with beautiful small drawers; the metalwork handles were in the simple, rounded *warabite* style. I could tell at a glance that it was old, but how old was the question. Reproduction staircase *tansu* chests were plentiful, but I'd only seen one or two really old ones in my lifetime in Japan.

I stroked the dark, slightly rough finish and examined the wood grain.

"It looks like a very old lacquer finish. Is the wood cryptomeria?"

"It's cypress, but that is hard to discern because of the aged lacquer. Can you guess the period?" Mr. Ishida, generously, was giving me a second chance to redeem myself.

I bit my lip, considering. "I've never seen a two-part *tansu* this tall. That makes me think it really was functional. Early Meiji Period, maybe?"

"I think it's even older than that—Edo Period. It bears the style hallmarks of a famous cabinetmaker in Yonezawa."

I sighed. "Where in the world did you find it?"

"My little secret."

"Okay, can you tell me how much the chest is worth on the current market—just in case I am lucky enough to run across something similar?"

"I told Mr. Sharp that if he wants to pay in dollars, it would cost thirty thousand. Of course, I know that Americans like to bargain, so I set it at that point, expecting to drop ten percent. But don't tell him that, *neh*?"

"Of course I won't. But even twenty-seven thousand is quite high. Does it include shipping or something?"

"It's just my fee for the *tansu*. The cost of sea post will be several thousand dollars more. Mr. Sharp told me he liked the piece, but wanted to check a few more shops."

The fact that Charles, too, had balked at the price made me have a little more respect for the man. "He's bought *tansu* from you in the past, right?"

"Yes, he has, and he's always examined the pieces carefully. Why, I had to bring down the top section so he could look at the condition of all its sides. And he took every drawer out and examined them for nails and what-have-you."

"He wanted to make sure all the drawers were original," I said. "May I look, too?"

"Yes, please. If it will teach you something, I will be pleased."

I pulled out one of the drawers from the bottom step. Its inside was smooth and cleverly fitted, rather than nailed together. I slid the drawer back into place, and then looked at it. From the outside, it looked as if the drawer was bigger than it actually was. What was causing the illusion?

"Is this a false-bottom chest?" I asked.

"I doubt it. It's not usual for a staircase style," Mr. Ishida said.

"But look at this." I removed the drawer again in order to tap the bottom of the step's interior. It made a hollow sound. I tried another drawer higher up and heard the same thing.

"Ah, good work." Mr. Ishida, instead of being embarrassed at being caught out, seemed pleased. "Thanks to you, we have discovered that the chest is even more unique. I shall tell Mr. Sharp what you've found."

"Oh, don't tell him anything about me, please." But what I was thinking was: Charles must already know.

The *tansu* would be the perfect carrier for smaller goods that he wanted to hide. And traveling as sea freight, it wouldn't be subject to the high-tech scrutiny used for goods traveling by plane. Yes, Charles Sharp had eyeballed a *tansu* that could serve him handsomely. However, the fact remained that he hadn't bought it yet. Until that happened, I'd have to hold my suspicions in check.

25

I was home an hour later. It was twilight, and the light from inside my apartment cast a welcoming yellow glow out toward me. Still, I took a glance over my shoulder as I put the key in the lock.

Regardless of outside opinion, I liked the feeling of having Hugh in my home. When I opened the door, I was hit again with the reassuring knowledge he was there—a briefcase propped against the tea table, a coat discarded on a chair, and from behind the bathroom door, an aroma of mineral salts from Hakone and the sound of rushing water.

"May I join you?" I called, already beginning to unbutton my blouse as I knocked on the door with the other hand.

Hugh opened the door, surprising me; he was wet from the bath, but wearing a robe and shaving.

"You don't have to do that for me," I said. "I like your rough side, especially at night."

Hugh winked at me. "No time for that. I want you to come with me to a tea ceremony tonight. At Morita Incorporated."

"Things must have gone fabulously if they're inviting you to a tea party," I said.

"We'll be crashing it, actually. I convinced a friend from the British Consulate to give me his invitation."

"What in the world—"

"I think what we might gain in knowledge of the corporate culture is worth the risk of any embarrassment. By the way, do you have a kimono that's ready to go? I don't know if they have to be ironed or anything like that—"

"No, they're just folded. But, Hugh, it's a tremendous amount of trouble to put one on. At least half an hour—"

"I'll help you, then." Hugh put down his razor and swept out of the room to get dressed in the suit and fresh shirt lying on my futon. He began pulling on his clothes, and kept talking.

"So, today was relatively calm. Charles didn't ask me anything about my request to San Francisco for the transcript and tape. That probably means that his paralegal didn't bother to tell him."

"Let's hope so," I said. "What happened with the job offer?"

"Well, just for the fun of it, I asked Charles to elaborate on the terms. I shudder to tell you how good the money is."

"How good?" I was bent over, putting on the tight silk socks that were the prelude to kimono dressing.

Hugh gave a quick laugh. "He offered me two hundred fifty thousand base, with bonuses tied to the success of the lawsuit. The COLA package per year—just our food and housing expenses, imagine—would be another four hundred thousand, if we live in Japan. And we'll both get business-class tickets to travel home to visit relatives each year. There's a children's private school tuition benefit as well, which wouldn't apply to us at this point, but maybe later—"

"You're not thinking of taking it. Are you?"

"Of course I won't, Rei. As I told you yesterday evening, I don't trust the fellow. Even if I were tempted, I couldn't go because I haven't been at Andrews and Cheyne for more than a year. If I left, I'd look like a promiscuous job hopper." Hugh sighed heavily. "But I kept him talking, because I want to know why he wants me so badly, all of a sudden. Since I've come on board, all they've had are major setbacks. The only thing I haven't bollixed up was the meeting with Morita today."

"Yes, tell me about that."

"I will, once you start dressing—we're running out of time. Where's the kimono you're planning to wear?"

So Hugh was dead set on my dressing up. I sighed and went to the small Sendai *tansu* in the corner of my bedroom.

"This is the most appropriate one I have," I said, pulling out a neatly folded rectangle of purple silk. It had been woven just before the war, I knew from the dyes used and the loopy floral styling of the robe. I thought the kimono would be perfect for the New Year because it was patterned with pine, bamboo, and plum, the New Year's trinity. There was a subtle stain on the side that I'd have to camouflage by stuffing that section into the obi sash. Ah, the obi. That would be harder to find, as I didn't have the original one meant to be worn with this kimono. I dug around in another drawer and came up with nothing. Then I remembered I'd hung a sash on the wall of my living-dining room, one patterned in red and gold chevrons with some green pine motifs embroidered throughout. It was not a perfect match, but a good enough one.

I slipped on a simple pink underrobe. When it came time to tie its belt, Hugh helped me with one of his crazy sailing knots. As tight as he made it, I knew it wouldn't come loose. And the fact was, I liked the feeling of his hands sliding against my skin, even though we were going out and it would be hours before he could untie the belt.

"Morita is based in Kawasaki, so we hired a car and rode out together," Hugh said, seemingly oblivious to how much I was enjoying being dressed by him. "During the trip, Charles prepped me on what he wanted to accomplish. It was agreed that I'd do most of the talking."

"Why you?" I didn't mean to sound rude, but I was startled. Charles had acted like Hugh's boss every time I'd seen him.

"Yes, that was a surprise to me, too," Hugh said ruefully. "But I think Charles was right. He wanted to create an impression of power—that he was so important he didn't have to speak, except to make decisions at the end."

"I see. I've seen that done in Japanese business settings."

"Right, and it certainly was the modus operandi when we got there. Gorgeous skyscraper building, by the way—but you'll see it tonight. The boardroom was quite dark—a bottle-green color, with a black table that must have been twenty feet long. There was a little doily with a glass marking each place. When we went in, I counted them up right away and realized there were fifteen of them and only three of us. It was interesting, psychologically—it created the sense that we were supplicants."

"I'm sorry," I said, reaching out to caress his face.

"It was quite intense. Turn around, I'm still trying to tuck the robe so it's level." I turned, and Hugh continued. "We had to wait for them—another clever move—and then they all came in. Business cards were exchanged. I was made aware that their most senior official in the room was the vice president for legal affairs."

I raised my eyebrows. "So they were taking you seriously."

"Yes. They had an interpreter, too, of course. He offered us greetings and good wishes right away, pointing out the longtime friendship between Morita Incorporated and the United States—they claim to be responsible for the employment of five thousand people in the U.S. Around the room, they had framed photographs of various magic moments, such as the many times their company presidents met various American presidents. I had a sense that we should have brought our own picture album, but what could it have shown—all of us together with your parents at Christmas, or perhaps you and I, frolicking together in the surf in Thailand a few years past?"

"What you could have shown would have been photos of the Morita Mine survivors," I said severely. "Rosa, who looked so beaten-down and awful, and poor Ramon, with his eyes sewn shut."

"But we have to protect their identities, remember?" Hugh said. "I got to the point. I started off just talking about the basis of the lawsuit we're working on, and they listened quietly. Then the vice president said, in the most sympathetic voice imaginable, that our firm is surely doing an honorable thing, but it has nothing to do with Morita—that the company never had mines in the Philippines. I then handed over some photocopies of old legal documents proving otherwise, and someone else at the table spoke up. They couldn't disagree that the documents were their own, but they stressed that after the war the company was reorganized, with new management and goals."

"Complete denial." Well, I wasn't terribly surprised.

"After that, I dropped the bombshell about our concern—and the police's—about the murder and the attempted murder of our plaintiffs. Either they really didn't know about it, or they knew too much. There was so much sweat in the room, Rei, that the walls were practically dripping. And this is in January, not the rainy season."

"Ha-ha," I said, not laughing. "Actually, you might have gone too far, if you embarrassed them that much."

"They said they'd call to schedule another meeting. At their managing director's convenience."

"This could go back and forth a long time. But time is what you need." I was fully dressed now, and searching for a wrap.

"I suppose so. Unless, of course, the time we waste results in the deaths of more plaintiffs."

I stopped. "Do you really think they're involved?"

"They have a very strong motive to want to suppress the truth about their past. But if they've hired someone to kill plaintiffs, they'll almost certainly be found out somewhere along the line. And I don't think they're stupid enough to commit corporate suicide."

We walked out, headed toward the train station, my *zori* sandals making quiet clapping sounds against the pavement. It was an age-old sound that I loved. Suddenly, I felt as if I had gone back in time—the combination of kimono and shoes forced me into a slower, mincing gait. Hugh had gotten a half-block ahead of me before he realized I couldn't keep up.

"Sorry." He walked back to me. "I've been running on too long. I imagine that you have things to tell me."

So, I told him about everything, except my trip to the Imperial Hotel. I spent the most time on Ramon Espinosa's situation, because I thought Hugh could help with the power of attorney document. Hugh explained that due to his situation of being a foreign lawyer, he couldn't write a legally binding document. And it would be better for a Japanese lawyer to write a contract binding Japanese people, he thought. He gave me the name of Mr. Harada, a local lawyer he'd known for years.

"Good, I'll follow up on that tomorrow," I said. "I also have your cell phone back from Chika. After I saw her, I visited Mr. Ishida. He showed me the *tansu* Charles is contemplating buying. It's an early-nineteenth-century, seven-foot-high staircase chest."

"Sounds nice. Must be obscenely expensive, though."

"Thirty thousand dollars. The lacquer is original, which is quite extraordinary, and it has another interesting feature, too: false bottoms underneath each step."

"Really. Enough room to store a few ingots?"

"A few. But if there's really a treasure-load of gold somewhere, the *tansu* wouldn't have enough room."

"He might just want it for the sake of collection," Hugh said.

"Maybe. I heard he's still shopping around. Maybe he's going to buy multiple *tansu* chests with fake bottoms for storage purposes." I changed the topic. "By the way, will Charles and Eric be meeting us tonight?"

"No, ah, I actually didn't mention what we were going to do tonight. Charles had already told me that he's busy with some appointments at antiques shops, and Eric will go with him to translate."

I stopped and looked at Hugh. "That's a close relationship. Have you considered that they might be partnering in a hunt for gold?"

"I suppose it could be," Hugh said. "It would go against all the ethics that lawyers are supposed to abide by . . ."

I snorted. "The average American would argue that dropping all ethics in pursuit of gold is *typical* conduct for a lawyer. The question is, Who would be holding the reins? I'd guess Charles, even though Eric might have been the one who came through with the information about where the gold lies."

"Well, the culprit, if there is one, will become clear once the transcriptions arrive from San Francisco. But tonight, we have Morita Incorporated to investigate. I'm eager to get your impression."

"How so? What do you want me to help you accomplish at the party?" I gestured toward my brilliantly colored kimono. Dressed like this, there was no chance of being a wallflower.

"I thought you might introduce yourself. Make the rounds, as I'll be doing."

"Whom shall I say I am?" I mused. "Your fiancée? The prodigal daughter of an old Imperialist family? A struggling antiques dealer? None of it is particularly impressive."

"Don't be so hard on yourself. But might I suggest that your past life as a part-time journo might serve nicely, especially since you're currently writing an article about Japanese history."

"But that's just a family history project!"

"How will they know? And if it's good enough, maybe you'll publish it somewhere."

"Hmm. I suppose I could hint that I'm delving into the history of wartime Japan. That might be enough to do the trick."

The train came barreling in, so I wasn't able to meditate on whether this was the kind of white lie that was appropriate under Buddhist law, or something else altogether.

26

As Hugh had said, Morita's corporate headquarters were not in Tokyo, but Kawasaki—the more industrial city just to Tokyo's south. It made sense because of the electronic goods that Morita made; but it also raised my hackles some.

"Kawasaki. That's where you were steered by the phantom phone caller on the day you arrived in Japan," I said as we rode in a taxi toward the address Hugh had on the invitation card he'd borrowed from his friend.

"Right. But that call was from an American woman," Hugh pointed out.

"It could have been an American woman who works for Morita. Lots of Americans work for Japanese companies. We both did."

The taxi slowed and finally stopped in front of a tall, mirrored skyscraper. I hadn't known buildings in Kawasaki could be as big as Tokyo's—that was my chauvinism at work. But this one, a perfect I. M. Pei design or imitation, was just as big and stylish as anything I'd seen in Tokyo's Minato-ku district: a glittering, inky pillar at night, though it must have been a dazzling silver earlier in the day. At present, it looked sinister and elegant—just the kind of place that made me feel as if I would trip in my zori going through the door.

There was a greeter at the door, a dour-faced man in a black suit, who looked us over and finally nodded. I tried to pretend that we had been invited, and had the right to stand in the huge golden foyer filled with abstract art on the walls and a stunning, fifteen-foot arrangement of pine, bamboo, and plum in the center of everything. I walked forward a few paces to see the sign next to it, and blanched. The arrangement had been designed by Takeo Kayama, a past boyfriend who was the new headmaster of the Kayama School.

I hoped that we wouldn't see Takeo here. That would be all the stress I needed, on top of what I already felt. I kept my gaze down as we slowly snaked toward a door at the back of the lobby, from behind which I could hear strains of *koto* music. This was the tea ceremony room, I guessed.

The line of guests, who were overwhelmingly Japanese, moved at a slow pace toward the room. Practically everyone was silent, reminding me of the atmosphere on the subway in the morning. Here we were, a mass of people being moved at a deliberately slow pace, ostensibly to relax and renew with a cup of tea.

A few minutes later we were at the entrance to the tea ceremony room. I could see it behind a handsome room with birch cases designed to hold shoes: a huge room featuring green walls flecked with gold and spotless *tatami* mat flooring edged in orange-and-green brocade. People had seated themselves, husbands next to wives, in a proper kneeling position in an exact square. In the center of the room five women wearing simple yet expensive kimonos moved like slow butterflies to each of the waiting sitters. The women's steps were slow and deliberate; each was carrying a small earthenware teacup. The tea ceremony hostesses sank to their knees and each offered a cup to a guest, smiling and bowing almost to the floor. The guests bowed back with considerable ceremony and made a gesture of showing the cup to the person on their left, who reacted admiringly. Then the cup was picked up, rotated, and sipped.

"What are they doing?" Hugh whispered.

"Turn the cup three times counterclockwise, then drink it in a few sips. It's going to be bitter. But don't worry—they're giving everyone a sweet cookie to eat first."

"It's like taking Communion," Hugh said, sounding more confi-dent.

He was right. Tea ceremony was a form of a purification ritual; originally Buddhist priests had made the tea, not ladies who stud-ied it as an art. I looked at the women, wondering who they were—no doubt longtime devotees of a tea school, perhaps many of them Morita wives. It would have seemed more natural for me to chat with the women than the men, but I guessed that their hus-bands kept all their business dealings from them; I probably wouldn't learn much.

"You are English?" a voice came suddenly from behind.

Hugh and I turned as one to look at a Japanese man, close to him in height, with a hawkish nose and thick, straight black hair mixed with gray. The man, who looked somewhere in his fifties, was wearing a good-quality black wool suit. Now I understood that this was the proper men's color for the event. Hugh had worn a wool-and-silk blended suit the color of *macha*—the thick, sludgy green tea that we would soon be drinking. I'd thought he looked very handsome an hour ago, but now I saw that he stuck out like a green thumb.

"Not quite," Hugh said, looking at the man and smiling. "I'm from Scotland. My name is Hugh Glendinning. "

"I apologize for the error," the man replied, inclining his head slightly.

"Sir. You are?" Hugh's voice was confident, but I felt suddenly weak and embarrassed. It was too blunt to demand a person's name like that.

"Hamazaki," the man said, wrinkling the intense nose as he spoke.

"Oh, you are the managing director!" Hugh said, with a half-smile. I recovered from my embarrassment.

"Ah, yes." Mr. Hamazaki stared in obvious surprise at Hugh. "But we don't know each other."

"We have a meeting scheduled. I represent an American law firm."

There was a sudden stillness in the line around us. I imagined that everyone was wondering what the business was about.

"I'm Rei Shimura," I said, to break the silence. "Hugh's—uh—friend."

"Rei, my wife to be, is a journalist who has written for a magazine—the *Gaijin Times*. I'm very proud of her for all those exposés—"

"Enough," I said, blushing as I thought of the how-to pieces I'd written on fixing up antique furniture. "I'm currently working on a project on Japanese history."

Mr. Hamazaki's nostrils flared again. "Well, the invitation here is for you to enjoy tea, not to do business. That is, if you actually received an invitation?"

"The invitation was in fact passed on to me by a friend at the British Embassy who had to send his regrets."

"*Ah so desu ka*. Have you ever experienced a Japanese tea ceremony?" Mr. Hamazaki's innocuous question seemed to be a detour from the tension—but I felt an undercurrent of mockery in it.

"No, but I'm looking forward to it." Hugh shot a glance at me, obviously seeking some kind of interruption.

"I have done it many times. My aunt is a member of the Urasenke Tea Society." It was true, though I had never taken the time to study.

"Very good. I hope you will find our tea adequate—and congratulations on your upcoming nuptials. It looks as if it's time for you to go in. Please enjoy."

He was gone, and we were pushed into the tea ceremony room before either of us had a chance to catch our breath.

"That went brilliantly," Hugh muttered in my ear as we kneeled down in a line amidst the others.

"You've got to be joking," I said, shaking my head as I watched Mr. Hamazaki move through the room, giving tight half-bows to various guests.

"He knows we're not here to play. That's what I wanted."

"Shh, others can understand," I mouthed at him. I was watching one of the tea ceremony servers, a woman my aunt's age in a beautiful green kimono decorated with a design of tall grasses. It seemed as if Mr. Hamazaki was indicating Hugh and me to her with a slight hand movement, because she glanced at us, then back at him.

"Did you learn from your friend at the embassy who the ladies serving the tea are?" I whispered as the woman in green went to the room's altar and poured hot water from a kettle sitting on an ancient brazier into a bowl.

"No, I didn't. But I'm sure they're too old to be Morita office ladies."

I thought some more. "They must be members of a tea society to be doing this, but I imagine some of the society members are also Morita corporate wives. Tea ceremony is a valued skill among upper-middle-class wives."

"Really? Are you telling me what you're going to spend the next ten years doing?"

I would have kicked him, but we were being ushered by another woman to step onto the *tatami* square, where tea was being served. I watched the woman in green tap tea powder into the bowl and mix it into a froth. Actually, she was too far away for me to see exactly what she was doing, but I'd been to enough tea ceremonies to know the ritual. Her role was to start the ceremony by bringing a cup to the highest-ranking person seated on the tatami. If Mr. Hamazaki had been seated, it would have gone to him; but since he had vanished back into the waiting crowd, the highest-ranking person would be someone else.

I bit my lip when the woman in green brought a tray with two cups on it to Hugh and me. In a fluid movement, she kneeled down, placed the tray on the tatami, and bowed her head.

Hugh bowed in return—too slightly, in my opinion, but he was a real novice. He took the cup, but didn't sip, just looked at me. Great. He was expecting me to go first.

The woman in green then placed a cup before me. I made a big show of bowing lower than Hugh, and then turned the cup three times in my hands. As I turned, I looked into the pea green depths and inhaled the aroma. Then I stopped.

I'd caught a glimpse of something white rearing itself from under the foam. White. What in the world was something white doing in a cup of green tea? I turned the cup again, and I didn't see it anymore. Either it had dissolved or I'd been seeing things.

I brought the cup to my nose and sniffed the aroma again. It didn't smell like the type of tea I'd had at the Urasenke Society. Perhaps the blend was different.

I began to sweat under the kimono, and glanced nervously at Hugh. He hadn't drunk his tea either, but was watching me for guidance.

I shook my head at him.

"What?" he whispered.

"Don't," I mouthed, and shook my head again. I avoided saying that I was scared because I realized that Mr. Hamazaki might have given instructions to the woman standing right before our eyes. Did potassium chloride have a color? I knew it was supposed to be quite salty—would the natural bitterness of green tea mask it?

"What's wrong?" Hugh asked, his eyes boring into me.

Unable to answer without being overheard, I placed my teacup down on the *tatami* mat in front of me. After a second's hesitation, Hugh followed my lead. By now, the two people to our right had been served; they drank their tea without delay. The tea service went on, almost interminably; at every moment, I was aware of the full cup before me, and the apparent strangeness of my action.

The women came around again and took the cups from everyone; at us, they paused, as if they thought we were waiting to drink.

"Please," the woman whispered. The command she'd used was one of hospitality, but it sounded desperate. *Please drink.* Was it because she wanted to save the ceremony, or because Mr. Hamazaki had told her to make certain we drained our cups?

"Allergies," I said quietly in Japanese. "So sorry. My fiancé and I both suffer."

"Oh, I am sorry." She added our cups to her tray.

Everyone was looking at us. My face burned, and I realized that in all my years in Japan, this was the most heinous etiquette violation I'd ever committed. Not to take tea with the others—not to follow the ritual—and then to come up with such an unbelievably lame excuse . . . oh, it was too embarrassing. Aunt Norie had been worried about Hugh embarrassing the family, but I'd done the job entirely on my own.

We hit the street five minutes later. It wasn't that we'd been thrown out of Morita headquarters, but it was clear that nobody wanted to talk to us after the tea-drinking debacle. We'd become larger than life—the foreigner who had been blunt with the company president, and his Japanese-American mistress. I knew that's what people thought, because I caught whispers of it behind my back.

"So what was in the tea?" Hugh asked as he raised a halfhearted arm to flag down a taxi. They were all passing us by, and it had started to rain. I pulled the light kimono coat over me, hoping that neither it nor my vintage robe would be ruined.

"I thought I saw something white in it. It could have been nothing but foam, but with the poisonings of Rosa and Ramon, I felt I just couldn't drink. And I didn't want you to risk drinking it, either."

"But Ramon wasn't poisoned," Hugh said.

"Oh, will we ever know?" I paused, trying to fight back tears. "I'm sorry. Probably there was nothing in the tea, but I just had an ominous feeling."

"Better safe than sorry, I guess."

"But it's so embarrassing! Do you know what I overheard someone calling us? The bizarre foreigner and the *nisei* whore who thinks she's too good to drink Japanese tea."

Hugh laughed. "And I thought this event was all about manners. Well, live and learn. And I'm hungry—how about you? Why don't we get supper somewhere?"

"Whatever. But I can't believe you can think of food at a time like this," I said as we headed back to Kawasaki Station.

"Just because I'm sensible enough to want supper doesn't mean I'm not concerned. Hey, I was attempting to launch a powerful image that's been sadly deflated. Now they'll all think the negotiator from the U.S. is too squeamish to even drink tea."

"But at least you're still alive," I said. "Think about it that way."

"All right," Hugh said softly. "I will."

Sleep. It was what I really wanted, after the long trip back from Kawasaki. Hugh had brought take-out Chinese food from the train station, and while it had tasted good at first, I'd gotten kicked in the stomach by its high MSG count. I had Hugh unwrap me as quickly as possible from the constrictive bindings of the kimono, and then I lay down on my futon, knees curled to my chest. I sank into an exhausted slumber just after midnight, but then the telephone shrilled.

"Take it, Mr. Energy," I muttered to Hugh, who was still reading by torchlight on the other side of the futon.

"It's for you," he said, not moving.

The phone trilled again.

"The phone's closer to you," I pointed out.

"Darling, every time I pick up the phone and answer, people ring off. It happened earlier today three times. Go ahead, give it your best." Hugh grabbed the receiver, pressed "On," and put it to the side of my head.

"*Moshi-moshi,*" I muttered.

"*Moshi-moshi,* this is Okada . . ." On the other end was a woman's voice, sounding tentative. But I'd woken up fully. Okada was Manami's family name. Maybe her parents had called me back about her whereabouts. Although the timing was inconvenient, I was glad I'd have the chance to learn what happened to my parents' missing houseguest.

"Yes, thank you for calling!" I said in a bright voice. "Is it about Manami-san?"

"Yes. I mean, I *am* Manami Okada. I hope to speak with Shimada-san?"

"This is Shimada," I said, sitting upright and shooting Hugh a significant glance. Her father had passed along my messsage—and my fictitious name—to her. Manami's voice sounded just the same as always, but I couldn't be myself; I'd have to playact a bit to get the information I needed. "Okada-san, where are you calling from?"

"From America," Manami said. "However, I'm very eager to return to Japan."

"I understand," I said, not believing her for a minute. She'd probably been in Kobe for a while, but was putting on a proper face with me, to show she wasn't a quitter.

"As you must have heard, I was taking advanced studies in

pathology in the United States. I would prefer to finish my course of study in Japan, as I will practice here someday."

"Was there something that didn't please you with the program in San Francisco?" I asked, playing the interviewer.

"Well, the pathology department at the University of California at San Francisco is excellent, but culturally, the city and people are not so nice. I heard people say that one never really understands what it is to be Japanese until one has been on the outside, living with foreigners."

This was the girl I'd thought was my only real Japanese friend in America. I swallowed my hurt and asked, "And how are the foreigners? Can you describe them?"

"Well, my host family tried to be kind, but they were just so . . . strange. It was a half-and-half family, to be honest. Their manners were different than ours. You wouldn't believe the behavior of their daughter, too—so wild, with this foreign boyfriend, right in her parents' house! I guess it's the custom with American girls. Let me assure you that I am not like that; I am a regular Japanese and a hard worker. I am ready to work hard at any hospital. I didn't catch the name of the hospital you represent, by the way?"

I had moved from embarrassment to rage. "The hospital of the sick and disillusioned."

"What place is that?" Manami asked, sounding innocent.

"It's a hospital where people go who've learned the hard way about opening their hearts and homes to strangers. Think about the efforts your host family made to include you in holidays, to feed you, to comfort you when you were sad! And that badly behaved daughter, who tried to teach you English slang because she thought you were genuinely interested—"

A gasp. "You—you aren't—"

"I'm not a Shimada, I'm a Shimura." I said it with anger and pride. "My name is Rei Shimura. My mother, the one who made lunches for you, is Catherine. And my father—you know him as Kenji—is on the verge of going to the San Francisco police about you! He knew you were troubled all along, but you're so much worse than I thought."

"Rei-san, I'm sorry. I didn't intend to—"

"You say the words, but you don't mean them. It's all lies."

I heard Manami gasp. Then she spoke in a voice that was in an entirely different register. "You shouldn't have played a trick to get me to call you. It isn't right."

"It's not Japanese manners, is it?" I was still on my rampage. "Well, excuse me. And one last thing: I don't expect you to do this, but what you really should do is go back and face up to what you did. Tell people the truth. For once."

I was sick of Manami. I clicked the receiver and threw it down on the quilt.

There was a moment of silence. Then Hugh spoke.

"I don't need to ask who your caller was, but as for your reaction, darling . . . maybe you were too frank—"

"Well, it's too late now." I groped around the quilt to recover the telephone receiver. I wanted to see if the Caller ID function would show me if Manami was in Japan or the United States. The phone she had used, however, couldn't easily be tracked; NO DATA SENT was the message that appeared in the window when I clicked back. I had no idea where she'd called from. But I was mad enough that I still wanted to talk to my father, and I dialed overseas to my home number.

The telephone rang endlessly. One of my parents was probably online. I decided to try again the next day. I was tired and cranky and needed sleep.

"Will it bother you if I stay up a while longer?" Hugh asked, tucking the covers around me.

"No. What are you doing, work on the class action?"

"Actually, I'm reading your great-grandfather's book. Tom sent more pages."

As I drifted off, I reflected that reading that book was supposed to be my job, not Hugh's.

It seemed like only a few hours later that sunlight was streaming into my eyes. I felt the space next to me on the futon, and it was empty. At 6 A.M., I still craved sleep; but since Hugh was up, I wanted to know what he was working on.

I pulled on a hip-length wool sweater over my Japanese long underwear, since I was now back in the land of no central heating, and opened the door.

Hugh was hunched over the tea table, still reading. "Guess who came to the door about half an hour ago? The courier. I've got my documents from San Francisco."

"Great," I said, settling myself next to him. "So what are the answers to the questions?"

"No answers, really. The paralegal sent a transcript, but no actual tape from the interview that Eric and I did. She included a note saying that she's trying to locate the tape and will send it on when it's recovered. But I bet it's gone for good, don't you?"

"Probably. What does Eric's transcript say, though?" I sunk my head onto his shoulder.

"Well, I've read it through a few times and haven't noticed any mention of ingots or gold or tunnels. The most significant things recorded are Rosa's memories of abuse, and her claim that she saw Japanese officers order soldiers to bury some of the Asian laborers alive. That's stuff he translated for me, verbatim, during the interview, so I have a feeling it was spontaneous and true."

"I agree. She brought up the burial again when I visited her." I shuddered at the memory. "About the gold, though—we can't be sure. The tape we have is quite hard to understand. We didn't come up with the theory until we listened to it many times. We might be wrong."

Hugh pulled away and looked at me. "I'm not about to order an excavation of the Philippine jungle, you know. I never said the gold was a sure thing."

"But you'd like it to be. If it turns out that Eric and Charles have dirty dealings, they could be ousted from being part of the class action, couldn't they? You could be a hero at Andrews and Cheyne."

Hugh snorted. "It wouldn't be quite as easy as that. And let me remind you that I want them to be good guys, and I'm only interested in justice, not personal gain."

"Oh, isn't that noble." I yawned and rubbed my eyes. "What's your plan at work today?"

"Hang on, Rei, you just insulted me!" Hugh's voice rose. "I don't think you even hear yourself anymore. The way you spoke to Manami on the phone last night, and this morning you're blithely accusing me of sinister machinations—"

"Don't say any more. You're right. I'm sorry." He *was* right, of course. I'd lost it when I had spoken with Manami last night, and my words today were less heated, but just as offensive. "I don't know what's happening to me."

"It's a difficult time." Hugh smoothed my hair. "Ideally, all you'd have to worry about right now is compiling your family history. But so much . . . trauma has filtered out of my work into your life. I've never shared as much with you before, and now I'm starting to think it was a mistake."

I glared at him. "I like knowing what's going on with you. I couldn't be married to you and not know."

"Well, whatever you know, it's got to be kept quietly between us from this point on. If Charles and Eric got wind of what I'm thinking, it would be curtains for me."

I thought guiltily about the keycards I'd cadged to Charles's and Eric's hotel rooms. Hugh would flip if he knew that I had them, and was still planning a covert inspection.

"So what is your work schedule today?" I could have asked, *When will all of you be out of the hotel?*

"Well, I'll be hunkered down in the conference room most of the day. But you could talk me into a half-hour lunch break. The weather's supposed to be good today—how about meeting in Hibiya Park?"

Instead of answering, I hedged. "What about Eric and Charles? Are they going to be in the office all day?"

"It's not a real office, it's just a rented room in the hotel. And I have no idea of their plans. Why do you ask?"

Instead of telling him that I wanted to get in their rooms, I said, "Well, it will be awfully hard for you to figure out what they're up to if they're breathing over your shoulder."

"Rei, I don't think you realize I actually have work to do. I've got to figure out the next move with Morita and, at the same time, gather names of more potential plaintiffs. As much as I'd like to figure things out about Eric and Charles, at the moment I simply don't have the time."

But I do, I said silently to myself. Out loud, I told Hugh I'd meet him for lunch at twelve-thirty.

27

As soon as Hugh was gone, I started making phone calls. The first was to Mr. Ishida, because I knew he was an early riser.

"What became of the staircase chest?" I asked after we'd exchanged morning greetings. "Did Charles Sharp decide to take it?"

"I haven't heard anything from him. Why, do you have a client who is interested?"

"I don't. I was just curious."

"Well, since you are socializing with Mr. Sharp, why don't you ask him his intentions?" Mr. Ishida asked.

"Um, I'd rather not. Mr. Sharp knows I know you, but he doesn't know that I have any knowledge he was considering that *tansu*. I'd rather keep that quiet, for Hugh's sake—Hugh feels I've been getting too much into company business."

"My, what modest, wifely behavior," Mr. Ishida said.

"Do you approve?" I smiled, knowing he was teasing me.

"Well, I like the man you've chosen. But can you do this for me? I know he's here on business for a short while. If he leaves, please tell me so I can release the hold I've placed on the piece and can offer it to someone else."

I promised that I would do that, and hung up.

The next person on my list was Mr. Harada, the lawyer Hugh had recommended. I wanted to talk to him about the possible form a power of attorney agreement might take if the person in question was a hospital patient floating in and out of consciousness.

Mr. Harada told me the situation was quite complicated and I'd need an appointment. I made an excuse and decided to delay the appointment, thinking now that if money was involved up front, I'd better make sure the Moriuchis were even willing to be of help. I obtained their number from Tokyo information, and placed the call.

It was still early enough in the morning that Mrs. Moriuchi was making her son's boxed lunch, but she returned my call twenty minutes later, after he'd left the house for school. I filled her in on Ramon's brief comeback, and she was delighted.

When I brought up the power of attorney topic, though, she was less enthusiastic.

"Of course I want to help, but I don't want to take away the rights of his family. We spoke to the nephew, and he's quite concerned about his uncle. I'm sure he would be the best one to oversee the future," she said.

"Oh, so the nephew spoke to you on the telephone? I can't believe Dr. Nigawa gave you his number, but wouldn't share it with me!"

"We didn't speak on the phone. Actually, I met him outside the door of Espinosa-san's apartment yesterday evening. He wanted to go inside, but the door was locked. I got my spare key and let him in."

"Why did you do that?" Suddenly, my antenna was starting to rise.

"Why? I did it because I have a key to that apartment. As you know, we are like family with Mr. Espinosa."

"What's the nephew's name?" I interrupted.

"Espinosa. I didn't ask his first name."

Of course she hadn't, because according to Japanese etiquette, first-name use was rude. I sighed heavily. "Can you describe the nephew to me?"

"Well, he spoke Japanese very well—like a native, but of course, there was a little something in the rhythm that told me he was a foreigner."

"What about his looks?"

"Black hair, medium height. He wore eyeglasses and was casually dressed."

"How old is he?"

"Oh, I didn't ask a personal question like that, but he seemed to be in his twenties. Yes, almost certainly his twenties, because he didn't have a wedding ring. But late twenties, just like you. Oh, excuse me, I didn't mean to say something so personal to you—"

"Never mind," I said shortly. "That's an awfully young age to be the nephew of a man in his seventies. Don't you think?"

"I have no idea. You could ask him yourself! The next time he comes by I will give him your name and number."

"No!" I said a bit too loudly. "Please don't tell him where I live. We have no idea, really, if this is his true nephew. Why in the world did he want to search that apartment, with his uncle in the hospital? Did you watch what he did in there?"

"No, I let him go inside on his own. I wasn't sure what he needed, but I assumed he was bringing items of comfort such as clothing. When he left the apartment, he was carrying a small suitcase of goods, and he thanked me for the assistance. A very courteous young man, indeed."

"But—the nephew hasn't even gone to see his uncle at the hospital."

"He said he had—"

"The doctor told me yesterday afternoon that the nephew had telephoned, but had not yet flown to Japan. If you saw the nephew yesterday evening—" I paused. "Well, there's a small chance that he really did fly into Japan yesterday, and went immediately to the apartment building. It would make sense if that were the place where he planned to sleep. But he didn't sleep there."

Mrs. Moriuchi sucked in her breath. "Do you think—the young Mr. Espinosa is actually the Kanda Ward Attacker? Why would a young man attack his uncle like that?"

"I can't answer that yet," I said slowly. "But I think there's a good chance that the young man you met isn't related to Mr. Espinosa at all."

• • •

I made my next call to Kanda General Hospital. Dr. Nigawa was not available, nor was Nurse Tanaka. I spoke to a junior nurse who confirmed that no nephew had visited—though a call had come from him checking his uncle's condition.

"Did you tell the nephew that he'd regained consciousness?" I asked.

"Yes, but of course we explained it was fleeting. He seemed most excited about this, and had many questions to ask about the likelihood of his recovery, and his ability to communicate."

"I have something important to tell you," I said. "I think the person who will claim to be Espinosa-san's nephew is not really a relative at all. I think it could be dangerous for the patient if you let this young man in the patient's room."

"It's not up to me to decide. It's up to Dr. Nigawa—"

"Please have him call me right away. And in the meantime, why don't you check the identification of any visitors to Espinosa-san. And go with them when they visit the patient. Please, please don't leave Espinosa-san alone."

Hugh had his cell phone back with him, so that was the number I punched in next.

"Can I call you later?" he whispered. "We're in the middle of quite a lot of work—"

"Oh," I said. "Are you doing something with Charles?"

"Both of them. We're drafting some documents in English and Japanese."

"When do you think the three of you will break?"

"It could be a while. I doubt I can make a twelve-thirty lunch after all."

"Don't worry, I understand. I'll see you tonight." I clicked off and looked at my watch. It was only 9:15. If Hugh thought they'd be working past 12:30, I was probably quite safe. Quickly, I slipped into another wife uniform—a cool black Ultrasuede pantsuit that had been my mother's, worn with a cream silk blouse underneath and a pink-and-purple Hermes scarf knotted around the neck. I slapped on some makeup, blew-dry my hair, and searched around for a different department store shopping bag, settling on a compact model from Isetan. I slipped my wallet and the hotel room keycards inside the bag. My favorite pair of go-everywhere black high heels, and I was ready for the Imperial Hotel.

I rode the subway, wishing it moved as quickly as the ideas flitting through my head. I'd abandoned my earlier theory that the nephew was a Japanese person posing as a Filipino. My thoughts were focused on a man sitting in conference with Hugh a few miles away. Eric Gan.

I ran through what I knew. The first I'd heard from Eric, upon my return to Japan, was on January 2. I'd assumed he'd been calling from San Francisco, because that's what the Caller ID on my telephone receiver said. But Hugh had pointed out it had been his cell phone, which meant Eric could have been in Tokyo on January 2. And on January 1, the day Ramon was attacked.

And of course, Eric had been in San Francisco when we had—when Rosa was killed. He knew where she lived. He also knew how to get into my house, which he'd probably searched. He knew what my mother's car looked like; for all I knew, he'd followed Hugh and me on Christmas afternoon and broken the window.

As I sat, consumed with these awful thoughts, the train moved methodically toward my destination. Traffic flowed on and off—businessmen, lady shoppers, armies of schoolchildren in uniforms. How I felt for the small kindergartners, clinging for balance to any seat handle or post, since they were too short to reach the hanging straps. It amazed me that Japanese parents trusted the world enough to allow such young children to travel on trains by themselves. But then again, Mrs. Moriuchi had let a strange foreign man she didn't know into Ramon Espinosa's apartment. And she'd trusted me—another strange foreigner—with all this information.

Hibiya Station was next. I stood up, offering my seat with a smile to one of the small children. She shook her head and shyly turned away. She was choosing to stand, taking the hard way. Just as I was about to myself.

● ● ●

Inside the Imperial Hotel, past the fancy red Frank Lloyd Wright lounge, up the elevator to the tenth floor. Nobody gave me a second glance. The maids weren't around yet, but that's what I was counting on, remembering that they had arrived at noon the other day.

Both Charles's and Eric's rooms were vacant; I made sure by knocking on both before I took out the keycards. The first one I opened was 1014, Charles's room.

I closed the door behind me and stood for a minute, taking everything in. The Imperial had rather plain rooms, considering their cost, but at least there was a breathtaking view of the rolling green topography of the Imperial Palace grounds. I turned from the view to examine the room. The sheets on the queen-sized bed were tossed back. Charles had left a 100-yen coin on the pillow— the correct Japanese method for tipping the maid.

A "Message waiting" light was blinking on the telephone next to the bed. I picked up the receiver and pressed the button that gave me access. Charles had two messages. The first was from a well-known *tansu* dealer in Roppongi, an elegant American man I knew slightly. He had called to confirm an appointment that evening to show several *tansu* to Charles. He left a phone number, but I didn't record it, because I knew the shop well. The next speaker also left a message in English, but with a heavy accent. He identified himself as Mr. Murano, and asked that Charles supply him with his home telephone number. Mr. Murano recited his own telephone number and extension, which I jotted down on the notepad next to the bed, taking care to place both the message and the sheet of paper underneath, which might bear evidence of my scribbling, in my pocket.

After listening to the messages, I didn't feel that I had very much to worry about with Charles. Still, I hadn't given his room a good check. His Hermès suitcase, standing in the closet, had been completely emptied: all his suits were hanging in the closet, his shirts and underwear were folded in the room's chest of drawers. There didn't seem to be much else besides toiletries, though. I realized that he probably had all documents relating to the class action downstairs in the office space he'd rented.

About the only thing present in the room that gave me any idea of Charles's character was a neat stack of antiques catalogs and magazines. I flipped open one of the Japanese catalogs. He'd marked ads for two *tansu* sold at different shops around the city.

Charles seemed to really be in town to shop. And what he was looking for, to judge from all the Post-it notes in the different periodicals, was Edo Period wooden furniture. I was beginning to believe that Charles wasn't interested in false-bottomed furniture as much as he was interested in acquiring a very rare and old piece.

I shook myself. What was I doing spending so long looking at Charles's antiques dreams? He appeared to have no dirty laundry, the small pile of worn clothes in a plastic bag notwithstanding.

It was time to move on to Eric's room. There was still a Do Not Disturb sign hanging on the knob, which I'd noticed earlier. I knocked and, hearing nothing, slid the keycard in.

Eric's quarters were significantly smaller than Charles's, but they still offered a Palace view. The room was neat as a pin—the bed was made, the bathroom orderly. No wonder he'd hung that sign out: He didn't want anyone messing with his things. A prickle of anticipation went up my back. Eric probably had something to hide.

My first step was opening up his bedside table drawer. Nothing there. His telephone had no messages waiting either. Perhaps he had erased any messages he had. Or, I thought suddenly, he might prefer to use his cell phone.

I poked around the drawers of the room's desk and bureau, looking for the cell phone. I couldn't find it. He probably had it with him in the conference room, I figured. I examined all the T-shirts and underwear folded in his drawer, and the slacks and polo shirts and jackets hung in the closet. Looking at the clothes, I felt a pang at seeing all the middle-range American brand names—Gap and Macy's and Dockers and Joseph Bank. It had been so long since I'd dated an American man, I'd practically forgotten what they wore. Charles and Hugh wore European brands; Eric didn't. On his translator's salary, he clothed himself in comfortable, modest clothing, the kind of brands I would have worn if

I didn't have such a super supply of vintage designer clothes from my mother.

Eric had two suitcases stacked on each other in his closet: a medium-sized Samsonite and then a smaller, zippered brown tweed case. I went for the Samsonite first. Inside, there was something that looked like a folded-up telescope. I decided not to bother opening it, since the likelihood was I wouldn't be able to put it back together the same way. I hastened on to the rest of the suitcase's contents. An umbrella, also folded up, plus a Japanese language map of Tokyo and several English language maps of the Philippines.

I spent ten minutes looking over the maps, but didn't see anything circled or underlined that might indicate he was hunting for gold. I spent even more time carefully sorting through a manila folder that was stuffed with papers. They were legal documents, many of them on Sharp, Witter and Rowe letterhead. I recognized them because of their length, and because I'd seen Hugh reading things that looked just like them. I paged through them carefully, trying to avoid messing things up. Here was Rosa's testimony, reading just as Hugh had described it to me the other day. There was also a list of people's names, birth dates, and addresses in Japan, China, and the Philippines. More plaintiffs, I guessed, looking at the birth dates. Maybe it was normal for Eric to have this information; I would have to ask Hugh.

I was really most interested in finding the missing cassette tape that Hugh had talked about. Very carefully, I felt around the edges of the suitcase. Nothing.

I glanced at my watch. It was noon already. The maids were probably coming soon, and I hadn't found anything significant.

I opened the second case. It was sadly empty. The suitcase had an interesting odor, though. I sniffed, meditated, and then I knew.

It smelled like Ramon Espinosa's apartment. And of course, Mrs. Moriuchi had said that the nephew who had visited Ramon's empty apartment had left with one of his suitcases. But there were no goods inside the case to prove anything. He must have hidden them somewhere else, or even disposed of them. The problem was, I didn't know what I supposed to be looking for.

I heard the sound of soft female voices in the hallway. The maids. I knew I couldn't linger much longer, but I'd gone through the whole room anyway. I zipped up the tweed suitcase and replaced it atop the Samsonite so it looked just the way I'd found it. I was closing the closet door and about to exit when the phone rang, making me jump. I knew then that I couldn't leave without hearing the message left by whoever had telephoned Eric. After ten rings, the phone was silent. A few seconds later, the "message waiting" light began blinking, just the way it had in Charles's room.

I picked up the telephone receiver and punched the code for voice mail.

"Eric, Hugh here calling from downstairs. Sorry to drag you back from your nap, but Charles wants to clarify some of the Japanese language you used for the last paragraph. Can you ring me right away? I think we can sort it out without your needing to come back."

If Hugh was calling Eric's room, and Eric had said he was going to take a midday nap, it meant that Eric was a minute or two from discovering me. I slammed down the phone, sending the eyeglasses placed next to it flying.

Glasses. I caught my breath and picked them up. Mrs. Moriuchi had described the nephew as having worn glasses. Eric had never worn them when we were kids. Maybe he wore contacts now; I had no idea.

I picked up the glasses and peered through them.

I squinted, and looked again. They were clear glass. These weren't glasses meant for reading or seeing at a distance. The only reason Eric would wear them would be to look like someone else.

I squeezed the pair of small glasses in my hand, thinking about whether I dared to take them with me to show Mrs. Moriuchi. Something Hugh had said to me about the law years ago came back to me: If I removed them, it would be a crime.

I put the glasses down, and saw that I'd held them so tightly that I'd smudged the lenses. I quickly pulled a tissue out of the box next to the bed and rubbed them clear. Then I set them down again and zoomed out of the room, not even bothering to listen for people in the hall. Fortunately, the maids turned out to be cleaning rooms—the only other company I had in the hall was a large cart heaped with dirty sheets.

Instead of going for the elevator, I went for the hall stairway. I'd escaped unnoticed. I wanted to celebrate, but the fact was I needed to call the police. I reached in my pocket for my wallet, but it wasn't there. I had the keycards to both rooms, and a MAC lipstick, but nothing else.

Then I remembered. I'd stashed my wallet in the Isetan shopping bag I'd brought with me. I'd left the shopping bag in Charles's room, right next to the bedside table when I'd picked up the phone to eavesdrop on his messages. And it contained my foreigner identity card, an expired California driver's license, and my at-the-limit Visa card.

How could I be so stupid? I mourned as I scurried back up the steps and peered into the hall. Nobody was there. I scurried to room 1014 and slapped the keycard in the door. My nervousness made me fumble, and it wasn't until my third attempt that I was able to get inside. I scanned Charles's room and saw the bag where I thought it would be.

The room wasn't terribly large—I fairly flew the twelve steps to the bag. But just as I grasped its handle in my palm, I heard the click.

The room's door was opening. I opened my eyes very wide and readied myself to pretend for the maids that I was Mrs. Charles Sharp. At least, I hoped it would be the maids, instead of Charles Sharp.

But it wasn't a couple of ladies at the door. There were two men instead: Charles and Hugh—both of them looking as stunned as I.

28

I opened my mouth, then closed it. At the moment, I couldn't think of anything I could say to alter the fact that I'd been caught smack in the middle of Charles's room. I stood there clutching my Isetan shopping bag to me like a life preserver.

But it couldn't protect me from Charles, whose face had gone from its normal pale color to a bright, angry pink.

Hugh spoke quickly, interrupting our frozen tableau.

"So, you made it in for lunch after all, darling! I guess the front desk people must have confused the room we're using as our office on the fourth floor with this one, which actually is for Charles's personal use."

What a perfect opener. Hugh, as always, had come through to save me. I was ready to continue the happy fable, but then Charles spoke.

"I don't believe that the hotel staff would have sent her to a private room—let alone given her a keycard like the one she's holding in her hand. After all, she isn't a guest."

"Actually, there's an explanation." I was ready to begin with the tale of what I'd found out about Eric and his disguise.

"Yes, I'm sure there's an explanation!" Hugh clapped his hands together and motioned for me to sit down at the chair next to the desk.

"I'd like to hear Rei speak for the record in front of some witnesses from hotel security," Charles said coldly.

"Is that really necessary? I'm sure we can work it out ourselves," Hugh said.

Charles laughed coldly. "Well, she's got a shopping bag there full of something that she might like to show them."

So he thought I'd come in the room to steal from him. How embarrassing. "It's just my wallet and some tissue paper," I said, spilling it out on the carpet. "See?"

But as I put on my show, Charles was dialing down to the front desk. He asked that the hotel's manager and its chief of security come to his room. When he hung up, he turned to Hugh. "I'm going to telephone for Eric to help us as well. We'll need to use his interpretation services so I can make sure I understand how to prosecute this devious young woman to the fullest extent of Japanese law."

"'Prosecute'?" Hugh repeated the word with horror in his voice. "But there's been no theft—"

"Not Eric," I interrupted. "Please, Mr. Sharp. Use any interpreter besides Eric. Eric's dirty. He's the one who attacked Ramon Espinosa!"

"And how do you know that? Was it because you broke into his room as well?" Charles snorted and said into the phone, "Eric? Please come to my room. I discovered Rei Shimura attempting to burgle my room, and I believe she may have been up to the same thing in yours. Come right away. I'll need you to interpret between me and the hotel administration."

He slammed down the phone and turned to Hugh. "I can't believe this. The question is whether you're in this game as well."

"He's not," I said. "And believe me, Mr. Sharp, after seeing this room I have no suspicions against you, just apologies. Like I've been trying to tell you, in Eric's room I found a pair of eyeglasses with lenses that had no power. Someone fitting Eric's physical description, but wearing eyeglasses, went into Ramon Espinosa's apartment. And I also found a suitcase that I think belonged to Ramon in Eric's closet. All we need is one witness from Ramon's apartment building to corroborate this, and then we'll know for sure."

"But that's incredible," Hugh said. "Charles, if what she's say-ing pans out to be true, we absolutely shouldn't be alerting Eric to any of this!"

"Whom do you work for, me or her?" Charles blazed. "What the hell are you doing protecting someone who committed a crime against our interests?"

My eyes moved from Charles back to Hugh. *Our interests*. Was there something Hugh was doing that he hadn't told me about?

But Hugh didn't flinch. In fact, the color of his face had returned to normal, and there was a steeliness in his gaze that I recognized from serious situations in the past.

"I don't work for you," Hugh said evenly. "And I'll thank you not to insult the woman I love. Yes, her actions at the moment appear a bit . . . unconventional, but she's already started a logical explanation. I'm sure there's more to it, if you would just take hold of your emotions and listen."

The doorbell sounded, and Charles moved briskly to open it. The hotel manager, Mr. Noguchi, and a security officer and Eric all arrived at the same time. Eric was looking at me with an almost gleeful expression. It reminded me of the times he used to throw spitballs at me in class and I'd return fire—because my aim was poor, somehow I was the only one who ever got noticed and in trouble.

But this was a hell of a lot more than spitballs, I reminded myself as Charles gave Mr. Noguchi a rundown of the situation—that I, a non–hotel guest, had managed to secure a keycard and enter both his and his colleague's rooms.

"Sharp-san, I believe I have some answers already to this prob-lem," Mr. Noguchi said, speaking in slow but good English. "After close examination of the front desk log yesterday evening, our staff realized that two women may have obtained keys without proper identification. They claimed to be wives of guests—of you, Mr. Sharp, and you, Mr. Gan."

"But Rei would never do this!" Hugh cried.

"Unfortunately, I did," I said in a low voice. "But I did go to the desk to get the keycards. I'm sorry, but I couldn't think of any other way to find out the truth."

"If you knew someone had a keycard to my room, why didn't you alert me?" Charles demanded of Mr. Noguchi.

"Well, sir, we actually had a front desk employee telephone you to ask if your room was all right, and you said yes. We considered the matter closed—"

"It shouldn't have been! If I knew someone had access to my room and my possessions, I would have asked to change rooms. Then this terrible invasion of privacy would never have happened!" Given how upset Charles seemed, it almost appeared he really did have something to hide, I thought. Now he was turning to Eric, and jabbing a finger in his face. "Eric, the gentleman here seems a bit slow on the uptake. Tell him in Japanese that I want the police here so I can press charges."

It all happened so fast. As Hugh stood by my side, unable to do more than mutter to me not to say anything until he'd gotten a good lawyer for me, the men in blue came. There were three of them, and they were about my age or younger, but their faces were hard, hard as soldiers' faces. They surrounded me and took me down the elevator and out to the car. Hugh had implored them to let him accompany, but they didn't seem to understand. Though Eric had translated Hugh's wishes to them, he'd done it with such harsh choices of words that it sounded as if Hugh was trying to undermine their authority. So of course he hadn't been allowed to go.

The charge against me was serious, the station's police chief informed me, once I'd told my story to him and the other officers in a private room at the Hibiya Ward headquarters. I'd unlawfully entered a domicile rented by another person, which was tantamount to housebreaking. Furthermore, I'd misrepresented my identity to the hotel staff.

"I agree it was a very serious risk that I took," I said. "But I'd like to explain what I did in more detail to some of your colleagues as well—officers from the Kanda Ward, where Ramon Espinosa was recently attacked. And in a few hours, you might want to consult with the homicide detectives in San Francisco."

"This is our business," the police chief said. "It doesn't matter if you have friends in those places. We will make the decision on whether to prosecute."

"But my—entry to the hotel rooms—was undertaken solely because I knew that one of the two hotel guests had to be connected with a murder in San Francisco and with the assault that happened in Kanda. What I did today was examine—but not remove—the personal effects of the men I suspected. And I learned that the man who found me—Charles Sharp—is not the one to worry about. It's the other man—the young translator, Eric Gan, whom you saw in the room—who is the culprit!"

At least the tape recorder was running, I thought as I talked on, explaining the whole story. I told them everything except for the name of the Japanese company that Hugh and his colleagues were planning to sue. But they weren't interested in that. There were enough fantastical elements that I brought up—Eric Gan's cell phone use; the phantom nephew who'd taken Ramon's suitcase, yet not visited him in the hospital; and finally, the plain-lens eyeglasses that I'd found in the room of a man with perfect eyesight.

"You have worked quite seriously to find these details," the chief said at last. "It is quite a story."

"It sounds as if you don't believe me," I said sadly. "I guess we just have to wait for another person to be killed, and then another. Maybe he'll be caught in the act someday. One can always hope."

"Nobody here wants loss of life," the officer said. "Unfortunately, there's very little we can do with this man. We arrest people in Japan when we are certain there is good reason to do that. We cannot pull people off the street based on circumstantial evidence."

"Why don't you call Mrs. Moriuchi," I suggested. "Just take her to the hotel to see Eric and then you'll know if it's the same man. And then go to his room and see for yourself the glasses and the suitcase and the maps of the Philippines."

"That could be considered a violation of privacy," the chief said.

"Just go back and speak to Eric Gan," I begged. "Ask if he'll voluntarily show you the contents of his closet. Or show you the entry stamp on his passport. If he doesn't, that should tell you something."

The officers exchanged glances and went outside the room to

talk. I heard the low rumble of their voices, then nothing. I knew better than to try to leave. I thought there was probably a hidden camera in the room, recording my every move. I didn't want to give the camera the privilege of seeing me cry, so I put my head down on my arms.

An hour later, I was startled to hear the door opening. The police chief had returned. "Shimura-san? Are you all right?"

I nodded warily.

"We spoke with our colleagues in Kanda and also Yanaka, where you live." He came and sat down across from me. "There are a number of things you didn't tell us, which they did."

"Oh?" I asked with a sinking feeling. What did they have on me now?

"You didn't mention that you were present to save the life of that elderly acupuncturist in Kanda."

"Well, yes, I was there," I admitted cautiously.

He folded his arms across his chest, looking smug. "And you also didn't mention that a criminal maliciously attacked your home with gas the other day."

"I didn't mention it because it seemed like a very small problem in comparison with my situation now—"

"And finally, you should know that our National Police English interpreter telephoned the San Francisco Police Department as well. An officer on duty explained that the death of the woman you mentioned to us did occur, and that it was recently ruled a homicide due to potassium chloride poisoning."

I nodded. "Have they found the murderer?"

"No, but they were most interested in speaking with the interpreter, Mr. Eric Gan, whom you mentioned. We would like to telephone the lady in Kanda you mentioned, Mrs. Moriuchi, to see if she recognizes him. And we will also have immigration records checked to find out his exact date of arrival in Japan."

"Thank you," I said. "Thank you so much for believing me—"

"Well, it is really an inquiry, not an absolution." The chief studied me a minute, and then his face softened. "You've had quite a hard afternoon, I think. If you'd like to make a telephone call to someone, you may do so from the pay phone in the lobby. And you may get something to eat or drink."

Of course, the first number I telephoned was the one for Hugh's mobile phone.

"Thank God," Hugh said. "I've been so worried about you. Listen, Mr. Harada's agreed to represent you; in fact, he's on his way to the station now. I don't want to depress you too much, but apparently in Japan, entering a person's space uninvited is equivalent to trespassing . . ."

"Don't worry about that now. The important thing is that they're coming for Eric."

"What on earth—?"

"As I told you earlier, Eric is the one who tried to kill Ramon. They're going to bring in Mrs. Moriuchi to identify him. I think I saw Ramon Espinosa's suitcase in Eric's hotel room closet. And Eric had left these glasses he probably wore as a disguise on his bedside table. You've got to keep Eric in your sights so he doesn't have time to get rid of these things."

"Okay, I understand. But Eric's been huddled with Charles and the hotel management most of the afternoon. The only time he could have acted would have been in the brief time he was in his room after Charles telephoned him there and inadvertently alerted him.

"Rei, listen, do you want me to explain anything to Charles? This certainly is a mitigating circumstance that explains your reason for being in his room. I'm sure he wouldn't want a murderer working as a translator for him, and will be glad you learned what you did—"

"Don't say a thing to him," I said. "He didn't listen to me before. The only one he'll believe is the police. And the police won't prosecute Eric unless they find enough evidence and Mrs. Moriuchi's identification of him is solid."

"Fine. I'll do my best to be your eyes and ears here. What's your number at the police HQ?"

"I don't know," I said. "I'm calling from a pay phone."

"I should have given you a mobile phone for Christmas—not an engagement ring," Hugh said. "Damn, but I was impractical."

"But I wanted the ring," I said, the tears coming back into my voice. "I wanted you."

"Well, you've got me without question," Hugh said, and I could hear the smile over the line. "And before I ring off, will you tell me where the Hibiya police station is? I'll pick you up when all the drama's over."

29

After getting off the telephone, I used the small amount of change I had in my pocket to buy a can of Aquarius Water. After drinking the so-called ionization beverage, I still felt dehydrated and spacey, and I realized I hadn't eaten anything since breakfast. But the only foods available in the police station vending machine were in liquid form—hot soups with flavors like corn, octopus, and kelp. My stomach turned.

I wandered back to the room where I'd been told I could relax. It wasn't a cell by any means, but it was definitely a type of holding area—a room with three hard chairs and a table, but no diversions like books or television.

After a while, I put my head down on my arms again. I was too sad and tired to sit up anymore. I must have slept, because all of a sudden there was a hand on my shoulder.

Someone was very tentatively tapping me; it didn't feel like Hugh's touch at all. I sat up quickly and saw a Japanese man, tall and thin with glasses and a gray business suit. He bowed awkwardly.

"I am Harada, your lawyer," he said, and held out a name card for my inspection.

I took it, looked it over, and then tucked it in my wallet. "Thank you for coming. I guess you know Hugh."

"Yes, yes, he is an old colleague from the days so long ago at

Sendai. I was happy to hear from him, and sorry that I didn't give you any information on the telephone earlier today. I think I might have been able to give advice to prevent this unfortunate situation."

"Well, I wasn't going to tell you my plans for the search," I said ruefully. "I thought I would be in and out to get the information I needed—after which, I fully intended to share it with the police."

"Well, the problem is the police came to you, and not the other way around," Mr. Harada said with a sad smile. "We must talk over the situation, and work on a positive strategy—" Mr. Harada broke off as his cell phone rang. "Excuse me."

Mr. Harada answered the phone with a brisk *"Moshi-moshi"* and then, after a second, spoke in English. "Of course. I arrived just a few minutes ago. She is right here and available to speak."

I took the telephone Mr. Harada held out to me. It was Hugh. He told me that the police had been in the hotel for an hour, and searched Eric's room. Hugh had managed to follow the search, and said the police had found neither eyeglasses nor any suitcase besides the Samsonite—which didn't include the maps of Tokyo and the Philippines that I'd found in them before.

"The police are frustrated; I can't understand what they're saying to each other, but I can sense it," Hugh said. "And Eric and Charles are booking tickets to get out of the country. Charles wants to rethink everything about the class action, including my involvement—he's already made a call to my boss at Andrews and Cheyne."

"Oh, no," I said. "I've ruined your life. So are Eric and Charles both returning to San Francisco?"

"Presumably. They're not giving me any information. They trust me about as much as they trust you."

"But the police want to believe me, I think," I said. "You've got to help them figure out where Eric hid the things I saw. I bet it's still in the hotel."

"Well, they say they checked the room's wastebaskets and that there are no wastebaskets in the halls large enough for a suitcase."

"You're right. All I saw were—" I broke off, remembering the maid's laundry cart heaped with sheets. "Oh, Hugh, I think I know where the suitcase went!"

"Where?"

"The laundry cart. There was a huge laundry cart in the hallway on the tenth floor. I bet he put everything under the pile of dirty sheets. So either the goods are in the bottom of the laundry cart, or in the hotel laundry, or in the lost-and-found—"

"I'll check," Hugh promised, hanging up.

Mr. Harada didn't make any comment about my overexcited demeanor on the telephone. He wanted to go systematically through the events of the day, and to hear about any extenuating circumstances that might save me from a burglary charge.

"The hotel knows another woman was with you," he said. "I don't suppose you'd be willing to reveal her identity? If it turns out that this person coerced you into doing this action, you might be able to be released without further problem."

"I will not discuss her," I said firmly. There was no question about it. Chika was my younger cousin; I was the one who'd led her into doing something stupid for my own gain. If Chika were to be arrested, that arrest would be a black mark on her life forever. She'd be expelled from the university, get rejected by future employers, and perhaps even miss out on the chance of getting married. A memory of Mr. Idabashi, the private detective, flashed into my mind. How stupid I'd been to worry about him being a gangster just because he had a pockmarked face! The true villain was a smooth-talking guy whom I'd been stupid enough to make out with in high school.

I must have made a face, because Mr. Harada asked me if I needed to use the rest room. No, I told him, but I was desperate for solid food. He nodded. "Let me go to the street and find something. I'll be right back."

Once he was gone, the enormity of my situation struck me once again. This time, I didn't hide my face in my arms when I cried. I stared at the wall and the plain Seiko clock on it, watching the minutes pass as I thought about the life that was passing away from me forever. I thought about how my engagement would probably never turn into a marriage. I thought about how, if I wound up in jail, Hugh shouldn't have to wait for me; he would be better off moving on to someone with no criminal record—and better sense.

I must have fallen asleep looking at the clock, because I jumped, and refocused, when I heard the door to the room open. I turned around to see Mr. Harada holding a lacquered take-out box that smelled like *yakitori*—skewered chicken grilled with soy marinade. Of course he did not know that I was a vegetarian.

Before I could say anything, I heard another set of brisk footsteps, and Hugh Glendinning entered the room.

"Hugh," I said. "You're supposed to be at the hotel! What's happened?"

"A quick question first. What do you call that card game in America that's like Snap?"

"Snap?" I repeated. He was talking about a game where you matched cards to each other. "Well, it's kind of like the American game, bingo, I guess. Don't tell me you brought a card game to pass the time. It won't distract me one bit." But the *yakitori* would. I took a long look at it, and then closed up the box regretfully.

"I'm not here to play games. I was searching for that word, that 'bingo' word, that Americans use when one gets something exactly right. Which you did." He leaned against the wall, smiling triumphantly at me.

"Which part did I get right?" I asked warily.

"Bingo, you were right about where Eric hid things. The cart with linens from the tenth floor made it down to the mezzanine, where the laundry room is. The staff there had been wondering what to do with an unmarked suitcase that had been found mixed up with sheets from floors nine through eleven. There were a few things in the case, but that didn't help them make any identification."

"What were they?" I asked.

"The glasses, as you suggested. There was also a small book written in Braille, a folded-up metal detector, maps of the Philippines, and a confidential list of potential plaintiffs around the world. Your police chief was quite excited about the find, and went straight to Eric, asking him why he'd thrown these things away. Of course, he tried to deny they were his, but then we had a visitor who proved otherwise."

"Mrs. Moriuchi? But how—"

"I had Mr. Harada call her. We weren't sure that she was going to come to the hotel, but in the end she did and saved the day. She said that without a doubt Eric Gan is the man who impersonated Ramon's nephew."

I thought for a second and said, "Impersonation's a minor offense, though, isn't it? That's one of the things that I'm accused of."

"Yes, it is rather minor, but the marvel is that once Mrs. Moriuchi identified Eric, he crumbled. He admitted not only to entering the apartment to get Ramon's address book—this is the book in Braille that we found—but to using the suitcase to make it look as if he were going to bring the man clothing in the hospital. And after the police demanded his passport and saw from the stamp that he'd in fact entered Japan before the New Year, he confessed to having had his sister telephone me anonymously with the information to go to Kawasaki."

"So Julia was an accessory," I said.

"An unwitting accessory. The police have talked to her in San Francisco to confirm details of the story, and it seems that she didn't really know why Eric wanted her to make the call—she just did it as a favor to her brother. Now, getting back to Eric, he'd already researched the address and phone number of Ramon Espinosa. He telephoned ahead of time to make sure Ramon was in, and had planned to visit him the day that you did, Rei. But, because you were there, he felt it was safer to wait to make his own visit until New Year's Day."

"When he thought he could kill him and avoid detection, because I'd be with my relatives—"

"Actually, Eric claimed that he didn't mean to hurt him but that a struggle ensued after Ramon refused to give out any information."

"About the gold?" I guessed.

"Well, it turned out that Eric had indeed learned about gold through Rosa's testimony—information that he didn't include in the transcript, so he could follow up on it later and find the gold by himself in the Philippines. He thought Ramon could be the key, because apparently Ramon had been an engineer before he was blinded—he might have remembered details about locations that Rosa wouldn't have known. So, in order to find out what he needed to from Ramon, Eric came to Tokyo early. He'd hoped to learn the name of the town closest to the mine's location. But Ramon refused to talk about the past, and Eric, in his frustration, became violent. He didn't mean to try to kill him, he said, just as he said he didn't kill Rosa."

"I can understand him not wanting to admit killing Rosa. Murder is the most serious felony." I said.

"Yes. Rosa's case, though, is not under the jurisdiction of the Japanese police. They've arrested him in connection with the attack on Ramon Espinosa, but it'll be up to the American police to decide whether to charge him in Rosa's death."

"Well, if the San Francisco police have ruled Rosa's death a homicide by poisoning, I hope they'll want to interview Eric. I'll go insane if they don't."

"I do, too. Mr. Harada, I'm sure, will have a better idea of whether Eric will even be allowed to be extradited to America for that kind of interview. Countries can be quite possessive of foreign criminals arrested on their own soil."

"Yes," said Mr. Harada. "The government here understands that if this man is extradited to America, he may or may not be convicted of murder. Yet here, he has confessed to the attack of a Tokyo resident. Whether he's convicted of attempted manslaughter or attempted murder, he'll be in prison for quite a while."

"Everything's going to come out in public about the class action now, isn't it?" I said in a low voice to Hugh.

"I'm afraid so. But at least we don't have to worry that our interviewing plaintiffs will bring about their death."

"So, it's back to work for you."

"Yes, it is. Just as it's back to the apartment in Yanaka for you, if Mr. Harada and I can do anything to prove our legal training wasn't for naught."

Finally, I relaxed. I decided that before I went anywhere, I would do something I'd been longing to do for years.

Once again, I opened the *yakitori* container that Mr. Harada had brought me.

I picked up a skewer of grilled chicken and bit in.

30

I'd been home for days, but nothing was the same.

For one thing, I was still eating meat. I couldn't stop—why, I wasn't sure. But I ate heartily at night, pairing the food with wines I'd thought in the past were too expensive. Now life seemed so uncertain; it was a waste to be parsimonious about food and drink.

The Tokyo police had announced to the general public that they'd caught the Kanda Ward Attacker and he was secured behind bars awaiting trial. However, we'd heard from one of our friends in the American consulate that despite Eric's ready confession to having knocked over Ramon, he still refused to admit that he'd murdered Rosa Munoz. Of course, there were all kinds of DNA tests that could be done to prove otherwise, but the U.S. was having trouble extraditing Eric back to California to pursue this line of investigation. Japan didn't want to let Eric go, the consul said, because it might mean losing the chance to prosecute him for the attack on Ramon.

"It's not over," I said to Hugh glumly when he came home for the evening. "It seems insane that Eric Gan can't be prosecuted for murder just because he's in custody here. I've read so many accounts of American police chasing down American criminals who've fled overseas to escape much lesser charges. What's going on this time?"

Hugh sighed. "Mr. Harada thinks it's a turf war between the

two countries. And I have to say, Eric Gan's damn fortunate to be in the middle. Even if he's charged with attempted manslaughter here, he won't get any kind of death penalty or life-in-prison sentence—which he might have in California, if they were to pin Rosa's murder on him."

As Hugh talked on about the death penalty, I stared at the rack of New Zealand lamb on my plate. I was still eating meat. The body that I'd once kept clean as a temple had turned into something else.

And so had I. Now that Eric had been nailed, I found myself obsessed with the recovery of Ramon Espinosa. I visited Kanda General Hospital daily, for hours at a stretch. I'd almost stopped going on my second day there, when TV reporters ambushed me, wanting comments on whether I felt the imprisonment of Eric Gan meant justice had been served. The idea of gold hidden in the Philippines was also a hot-button topic. Every day there were maps of the Philippines in the papers depicting places other stashes of gold had been dug up in the past—and where more might lie today. Whose gold was it? Should it be shared between all looted Asian countries, or remain the property of the Philippines?

I broke into a run to get away from them, because I knew that to talk would make my situation even more tenuous with the police. While the Hibiya police understood that I'd given them the necessary evidence to catch the Kanda Ward Attacker, Charles Sharp still wanted me prosecuted. This put pressure on the police to ensure that my situation was handled within proper legal boundaries.

"I still don't trust Charles," Hugh said one night when we were lying in bed after I'd grilled us both steaks. "He's a dodgy one. But Eric remains steadfast in his statement that he had no accomplice, save for his sister who placed the call steering me to Kawasaki. But Charles . . . he's changed his behavior so dramatically these last few days. First he was heading back to San Francisco and making sure that I was thrown off the case—but the coalition of law firms is backing me, so his hands are tied, and now he's decided to stay a while longer here, because things are going well with Morita."

"What do you mean, 'going well'? Are you able to tell me?" I asked.

"Well, I personally think we started settlement negotiations with Morita too soon. But Charles feels that the media attention given to the case has the potential to embarrass Morita, should their name get out. And that's our trump card. They've started throwing out numbers to Charles that I think are too low. But being odd man out these days, it's all I can do to get bits and pieces of information. I heard Charles say something on the phone about wanting twenty thousand per survivor—which is pitiful."

"But that's what the U.S. paid to the Japanese-Americans they held in internment camps. And isn't it the same amount the Germans paid Jewish survivors?"

"Those were governments that paid that amount in the past to vast numbers of survivors," Hugh said. "Morita is a very rich company that didn't commit these injustices for the sake of politics or national defense. They did it out of greed. And the war slave survivors we'll find are so few in comparison to the Holocaust and internment survivors. They can damn well afford to pay more than twenty thousand per survivor."

Hugh's words made me shiver, because I'd been reading more and more of my great-grandfather's history text over the long hours that I was spending in the hospital, sitting with Ramon. There was one passage to which I kept returning:

> The challenge today is to continue the rightful expansion of our Pacific empire. China and Korea are much the better under the guidance of our culture; what now of the countries awaiting our touch, the lands of Siam, the Philippine Islands, Indonesia, and so on? After they join our empire, with courage and duty we will move onward to Hawaii, occupied currently by Americans. When Hawaii is rightfully restored as an Asian kingdom, its people will become grateful subjects of Japan.

Pearl Harbor wouldn't happen for several more years, but still . . . here was the idea of the attempt lying dead ahead. As I examined the passage, I couldn't help wondering if my great-grandfather had advised anyone that the attack would be a good idea. Or perhaps, when my grandfather had tutored Hirohito, he'd encouraged the young future emperor into believing Japan's conquest of Hawaii was a matter of destiny.

There were still many pages left to read. I could only imagine how my embarrassment would grow, reading them. It was all so ironic. Great-grandfather Shimura was part of me, genetically and emotionally. He probably had bequeathed to me the spirit that made me love Japan so fiercely—more fiercely than my own father ever had. But because of his love of nation, my great-grandfather had done a terrible thing. He'd possibly imprinted his attitudes on the mind of the nation's emperor, and he had definitely warped the thinking of the generation of students who came of age in the 1930s and '40s. I found myself wondering whether it was worse to try to kill with your own hands, as Eric Gan had done, or to emotionally enable millions to kill with theirs.

On the morning of the sixth day, I was at Kanda General Hospital again when Ramon had a breakthrough. I had been talking to him—reading aloud from my great-grandfather's book, in fact, and telling him what I thought of it—when his left cheek began twitching hard. I called for a nurse, and with her as my witness, I told him about Eric Gan's being arrested for attacking him. An hour later, the police were there with a tape recording of Eric Gan's voice, which Ramon signaled to them was the voice of the man who had hurt him.

Ramon remained lucid all afternoon—enough time for Mrs. Moriuchi to come in, and make the offer to handle his health and legal affairs. He agreed, and a lawyer representing the hospital helped draft a power of attorney agreement. But by evening, Ramon had slipped back to the place where he'd been until recently.

Now Dr. Nigawa was confident that Ramon would recover—if not physical movement, at least the ability to communicate. I knew I should have been happy about the turn in Ramon's condition, but knowing what he'd been like before, I was still regretful. The stroke's effects couldn't be completely undone—just as my own actions at the Imperial Hotel continued to haunt me.

The problem, Mr. Harada said when he made his regular early evening phone call to me, was that the police wanted to know the name of the female accomplice who'd also gotten a hotel keycard. All I had to do was tell them her name so they could take her in for questioning and decide for themselves whether she was subject to any charges.

"I can't do it," I said to Hugh after I'd hung up the phone. "I know the power of reputation in Japan, and throwing away my friend's life for a little less hassle in my own is not worth it. We'll just have to be patient. Maybe after Eric's convicted, the pressure will be off the police to be so hard on me."

"Rei, I suspect I know whom you're protecting. Just *tell* me, and maybe I can talk to her, uh, parents and we'll all come up with a way to handle this as a family. We can turn your situation around. If Mr. Harada thinks the police are holding firm to their line, it's not something to ignore." Hugh was lying behind me on the futon, stroking the slight swell of my bare stomach. It was pleasantly filled with pork tenderloin grilled with a Jamaican jerk seasoning—hard to find in Tokyo, but I'd cobbled together the ingredients from three specialty stores.

"They can't arrest me. If they really wanted to, they would have." I moved his hand down farther, trying to distract him. We'd had this conversation too many times.

Hugh moved his hand back to the safe zone. "Even if they decide not to arrest you, they can deport you. That's what Harada said to me earlier today."

"Well, why didn't he say it to me, too? Deportation is—absurd," I said. "I've been here for years. I have family roots, people to stand up for me."

"Deportation is a peaceful action that many governments take against foreigners who don't toe the line. Look at America," Hugh said. "Grown adults have suddenly been bounced back to their homelands after the INS has dug up information on marijuana possession or some other stupid misdeed done while the person was a teenager."

"If I'm deported, I'll die from the shame. What will my parents think?" I groaned. The fact was, just as Aunt Norie and Uncle Hiroshi had no idea that I was on the verge of arrest, neither did my parents. I'd let them know that Eric Gan had been arrested after confessing to attacking Ramon Espinosa, and that the San Francisco police were going to investigate his role in Rosa's murder. But that was all.

"I think your parents will be more relieved to have you home with them than in a Japanese prison," Hugh said. "Listen, you can go to San Francisco, build a new life there. I'll follow you. Your mother once said something about giving us the third floor to make over into our own flat—after we're married, of course."

"Are you thinking that we'd have to live in my parents' house?"

"Why wouldn't we *want* to?" Hugh snorted. "There can't be a more beautiful house to live in, and besides that, I like your parents! Your dad has his moody moments, but don't we all? Your mother's always been wonderful to get along with—"

"It's not the right solution," I said.

"It's not what we would have wanted originally, yes, but it makes sense. We could live there while I continue work on the case. I'll talk to the managing partner at Andrews and Cheyne about it. The advantage to shifting me to San Francisco is I'll be close to the headquarters of Sharp, Witter and Rowe and have quicker access to the Asian Pacific Rim."

"You'll travel all the time," I said.

"A lot," Hugh said. "But even if we lived here, I'd travel a lot. You know that."

"I want to stay here as long as I can," I said.

But Hugh was right. The letter from the government came the very next day. It advised me that my working visa had been revoked and I was being requested to leave the country within seventy-two hours. My option, should I decide not to be voluntarily deported, would be to face a criminal trial.

"Seventy-two hours," I said. "Do you think they mean seventy-two hours from when they posted the letter—it's dated two days ago—or from the time I actually received this letter, which was just a few hours ago?"

"I'd say today. But hush, the agent's finally taken me off hold.

Yes?" he raised his voice. "I'm calling about my frequent flier account."

I walked away, totally discouraged. Hugh had reacted in the most bizarre way possible. Instead of rushing to comfort me, he seemed obsessed with getting me out of the country without having to pay for it, since the government kicking me out wasn't giving me the courtesy of a paid ticket. The problem was the government required that I travel on a one-way ticket, and that was not the kind of ticket the frequent-flier program was used to issuing. Hugh was outraged. I just wanted to cry. I didn't want to leave the country. I wanted to stay put. But it seemed clear that fleeing Japan was the safest option.

As Hugh put on his best BBC accent, I stared at the letter, which hadn't been out of my hand for the last few hours. I knew why the police were punishing me. I'd refused to tell them the name of my so-called accomplice, the mystery woman who'd helped me secure the hotel keycards.

I couldn't do it. If Chika were charged with a misdemeanor for aiding and abetting me, it would decimate the Yokohama Shimuras. Aunt Norie would be cut dead by the neighbors. Uncle Hiroshi, whose new job was still tenuous, might be fired. As would Tom—because who would entrust themselves in the care of a physician known to have a convicted sister and cousin?

No, I decided, staring out at my gray street, no matter how many people were to give up their comfortable ways to help me, as a foreigner who'd broken a law I had no rights. It would be the same situation if I were an Arab who overstayed her visa in the U.S. It wasn't racism working against me—deportation was the way nations got rid of threats without causing international outrage.

Fifteen minutes later, Hugh got off the phone, triumphant. He'd secured a business class seat for me after having convinced the airline that I was his wife, albeit with a different surname, and needed a one-way evacuation for emergency reasons. I would be checking in at 2 P.M. exactly three days from now.

"It was just a little white lie," Hugh said, kissing me on the neck. "Come, let's go out to dinner to celebrate beating the system. They might make you leave, but they can't make you pay. And Mr. Harada and I will work double-time to figure out a way to get you back in—even if it's as a tourist!"

A little white lie. I thought back to the conversation I'd had with my father just a few weeks ago, the conversation about Buddhist rules. You could still go to heaven, he'd said, if your gentle lie was employed to ensure the well-being of society. The rule didn't work, obviously. The white lies I'd told to get myself into Eric's and Charles's rooms had brought me nothing but hell.

31

The next day, Hugh worked. I was on the phone all day, paying off accounts. With what little I had left, I went upstairs to my landlady to pay the next month's rent, and to try to explain.

"I don't want to move," I said tearfully to Mrs. Takashi. "It's because of a sudden problem. I'm needed at home. I'm sorry for the inconvenience. Of course, I expect you to keep my security deposit."

"I know it's hard," she said softly, looking away. "The neighbors—they have been bad. Little Kentaro-chan, he was the one who did that crazy thing with your food delivery. I heard about it later, and I spoke to his mother about it. I wish you wouldn't leave."

"Well, it's not just Kentaro," I said, although I was relieved to have an answer about the tear gas attack. "I know the majority of the neighborhood is not comfortable with—with my fiancé staying here."

"Why do you think that?"

"Mrs. Yuto told me. She knows everything and everyone—"

"Yuto-san has lost her mind. She doesn't think clearly anymore. Everyone likes you, Rei-chan. You grow such pretty orchids at your window. You buy food from neighborhood merchants. You are very quiet—generally."

I blushed, wondering if she was considering the occasional times I had friends over for dinner and drinks—or the more recent, intimate nights with Hugh. She did live upstairs.

"When I come back to Japan, I'll say hello," I promised. "But I think Hugh and I should get married and then try to find a place to live that's spacious. We need room for children."

"Children?" Mrs. Takashi's face creased with delight. "Oh, how delightful. I didn't know you wanted children!"

Nobody knew. I hadn't even thought of it that much myself. But now I was faced with the depressing certainty that my children would grow up with peanut butter and chicken nuggets, not *tofu* and sushi. They would never taste the real shavings of a genuine aged fish.

I turned away in tears, and got on with the rest of my business. I hired a company to pack up everything in the apartment—they couldn't come until five days later, but Hugh assured me he'd oversee the process. My worldly goods would go into storage and either be shipped to San Francisco or remain in wait for me, should I ever be allowed to reenter Japan.

I made a list of the people to whom I owed an explanation for my leaving Japan. The Yokohama Shimuras were the ones I loved most—but the hardest to explain things to, so I set them aside. I went out for good-bye drinks with Richard Randall and his partner Enrique, plus Mariko, Karen, and Simone. The day after that— my second-to-last day—I made phone calls to everyone else I could think of and paid a quick visit to Mr. Waka, proprietor of the neighborhood Family Mart. Like Mrs. Takashi, he was convinced that it would be easy for me to get a visa back into the country, once Eric was formally convicted of his crimes and concern about the case died down. He sent me out with a cheerful good-bye and a box of chocolate-flavored Pocky Sticks. I munched them, thinking how much they tasted like cardboard, as I walked along to Mr. Ishida's antiques shop.

"Ah, what a nice surprise," Mr. Ishida said as I made my way through all the big pieces to the back room, where he was sitting at the tea table reading the newspaper and sipping a cup of tea. A small iron kettle sat steaming on the space heater nearby.

"I see the staircase *tansu* is sold. Congratulations," I said.

"Yes. I never heard more from Sharp-san, so I sold it to a Japanese gentleman who came in the store the other day. I was quite impressed—he was willing to pay full price for it without much of an inspection. His name is Murano. Have you heard of him?"

"The name sounds familiar, but he's never bought from me. He sounds like a high roller."

"Well, I hope he comes back for more. With the current economy, the high rollers are few and far between. My profit from that sale took care of my rent for the next eight months!"

"That's good fortune," I said. "I wish I were so lucky. Actually, I have something difficult to tell you."

"Yes, of course. But first, you must have some tea."

I was about to cut him off and say that on this, my last full day in Japan, I had no time for a cup of tea, but then I realized it would never happen again. This would be the final ritual, the ending exchange between me and the man who was like a grandfather to me. So I sat down and took the blue-and-white cup he offered me. After I finished my tea, he said, "So, what is it?"

I'd been able to talk about my deportation with righteous anger to everyone else, but I didn't have the energy anymore. I told Mr. Ishida, in a low voice, that because I had chosen to withhold information from the police, I was being asked to leave the country the next day.

"You are withholding information for an important reason, yes?"

"It's very important, I think. If I were to give up a certain name, it would put an innocent person in trouble. I made her do something silly that she didn't fully understand. Though it led to my being able to break a law, she didn't commit any crime. She's innocent, but I don't trust the legal system here to regard her as that."

"You used to revere Japanese culture," Mr. Ishida said slowly. "Something's changed."

"I still love Japan and its people. But I'm afraid of the military. I know what the military did in the past when powerless women were shipped overseas to service Japanese soldiers. I'm being sent away, too—not for such a horrific purpose, but because I'm seen as a person with no rights. A foreigner who can't be trusted."

"Did you know that after the war, many of the military officers found employment in the Japanese police? That's why it's so tough. And secretive."

"I didn't know that," I said. But it was interesting—and believable—that the group I considered my enemy was really just a reincarnation of the forces that had abused Rosa and Ramon.

"I was a young man during the war, " Mr. Ishida said. "Just sixteen. My father was already dead from tuberculosis, and American bombs had killed my two sisters. I was the only child my mother had left, and I was drafted to serve in China."

"Oh, my goodness. I had no idea," I said.

"As you know, we Japanese like to think of the past as being over. But it's never been possible for me." Mr. Ishida turned to survey all the old furniture around him. "I buy and sell old things because I want to be surrounded by reminders of what things used to be. I don't have a television or computer because I strive to live in the manner that my family did, before we all lost our innocence. I think you are much the same."

"Well, I collected my family history looking for those kinds of things," I said. "But what I found, ultimately, is the worst kind of skeleton."

"Oh? You don't mean real bones—"

"No." I smiled, reassuring him. "What I mean is I learned that my great-grandfather was quite terrible. He wrote a coda of Japanese superiority and recorded it for millions of schoolchildren to read. And to make matters even worse, he tutored Emperor Hirohito. For all we know, Hirohito kept the war going such a long time—and permitted the military to brutally abuse other Asians and all its prisoners of war—because of what my great-grandfather taught him."

"Words are not like bayonets," Mr. Ishida said.

"What do you mean? It's clear that my ancestor was a significant contributor to the buildup of nationalism before the war. I know I'm supposed to revere my ancestors, but when it comes to this man, I'm quite ashamed."

"We are all ashamed of the war," Mr. Ishida said. "Ashamed because we had believed the emperor was God, and then saw him humiliated by the Americans. Ashamed because we were humbled into a starvation state, and then so eager to accept the food given to us by the occupying forces. Ashamed because our Buddhist culture tells us not to kill except in self-defense, and we did otherwise."

I paused, not quite sure of what he was saying. "Did you have to, Ishida-san?"

"Are you asking me, did I kill someone? Yes!" Mr. Ishida's voice was louder than I'd ever heard it. "Many people. I was in Nanking. The situation that is barely mentioned in today's junior high textbooks, always with the codicil it might not have really happened. Well, Shimura-san, I can tell you that it did happen, because I was there."

I was stunned. The most horrific war scene of the twentieth century, and my mild-mannered, antiques-loving mentor had been part of it. Of all the men I might have guessed had war guilt, I would have never thought of Mr. Ishida.

"There are so many memories." Mr. Ishida sighed. "They still come to me at night. I remember it being like an ocean, our army and theirs, surging together. You saw the different colors of the uniforms, but soon you couldn't tell, because it was all covered with blood. But the faces—I'll never forget. The Chinese boys' faces looked so much like our faces. In a different era—before the war—we might have played in sports competition together, shared rice afterward. But that time was gone forever."

"Please, Mr. Ishida. You don't have to tell me any more—"

"Ah, but I do. It shouldn't have been like that. I knew it was wrong. But I kept going with my bayonet, because that's all I had at that point in the battle. And I was afraid I'd be shot by my commanding officer for disloyalty."

"Please, you've told me enough—"

"I wasn't alone in my feelings of fear and disgust, Shimura-san. There were other young men who didn't want to be there. We talked about it between ourselves. We kept out of the center of the city, where others were torturing and killing women and children.

But still, we had to show we were part of the team. So we served with our troops, and we carried our bayonets."

"Did you serve until liberation in 1946?"

"No, I was shipped home shortly after Nanking because of serious injuries I suffered. I was wounded in a way that precluded me from ever becoming a father. So I never married. And in a sense, it was good that I didn't have children. This way, there is nobody to be ashamed of me."

"Oh, Ishida-san! What I said about my great-grandfather must have made this all come back. I'm so sorry."

"I wish you wouldn't be," Mr. Ishida said. "I wish instead you would understand what I'm trying to tell you."

"You told me a horror story out of your past, something you'd rather forget." *The hard things survive*, I thought. "That's enough for my last day in Japan—I don't think I can handle any more."

"What I'm trying to show you is that I obeyed without question," Mr. Ishida said. "I was ordered to kill, and I complied. You also are being ordered to do something—to give up a name. You've chosen not to do it. I'm proud of you."

"But my life isn't at stake. Yours was."

"Your happiness is—and that of several other people. What's life without happiness?"

Through a blur of tears, I said, "I can't imagine life without having you to talk with."

"Well, there's no reason our talks should stop."

I looked at him. "It won't be the same. The way I could come in and have tea and learn about a piece of furniture . . . the way it was just last week."

"Why not? We can't have tea, but you can serve as my agent within the U.S., importing pieces from me that you think your clients will like. It could be as simple as your calling me about a need and my faxing you a picture, or it could involve your working as a courier to bring the pieces over—in fact, the *tansu* Mr. Murano bought must go to the West Coast tomorrow. Your first job for me could ensure it passes safely through customs and reaches its destination, the home of a Mr. Ikehata. Being Japanese, he's bound to be exacting."

I was silent a minute, digesting it. "It's an idea. But I want to be more than a gofer or someone who leaves you orders. After all I've learned, and dreamed of doing, I want to have more."

"What's 'more'?"

"I might want to have my own retail shop," I said. "The rents have gone down in San Francisco, you know, especially in this area south of Market Street—"

"Good," said Mr. Ishida. "And the end result of it is we could be partners, though on paper I'll appear as your employer—which means I can perhaps sponsor your reentry into Japan."

I bit my lip. "You know, my lawyer said I could reapply to return to Japan after a year's time. I was planning on doing that . . . but a letter from you would only help."

Mr. Ishida smiled. "As you know, I've never had children. But I've always thought of you as a granddaughter."

I caught my breath. "Will you call me that?"

"What do you mean?"

"You can call me Rei-chan, if you like. It would make me feel so happy. So honored."

"Yes. But only if you will call me Ojiisan."

He'd given me license to call him Grandfather. I whispered the word, wondering at how good it made me feel. And then we embraced. As I felt the warmth of his thin arms, I thought of them sixty years ago, younger and stronger and holding a bayonet. And I didn't flinch.

The things that I couldn't understand before about Japan, I did now. There were no good Japanese and bad Japanese. They were all the same people sharing a capacity for both kindness and evil.

Mr. Ishida had taught me that the choice lies within all of us. And although the choice I was making was hard, I knew it was the right one.

32

On my final night in Tokyo, Richard Randall threw a long good-bye party at Salsa Salsa. I was too depressed to even finish my first *caipirinha*. I sat, sober and grimacing, as everyone around me told tales of my past. The insane things: the time I'd sneaked into a hostess bar, the time I'd been tied up in a mountain cave, the time I'd almost drowned in the Hayama Bay, but for the last-minute rescue by a gangster. They ran through all the good old, bad old, times. They gave me good-bye presents: a rape whistle, to use for the mean streets of San Francisco, and a Hello Kitty mobile phone, with a month's worth of international calling. And I had to come back, everyone said. The furor over my misdeeds at the Imperial Hotel would die down, and Mr. Ishida's employment of me would cinch the reentry visa.

Everyone believed it but me, and after a round of hugs and long good-byes, I left early with Hugh. I was practical enough to want to make the last train and have time to lay out my clothes for the next day. I decided to wear the black Ultrasuede suit I'd worn to the hotel the day I'd found out the truth about Eric and everything fell apart. It seemed fitting, and I'd arrive unwrinkled. As I smoothed my hands over the jacket, my fingers felt a bump in a pocket. I pulled out its contents: the MAC lipstick I'd hurriedly smoothed over my lips that morning, a rose-colored shade called

Desire; an old subway ticket; and a note folded in two. I unfolded it and read the name, "Murano," followed by a phone number with a Kawasaki area code. Oh, yes. Charles's telephone message; I'd jotted it down when I'd listened to his voice mail.

"Murano," I said. The name haunted me. I remembered that Mr. Ishida had told me that a Japanese buyer called Murano had purchased the staircase chest.

"What's that?" Hugh said from the bathroom, where he was brushing his teeth.

"This is weird," I said. "Remember the staircase chest that Charles Sharp considered buying from Mr. Ishida? A man named Murano bought it. And here I have his name and phone number, because he tried to get in touch with Charles Sharp—he left a message on Charles's voice mail at the Imperial Hotel the day I was there."

"Murano? That rings a bell for me, too." Hugh came into the bedroom and took the little paper in his hands. "This is a number at Morita Incorporated. I can tell by the prefix."

"Really? Who is Mr. Murano?"

"He's a section head at Morita," Hugh said, still staring at the paper. How expensive was this *tansu*?"

"Thirty thousand U.S. I hear he paid full price."

Hugh whistled. "That's a lot of money for someone making around 100K a year. I wonder how he swings it."

"Well, Mr. Ishida's glad for the sale. It netted him enough profit to not have to worry about his rent for the next few months. He'll have more funds to use for the new overseas expenses."

"It can't be enough on its own to cover the storage and retail space you were talking about finding in San Francisco, though."

"You're right. Actually, I was going to sell some of my mutual funds to cover that myself. After all, Mr. Ishida is doing me a favor in coming up with this export plan. It might not work, and he's an old man. I don't want him to lose everything on a risk."

Hugh studied me. "Well, if you decide to be the one to take the risk, you should really be partners with him. Not his employee."

"I agree with you. However, I don't have inventory yet, and being his employee might help convince the government that I should be allowed back in."

"I see. Just make sure you don't sell your soul for that visa, Rei."

"Mr. Ishida wouldn't be a bad boss to have," I said.

"Of course not. But you must ensure that you understand your role in his organization."

I studied Hugh. "You used to trust Mr. Ishida. Now you're paranoid. I think—I think you're reading a lot of your own problems with the law firms' consortium into my life."

Hugh sighed and sat down on the bed. "You're right that there are problems. Ever since our little publicity nightmare, both Charles and Mr. Hamazaki at Morita are seriously talking settlement. I told you about it a few days ago when it was just a discussion—now it's seeming like a reality."

"So Ramon will get twenty thousand dollars," I said.

"Yes, and I don't think it's enough. Some of the other participating law firms agreed with me in the past, but now they're shifting their opinion to what Charles is saying. As you know, he's got more stature than I—he's on his firm's letterhead as a managing partner, while I'm just an international consultant, a hired gun to Andrews and Cheyne. It's natural that his words are listened to more."

"I still can't get over the fact that someone from Morita chose that exact *tansu* that Charles wanted." I stared at the slip of paper in my hand. "What if . . . Morita Incorporated—the company itself—purchased the *tansu* for Charles?"

"You mean, they shielded his purchase and he's going to reimburse them?"

"No, I mean, bought it as a gift for him. A gift that he's taking in exchange for settling the class action instead of filing it."

"It couldn't be," Hugh murmured. "It would be against everyone's financial interest . . ."

"I don't want to hurt your feelings, but the chances are the class action will fail! Then the firms will really have wasted their money. Charles might see this as the most practical way out, and as for the gift—you know the Japanese are famous for gift-giving. And it's very hard to turn down a gift. I didn't want that silly mobile phone, but I accepted it tonight."

"But they wouldn't have surprised Charles with the *tansu*,"

Hugh murmured. "He checked it out himself and then asked for it specifically. Not to mention that for a lawyer to take a payment or gift from an adversary during negotiations is completely unethical."

"I wish I could meet this Murano-san," I said. "I could tell you within five minutes of chatting with him whether he really knows or cares about Japanese antiques."

"No!" Hugh's voice rose. "Please don't! You only have a few hours left in Japan. Let's make them hours we spend together loving each other, not chasing more trouble."

So we did, but the next morning came too soon.

Like a coward, I placed a call to Aunt Norie's house at precisely the hour when I knew the men would be at work and she would be out at an *ikebana* class. I'd bargained on getting the answering machine, and I did; but after I started speaking, Chika picked up.

"Rei-chan, it's me."

"Oh! I thought you'd be back at the university," I said.

"It doesn't start for a week. Hey, you want to go downtown again? I'm not doing much today."

"Chika-chan, I was calling because I'm leaving. I have to go back to America this afternoon."

"Oh, really? Are things okay with your parents?"

"They're perfectly fine; thanks for asking." At least they'd sounded that way when I talked to them a few days ago about the arrest of Eric Gan. I knew, however, that they wouldn't be fine when they heard that the government was kicking me out. They'd wanted me to come home for years—but not in disgrace.

"Then why are you going?" Chika caught her breath. "I hope Hugh-san didn't get the wrong idea about the hotel. If he did, I can explain—"

"Chika, you know nothing about the Imperial Hotel, okay? It's very, very important that you never discuss with anyone that you went there with me. Now, let me tell you that I hope to come back to Japan soon, though I'm giving up my apartment. I will be back and forth on a new business adventure with my mentor, Ishida-san."

"I don't understand. You must have done something wrong if you want me to keep secrets about the hotel," Chika said.

"You're right, Chika. Let's leave it at that."

"Are you still getting married?" she asked plaintively.

"Yes, I—I think so. But obviously, it can't be here." My fantasy about getting married under a bower of cherry blossoms would never be realized. All because of my mistake.

My stupid, stupid mistake.

The police had said it wouldn't be possible for Hugh to accompany me to the airport, so the next morning we had a tearful goodbye while a massive gray police bus pulled into my street, blocking everything. Two men in pale blue shirts and badges stepped out and knocked on my door.

"Time to go," they said.

"May I ride with her?" Hugh asked, his voice cracking.

They shook their heads.

"Tell them in Japanese, Rei," Hugh said. "I don't think they understood I just want to ride along with you to the airport . . ."

But of course they wouldn't allow it. And when I got on the bus with my two suitcases, I could see why. The bus was loaded with a dozen immigration police officers and about thirty foreign prisoners. I was surrounded by Filipina hostesses, Chinese restaurant workers, Thai nannies, and Iranian construction workers—all of whom had been caught overstaying tourist visas. As people chatted in our babble of various languages all the way to the airport, I learned that most people had been brought directly from an immigration jail in Kita Ward. Because they'd been convicted of immigration fraud, they were banned from returning to Japan for fifty years. I had the chance to reapply after a year—which they all considered special. Lucky, even.

I didn't feel lucky as I stared out the window at the gritty Tokyo landscape, which after an hour turned to rolling green rice fields. The green fields would be my last vision of the country that had brought me so much success—and pain. It was the land of my roots. I could only imagine what my great-grandfather would have thought, to know his country had turned its back so decisively on his offspring. I guessed he would have been ashamed of me.

When we reached Narita Airport and stepped off the bus, an officer clamped each of our wrists with a pair of truly unusual handcuffs—steel underneath, but covered with a dark blue fabric. I imagined that the blue fabric was supposed to keep the other passengers in the terminal from realizing who we were. However, the fact that we had to carry our own luggage with this restriction on our arm movement made the cuffs quite noticeable—that and the fact the immigration police had formed a large ring around our group, as if to prevent anyone from wandering astray.

As I huffed and puffed along with my two suitcases, I worked my way to the fringe of the group so I could explain to one of the officers that I had a crate of special goods waiting with a customs broker and I'd need to check it before leaving.

"That is most unusual," the officer said. "Everyone coming from the prison has their two-piece allowance—"

"But I didn't come from the prison! And it's not personal goods," I said. "It's a prepaid shipment of an antique chest to a client in San Francisco. My boss wants me to be sure it gets on the plane."

"Just how old are these antiques? Do you have clearance for them to leave Japan?"

"Of course. I have the certificate in my carry-on bag, along with the client's duty payment. Would you care to see it?"

The officer conferred with his supervisor, and it was agreed that the supervisor would take me to the proper desk and that we would then rejoin the rest of the group at the baggage check.

Mr. Ishida's crates were immediately visible at the special luggage area—they were huge, and stamped with his shop name and FRAGILE and THIS SIDE UP in both Japanese and English. The customs agent who'd brought them to the airport was already there. His eyes widened at the sight of me in handcuffs.

"You really are Shimura-san?" he asked.

"Yes, just ask the officers. I am," I said glumly.

"Ah, I have to give you these documents to present in San Francisco," he said. "How can I give them to you . . . ?"

"Yes as you see, my hands are literally tied," I said. "Can you unzip the carry-on bag on my shoulder and tuck it in?"

"Shimura-san, would you mind double-checking the address on each crate, to make sure it is correct?" the agent asked.

I got up on a chair so I could see the tops of both crates. The base of the chair wiggled as I gingerly stood on it in my stocking feet. I put my bound hands on top of one crate to steady myself and looked at the address label, which was printed in block letters and covered with clear plastic to ensure its safety.

The addressee's name was Japanese and meant nothing to me: Teshi Ikehata.

But his address did. It was on Washington Street, in San Francisco. Washington Street—where I remembered hearing that Charles Sharp lived.

33

As I waited in line for the luggage lying on the belt to be X-rayed, I had time to open my carry-on and double-check the paperwork. It was all coming together. Mr. Murano of Morita Incorporated had bought Mr. Ishida's chest, but was shipping it to Mr. Ikehata at an address that was close to where Charles Sharp lived. How I longed to use my new cell phone to call Hugh about the situation—but with the police breathing down my neck, I couldn't. And the truth was, when I reached San Francisco and was on my own, able to escort the crate to its final destination, I'd be able to put all the pieces together. The depression I'd felt about leaving Japan was suddenly tempered by the realization that I would be learning something new about Charles Sharp—something that could possibly quash the looming settlement that Hugh was so against.

The agents were now methodically going through everything in my suitcase with wands and special lights and X-ray devices. I handed over my carry-on bag and watched them begin to wand it. A beeping noise broke the quiet, and I jumped. Oh, no. Had I left in the metal measuring tape I carried everywhere? It might have set things off.

The inspector reached a gloved hand into the bag and handed the new cell phone to me.

"Oh, sorry, I didn't know it was on." I clicked on the receiver and gave a low *"Moshi-moshi."*

"Rei. It's me." I recognized Eric Gan's voice right away. The ordinariness of it sent a chill through me.

"You're out. Where are you?" Suddenly, I was glad to have so many policemen around me.

"No, I'm not out. I finally got the right to make a phone call, and I wanted to talk to you before you go."

"If you want to talk to somebody helpful, you should call the U.S. consul," I said. "How did you get this cell number, anyway?"

"They're already helping me, if you can call it that. And to answer your second question, I called your regular home number. You left a message on it saying you were moving and that this number would work for a while."

"Eric, I don't know how I can help you. At this moment, my hands are literally tied—"

"But I'm in solitary confinement! Rei, you've got to do something to get me out. I only knocked the guy over. I never tried to *kill* him. It was all a big mistake; he threw a metal box at me filled with millions of tiny needles, and I lost it. I pushed him in self-defense, that was all."

"I suppose that it was an accident that you poisoned Rosa?" I kept my eyes on the immigration officer, who was not interested at the moment in me, but in my carry-on bag. And of course I was speaking English, which he didn't understand well.

"I didn't ever go to see her on my own, let alone poison her! I know this may be the last time we ever speak, but you've got to hear me out. On Christmas Day, I was with my family. I didn't kill her."

"That alibi means nothing. Your family would say anything to help you out," I said, thinking about the situation with Chika. It's what I *didn't say* that had saved her, but she would never know. She'd just continue thinking I was a dishonest, sour older-girl cousin.

"I know it doesn't mean much, a family alibi. But I'm telling you, I think I know who did it. I didn't say anything when I was arrested because I didn't think anyone would actually try to charge me for it, but here, alone in solitary, I have nothing to do but think—"

"Cell phones must be turned off!" the immigration officer said to me. "They interfere with the inspector's instruments."

I sighed. "Eric, I'm going to have to call you when I get to the U.S."

"No, Rei, it might be too late. They're talking about transferring me to a different prison and—damn—"

I heard static, and Eric's voice was gone.

"Too bad," I said, snapping off the phone. Eric was the one who knew Charles Sharp best. He might be able to confirm my suspicions about Sharp's acceptance of graft from Morita—and worse. Well, soon enough I'd be in the U.S. and I'd be able to put the pieces back together when I placed a telephone call on a real phone to Hugh. He'd be able to reach the consul to track down Eric in whatever prison he was staying.

Ten minutes later, the immigration police had my passport in their hands. They'd drawn a line through my old visa and added a stamp that said B-1. Mr. Harada had already explained to me that this meant I'd been deported and would be immediately recognized by airport officials should I ever try to come back using the same passport.

I moved on quickly with the immigration officer, making a left to go to the departure gate. It turned out we'd spent longer at the examination table than I'd realized, and the plane was almost ready for boarding.

"Hands, please." The officer used a key to unlock my handcuffs. I rotated my wrists, which were feeling quite bruised.

The officer insisted that I be boarded first—before first class even. I saw the well-dressed businessmen noticing this affront— that I, a young woman in vintage Ultrasuede, had trumped them. But I had no desire to gloat. I just wanted to get to San Francisco and figure out what was going on with Mr. Ishida's staircase *tansu*—and then think about what I was going to do for the rest of my life.

The JAL flight was not crowded. I had the whole center row to myself—I was sure in part because others on the flight had seen my handcuffs and didn't particularly want to share space with me.

When the flight attendants came around offering beverages, I had a glass of white wine. And then another. As the plane floated over the Pacific, I wondered where Japanese airspace ended and other nations began. I wanted to drink for as long as I could over Japanese airspace, then stop as I left the place that I'd so passionately, and irrationally, loved for the past four years. No, six. I'd grown up here, but now I was going to the place where my passport said I belonged.

I'd resisted calling my parents to tell them about what had happened. Now I had to face up to the fact that in a little over twelve hours, I'd have to tell them, face-to-face. And then I'd have to figure out whether I would stay with them or strike out on my own. I had a strong temptation to look for an apartment. Then I could say to my parents that while I had come home, I wasn't really the prodigal daughter needing shelter.

The flight attendant came back to retrieve my empty glass.

"May I get you anything else?" she asked with a gentle—but, it almost seemed, knowing—look.

I shook my head. It would be stupid to get drunk on the flight. It would exacerbate the dehydration effect of air travel and leave me a wreck on the ground in San Francisco. I shut my eyes, and wished myself into a dream of being home at bed in Yanaka, freezing cold but happy.

34

I'd never arrived at the San Francisco Airport without being met by at least one of my parents, so I felt quite odd and lonely as I walked from the gate. But it was my own doing. I could have called them, but I didn't.

The flight came in just after 9 A.M. I let everyone else get off the plane before me, trying to prolong the inevitable. Then I picked up my carry-on bag and started walking, briskly, off the plane and into the arrival lounge.

My first stop was bulk cargo, where Mr. Ishida's crates would be unloaded. I had to wave my paperwork a few times to get them to release the crate to me, but it happened after a half hour of waiting. By this time, of course, my personal luggage had long been unloaded, and I added it to the large cart that held the crates and headed for customs.

A flight had come in from China, so there were plenty of people ahead of me in the Items to Declare line. As I waited, I popped out my cell phone. I wanted to call Mr. Ishida back in Tokyo to find out what exactly the crates held. The documents the courier had given me listed the contents as two chests; this could mean the same thing as one staircase chest, once it was assembled.

The line rang and rang at Mr. Ishida's place, and I remembered too late that I was calling at two in the morning his time. The telephone number I had for him rang downstairs in the shop section. He couldn't possibly hear it if he was in bed.

Resolutely, I dialed the next number: my parents. I thought at least one of them might be home, but they weren't. I left a message on the answering machine that I was in town again; the less said at this point, I figured, the better. And by the time I saw them in the late afternoon or evening, I might have a lead on where I'd be living.

When it was finally my turn to have my luggage inspected, I hoped that the INS inspectors would insist on opening the crates. For the last twelve hours, I'd been dying to know whether the staircase *tansu* was inside them. But nobody seemed interested in looking into the crates, or into my luggage. It must have been my U.S. passport, I thought darkly. Compounding the no-scrutiny problem was the fact that Petra Simms, the customs agent who showed up with all the right paperwork, was an attractive blonde woman who was clearly on familiar, good terms with the customs guys.

Petra, who in addition to being about six feet tall wore a neat diamond stud nose ring and a green tweed minidress, whisked me through customs and out to the curb, where she told me she would pull around with her van. One of the airport workers—as a favor to Petra—helped me load the crates into the back of the van. Then Petra blew him a kiss, and we were off.

"Have you been here before?" Petra asked as she drove me from the airport. It was the same route I'd taken with Hugh just two weeks earlier. The weather had been gorgeous, and I'd been light-hearted. Today was dark and rainy—typical winter weather, but I'd forgotten what it was like to be caught up in a morning so foggy that it felt like the night hadn't quite ended. "Actually, I'm a native. And today's more than a simple courier job for me. It's my move back home."

"Ooh. How nice. Your parents must be ecstatic."

"Actually, I'm hoping to live independently. And I won't have much money till I get my fledgling antiques business really going. You wouldn't happen to know anyone who's looking for a room-mate or who has a small apartment to sublet, would you?"

Petra made a sorry-looking face. "I wish I did. The problem is it's hard to find the cheaper rentals right now. The Internet bust has created more available space, but the prices are still high. The few good deals left are found through Craig's List or the schools, which sometimes have alumni and faculty with spare rooms in their houses. If you were planning to go to school here—San Francisco State, or the University of California at San Francisco, someplace like that—you could take advantage."

"I can't bear to go to school again." I shut my eyes for a minute, thinking about my expensive bachelor's and master's degrees, which had really gotten me nowhere. "However, my father works for UCSF."

"Oh, that's great! Maybe you can qualify for housing aid as a university family member."

Once we got into the heart of the city, I directed Petra to Washington Street, asking her to avoid some of the bumpier hills. The van, with its load of heavy precious cargo, was a stick shift, and even if Petra wasn't nervous about it, I was. Unfortunately, Washington was one of the steepest street in Pacific Heights, so bad that no parallel parking was allowed. The parking spots were all perpendicular, and the cars parked with their noses facing the road, ready to gun their way out against the relentless force of gravity. Still, I didn't feel safe. To me, the cars appeared like a long row of dominos, ready to tumble at the slightest tap. I thought wistfully about Japan, where 80 percent of the land was mountain-ous. The Japanese answer was not to build on these mountains—it was to live beneath them.

"Don't forget to put your hazard lights on!" I said after Petra had double-parked in front of the house.

"Don't worry so much! I've been here before for a few other deliveries—this street is loaded with the kind of people who spend lots of money overseas." She grinned at me. "I'll stay here anyway. But after we're done, could I drop you off somewhere? You can't walk these hills with that load of luggage."

"Oh, I'll manage." Actually, I should have been able to trundle the luggage the few blocks to my parents' house, but I'd have to go down to Octavia, which was so steep that I'd surely lose control. "I've got to stay here for a bit. I'm duty-bound to see the furniture once it's out of the crate, to make sure it isn't damaged."

"You're breaking my heart with your goodness," Petra said.

It was a few steps uphill to Ikehata's house. It was an early-twentieth-century Greek Revival house—white stucco, with eight classical columns and an elaborate, half-circular portico. A six-foot-high wrought-iron fence and gate guarded the property.

As I opened the gate and began a brisk walk to the portico, I saw a curtain in a window on the first floor move. The door opened before I reached it. I stood facing a slender, golden-skinned man, somewhere between my age and his late thirties; it's hard to tell age with Asians who have taut skin, as this man did. He was also in great shape; his lean body was clad in a fashion-able, form-fitting blue viscose sweater and slim gray flannel slacks. Nice outfit—nice-looking man. Hardly the stereotype of a wealthy, aged collector.

"Are you Mr. Ikehata? I'm the courier," I said in English.

"I was expecting you," he said in a soft Japanese accent.

"Yes. The crates are quite large. I'm afraid the customs agent and I may need some assistance."

I'd anticipated that Mr. Ikehata would call for a manservant, but he didn't.

"I can do it myself. I keep a cart in the greenhouse for such pur-poses." Mr. Ikehata motioned for me to come inside.

I couldn't believe my luck. As Mr. Ikehata disappeared down a long, long corridor, I gazed around at the dramatic foyer. The floor was Carrera marble, and the walls a gorgeous pale gray; the color extended all the way up to the circular ceiling, which was orna-mented with amazing old plaster moldings that continued the classical Greek theme I'd seen outside. The furniture was a mélange of American and English antiques and Asian pieces. I walked a few steps to look through an arch into the living room, where a pair of camelback sofas flanked a baroque-looking fire-place. Along the wall there was a Yonezawa *tansu*—Meiji Period, I thought, walking closer to examine the metalwork and handles. The chest was adorned with an ancient Chinese terra-cotta horse, various gorgeous carved ivory netsuke, and some silver-framed photographs.

My eyes were drawn to a group of wedding pictures. The

biggest was of a good-looking all-American couple standing in front of Grace Cathedral; from the minimalist, Vera Wang–ish gown I knew it had to have been taken within the last ten or fifteen years. The bride and groom were exquisite, but their photograph was less interesting to me than one of another bridal couple in front of the same cathedral. The man's expression was tight, and oddly familiar, but I couldn't place it. The next photo was of a little girl wearing a *Flashdance*-style off-the-shoulder T-shirt, part of the same sad fashion warp that had surrounded me when I was young. From the turned-up nose and cool blue eyes, I realized that the little girl had grown up to be the bride in the Vera Wang gown. And I'd known her in junior high and high school. It was Janine Sharp, the girl who'd been at St. Ursula's with me. So this was Charles Sharp's house, after all—though he shared it with a good-looking Japanese man, whose connection to him I couldn't quite understand.

Suddenly I heard Mr. Ikehata's steps, and the sound of something rolling, so I hurried back to the foyer. Of course, given the direction that he was coming from, he'd be able to tell that I'd moved from where he'd left me. And his face was far less open and welcoming than before. Suddenly, things began to fall into place like dominos. Charles Sharp. His desire to make a quick deal with Morita Incorporated. This handsome Japanese man living in his house.

"I, ah, was just looking out the window for my colleague, who has the crates in the van," I said quickly. "What a beautiful house you have."

"Thank you, but it's not my house," Mr. Ikehata said.

"Oh, is it your—friend's?" I was using the gentlest language possible, so as not to offend a man who hadn't grown up loud and proud in California.

"Mr. Sharp is my employer. He is the one who ordered the *tansu*," Mr. Ikehata said crisply.

"Ah," I said. Maybe I'd guessed wrong about the relationship. Who cared, anyway? "Well, it's awfully heavy. I'll show you the right way to carry it inside."

Mr. Ikehata and I trundled the cart out to Petra's van. When she saw us, she stretched her mile-long legs out of the front and came back to help us. "They're heavy," she warned Ikehata. "Rei and I had a bit of a struggle to get them in."

"Your name is Rei? Are you Japanese?" Mr. Ikehata said between deep breaths as he pulled the crate forward; I was crouched in the back of the van, pushing it outward.

"Ah, yes I am."

"And I'm Petra! You probably don't remember, but I was the customs agent who brought some marble statuary here last year—I think it was from Rome—"

"Ah, of course," Mr. Ikehata said, giving her a quick bow. "Miss Petra. You look different this time—did you alter your nose?"

"Yes, I did! I had a piercing. Thanks for noticing!"

"Let's try to lower the box," Mr. Ikehata said in his gentle voice. "Miss Petra, you can help us by steadying the cart?"

"Okay, we'll bring the first one in," I said. Mr. Ikehata rolled the cart back into the house, and I followed to help him slide it gently off the cart into the center of the foyer.

The second crate was a little bit heavier, making me think it was the base of the staircase *tansu*—for in my mind, there was no doubt anymore that Charles Sharp had gotten Mr. Murano to import the staircase *tansu* for him. The trick was going to be actually getting Mr. Ikehata to open the box to see it.

"Petra, you can go ahead if you like. I, unfortunately, have to make sure the contents are in sound condition," I said.

"Oh, I'm certain it's fine. We've never had a problem with wooden pieces in the past," Mr. Ikehata said. "Please, go ahead with your friend."

"It's my duty to see it," I said with a rueful expression.

"None of the couriers in the past felt that way—"

"Well, Mr. Ishida specifically asked me to do this—"

"Very well." Mr. Ikehata exchanged smiles with Petra, as if they both knew that I was an overzealous amateur. "Let me get an instrument to open it."

He used a pry bar and the curved edge of a hammer to open one side of the crate. As he lifted off the rough plywood, I craned my head to see inside. Lots of shavings of wood—Mr. Ishida's preferred insulation against breakage. Mr. Ikehata and I pulled off the wood shavings, and I apologized for the mess it was making on the floor.

"Ah, it's no problem. It would have to come out at some time."

I sighed aloud when I saw the side of the chest. It was just as I remembered it—the gorgeous cryptomeria with expert joining at top and bottom.

"Steady," Petra said, and held the crate as Mr. Ikehata and I carefully pulled the chest free. It was the four-foot-high base of the *tansu*.

"People used to use them as staircases to the second floor of small Japanese houses," I said. "The drawers in each step were useful for storage. And can you believe that some of these chests have false bottoms, under which even more things could be stored?"

"Cool. I could use that, in my tiny co-op. Not that you need the space here," Petra said, batting her eyes at Mr. Ikehata.

She was on the make, I realized suddenly. Well, who wouldn't be? A single man, this cute, in such a big house?

Mr. Ikehata was smiling politely, clearly unaware of the machinations of tall, sexy American women with nose rings.

"Let me show you where it might be." I crouched down and pulled out a bottom drawer. "That is, if you'd like to know about it, Mr. Ikehata?"

This was what I'd wanted to do ever since I'd realized Charles Sharp had chosen a false-bottomed *tansu*. Using the flat side of the ruler I always kept in my backpack, I pried up the false bottom just as I had in Mr. Ikehata's shop. The only difference was, when I'd done it there the room was dim. Here, I was under an alabaster chandelier. When I looked down at the true bottom of the *tansu*, I saw holes: old, tiny insect holes. My first thought was that at least the infestation was inactive—and that the wood containing it was completely hidden.

"But—it's ruined!" Mr. Ikehata's voice cracked as he stared at the *tansu* bottom.

"But the wood-eating insects are very long gone," I said quickly, mindful of the stress that might lie ahead for Mr. Ishida should we have to ship the *tansu* back to Japan.

"I am very glad you were so kind to open the *tansu*, Miss Rei," Mr. Ikehata said, looking at me with new eyes—as if I was the smartest person he'd ever met. "Thanks to you, we have been saved from a terrible situation."

"But as I said, it's clear that the insects are long gone! If you don't believe me, all you need to do is have an insect control company make an inspection. I'll pay for it, if you're that nervous—"

"Let's inspect the other cabinet section," Mr. Ikehata said. "We cannot risk any damage to the pieces in this house. Mr. Sharp would be—furious. And please, can you put the bottom and drawers back right away?"

I did that as he and Petra quickly unpacked the other *tansu* half. It was the top half, which meant it was less likely to have a false bottom, as it was meant to sit atop the base. Still, I pulled out all the drawers and searched for a false bottom. There was none, but Mr. Ikehata was unconvinced. He tapped at the underside of the piece.

"Listen, there's no hollow sound," I said. "Whereas on the other piece, there is."

Mr. Ikehata folded his arms. "I don't feel comfortable about taking this. I'm sorry, because you've traveled so far with it . . . but that insect infestation . . . it's too risky."

"Wouldn't you want your employer to decide?" I asked. "Of course we can send it back to Japan, but if he chose the piece himself, understood its condition, and liked it, wouldn't he be upset to lose it?"

"I don't know," he said softly. "He will be coming home in the next week or so. I couldn't bear for an insect infestation to take up in the house. Please, can't you put it in storage and leave it for him to decide?"

"I better step in here and say that I don't think we can help you that way," Petra said. "I just deal with paperwork, and Rei here can't do anything. She doesn't even have a place to live right now."

I knew there was my parents' house, and I could have schlepped it over, if only someone had been home to let me bring it in. But I wouldn't have dared to leave a $30,000 *tansu* to languish for even a few hours in the damp outdoors.

"I think the answer is what Mr. Ikehata suggested: safe storage. I'll make a few calls and see where I can place it. And don't worry: I, as a representative of Ishida Antiques, will take responsibility for the transport, storage, and insurance." My first crisis; this seemed the most honorable way to handle it.

"Sorry I couldn't do more," Petra said as she got ready to leave.

"Wait, I'd better get my suitcases out." I walked to the van with her.

"Didn't I warn you not to do too much?" Petra said, giving me a sympathetic smile as we hefted the suitcases down.

"Yes, you did. First-time jitters, I guess."

Petra shook her head. "Well, good luck. You seem to need it."

35

Back in Charles Sharp's house, Mr. Ikehata pulled up a chair for me at the granite counter in the kitchen. He offered me a cup of tea, a telephone, and the Yellow Pages. I already had a good idea of my first resort—Mary at Hopewell's.

While I dialed, Mr. Ikehata retreated to the hall to begin repacking the pieces. I was glad for the privacy. My conversation with Mary was going to be quite delicate.

She gasped when she heard that I was back in town. "What a surprise! I just saw your mother two days ago and she didn't mention that you were coming home so soon. Wedding plans, I bet."

"Well, I'm actually here on business," I said. "I brought over a gorgeous, hundred-fifty-year-old *tansu* chest that I'm hoping to put in storage for one week's time. Can you suggest a very safe, temperature-controlled place where I could do this?"

"Well, why not your parents' house? It's certainly got the room," Mary said.

"Oh, well, you know how Mom has everything arranged just so. I was thinking of a real storage facility—you know, the kind that charges forty dollars a month or so . . . if it's safe and controlled."

"No," Mary said. You absolutely should not do that for any antique piece—I wouldn't even put my own ten-year-old sofa in such a place. How big is this *tansu*? Maybe I could find space in our back room."

I told her about the two five-by-five crates.

"Rei, I'm so sorry—it's just too large. Just go home with them, I know you can convince your parents to take care of it, if it means they get to take care of you in the bargain!"

Mr. Ikehata had come back into the room. I put down the phone and looked at him.

"So far, no leads on storage."

"It cannot remain here. I was just on the other telephone line to my employer, and he agreed with me. He wants to send it back to Japan."

I gulped, knowing that the airfreight had already cost three thousand dollars. On the way back, it would be on Mr. Ishida's bill. Meaning my bill, since we were now in business together. And if Charles Sharp decided to extort another valuable antique from Mr. Murano and the honchos at Morita Incorporated, the company might demand that Mr. Ishida refund them the purchase price of the staircase *tansu*. That would be unacceptable.

"Let me make another call," I said. Again, I dialed Hopewell's and got Mary.

"Mary, what would you say to storing the *tansu* at the auction house if there was a chance you could have it for a sale? It could only sell if it were priced higher than its minimum, of course."

"What's the minimum?"

"Thirty thousand dollars. The price is based on Tokyo appraisal, of course."

"Sounds like an important piece," Mary purred. "Why don't you bring it by for me to see."

"Well, unfortunately, I have no transportation. Not that it would fit in my mother's SUV."

"Okay, just tell me the address and I'll send around a van and two big strong guys."

"Mary, I can't thank you enough," I said.

"Oh, don't thank me. It sounds as if you've brought us the kind of high-profile piece that will give us a run for our money against Butterfield, at last."

• • •

An hour later, I was still waiting for the truck from Hopewell's. It might have been lunchtime in San Francisco, but it was five-thirty in the morning in Japan. I was falling asleep over my fifth cup of tea. Mr. Ikehata had done his best to make me comfortable, serving sandwiches and offering me the newspaper to read. I'd gone through the apartment listings in the back already. Everything well priced was gone by the time I'd put the call through. I made a call, as Petra had suggested, to the UCSF residential housing office, where a sympathetic student told me that having a father who worked there was not enough to qualify for any kind of housing aid.

"Can't you, like, live with your parents?" the girl suggested.

I groaned. "Could you?"

That brought a small laugh. "Hey, what I can do for you maybe is . . . give you some stuff from the trash."

"What do you mean?" I shuddered at her choice of words.

"Well, there are people advertising apartment shares with us who withdraw their offers. Not always because the place was filled, but because they decide they want different kinds of tenants. All those people who used to have good jobs with the Internet, because they're more mature—like you—they sometimes have stock or whatever they can sell to pay more for the apartments. It's really hurt the students."

"I see," I said. "Well, I don't mean to steal from the students, but if you say you know a few names of people who might have space but have decided against younger renters, I'd be so grateful."

"Hang on and I'll go find the rejects folder." I sipped my tea, knowing there was no reason to be excited. If these landlords felt they could make more money by renting to outsiders, they might have repriced their apartments beyond my reach. When the student came back and began reading off details, I scribbled them down, using the paper and pen Mr. Ikehata had brought me. Some of them were single bedrooms, others whole apartments. Thinking of price, I went for the single bedrooms first, no matter what part of town they were in, and even the ones that were out of town, in suburbs like Alameda and Orinda, which would necessitate my buying a car.

No luck. I began calling the apartment shares. They were gone, for the most part—though I did have a lengthy call with a single man seeking a female between twenty-one and thirty to share his apartment, an offer I declined the minute he started whispering soulfully about his shower built for two.

The last person on my list was a female looking for another female to share an apartment with her and her roommate—, as Marcia corrected me after I'd flubbed my introduction by using that word. I kept going, patiently, because the rent on this apartment was actually affordable: $800 and a third of the utilities.

"We've been burned before, so we're looking for someone who's truly simpatico in terms of gender politics, human rights, and food," Marcia said. "I hope you don't mind a lot of questions before I invite you to visit. We had a bad experience with a student before."

"Oh, I'm not a student," I said. "I have a master's degree, but I'm working now."

"Good. I'll need to see your last two months of pay stubs—"

"Ah, how about last year's tax return?" I said brightly. "You see, I'm self-employed in the, ah, antiques business."

"Antiques? I hope we're not talking endangered-species-type antiques like ivory and so on."

"Oh, no. Just wood. And not rain forest wood, I promise you! Just regular wood from trees in Japan."

"You work with—Japanese?" There was a silence. I couldn't tell if I'd pleased her by being ethnic, or done something else.

"Yes, I'm a Japanese-American. I'm hoping to start a business selling pieces that my partner in Tokyo will export to me."

"You mean—you're from Japan?"

"Yes, I have worked there the last four years. But I sound American, I know, because I was born and raised here."

"Aha. Just a minute. Let me talk to my roommate, Nicole." Marcia got off, and I heard the sound of mumbling and a sharp "No!" in the background.

"Hey, it's me. I'm back. And I've gotta be up front with you, Rei. Nicole and I think you wouldn't get along well with us. We had a Japanese student roommate before, and she was psycho, and the worst part was, she didn't want to leave! We had to get a lawyer to help us evict her. I don't know if you'd be like this, but, well, it's probably not worth the risk. So thanks for calling, but—"

"Just a second," I said, my mind whirling. "Don't hang up. Please. This old roommate of yours . . . was her name Manami Okada?"

"Yes! Do you know her?"

"I do. She moved to my parents' house after you. But she didn't stay more than a month."

"Really." Marcia laughed heartily. "Do you eat, like, normal food? I eat mostly frozen dinners and snack foods, and Manami was always retching at the sight of it. She was into home cooking, she said, though I never saw her do any."

"Well, there was plenty of home cooking from my mother, which she did eat. She just thought we were weird people—"

"You mean queer," Marcia said, laughing. "You are queer, right?"

"No, I'm—we're—not. Though we're definitely not homophobes," I added, blushing because I spotted Mr. Ikehata looking at me curiously.

"Well, my roommate, Nicole, is a lesbian, and whenever she had a date over for the night, Manami would storm around, furious. And twice Nicole woke up in the night and saw Manami standing in the doorway—with my sewing scissors in her hand. It was like a bad movie, and it scared us enough to ask her to leave. It was all too possible she'd want to kill gay people because of her conservative politics."

"Conservative politics? You mean, she joined Pat Robertson's party, or just that she supports the current Republican governor?" Even though I disliked Manami, I was beginning to get annoyed with Marcia and her PC attitudes.

"No, she's Japanese conservative! She believes Hawaii is destined to be a Japanese country, and that Japan is better than any other country in the world. She doesn't believe the Nanking massacre happened—"

"And she refuses to believe comfort women were ever really forced into prostitution." A deeper woman's voice had come on the line, a voice that I guessed belonged to the other roommate, Nicole. "Manami actually believes the current Japanese emperor is a god. She had a photograph of an older guy in her room that we thought was her father, but it turned out to be the emperor! She made a shrine in front of it where she burns incense. She kept her door closed so we couldn't see it, but every time I smelled the incense burning it gave me the creeps."

Manami hadn't made a shrine in our house. Well, after getting evicted by Nicole and Marcia, she must have learned that it was smarter to hide her true feelings. I thought back to the conversations we'd had over the dinner table about comfort women and slave labor—how she'd quietly disagreed with some points, but not pushed things. Inside, she must have been seething.

"I—I understand it must have been a hard time. Thank you for telling me. It's been quite—helpful," I said.

"I'm glad she's not rooming with your parents anymore," Marcia said. "Hey, Nicole, what do you think of giving Rei a chance? After all, if Manami didn't like her, she's probably cool."

"Oh, I don't think it would be the right fit," I said. "Not because of gender or politics, just because . . . I'm starting to think I had better go home."

"You mean, back to Tokyo?"

"No, to my house here. I mean, my parents' house."

Mr. Ikehata was kind enough to drive me and my luggage the five-block distance to my parents' house. Normally, I wouldn't have taken a ride with a stranger, but I was in a daze. The jet lag and shock of what I had learned about Manami were vying for room in my head.

Manami had been staying on the same floor as Hugh. She could have gone through his papers to find Rosa's address. On Christmas, aided by the new map I'd given her, and the address, she could easily have gone to the Tenderloin.

I remembered how I'd heard her crying on Christmas night.

Was it because of what she felt she had to do the next day? And was shock over the murder of Rosa the reason that she'd fled my parents' house?

A voice came back—the voice that had spoken in my ear as my bags were being examined in Narita Airport.

"I think I know who did it," Eric Gan had said. Now I wondered if he'd been in our house on Christmas, looking around. Maybe he had found something in Manami's room that proved she was interested in Rosa—but because he shouldn't have been in our house, he'd never dared to tell anyone.

Except for me—when it was too late, and I was too afraid of him to believe that anything good or honest lay within him.

I shivered. My father had been so worried when Manami had run away. But now, I realized, her abandonment of the house had been the best thing for their safety.

The Christmas decorations were gone, but I felt my spirits rise at the sight of my father's Honda Accord in the driveway. Good. I'd be able to get in from the rain.

Mr. Ikehata helped me get my bags to the front door. "Your parents are home, I hope?"

"It looks like it." I rapped the door knocker and waited. There was no answer. I turned to Mr. Ikehata and said, "I'm sure they'll be home soon. Please, go ahead back to the house."

"I can't leave you outside here in the rain, miss."

I nudged aside the flowerpot to look for the spare key. Of course, it was gone. That left only one option—the milk door. But I didn't want the elegant Mr. Ikehata to see me cramming my bottom through the narrow space.

"There is an unlocked back entrance; I'll use it. Thanks again for the ride, and please know that even though the *tansu* will be at Hopewell's, if Mr. Sharp has a change of heart and wants to take it back, he should just call me."

"I don't have your full name," Mr. Ikehata said.

There was no point in lying anymore. I sighed and said, "Rei Shimura. He knows me already."

36

As I walked around to the back of the house, I reflected that Charles wouldn't be pleased to know that I'd overseen the delivery of his *tansu* purchase. He'd understand that I'd figured out that the gift he'd received from Morita Incorporated was a form of graft. I had to let Hugh know. I glanced at my watch. Two-thirty in the afternoon here meant it was seven-thirty tomorrow morning in Japan. Everything had gone so wrong in my life, but at least I was in the perfect zone of time to call Hugh, who was probably having his morning tea in the chaotic remnants of my Yanaka apartment.

But first, I'd have to get in. As I'd expected, the kitchen door and windows were all locked. I crouched down to examine the old milk door—the one I'd used for my teenage forays. I'd been slim enough to get through when I was one hundred pounds. Now I was twelve pounds heavier, but I liked to believe that some of the weight was muscle. Maybe that would help me to pull myself through.

I pushed gently at the door's surface, and it opened inward with a creak. Suddenly, I realized what I was doing: breaking and entering. The action was a repeat of what I'd done at the Imperial Hotel, but this was my house. I was sure my parents wouldn't charge me.

I pushed my head and shoulders through and into the kitchen.

The lights were off and the shades drawn. It was warm, though, and there was a faint aroma of green tea. My father had to be home. Why hadn't he answered the door?

I hollered his name a few times, but there was no response. Maybe he had one of his headaches and was napping upstairs. I stretched bit by bit; once my shoulders had made it through the space, the rest was easy.

Inside the kitchen, I stood up, dusting off my hips and thinking that if I could make it through the door so easily, burglars could, too. I'd have to get my parents to board it up. I took a few steps into the kitchen and went straight for the wall with the old-fashioned push-button light switches. I pushed the top one, but nothing happened.

So, the lightbulb had burned out. But not the hot-water radiators, I saw when I put my hand on the old Victorian model that ran under the window. Nor the gas range. I turned on the stove and put the kettle to boil. Then I went to the front of the house, opened the door, and lugged in my two suitcases.

"Dad?" I called again. No answer.

The kettle had come to a boil, so I went back to the kitchen and made myself a cup of Darjeeling. Then I flipped open the new cell phone and dialed my apartment in Japan. But instead of getting Hugh, I got a signal that the phone wasn't working. Apparently I'd run the battery down. Its recharger was in one of my suitcases, but I felt too lazy to unpack at the moment. Not to mention that once I unpacked in my house, it would be hard to repack. Not just because there were so many things crammed in—but because I knew I didn't really want to live in an apartment with strangers. Making all those calls to various landlords had been a dose of reality. Life was better living with people you loved than with strangers. I'd be a was a fool to give up this house, which held everything I needed, from my beloved Peter Rabbit mug to my parents. Growing up didn't necessarily mean living apart. The Japanese understood this clearly.

The cell phone hadn't worked, but I was sure the house phone would come through. I picked it up and got a dial tone. Super. I called my apartment in Tokyo. At the fourth ring—just as my answering machine was coming on—Hugh picked up.

"I've arrived," I said.

"But you were on the ground hours ago. I checked with the airline, and I've been waiting for your call."

"I didn't want to wake you," I said. "Anyway, in the time that passed, I've figured out something amazing." First, I told him about Charles being the recipient of the *tansu* bought by Morita Incorporated, and the problem with its base that I'd inadvertently revealed. I explained how Mr. Ikehata had been worried enough to telephone Charles about it, and how Charles had said it should be taken out of the house.

"I didn't mean for Mr. Ikehata to know my name," I said. "But there was no point in trying to cover up. If Mr. Ikehata gave a physical description of me to Charles, he'd know."

"Oh, don't worry." Hugh's voice was tender. "I don't care if Charles knows what you've done. And as far as my day goes, I'm not showing up at the Imperial Hotel. There's no point in my pretending to go on normally if it's true that he's gone to bed with Morita Inc. I'll spend the morning placing calls to all the other principals involved in the class action. They all need to know, so we can figure out the next step."

"Was there a crime?" I asked, voicing the fear I had. "You see, because I'm taking the staircase chest to Hopewell's, following the rejection from Charles's manservant, it's almost as if he didn't really take it." I sighed. "I screwed you over again, without meaning to. If I hadn't been so hell-bent on examining the false bottom of the chest, the old wood would never have been a problem—and the piece would still be in Charles's house."

"You examined the *tansu* because you thought there was going to be something significant in the bottom," Hugh said gently. "That didn't pan out, but if it had, there would have been an even stronger argument against Charles. Still, the fact remains that he went through all the motions of soliciting and accepting an inappropriate gift. That should be enough to get him thrown off the case."

"Before we get too deep into legal rhetoric, there's something else you need to know." I told him about the last-minute phone call from Eric Gan, and how Eric had been so vehement that what he'd done to Ramon had been accidental, and how he thought he knew who really killed Rosa.

"I think he didn't do it, Hugh—and not just because he's an old beau and I feel sorry for him. I think the culprit was probably Manami."

"Manami?" Hugh laughed. "That quiet, gentle girl who barely said two words to me the whole time we were cohabiting?"

"She's a nationalist of the most severe stripe, according to her old roommates. She's also unbalanced. Apparently she went into one of the women's rooms at night with a pair of scissors. It scared them enough to evict her."

Hugh was silent for a minute. "Do you think they're telling you the truth?"

"Of course I'm not sure, but it seems plausible. The facts fit. Manami could easily have lifted Rosa's address from the files in your bedroom right after she'd heard the story about what you planned to do. I'm thinking that she thought if she could eliminate Rosa, there would be no way for you to pursue the case—and embarrass Japan. She definitely had time on Boxing Day to do the deed—"

"But she was working," Hugh said. "That means she had to be at the hospital—"

"At the hospital, moving about from ward to ward. I remember from my father's days on call that he carried a pager to respond to requests from staff who wanted him to see patients. He could easily talk to the staff whether or not he was in the hospital. Manami too could have kept in touch with people by using her pager, yet been away from the hospital for an hour or two."

"Where is she now?" Hugh asked.

"I don't really know. Either Japan, or floating around somewhere in the U.S. I'm just glad she left my family."

"I am too. And I think what you've learned is quite provocative. However, it seems the American police have pretty much hung Rosa's death on Eric—whether or not they can extradite him to press charges."

"That's just perfect for Manami," I said grimly. "I'm sure she's back in Japan now, in the bosom of her family. They'll never know, and she'll never tell."

"Don't be too pessimistic, Rei. I'll talk to my friend in the American Consulate. If I bring up your points, perhaps some kind of search for her could be made. I'm sure it would be just for an informational interview, not an arrest, as there's no cold, hard evidence against her—"

"But there's none against Eric, and look where he is!"

"What do you mean? He attacked an old man. Don't tell me you want him to be forgiven for that?" Hugh's voice was horrified.

"I feel compassion for him. Although it tears me up, knowing how he hurt Ramon." As I spoke, I knew that a few weeks ago I would not have been capable of sympathizing with someone who'd done what Eric Gan had. But so much had changed. I had embraced a man who'd been part of the Nanking massacre. And I was the descendant of one of the evil men who'd led Emperor Hirohito to make very bad choices.

"Darling, take a break from worrying. You're home, aren't you? Do what I always do after a long trip—take a hot bath, have some hot milk, and lie down. When you wake up, your parents will be home and you can let them help you brainstorm about what to do next."

"Will you call me after you're done working today? I want to hear what's happening with Charles."

"No, Rei, I'm not going to call you today. I want you to have a chance to sleep. I'll call you back tomorrow morning my time. Until then, sweet dreams."

After I hung up, I stretched, putting my head down on the table. I was so tired. So much had gone on. Hugh was right—it was time for bed.

I kicked off my shoes, then thought better of it and put them next to the front door. I dragged my suitcases to the kitchen's dumbwaiter and set the crank to send them upstairs. After that, I went upstairs myself, savoring the feel of the old Persian runner under my stocking feet.

I walked straight into my room, and caught my breath. It was neat as a pin, and made up with turned-down fresh sheets. It was as if my mother had gotten it ready for me—I enjoyed thinking that, rather than the more likely prospect that she'd made up the room in advance for the next time she had a surplus of guests.

Since I'd soon be sleeping, I left the curtains closed and went into the bathroom to turn on the bathtub taps. The water that came out was brown at first with rust, but then it became clear. And hot. There was even a scented candle on the old marble-topped vanity.

Suddenly, I was very glad none of the apartment shares had been available. I tooled around looking for my favorite towel and one of my old Lantz nightgowns. I opened my top dresser drawer, then remembered that my home wardrobe wasn't kept in drawers, but in some boxes on the third floor.

I headed resolutely up to the third floor, then walked down its long hall, passing the various guest rooms. The room in which Hugh had slept was in as guest-ready condition as my own. The room that had so recently been Manami's had its door slightly cracked. Out of curiosity, I pushed it all the way open.

It looked the same as before. Manami had not come back for her things. Her family photographs were on the bureau and her pathology textbooks were stacked on the desk. The quilt on the bed was rumpled, and her slippers lay kicked off on the floor. There was a cup of tea on the bedside table. I walked over and looked down at it. It wasn't like my mother to have let the room stay in such condition. But then I saw condensation on the cup's ceramic surface. The cup was warm.

As I picked it up, I heard the sound of a light footstep. I whirled around.

There she was.

37

"Oh, I'm sorry," I said quickly. "I didn't mean to snoop. I thought you didn't live here anymore—"

"You told me to come back. You said it was the honorable thing to do," Manami said quietly. She looked younger than ever, standing straight with her hands behind the folds of a voluminous, calf-length skirt. With her simple cardigan, knee socks, and braids, she looked like the kind of old-fashioned Japanese schoolgirl who had shown up in my father's old photos.

"I did say that," I admitted. "Tell me, Manami-san, how long have you been back living in our home?"

"Three days. I was in a youth hostel for a while. But then I spoke to you on the phone, and you encouraged me to come back. To face your parents." Her smile was brighter than it had ever been, and I realized that it was mocking me.

"My parents—they're gone. You didn't . . ." I trailed off, because I was afraid to voice what I feared.

"They went out for some kind of—romantic lunch." Manami made a face. "That is what your mother said. Can you imagine, people that age, persisting in romance?"

"I can't! Did you work at the hospital today?" I was wondering whether she'd been listening in when I was on the telephone with Hugh. All the third-floor rooms had telephones.

"I'm not working there—I lost my position while I was gone. And now I've just heard that my visa's being revoked. I will have to return to Japan. In fact, I could really use the kind of Japanese hospital position that you pretended to offer to me."

"I'm sorry." I clenched my fists so hard that my nails bit into my palms. Would fists be enough to defend myself, if I needed to? "I shouldn't have told your parents that, but I wanted to be in touch with you directly, so I could know you were all right."

"You didn't honor my parents," Manami said. "Just as you didn't honor your own forebears, despite the business about working on a family history."

"I'm, uh, interested to hear your opinion of my family history, but I'm so thirsty. Shall we talk about it over a cup of tea downstairs?" I took two steps toward the door, but she blocked me. I smiled, again feigning friendliness. "Let's go downstairs where we can make a fresh, hot cup—"

"That's not a good idea. I want to show you something you never did justice to in your family history."

I breathed easier for a second. "What is it?"

"Your father hangs it in his bedroom like a trivial ornament, but it's really much more meaningful." Manami brought out what she'd been holding behind the back of her skirt: the Shimura samurai sword. She swirled the long curved blade through the air.

I stepped back, banging my calves against her Empire bed.

"At university, I was in a club where we learned how to use it."

"Would that be the New Imperialists?" I shot a glance over my shoulder to the pair of casement windows behind me. There was a balcony underneath them. If only I could get outside. The problem was Manami would be out there with me before anyone could come to help.

"How do you know about our group?"

"I was chatting with a student there recently, who told me. So, this is really—impressive. Do you play a sport that's like fencing or kendo or something like that with samurai swords?"

"It's called *iaido*, which is the solo practice of the *aiki batto* sword exercise tradition." She smiled. "In the old days, every woman and man of a certain class had to know how to use these weapons—not just on others, but on themselves, should they suffer a terrible dis-honor, a situation where there was no way out."

"*Seppuku*. The ritual disemboweling." Was she intending to do that to herself—with my help? My stomach flip-flopped.

"Yes. Like Mishima-sensei did for himself after he tried to save our country for the emperor back in 1963. It happened before I was born . . . but my father was there."

I blinked. "Your father was with the writer Yukio Mishima at the takeover of the Self-Defense Force Building? When he tried to liberate the military, but was, um, interrupted and gave up?"

"Mishima-sensei didn't give up! He took himself to the next world. And my father and our family never gave up our beliefs. Not like so many families who capitulated during occupation. The Okada family always held to its ideals."

I thought about how I could phrase things to break her. I wanted to make her lose confidence, to wilt and put down the sword. "But, Manami-san, if you, an Okada family member, com-mit suicide . . . you'd shame your family. The right thing to do is get psychiatric help. As a physician, you must understand this—"

"Help from whom? Your father, who is so anti-Japanese that he became an American citizen? No, I wouldn't take help from him."

The house had become more quiet somehow. I heard the sound of Manami's fingers as they stroked my father's family sword. "I admit that I embarrassed myself. I did not fulfill my professional goal. But in another way, I served my nation. A lying voice is gone."

"Ah, why don't you let me hang up my father's sword down-stairs again," I said. "Then we can have some tea in the kitchen and you can tell me the things I need to know." It was hard to keep my voice light, when I was about to faint. I'd been in dangerous situations before, but never had I been five feet away from a sword that had probably killed dozens of people in the past—and might take another life, now. Suddenly, I hated the Shimura sword.

"I don't want tea, haven't you listened?" Manami screeched. "It seems there's no point in my telling you anything. You figured it all out. I heard you on the telephone."

I took a deep breath. "Yes, I told Hugh some things that—that I suspected. And because Hugh knows, there's no way that you could escape discovery if you decide to use the sword." I couldn't bring myself to say, *if you kill me*. I was being extremely Japanese in avoiding harsh language, I realized with a brief pang.

Manami's lips wobbled. "It doesn't matter. If you die here, your parents will know I did it, too. But your father already knew. That's what you told me on the telephone."

"What?"

"Let me repeat the words exactly, as you said them to me. You said your father always knew that I was troubled and that he was on the verge of going to the police. So that's why I came back—"

"My parents? You didn't already—" A sob broke from me.

"Not yet. But you've set things up very nicely, Rei. Your parents— who are out having lunch and shopping—will come home to see your shoes by the door, and your coat and some various other things. They'll be overjoyed that you are home and will rush upstairs to look in on you sleeping in bed. And when they're bending over you to see why you don't wake, that's when I'll finish *them*."

"You're not well," I said in a tight voice, having pulled myself together, now that I knew my parents were alive. Manami was insane. She had a basic antisocial streak that she'd melded to per- verted nationalistic beliefs. I found myself thinking she would make a fascinating case study for a forensic pathologist. The only problem was that I didn't want to be a footnote in that study.

"Take me down to the second-floor bathroom," I said, choosing my verbs carefully. Before, I'd suggested that we do things together. What I'd figured out was that she was hungering for con- trol. "Please end my life honorably in my room, as you suggested. We wouldn't want to mess up the carpets and floor—that would tip them off about your actions."

I saw some confusion in Manami's face, and the sword dropped a fraction. To me, that was the world. In that second of hesitation, I charged past her for the door.

"Stop!" Manami screamed, and I felt the sword tearing through Ultrasuede. But just as I anticipated pain racing down my back, a different one came. The bedroom door banged into my head, and then I heard another crash.

Manami collapsed with a scream like none I'd ever heard

before. And my mother was standing in her stocking feet over Manami's prone body, a heavy wallpaper sample book in her hand. From the expression on her face, she looked ready to bang Manami again.

But Manami was no longer a threat. She had fallen on the sword, and a growing dark red stain was flowing over the old hooked Pennsylvania Amish rug next to the bed.

"Call the ambulance. She's losing blood fast."

I heard my father's voice. My gaze jumped beyond my mother to see him push past her and grab a sheet of the bed to press to Manami's middle. Of course. He was a doctor, concerned about someone who might be dying—no matter that the person had almost killed his daughter.

I picked up the telephone next to Manami's bed and dialed 911. After I'd given all the details, I rushed to my mother to throw my arms around her. "How did you know?"

"Well, to be honest, your father and I enjoyed lunch so much we decided to cancel our afternoon appointments and come back home for a little . . . break. We saw your shoes by the door, and the filling bathtub. We felt you were here but weren't sure where, so we came upstairs, and we heard it all."

"You came in here like a commando instead of calling for help," I said, coming up beside her to look down on the woman she'd felled.

"We didn't bother, because by the time we got up here we realized that to make any move or sound might give us away—and result in danger to you," my father said. "That sword. I never would have dreamed it could be put to such terrible use."

"But that's what swords are all about," I said. I remembered our ancestor who'd used it to save the daimyo and lost his arm in the process. In a sense, Manami had committed a similar act. She'd used the sword to protect her fantasy of what Japan once was, and should be again.

I thought about it until the sirens wailed up to the front of the house, and then I went down to let in the paramedics.

38

A week later, I was at a cafe on Union Street with a used laptop on the table in front of me and a double latte in hand. In the days since the confrontation with Manami, I'd felt too spooked to be alone in the house. So I'd cadged the old laptop from one of my high school friends and persuaded my mother to teach me my way around the Internet. The net result was that I had finally figured out how to answer, file, and forward E-mail messages, and there was no better place to do it than this cybercafe. In just a few days, I'd become a cafe sitter—just like the people I'd gawked at a few weeks before.

I clicked onto a website I'd bookmarked that advertised Hawaiian honeymoons:

> *Try our Bird of Paradise Package! Complete seaside wedding ceremony followed by dinner for two—or two hundred! Five nights at an ocean-view suite with private pool, daily massages, convertible car, and kayak.*

Even though it was high season, it was still cheaper than what my mother wanted to do in San Francisco, and what Hugh had suggested doing in Scotland. Maybe I could please all of them by inviting them to Hawaii. Was a wedding in three weeks fair notice?

"More coffee?" A waiter hovered over me solicitously.

"Decaf this time, please," I said. "Oh, and do you think it's fair notice to invite people to a wedding with only three weeks' advance warning?"

"Ooh, is something, uh"—he coughed delicately—"baking in the oven?"

"No," I snapped, annoyed at his casual intimacy. "Though I would like another chocolate croissant. Can you add it to my tab?"

Life was too short not to eat chocolate, I knew—and my time in San Francisco wouldn't last forever. Hugh had complained about this mightily, because he'd been transferred from Japan back to Washington, D.C., where his firm had taken over the leadership role in the class action. All the lawyers at the different firms had voted Hugh to be the one running the show—and agreed that Charles Sharp had to disqualify himself and his firm, given the gift he'd taken from Morita Incorporated. Upon investigation, it turned out the $30,000 *tansu* was just one of three gifts that he'd already had shipped from Japan.

Hugh's promotion would mean even more work and travel than he would have had otherwise. We'd need the honeymoon in Hawaii, just to have a few moments of peace. The San Francisco Police Department's investigation of Manami had taken a toll on me as well. Dozens of police had turned over our house, looking for evidence. They found potassium chloride in Manami's bathroom cabinet, which matched the sample found in the soy sauce at Rosa's apartment. Additionally, three different people recalled seeing Manami in the Tenderloin on December 26, the time she was supposed to be in the hospital on call.

Despite all the evidence, I knew, it could take years for the governments to figure out which country Manami should be tried in. The Morita Incorporated class action would similarly be pending for a long time. Guilt was such a difficult thing to understand. Eric Gan's attack on Ramon Espinosa was indisputable—and Eric would probably serve a year or two in a Japanese prison for it. I thought the sentence was just, but still I felt sad about it. Eric had been a normal boy and young man; greed was the element that had challenged him, and won.

Manami's sense of guilt was just as difficult to understand. My father thought that quite a few psychiatrists would view her behavior as that of a mentally ill person and that institutionalization would be a more humane remedy than prison. However, he pointed out, she was devious enough to trick Rosa into eating poisoned food, and later on returned to our house behaving normally, but waiting for the chance to kill. Her acts showed awareness of right and wrong.

I remembered how I'd felt my life was about to end when she'd slid the sword out from behind her back. I still dreamed about it. I'd asked my parents if the sword could leave the house, and they'd readily consented. They were willing to sell it at the next Hopewell's auction and give me the money as a nest egg for my local antiques business, but I wanted the sword to return to Japan. Uncle Hiroshi should decide what to do with it, I said. He might want to exhibit it on the family altar, or sell it on the Japanese antiques market, where he'd realize a higher price than was available in the United States, whose market was glutted with Japanese swords that had been brought back by the occupation forces.

The waiter brought me the fresh coffee and croissant, and I toggled over from a vision of a Hawaiian sunset to check for E-mail. I'd been getting regular notes typed in *hiragana* from Yuki Moriuchi, Mrs. Moriuchi's son. It was Yuki who'd informed me that Ramon had come out of his coma, and was undergoing physical therapy that allowed him to tap out messages with his toes. Ramon had also agreed to have his closed eyelids opened, and to let a cornea specialist use surgery to attempt to treat his blindness. A date for the surgery would be set soon.

I sent my best wishes to Ramon via Yuki and then noticed that a new message had popped up from Hugh.

Sorry to say I had some unexpected travel for work—won't be able to speak on the phone tonight. But ponder this question—Washington or San Francisco? There's a fantastic stone former boys' school—a building from the 1890s—for sale on 16th Street. The ground floor has enough space for retail and upstairs there's enough room for us and many, many children. Love, Hugh.

San Francisco or Washington. One place was so familiar and dear and the other was new to me, but not entirely: Washington was close to Maryland, the seat of my mother's people. I'd never paid much attention to them. Perhaps this was the right time to get to know them, since I had at least a year or two to kill in America.

Not time to *kill*, I corrected myself—time to spend. If I spent a few years away from Japan leading an exemplary life, the Japanese government might relent and allow me to return. The deportation had, overall, been providential—if I hadn't been forced to return to America, Manami might have killed my parents before I got there. I knew this, and in gratitude for all of us having been spared, I'd do everything I could to be good. I'd be considerate to my parents, and I'd resume a vegetarian diet. I'd volunteer as the Japanese-speaking contact at Eric's sister's hot line—if she would still let me help.

A taxi pulled up, enveloping me in a cloud of carbon monoxide. I wrinkled my nose and added, *I will drive only a hybrid car* to my brand-new list of precepts.

A door slammed and the taxi sped off again in a burst of fumes. When I was done coughing in my napkin, I heard the scraping sound of a chair being pulled close. I put the napkin down, and discovered Hugh settling in next to me.

"You tricked me," I said, looking from him to the computer screen. "You just sent me mail saying that you had to travel for work!"

"It's true," Hugh protested, grinning. "I just didn't tell you where my work would take me. There are a few more plaintiff interviews to do here, and since Charles is out of the action, I'm the obvious choice to do them."

"I bet," I said, and we kissed. We made it a luxuriously long kiss, since this was the first one since our brief, painful good-bye in Tokyo over a week ago. When we were through, the waiter who'd smirked about my being pregnant was looking grim.

Another gorgeous man wasted on a woman, I imagined him thinking.

But Hugh, typically impervious to his own charms, smiled and crooked a finger at him. "Hallo, can you bring me a pot of Darjeeling, please?"

"I suppose so," the waiter said, eyebrows rising at Hugh's accent. "Would that be iced or hot?"

"Boiled," Hugh said with vehemence. "And can you bring some milk and sugar on the side? I'm afraid I'm quite particular. I have a serious thing about tea."

And I have a serious thing about you, I thought as I shut down my computer.

Tokyo, San Francisco, or Washington—the places didn't really matter.

What mattered were the people I loved.

A Reading Group Guide to

The Samurai's Daughter

Discussion Questions

1. "My feelings about food, my hometown, and my father were about as mixed up as the Buddhist rules" (page 3). Discuss Rei's confusion with these elements in her life. Do you think Rei is prejudiced against Americans or simply prefers the Japanese lifestyle?

2. Rei's father describes Manami as a "girl in a box" (page 4). What does he mean by that?

3. "Shinto, the ancient religion of Japan, fostered a belief that swords contained the soul of a samurai" (page 21). Discuss the irony and relevance of this statement in regard to the novel's climax.

4. "When a country loses its culture, it loses its soul" (page 23). Rei's father believes that artifacts taken from other countries should be returned to its people. Do you think he disagrees with his daughter's choice to be an antiques dealer?

5. "I just wanted to get back to my old life, where there was nobody I cared about enough that I could get shaken to the core" (page 95). Discuss how Rei's feelings about Japan and its culture change throughout the novel.

6. How does the author use food in this novel? What do you make of Rei's on-and-off vegetarianism?

7. The author poses questions about guilt and responsibility in the larger context of Asian history as well as in the personal choices we make today. Take a closer look at some of the characters in this novel—Rei, Toshiro, Hugh, Eric, Ramon, and Mr. Ishida—and discuss what guilt, if any, they carry due to the choices they have made or the history they have inherited.

8. "History is worth much more than money. It's our nation's heritage. The problem here is that nobody will speak up about his or her life. We say water washes everything away—that it's unimportant. So the stories, like pieces of old furniture, are lost" (page 177). Mr. Ishida is referring to his nation of Japan. Do you think we have a similar problem here in the United States? Or do you think we suffer from the opposite—dwelling on our past, be it historical or personal?

9. Do you think Eric Gan's ending is just?

10. Whom did you suspect of murdering Rosa Munoz? Did your suspicions change throughout the novel? What clues did the author leave for you?

11. What do you think Rei learned from researching her family history? Do you think it will change her relationship with her father?

Here's a sneak preview of

The Pearl Diver

by Sujata Massey

Available in August 2004

in hardcover from

HarperCollins Publishers

1

I'd scored a single line and a shadow.

Or were they double lines? I squinted at the plastic wand lying on the edge of the bathroom sink. One line meant negative, two positive. There was no definition for one line and the vague suggestion of a shadow.

"What's the verdict? I'm about to dash," Hugh called from the other side of the door.

"Inconclusive," I said, opening the door and holding out the EPT stick like an obscene hors d'oeuvre. "You do the math."

"One. That's easy."

"Don't you see that shadowy line next to it?"

"A line would be pink. That's just a wrinkle in the material." He was already pulling on his Burberry. It was early spring in Washington and had rained for almost a solid week.

"I wish there was an explanation for shadows—"

"Shadows that only you can see. Darling, if you're really anxious, you could call the consumer help line."

"If I do that, I'm sure they'll tell me to consult my doctor."

"Maybe this means you're a little bit pregnant." Hugh paused in putting on his coat and slipped his hand inside my flannel pajamas to stroke my bare stomach.

"A surprise pregnancy would be a delight, without even a wedding date on the horizon," I said, removing his hand. Hugh and I had been engaged for exactly three months. We had considered a quickie elopement, on the beach in Hawaii, but once our families had gotten wind of the idea, they'd guilt-tripped us out of it. Now we thought we should set the wedding in Washington. But progress was slow. I didn't know the area well and was totally stymied about locations and caterers. I had nothing to show for myself except the guy.

"My cousin was married with new baby in arms and it was the best wedding anyone had been to in years," Hugh said, spinning his rolled-up umbrella through the air before catching it neatly. He was such an optimist: about babies, about the outcome of the class-action suit he was trying to organize, about life in general. He didn't even mind the Washington rain, because it reminded him of Edinburgh. I preferred the hard, blinding rain that made a rock-and-roll sonata on the tile roofs in Japan in the fall, or the warm, humid rains that marked spring's rainy season. But I'd take the Washington rain, because it came with Hugh, and the promise of our future.

After we negotiated the night's dinner plan—risotto with browned onions and sea scallops if I could find them, and a simple green salad—Hugh left, and I made myself a quick *o-nigiri*. I'd kept last night's rice warm in the rice cooker, and I had a small piece of leftover salmon in the fridge. I tucked the salmon into the rice and folded the triangular wedge into a sheet of seaweed that I quickly roasted on the stove.

I ate the rice ball with my left hand and used my right to scroll through the *Daily Yomiuri* online. I'd been away from Japan about six months now, and I could feel the language beginning to slip. It was my duty as a *hafu*—a half-Japanese, half-American—to keep up. I bypassed woeful economic news and went straight to the language-teaching column aimed at foreigners. The word of the day was *zurekin*, which meant "off-peak commuting," an idea strongly encouraged by the government but not quite adopted by the working world. It was easier, calmer, better for people and the environment

At least, that's how it sounded on paper. My whole life had gone from frenetic to *zurekin*—and I wasn't sure I liked it. I'd spent my twenties working in Japan, where I'd lived simply and worked hard, and come to believe that everything Japanese was wonderful, even the crowded trains. The problem was, I couldn't live in Japan anymore. I'd been thrown out, for an indefinite length of time, by the government for a misdeed I'd committed in the name of something more important. Now, because of the black mark in my passport, I had to make the best of it in Washington, complaining like all the other Washingtonians about crowded Metro trains that I considered only half-full, and so on. The only thing I truly agreed with was that Washington real estate was as insanely priced as Tokyo's—though the spaces were bigger.

Hugh's apartment, for instance, a two-bedroom on the second floor of an old town house, had lots to admire—high ceilings, old parquet floors, a bay window in the living room. It was lovely, but so . . . foreign. The telephone rang, and even that sounded different. I picked it up.

"Hi, honey, what are you doing for lunch?" The throaty voice on the other end of the line belonged to my cousin Kendall Howard Johnson, who lived in Bethesda.

"Kendall?" It annoyed me when people didn't introduce themselves on the phone.

"Yes, Rei." She drew my name out in the exaggerated way she'd pronounced it since we were little. Raaay, it sounded like.

Kendall had grown up in Bethesda, so I'd run into her plenty of times on my childhood visits to my mother's home forty minutes to the north, in Baltimore. Grandmother always called Kendall and me the ladybug team because of Kendall's red and my black hair; a set of cousins the same age who seemed destined to go together, but didn't really. I'd never forget the humiliation of the summer when Kendall was fifteen and she'd taken me in the backyard bushes and produced a joint. I hadn't known how to strike a match, let alone inhale, and I was from the Bay Area, where everyone was supposed to know how to roll. But at the coed boarding school Kendall went to in Virginia, she'd already learned lots of things that I hadn't. Horseback riding, joint rolling, how to sneak backstage at concerts without being stopped. Kendall, who'd worked as a corporate fund-raiser for a few years after college graduation, was always more advanced than I, and she'd maintained her advantage. The trust fund our grandmother had set up was now open for her use. Kendall dipped into it for her wedding, her first house payment, and even political donations that she'd begun to make as she began her careful ascent in grown-up Washington. My mother hinted that if I spent more time with my grandmother, she'd feel more benevolent toward me, but the fact was, I didn't feel comfortable with Grand, as everyone called her, and the last thing I wanted to do was suck up to her for the money that all the Maryland cousins received, and that I, the lone Californian who hardly ever visited, didn't. Then again, my exclusion from the trust might have occurred because my mother had jumped into a marriage that had felt like a death blow to the Howards. If my father had been black, the marriage would have broken Maryland law at that time. An Asian husband wasn't quite as shocking as a black one, but my parents' wedding hadn't been a family affair.

Still, I couldn't resent Kendall for being one of the Howards, for as busy as my cousin was with the babies, running her household, and fund-raising for her favorite political hopefuls, she hadn't forgotten me. Kendall was the only relative who'd sought me out since I'd arrived in Washington a few months earlier, and I was grateful for that.

"How are the twins?" I avoided asking about her husband, Win, whom I couldn't stand. Win was a real estate agent and saw everyone as a potential target. The fact that Hugh and I hadn't been interested in buying a McMansion in the suburbs was still a point of contention.

"The babies are sick with strep. It's highly unusual in children under three, but my two have it, of course!"

"You must be tearing out your hair running from one to the other," I sympathized.

"At night, yes. By day our au pair is playing Nursie, thank goodness. I've escaped to the gym and had an hour to spin and then an hour for weights. I'm starved. Could you make a twelve-thirty lunch?"

"I don't know. The weather's kind of bad. I was thinking of doing some things around the apartment—"

"Rain's good for you, honey!" Kendall snorted. "And it's not just a gals' lunch at the coffee shop I'm talking about. It's at a good restaurant with Harp Snowden."

"You socialize with Harp Snowden?" I was amazed. Harp Snowden was a Democratic senator representing California, a liberal stalwart who voted against each and every war proposed. He was one of the few politicians who'd entered the new century unabashedly pro-environment, pro-immigrant, pro-peace. Kendall's meeting with him was interesting; she was a conservative Democrat, practically Republican.

"It's a new relationship. When he suggested lunch at Mandala—one of my favorite places—I knew he was on the make. I thought you might like to come along, too."

"What do you mean, he's on the make?" I asked. Kendall had been married for five years. I'd thought she was still crazy about Win.

"Not that way, silly. He wants me to raise money for him, you know, get involved with his campaign in this area, especially reaching into northern Virginia. It's kind of a challenge, not being a Republican there, although he does have the history of actually having fought in Vietnam and lost a foot, which earned him a Purple Heart. He's kind of like John McCain meets Howard Dean meets the late Paul Wellstone."

Kendall was like that. She talked in shorthand, clichés, expressions that I was just beginning to learn everyone used, 24/7, in America. "But you're from Maryland," I said. "And if Senator Snowden and you are both Democrats, what are you doing talking about going after Republicans?"

"It's possible to get people to shift their vote, if the candidate is right," Kendall said. "Of course I'm a Marylander, but I went to boarding school and college in Virginia, which practically makes me a citizen. I know everyone, from the horsey set in Charlottesville to the techies in Reston. Harp desperately needs a friend like me."

Everyone meant people with money, I thought cynically. "So how much money do you have to give the senator to become his friend?"

"An individual can't give more than two grand because of all the soft-money reforms, but people like me can encourage our friends to give money. Lots of people, lots of money. You weren't here during the McCain campaign, but I threw a dinner for him that people are still talking about."

"McCain wasn't a Democrat," I pointed out. "What are you, a switch-hitter?"

"Usually I describe myself as a conservative Democrat with Independent leanings," Kendall said. "Anyway, I promise you lunch won't be too political. I want you to relax. You can talk with him about Japan. He did some kind of Zen yoga thing there when he was in his twenties. Maybe you have some friends in common." She paused. "Oh, Rei. About your clothes?"

"Yes. What should I wear?" A private lunch with a senator was a first for me.

"Think Democrat, but dress Republican. Got it?"

Books by Sujata Massey:

THE PEARL DIVER
ISBN 0-06-621296-0 (new in hardcover from HarperCollins*Publishers*)
Just as Rei Shimura starts to settle down in Washington, D.C., things start to go
haywire. First, her cousin vanishes, and then Rei is drafted to help find a Japanese
war bride who disappeared thirty years earlier.

THE SAMURAI'S DAUGHTER
ISBN 0-06-059503-5 (paperback)
Rei Shimura enters the world of war reparations and family secrets when her
lawyer-boyfriend's plaintiff is murdered and Rei begins to uncover unsavory facts
about her own family's actions during WWII.

THE BRIDE'S KIMONO
ISBN 0-06-103115-1 (mass market paperback)
Rei Shimura, acting as courier in the transport of a set of priceless early 19th-
century kimonos, embarks upon the adventure of a lifetime, involving stolen
artifacts, a wacky tour group of Japanese women, and a very dead body.

THE FLOATING GIRL
ISBN 0-06-109735-7 (mass market paperback)
Moonlighting as an arts writer, Rei Shimura is set to interview a young comic book
artist in Tokyo. But the artist has vanished, and his best friend turns up dead in the
Sumida River, dressed in the gaudy costume of the super-heroine.

THE FLOWER MASTER
ISBN 0-06-109734-9 (mass market paperback)
Rei Shimura has her hands full with an ikebana class (Japanese art of flower
arranging) when one of the teachers is murdered.

ZEN ATTITUDE
ISBN 0-06-104444-X (mass market paperback)
Bad karma comes with a to-die-for chest of drawers as Rei goes from murder
suspect to murder target while staying on the grounds of the Zen temple Horinji.

THE SALARYMAN'S WIFE
ISBN 0-06-104443-1 (mass market paperback)
On a visit to an ancient castle town, Rei Shimura is the first to find a high-
powered businessman's wife dead in the snow.